Visits With Mary

David Stockar

Visits With Mary

Published by Wailele Press, Inc. - www.wailelepress.com
Wailele Press and the "hibiscus" logo are trademarks belonging to Wailele Press, Inc.

Cover design by Jason Welsch
Photo on Eden Crossing cover by David Renz
Author photography by Gretchen Johnson

ISBN 978-0-9908254-0-1

I dedicate this, my first released novel, to my wife, Karyn, in gratitude for all of her unconditional love and unending support.

In addition, I wish to pay tribute to the storytelling genius and inspiration of Lewis Carroll.

Contents

Preface

The rain danced on the tin roof. He awoke as thunder echoed through the last remnant of his dream. It was nothing more than another spring storm, yet this time there was something that touched a nerve never previously awakened. He relaxed and listened to the rain. The old tin roof was alive with the harmony of countless fleeting raindrops, each adding its note to the enchanting melody. For the first time in his life, he was engulfed in the moment, savoring each drop.

It was 3:30 in the morning when he was aroused from this tranquility by a violent flash of light, instantly echoed by the crack of sound that ended with a thundering crash. The warm body next to him made her presence known with a soft sigh as she rolled over to meet him, her arm searching for his comfort. He reached out to reassure her and without the intrusion of words, kissed her. The kiss led to another, and soon the music of the rain and the rhythm of the wind provided the tempo for their passion. Now the roll of thunder was overpowered by a more piercing, more intense confirmation of the miracle of existence. The two lovers fell back exhausted but still intertwined, inseparable as the thunder and lightning slowly drifted into the past, or simply moved on. No matter, the sacred moment was gone. As she drifted back to sleep, he listened to the rain, savoring the night as if it was his first and last.

There is something magical about complete contentment, the kind that permeates your entire body, mind and soul, and in that precious moment all is fulfilled, lacking nothing, perfectly whole. This was that rare moment, and, for the first time in his life, he was wise enough to recognize it and awake enough to savor it.

CHAPTER I

The Field Trip

*J*ack Fulton was leading a class of young minds on his first field trip as a graduate student of Geology at McLaren University in rural western Pennsylvania. It was part of an undergraduate course taught by Professor Adams, his advisor. He was a little nervous. At twenty four years of age, he was barely two years older than some of his students. Nonetheless, he knew the subject with a passionate curiosity for nature and a patient love for teaching. The two made him instantly popular with his class.

Now halfway through his second semester at McLaren, he was eager for the teaching opportunity, being solely in charge of this one-day geological field trip within the Valley and Ridge Geological Province of the ancient and once mighty Appalachian Mountains. His natural gift of storytelling had many of the students firmly teleported to the Late Devonian, a time when the surrounding lands were shallow seas filled with primitive creatures unlike any known to man. He weaved a tale that made even the most rebellious student, a jock named Randell Twiner, question the safety of the old school bus against the giant cephalopods. All the students were engaged, except one. She sat alone near the front of the bus and respectfully listened, not hearing a word. Mary Collins was not interested in geology, but her friends told her that this was the easiest science course, and she desperately needed the science credits to graduate in May.

At the first stop, the bus pulled onto a dirt road and soon came to a halt at the base of an abandoned quarry outside the small town of Kamerynville. Jack stood up in front of the still seated students and described the highlights of the site. "What we will observe here are rocks that were deformed in the last stages of Appalachian mountain building, during what we call the Alleghenian orogeny of the late Carboniferous and early Permian. They are the folded and later faulted strata that were deposited in the shallow seas of the late Devonian. At this particular location, there is too much deformation to substantiate viable fossilized specimens, but that does not mean that these were not once extremely fertile seas for early life forms. Pay particular attention to the sequence of tectonic events and the chevron fold that will be very obvious. It is a textbook example of a large chevron. Any questions?"

There were none, except that Randell whispered a comment to his side kick, Jimmy Taylor, which resulted in much chuckling in the back of the bus. Jack noticed this and decided to put Randell on the spot for the fifth time that morning.

"Randell, it seems that you have more to share, please don't deprive the rest of us."

Randell looked over at Jimmy and then at Al Kowalski, his other dedicated fan. The two rolled their shoulders in unison in the universal sign for "don't ask me". Jack waited, still staring at Randell. Finally, Randell found his courage and spoke up.

"I was simply wondering if we'll see an orogeny on this trip?" Randell smirked at Jimmy and Al. The latter two could not hold back any longer and broke out into an explosion of laughter. Soon the entire bus was laughing, even old Mr. Chesterfield, the bus driver, for whom this was the only part of the morning discussion that was of any interest.

Jack quickly realized that he had made a mistake giving Randell the stage. Randell, whose large ego had inflated to twice its size with the supportive laughter of his class, felt omnipotent and smiled proudly at Mary, who along with the rest of the class had his attention. Mary, rather strikingly attractive in both looks and self-confidence, was completely uninterested in Randell, who was not used to being ignored. This made her the supreme target of his hormonal interests. He watched eagerly to see if she too would laugh, but to his momentary disillusionment, she soon looked away unmoved, turning her attention back to her smart phone.

"Very funny, Randell, very funny," was all that Jack could muster. "Any more questions?"

The bus fell silent.

"Okay. If not, let's all get out and explore this site. Please be careful and don't climb on the rocks or get near the edge of the steep quarry walls," Jack warned.

No one was listening as everyone began to pile out of the bus. Mary remained seated despite being near the front. As Randell passed her, he stopped to talk to her. He knew that the target of his affection was a year older, being a senior to his junior ranking, but with the added courage of his recent public triumph, he decided to slip next to her and let his classmates pass. Turning to her, he whispered, "Can I show you around?"

She turned to him, and for the first time that day, he was rewarded by her smile. That smile nearly made him stutter due to a sudden drop in self-confidence. It was completely absorbing and he was suddenly tongue tied.

"No, thanks, Randell. I know what you're after, and I'm not interested. Please stop hitting on me, and move so that I can get out," she calmly replied.

Randell felt completely deflated and was left uncharacteristically speechless. The recent master of ceremonies became the confused observer, the tongue-tied fool. It took him a few seconds to recover, but recover he did, for he had an image to maintain with Jimmy, Al and the rest of the class, several of whom had witnessed the exchange.

"Did she kiss you like you said she would?" Jimmy asked eagerly as Randell joined his friends wearing a forced smile on his face.

"Of course! She loves me. They all do," Randell boasted. But, as he followed his admiring friends toward the upper wall of the quarry, the site of the huge chevron fold, he felt internally deflated. It was the same deflation that his domineering father made him feel every day for much too long. His defeat soon turned to rage, rage toward his father and rage toward the one woman that reminded him of these feelings that he could not forget. He wanted control, control over this humiliation, control over this impish girl. He despised her for crushing him at the height of his glory. "How dare she?" he muttered under his breath, completely ignoring Jack and the chevron fold.

Unaware, Jack completed his passionate lecture to the class on the wonders of this massive chevron and the layers of tectonically deformed sedimentary rock that composed it. He allowed the students to explore, as he searched for Mary Collins. The day was peaceful and bright, not unlike the effect this particular young woman had on her equally young instructor.

Minutes later, all serenity was shattered as one of the students, Suzy Kurtz, screamed a horrific, piercing, bone-numbing scream. Everything stopped and all eyes were on Suzy. She too was frozen in time, screaming while pointing over the edge of the quarry wall, screaming and robotically pointing below.

A crowd gathered, which included the young instructor. To the horror of all, a bundle of blue clothing lay at the base of the quarry wall, some thirty feet below, crushed on its unyielding floor. It lay lifeless. As Jack looked closer, he saw Randell to his left carefully climbing down from a lower ledge toward the motionless bundle. Suzy stopped screaming, and looked with a crazed stare at Jack and the growing crowd of classmates.

"It's Mary!" she exclaimed, as she looked back over the edge.

"Call 911!" Jack shouted but did not wait for a reply. He ran along the lip of the quarry wall to a scree of fallen rock on the far right and leapt over the edge. Pretending that he was skiing, he hurled himself down the loose stones of the scree, barely in control. Once at the base, he sprinted toward Mary's fallen form beating the cautious Randell to arrive first. As a ski instructor during his undergraduate college years, he was well versed in first aid and he quickly checked her breathing and pulse. Miraculously, he found both, but Mary lay limp and unconscious. He knew not to move her as he inspected for other injuries. There were a few abrasions and her left ankle seemed twisted, but no major bleeding and no major breaks.

Randell finally arrived in a panic. "Is she all right? I saw her down here, and I tried to get down to her. Is she dead?" He appeared genuinely shaken.

"She's not dead, but she's unconscious and badly bruised," Jack summarized while his mind raced through various outcome scenarios.

"I didn't see the fall," Randell paused, but made no eye contact with Jack, "but it's possible that she…" He did not finish his statement.

"That she what, Randell?"

"Well, she may have let herself fall."

"Jumped?" Jack looked up at Randell who finally met his eyes. He seemed sincere. Then Jack looked back at the beautiful, young, and oddly tranquil face of Mary Collins. Something about that idea did not fit that face. He had no time to reason for soon he heard the sirens.

"Thank God the paramedics are here!" he proclaimed, and looking up he saw the rim of the quarry crowded with his students. The crowd parted and several paramedics appeared, followed by firemen and the police. Quickly, the rescuers reached them and began to apply first aid. Within minutes, a medical helicopter landed several yards away inside the old quarry. It airlifted Mary's limp body to the trauma unit of a nearby medical center. Jack was left with a sinking feeling and a plethora of police questions.

CHAPTER 2

Mystery Woman

It was well after midnight when Jack finally arrived at his small studio apartment near campus. This was supposed to be a great day. He had planned it out in detail, so that it would be the best field trip in the history of the McLaren Geoscience Department. Instead, it was the worst.

Now he was ready for bed after the long, exhausting day of interrogations and endless questioning by university administrators, police investigators and fellow professors, not to mention distraught students and media-panicked parents. Everyone had a piece of him, except the victim, and to his surprise, her parents. They had never surfaced.

Suddenly, he realized that with all the focus on the accident, he had forgotten about Mary, the victim. It was after 3 am and his body yearned for sleep, but his heart would not yield. He picked up the phone and called the hospital. Soon he was connected to the nurses' station at the trauma unit.

"I'm calling in regards to Mary Collins, a patient," he began.

"Are you her husband?" the nurse asked.

"No, her college instructor," Jack replied honestly.

"I'm sorry, but we can't release patient information over the phone to anyone who isn't a direct relative," she replied.

"I understand, but is she all right?"

"I'm sorry, but I cannot release that information," the nurse held her ground.

"Okay," Jack replied and reluctantly hung up the phone.

This was unacceptable. He was responsible for his students, and one of them was critically ill while he was here, in the comfort of his home. He knew he should be at the medical center.

He took a two-minute shower, changed his clothes and, within another five minutes, was speeding toward the hospital. There was no traffic in the middle of the night, and he arrived at the trauma unit just before 3:30 am. The night shift appeared to be doing its rounds when he approached the nurses' station.

"Damn it, where are they?" he cursed in frustration under his breath.

He looked about the empty halls but saw no one. Looking over the counter onto the nurse's desk, he saw a list of patient names. Reaching over, he saw that Collins, Mary was in room 328. He placed the sheet back on the desk and rushed quietly down the hall. Within minutes, he found room 328. The door was open, but a curtain was drawn around the bed. There were instruments everywhere, and the only sounds were the rhythmic pulsing of a respirator machine and steady beeping of the heart monitor.

He inhaled deeply. "At least she's alive," he thought. Slowly, he peered around the curtain. He stopped in awe, instantly mired by deep sadness. There was Mary, beautiful in her tranquility, yet completely lifeless, like a mannequin. What struck Jack as odd was the Mona Lisa smile frozen on her serene face. It was in shocking contrast to the countless tubes and electrodes that surrounded her and appeared to pierce every part of her. He stood there staring, and as he stared, he realized that he was not alone in the room with her.

There, slumped on an adjacent chair, was a dark-haired woman, equally tranquil, beautiful and seemingly asleep. She had her right hand over Mary's left arm and the energy between them was evident from afar. "Good," Jack thought, "at least she's not here alone but has someone who cares for her. Good!" he echoed to himself.

As he looked at her, he felt an attraction to Mary. It was the attraction one feels to complete innocence and purity. No, who was he kidding. It was the attraction a man feels toward a woman. He hated that he even felt it at a time like this. He forced it to disappear.

Then he realized that during his introspection he had lost his awareness of the other woman, and now he was the one being scrutinized. The dark-haired woman's eyes met his, and he felt that her strong gentle gaze pierced right through him. Nothing could be hidden from it. Her eyes were strikingly bright, light violet in hue. In fact, there was a slight magenta aura about her that baffled him.

She did not say a word, but looked away to refocus her attention on Mary. It was as if she already knew all about him, and there was nothing further to ask. Her attention was completely with the young woman lying on the bed, fighting for her life. The dark-haired woman rose gracefully and bent over Mary, kissing her forehead with a love that seemed to radiate and fill the room with a powerful, yet serene force that Jack had never experienced before.

Jack stared. An inner voice kept him silent and still, guiding him to not interrupt any further. He stood frozen, the neutral observer.

The woman silently placed her ivory hands over Mary's chest some three inches above it and cupped them. Her lips moved, uttering silent words in a silent world. She took her time, completely calm and completely ignoring Jack's presence. All the while, Jack thought that he imagined a purplish white light, not unlike that of the mysterious woman's eyes, pass from her cupped hands into Mary's form. The light turned to deep hews of magenta and then to indigo. Jack rubbed his eyes to assure himself that what he saw was real. When he looked up, the light was gone. He was tired and his mind was frazzled by the day's events. "Surely, I just imagined that," the logical thinker consoled himself.

It was then that Jack felt the weight of his fatigue and, reaching for the small chair behind him, he sat back, observing in silence. As the odd woman reached down once more to kiss Mary's forehead, he began to drift into sleep. He could not fight it. It was overpowering. The last thing he remembered was the dark-haired woman looking over at him with large, piercing, indigo eyes and smiling, before sitting back into the sofa chair adjacent to Mary's bed.

Jack awoke to the sensation of someone gently shaking his arm. Completely disoriented, he looked up to see two brown eyes.

"Hello, there!" she greeted him. "Brother, right?"

"No," Jack replied as he gathered his bearing. He was about to confess that he was Mary's instructor, but remembering the response he had received over the phone, he decided to use a different descriptor. "I'm a close friend," he replied.

"Oh, I see. Her boyfriend," the savvy nurse concluded aloud.

Jack was going to correct her but did not get a chance.

"You're welcome to stay despite the hour. I'm sure they told you at reception that we've recently started round-the-clock visitation for friends and relatives of patients in this ward. It's targeted to stimulate our trauma patients, including coma patients like your girlfriend. It's a new experimental treatment that our in-house psychologist introduced last month. I guess it's a good idea, but I'm not used to people like you showing up on my ward at odd hours of the night. But, I'm glad that someone finally showed up to visit this poor young thing." The young nurse said so much so fast that Jack's tired mind could barely keep up.

"Coma!" He exclaimed. The word sunk in like a death sentence. "She's in a coma?"

"Unfortunately, yes. She was in a coma when she arrived here," the nurse replied. "Poor thing. So young and pretty. We tried to reach her parents, but the university representative that we dealt with said that her parents are both deceased. I guess that you already knew all that being her boyfriend," she added.

Jack did not respond. He reflected on how little he knew about Mary or about any of his students.

"This one has had it tough, poor dear. I'm truly sorry. This must be very difficult on you as well. I talk too much. You must be distraught. My name's Jennifer. Most people call me Jen. Can I get you something?" she paused, warming to Jack.

"No, thanks, Jen. My name's Jack," he replied and extended his hand. He decided not to correct her assumption regarding his relationship with Mary.

Then he remembered the dark-haired woman and looked at his watch. It was just after 4 am. "Jen, who is the woman who was sitting over there?" Jack pointed to the sofa chair beneath the window and next to the bed. "She was here when I came in about a half hour ago. I fell asleep shortly after I arrived and never had a chance to ask her name. Who is she?"

Jennifer looked at Jack empathetically. "You poor dear! It's a lot for the mind to absorb. I'll get you some water. You can rest in the sofa chair. It's a lot more comfortable and reclines if you wish to get some sleep," Jennifer replied, and was about to walk out of the room.

"Jen, about the woman? Who is she?" Jack insisted.

Jennifer turned compassionately toward Jack. She was taking a liking to the young man, who was about her age. "Jack, get some rest. She'll be okay. Don't worry. I'll take good care of her." Jennifer smiled and headed out the door.

CHAPTER 3

The Prognosis

*O*nce more Jack fell asleep in the sofa chair next to Mary's bed. At 6:20 am, he was awakened by Jennifer who announced the arrival of Dr. Murphy, the neurologist. She introduced Jack to the doctor as Mary's boyfriend. The doctor shook hands with Jack and wasted little time on small talk. He was a doctor who loved his profession and the patient was his primary focus. After reviewing the charts from the night and checking the instrument monitors, he performed several small diagnostic tests, including checking pupil dilation response, and listening to Mary's breathing and heartbeat with his stethoscope.

He turned to Jack and finally addressed him on the subject of Mary's prognosis. "Jack, is it?" he paused to assure that he had remembered the correct name of the young man standing nervously before him.

"Yes."

"Well, Jack, I don't have much in the way of good news, I'm afraid, except that she's stable. There's limited activity in the pre-frontal cortex and occipital cortex, and we're screening her for the potential onset of a compounding infection due to one of the lacera-tions. Outside of the critical head trauma, her body was remarkably unscathed, barring fairly minor lacerations and a sprained ankle. Such minor injuries will heal perfectly in a woman her age. The issue is the brain trauma that caused this comatose state," the doctor paused, turning toward Mary.

"As I mentioned," he continued, "the head trauma due to the impact appears to have resulted in minimal brain activity in the prefrontal and occipital cortexes, the PFC and OC. Fortunately, the MRI did not reveal significant physical damage to either, but inexplicably the functionality of both has been grossly impeded," he paused again and looked at Jack to see if he had any questions. "It doesn't warrant surgery at this time, but we need to conduct further testing to try and identify why she's in this comatose state. Right now that remains a mystery."

Then he added, "Unfortunately, we know more about outer space than about our own brain. Frankly, it was a small miracle that no severe hematoma developed in the occipital cortex given the bruising and lacerations at the rear of her cranium. Regardless, her condition appears to have stabilized although the coma has not lifted. All vital signs are stable although pulmonary activity is strained. It is the PFC and OC activity that is severely impacted and of primary concern." Dr. Murphy stopped once more, awaiting a response from Jack.

"Doctor, is she going to wake up, and, if so, will she be all right?" Jack asked the pertinent question.

"What I'm trying to tell you, son, is that I don't know. The physical cause of the brain trauma is clear, but her brain's response to it and its ability to recover are a mystery. I'm hoping that if we continue to stimulate the brain electromagnetically, she may awaken from the coma, but it's hard to predict, given the com-pounded impacts of the fall. Our first attempts, when she first arrived, obviously failed. I'm sorry that we do not know more at this time. I'll send her for another MRI and an EEG later this morning to make sure that the small hematoma at the rear base is stabilized, and to get a baseline on the activity in the PFC and OC. At that time, we may perform some additional testing and targeted stimulation as needed to try and stimulate activity in the PFC and OC, as well as other parts of the cerebrum and cerebellum, but until then, I have nothing new to tell you. She could remain this way for some time, or she could awaken quite suddenly, or she could…" He did not finish the sentence.

"Thank you, doctor," Jack replied. He had nothing more to ask for he was starting to feel empty and helpless.

"Of course, son, of course. We'll do our best. Jen here is the best." Dr. Murphy smiled at the young nurse, who obviously idealized him, and then he slipped silently out of the room.

"He's a great doctor. We're lucky to have him here. His wife's a sociology professor at the university. That's why he's here. Your girlfriend's in good hands. See, he was more optimistic than yesterday." Jennifer smiled as she went about tending to Mary's many machines and tubes.

"Thanks, Jen, but nothing has changed since yesterday, so why would he be more optimistic?" Jack, the scientist, analyzed the facts.

"Because it's another day," Jennifer concluded as she adjusted Mary's pillows.

"About that woman that I saw in here last night," Jack began, "who was she?"

Jennifer stopped and looked at Jack with deep compassion. "Oh, my dear," she caught herself revealing her growing interest in this handsome young man. Sensing the complete inappropriateness of her feelings and words, she wisely corrected her tone. "Jack, there was no woman in here last night."

"There was! I saw her with my own eyes. She was asleep in this very chair when I came in." Jack raised his voice in protest as he pointed back at the sofa chair near the window. "She awoke and lovingly tended to Mary. She kissed her on the forehead a number of times and held her hands over Mary's heart, and said some inaudible words as if she were a shaman healer or something. I don't know. But I saw her as I see you right now." Jack was frustrated and his voice betrayed him.

"Okay, Jack, if you insist, but I didn't see anyone except you in this room all night. Sorry." Jennifer resumed her work quietly. She felt for the young couple and wished that she had someone like Jack that loved her this way. Mary was in a coma, but to Jennifer she was lucky to have such a loving and caring boyfriend, even if he was a little odd with this imagination.

"Jen, I'm sorry to have raised my voice. It's just bugging me. Do you have cameras in these rooms?" he asked sincerely.

"No. That would go against patient privacy rights, but there are cameras in the hall and at the entrances to the ward. Why?" Jennifer asked as she finished her work in Mary's room.

"Can you check the camera footage to see if there was a woman in here last night? Please?" Jack was desperate. He knew that for a scientist to become delusional was a kiss of professional death. Besides, he wanted to prove his point and confirm his sanity.

"No, I can't. Security has access to that. We nurses don't have that access. Look, Jack, Mary needs you to keep it together. I know that this must be really hard on you since she's your girlfriend." Jennifer slowly rolled the "girlfriend" word off her tongue as if it did not want to be uttered.

"Sorry, but how can you be so sure I was imagining it?" Jack slumped into the sofa chair like a defeated defiant teen.

"I was at the nurses' station the entire night and know exactly who came in and out of here last night, and the only one was you."

"That's not true, Jen," Jack objected. "I walked in here, and there was no one around. I walked in here, and you didn't know."

"Yes, I did. I saw you leaning over the counter looking at the patient list to find this room," Jennifer replied.

This shocked Jack who had thought that he was unobserved when he first entered Mary's room. "Where were you?" he asked sincerely.

"At the nurses' station!"

"Stop messing with me, Jen! I barely know you, and this isn't funny. There was no one at the nurses' station last night when I came in," Jack objected. Was he really losing his mind?

"Sorry, I didn't mean to upset you. It's our terminology," Jennifer replied calmly. "I was in the back room of the nurses' station, where we keep the records. I saw you come in on the camera monitor that's above the reception desk, but before I could come out to greet you, you pulled your little trick. At least you signed into the guest log, even though you lied and signed in as Mary's brother. Shame on you, Jack!" she added and paused. "Soon after, I checked on you, but you were asleep in the chair, so I figured all was fine. I could tell you were a good man," she added and blushed.

"And you didn't see anyone else in the room when you checked on me?" Jack replied, blind to the young nurse's growing attraction.

"No. Sorry." She shook her head.

"But you couldn't see Mary or the sofa chair from the doorway since the curtain was blocking your view, so you wouldn't have seen the woman." Jack perked up grasping for the last thread of hope.

"No, but…"

"So you don't know who was in this room last night," Jack concluded firmly.

"Let it go, Jack. I have other patients to tend to before the day shift comes on. Fine, you're right. But I do know that, except for you and I, no one else came in or out of this room last night. Unless your mystery woman can scale buildings to the third floor, she wasn't real. I need to run." Jennifer left the room shaking her head. "I hope he snaps out of it," she thought to herself. "What a waste!"

CHAPTER 4

The Inspector

The next evening, Jack was eating dinner in his studio apartment near McLaren University campus when he was interrupted by a strong knock on his door.

"Who is it?" he yelled and reluctantly rose to answer it.

"Inspector Cabot!"

Jack recognized the name of the police inspector handling the case. He had heard that gruff voice for hours during his first day of interviews. "Now what could he want?" he thought as he opened the door.

There, before him, stood a middle-aged, rounded man of short stature with a large dark mustache. Despite the cliché gray trench coat, he had an aura of authority which was mixed with childish curiosity bordering on naivety, yet, he was anything but naive. The combination of traits and appearances made him extremely successful at unearthing the truth in a growing portfolio of solved cases.

"Mr. Jack Fulton, my apologies for disturbing you at this hour. May I come in? I promise I won't be long." The Inspector charmed his way in before Jack could reply.

"Have a seat, Inspector." Jack offered an empty chair in his small living space.

"Thank you. Nice place." The inspector's trained eyes scanned the room before he seated himself.

Jack dropped into the seat opposite him. "How can I help you?"

"Well, I wanted a chance to ask you a few more questions regarding the Mary Collins case. By the way, I heard she has stabilized," the Inspector began fishing.

"Yes. She has. I just returned from the hospital an hour ago."

"Very caring," the Inspector replied without any expression on his face.

Jack felt as if he were being interrogated about his relationship with Mary. He became nervous, fearful of betraying his growing feelings toward his student. "Yes, well I feel responsible."

"Are you?"

Jack suddenly realized that he was walking into a verbal trap. "Of course not! What are you implying?"

"Nothing. You mentioned that you felt responsible for Miss Collins' condition, and I was simply clarifying." The Inspector smiled again.

"That came out wrong. I simply feel that it is my responsibility, as her instructor, to assure that she's all right, especially given that she doesn't appear to have any parents or relations," Jack quickly clarified in a rushed and nervous voice.

"I'll be blunt, Mr. Fulton. I came here because there are a number of contradicting and even suspicious factors about this case."

"There are? But why did you come here at this hour?"

"Because I was hoping that you could shed some light on the confusion. That's all. That and because I was heading home, which is only three blocks from here." The Inspector did not wait for a reply. He broke eye contact and searched for his small pocket pad and pencil. As soon as he found them, he scribbled several comments on the first available page.

Jack observed him. The mysterious scribbling made Jack half curious and half fearful.

"You seem nervous, Mr. Fulton. Do I make you nervous, or is there something that you wish to share with me?" The Inspector had his small notebook opened, and, with pencil in hand, was ready to capture any and all relevant information.

"I'm confused, Inspector. Why are you here?" Jack tried to regain his composure.

"Well," the Inspector played with his mustache, "as I mentioned, based on the interviews of all the witnesses to the accident, there are several gross inconsistencies. That and the fact that most of the students seemed oddly disengaged when questioned. Was Miss Collins a bit of an outcast?"

"Not that I know of, Inspector. She seemed rather disengaged in my class at times, but that hardly makes her an outcast, does it?"

The Inspector twiddled his mustache again. "Right. True indeed." He adjusted his seating position. "The key issue lies with four testimonies: that of Mr. Randell Twiner; that of Miss Suzy Kurtz; that of the bus driver, Mr. Roger Chesterfield; and yours. Specifically, your testimony is the one that fits the least, but I can't for the life of me imagine why you'd be lying."

"What!" Jack jumped out of his chair. "Is this some kind of a joke?" He glared at the Inspector.

"No joke, I assure you. You see, I can't get my finger on a motive, and the poor girl's in a coma and can't help me. All that I have managed to discern to date is the fact that there was some tension between our victim and both Mr. Twiner and Miss Kurtz, who appears to be Mr. Twiner's rather jealous girlfriend. Nothing all that serious, just the usual love triangle sort of thing, but that's motive in more cases than you may imagine," the Inspector chuckled.

Jack remained standing, staring down at the Inspector, who seemed to be relishing his position of power.

"Do sit down, Mr. Fulton. I didn't mean to alarm you." The Inspector smiled and twirled his mustache.

Jack returned to his chair, still visibly upset. "Are you accusing me of something?" he asked.

"No, but should I be?"

"No! This entire visit is preposterous!"

"I agree. You and Mr. Chesterfield, the bus driver, you know…"

"I know he's the bus driver." Jack interrupted.

"Do you know him well?"

"No. I never met him before or since."

"Then, how do you know that he's the bus driver?"

"Because he was driving the bus!" Jack was getting extremely angry.

"If I profess to a class, then am I a professor?" the Inspector toyed.

"This is ridiculous, Inspector! I must ask you to leave."

"I understand, but before I do, tell me, Mr. Fulton, how long have you and your student, Mary Collins, been sleeping together?"

CHAPTER 5

Carl

Jack's head was spinning after he forced the Inspector out of his studio apartment. He felt sick to his stomach. How was he at the center of a criminal investigation in the tragic mishap of one of his students? How could that happen?

He felt trapped, like some exotic wild animal at the mercy of its captors. He never saw the trap. He never even knew that he was being hunted. He did not even know half of his hunters. "Mr. Chesterfield? Who's that? Why would a random bus driver testify against me? Randell Twiner and Suzy Kurtz? They're just naive kids. It must all be a misunderstanding. It must be that crazy inspector's version of a head game," Jack reasoned. He was ready to report the harassing behavior to Inspector Cabot's superior. But who would believe him?

"Maybe that's what that damn fool wants is for me to be upset and rush to police headquarters." Jack's mind was racing. He was losing his grounding. Later that evening, he decided to call upon a friend.

"It's bloody ten o'clock at night, Jack, on a Sunday no less!" Carl Rupert exclaimed in a sleepy voice and a hearty Australian accent. He stood in his doorway wearing a pair of the ugliest striped pajamas known to man.

"Sorry to wake you, Carl, but I had nowhere else to turn," Jack confessed as he took notice of Carl's pajamas, casting his glance the length of the stripes. "You sleep in those disgusting pajamas?"

"Yes, what else would I sleep in? What are you doing here at this hour? Any change with Mary's condition?" Carl suddenly sounded deeply concerned.

"No, she's still in a coma."

"Damn it! I was there this afternoon to see her. What a mess! This entire thing is horrible."

"I know," Jack sighed audibly. "I don't know what we can do? Can I come in?"

"Yes, but I have to give a lecture at eight in the morning tomorrow on the evolutionary significance of brachiopods. I'm a sedimentology graduate student. What do I know about brachiopods? This lab I'm teaching covers ancient environments and the significance of the dominant species that inhabited them. Just my luck!" Carl opened the door to let Jack in.

"This place smells disgusting! What died in here?" Jack's stomach was starting to turn again.

"I had Kimchi for dinner. It was delicious." Carl referred to the spicy Korean fermented cabbage dish.

"No wonder you don't have a girlfriend, Carl. Between your diet and those pajamas, it's a wonder that you're not completely celibate."

"Well, at least I haven't slept with half the campus in less than a year. Why are you here, Jack?" Carl replied, visibly annoyed at the comment.

"That's a jealous cheap shot, Carl." Jack stormed into the small dingy apartment and dropped into the nearest seat, which was much too worn to properly support his large, muscular frame. As a result, he sank into an uncomfortable position barely clearing the floor. "Damn it, Carl, get some real furniture instead of these rejects!"

"Look, Jack, if you came here to insult me in the middle of the night, then please leave."

"I'm sorry, Carl. I really am. We really need to talk."

"Okay, but I need to get some shuteye soon."

"Fine, I'll get right to it. The police are implying that I'm involved in Mary's fall. I don't know how they came to that conclusion so fast." Jack buried his face in his hands.

"Jack, they're probably just looking under every rock, no pun intended. Remember that these guys are trained to rattle you. You're innocent, so you have nothing to worry about," Carl comforted his fellow graduate student. "Are they suspicious of anyone else?"

"I don't know, but that damn chief inspector believes that Mary and I are a couple. That makes me look suspicious," Jack confessed his concerns.

"Deny it as totally bogus! Assure them that not even you are so brash and stupid as to sleep with an undergraduate that's in one of your classes." Carl stated the obvious.

"Right, I know."

"Go home and get some sleep, but keep me posted. I'm sorry about this entire mess! You want a sleeping pill?" Carl asked.

"No, thanks. Look, Carl, let's not kid each other at this point. I know that you know that Mary and I slept together." Jack looked straight at Carl.

"I know and I warned you that no matter how attractive she may be, you're playing with fire, mate," Carl replied.

"I know it was stupid. She came into my lab a few times asking for some help with the lab project and well... damn it."

"So you had to conquer her. You had to have her. Like you do all women, right Jack? The disgusting thing in this room in not my pair of pajamas, mate." Carl rebuked in his Australian accent.

He had been jealous of Jack since they both arrived as graduate students at the Geoscience Department at McLaren nine months earlier. Being shy with low self esteem, Carl had hoped that his association and friendship with Jack Fulton, the flamboyant and handsome bachelor, would improve his chances at finding a potential wife or at least a steady girlfriend. He greatly envied his friend's seemingly endless male magnetism, and despised how easily he took it for granted. But mostly the relationships were his envy, for Carl had none, and Jack seemed to have endless opportunity.

Carl knew Mary Collins. She was hard to miss, but she seemed beyond the powers of Jack Fulton and men like him. He had been sure of that, until a few weeks ago when he discovered otherwise. He was angry with Jack then and he was angry now, although this was the first chance that he had to confront him on the subject.

"Damn you, Jack! She was innocence and you destroyed it! She was the one person that you had no right to spoil. Damn you, Jack! What a mess!" Even Carl was surprised at this new bout of anger towards his friend and colleague. All of the jealousy surfaced at once.

Carl was angry at himself as much as he loathed Jack's actions. He too had taken a liking to Mary the first time that he laid eyes on her when she had come to inquire about the Introductory Geology class for which he was a teaching assistant. It happened the previous semester, his first semester at McLaren. To his disappointment, she seemed completely oblivious of his existence, and to his dismay, she postponed her enrollment in the class by a semester. Now Jack Fulton had the role of her teaching assistant. "Teaching Assistant in what?" Carl reflected in disgust. Presently, having confronted Jack with his true feelings, he was spent like a erupted volcano, and wanted nothing more than to deflate into his sofa chair.

"Wow! That was uncalled for after all I've done for you. I didn't expect that reaction, mate," Jack replied startled and deeply hurt. He considered Carl one of his closest friends at McLaren. Carl's reaction seemed like a betrayal. Instead of receiving the sympathy that he so desperately desired, he witnessed the opposite. Silently, he rose from his seat and walked toward the door. When he reached it, he looked back at Carl, who was slumped in the sofa chair.

"Not that it matters to you, but I never 'had' Mary. No one can possess her. She is beyond that. We simply crossed paths on one magical night that should not have happened. Yet, it was something beyond description, and neither you nor the rest of the world would ever understand. Although you criticize me, you're the one that wishes that you 'had' her or a woman like her. You're the one who looks at women as something you can 'have', as if they're possessions," he rebuked and walked out the door into the cold spring night. "Damn, Carl! Damn that inspector, too! How the hell did he find out anyway? What a mess! I should've controlled myself!" he exclaimed aloud into the night. Unfortunately, he was too upset to notice the short, shadowy figure watching him leave.

CHAPTER 6

Tiger Lilly

Lilly Austin was brushing her hair. It was a nightly ritual. Since she was a girl, she had always possessed the most beautiful auburn hair. She would sit in front of her mirror in her quiet bedroom, and brush her hair every night for at least fifteen minutes, twenty if possible. It brought her peace and a sense of balance and self assurance. Tonight was no different. She was in perfect harmony. Her naturally pouting lips dominated her Celtic features, and her deep brown eyes were peacefully closed. She brushed and brushed, recalling her joyous youth in the hills outside of Galway, Ireland. Like a princess, she was born in a castle, and like a princess, her father pampered her all of his days.

She remembered him now in her nightly ritual, feeling him near her despite his departure two years ago. "Love binds all, even the doors of death are immune to its pervasive power," she reasoned. Lilly loved her father, but not as much as power and passion. She looked at the old clock on the large mantelpiece. He was late. The latest source of her passion was late. He had been absent much too often of late. "Late, late, late!" She brushed with increased vigor as she reflected on their relationship.

Lilly Austin was not in love. No, that was not to be, not now and maybe never. But, she was caressed and a princess once again, even if this prince was hardly more than a lusting oaf. She did not care. It was the attention that she craved.

Tonight her prince was once again late. "Late, late, late!" She brushed her hair. The clock struck midnight. She decided to cease her ritual, which did not fully satisfy on this night. Having waited an hour now, there was no reason that a women, regardless how forgiving, should wait so long.

Lilly undressed slowly in a fashion that betrayed her bearing. At the age of twenty five, she made a stunning sight wearing nothing but the glow of the rising moon. Catching a full reflection of herself in the floor-length mirror, she felt satisfaction with her vision, as might an artist that just completed a masterpiece. Lilly was vain, and this reflection confirmed to her that right. With one last admiring glance, she slipped into her silk negligee and carefully receded into her large, soft bed. He would not come tonight. She released him and fell asleep unmoved.

She awoke to a doorbell ringing. Glancing at her clock, she was surprised that she had been asleep for only twenty minutes. Rising, she reached for her robe and descended the stairs of her picturesque mansion, which at present she shared solely with two Siamese cats, named Ying and Yang, and an elderly couple who acted as her domestics. The two cats accompanied her toward the ringing doorway. She used the peek hole to confirm her suspicions. He had arrived at last, only ninety minutes too late. The thought of leaving him out in the cold pressed into her consciousness, but her quiet anger desired satisfaction. Grasping the heavy door handle, she turned it and pulled the door toward her, but only a crack.

There he stood, looking rather ruffled and most definitely romantically uninspiring. "I'm so sorry!" is all that he offered as an explanation. "May I come in?"

She paused. Her desires for him were not there tonight. "No, not tonight," she was about to reply when their eyes met. "There lies the problem," her logical mind whispered. "Close the door and leave him in the cold," her mind insisted. But she could not obey. For, once their eyes met, she was unable to resist the lust that was ever-present between them. Slowly, she opened the door, and soon she fell into his strong arms. She felt excited again, as she had when she brushed her long auburn hair.

CHAPTER 7

Jennifer

Jennifer, the night nurse at the trauma center, was doing her early morning rounds when she noticed an odd glow radiating from room 328. It was extremely subtle, but with the ward nearly dark, it demanded attention.

Jennifer Angel was a hard-working young woman, down on her luck. Her fiancé of two years left her for another, and work kept her from finding a suitable substitute. She had worked her way up from poverty to self-sufficiency. Her parents gave her little support in this journey. In fact, they mostly added to her challenges. Her mother was an alcoholic, recently recovering, and her father was nowhere to be found. He left the family years ago, two days before Jennifer's twelfth birthday. It was an odd birthday gift, but in hindsight it was a gift nonetheless, for the man was abusive to her and her mother. Jennifer was the oldest of three. Her younger brothers were five and two when their father vanished, presumably with a new woman. It mattered little, for in the end it was a blessing even for them, although unlike Jennifer, they never realized it.

Jennifer had two key ambitions. The first was to get accepted to medical school and become a doctor. The second was to have a perfect and content family of her own. The former she pursued with vigor, studying for her medical school entrance exams at every chance she could, including her breaks at work. The second was the one that had always eluded her, yet so many of her friends and patients possessed it and took it for granted. Now, at twenty four, she found herself once again alone. Her mother and two brothers lived in Pittsburgh, which was perfect. They were close enough for a visit and far enough not to interfere. She was done being a mother to all three. She was done being the responsible one, the provider. It was her mother's turn to finally assume the role so lustfully begotten and so willfully neglected.

Ironically, Jennifer's departure from her family a year ago was the very nudge that her mother needed to finally raise her boys. At last, it was something, for she had never raised Jennifer. Jennifer raised herself and would not have it any other way, except that she yearned to be a mother. She knew she would excel at it and her heart swelled at the thought. In her daydreams, this wish was already fulfilled by a doting husband and four children: two boys and two girls. She even knew the names, and where she would live. Jennifer had her family life all planned out, except for one problem. She was alone.

Alone she approached the odd glow in room 328. She was not afraid. Basic fear was something she felt that she had conquered years ago. She was simply curious.

The glow was a soft magenta color with short bursts of deep violet. As she approached the room, where Mary Collins lay in a coma, the possible causes of the mysterious glow flooded her mind. "Television set? Was Mary awake? Malfunctioning light, but of that color? A gauge bulb at the end of its life, glowing bright before it burst? Maybe it was some police activity out in the parking lot. That must be it," she reasoned.

Just as she was coming around the last corner toward the gentle glow that now barely illuminated the open doorway of room 328, the telephone at the nurses' station rang. "Darn it," she muttered and turned toward her desk to answer the insistent ringing.

Jennifer picked up the receiver only to discover no one on the other end, not even a "Hello" or a "Sorry". "Hello," she fished for a response. The line was still open, but no one answered. Someone was there, but no one answered. "Hello! Trauma Unit, may I help you?" Nothing. Not a thing. She did not hang up. She was curious about the outcome. Finally, the other party broke contact, and Jennifer was answered by a busy tone. "Strange night tonight," Jennifer whispered under her breath. She turned her attention to room 328 once more. She was met with complete darkness. The glow was gone.

Rushing toward the open door of the room, she peered inside not knowing what to expect. To her relief and disappointment, nothing had changed. Mary Collins remained motionless on her bed with a fixed mesmerizing smile that could not be extinguished by the tubes that pierced her body and kept it alive. All was unchanged.

Jennifer looked around the room. There were no magenta gauges or lights. The television was off, as always, and the shades were drawn. Nothing had changed, yet something was different. Jennifer was sure of it. No, maybe she was simply working too much in order to save some money. "Maybe these double shifts are a bad idea after all?" she thought. "I'm seeing things, just like Jack."

The picture of the young man projected in her mind. She sat back into the chair next to Mary's bed and enjoyed that mental vision. Sighing, she looked at Mary and touched her hand. "You poor dear. You are so blessed to have such a man that loves you, a handsome and smart one too. Now, it could all be taken away. Why? Why do things like this happen to a promising young person like you? Why?" Jen asked of Mary, who answered with silence. "What I would give to have a man like your Jack. You're lucky, Mary. I mean you were lucky. Look at you. You're certainly not lucky now. Yet, you continue to smile like joy eternal. You continue to smile like you know a secret beyond any I can fathom. You smile like you see beyond the grave." The last thought made her shiver. "Maybe you never really conquer fear," her thoughts drifted. "Certainly not until you resolve that mystery beyond the grave. Such morbid thoughts! I'm working too hard."

Jennifer remained seated and fluffed up Mary's pillows. "We're like sisters, you and I," she whispered aloud. "Together we would have everything, yet apart we have little. That this touch would heal." She touched Mary's dark black hair. "I used to believe the Bible miracles, but then I was just a kid. Look at you, Mary. You're hardly a miracle, nor am I able to provide you one. You have a man who fulfills you, yet no awareness of him now, and I have the awareness to know he's yours, not mine. We're like sisters, you and I, Mary. I could use a sister like you. I always wished for a sister like you. You rest and soon you'll get better. I know it, even if the doctors think otherwise." Jennifer got up and adjusted Mary's pillow once more, for a moment forgetting any differences between them. In that moment, they were kindred souls — nothing more, nothing less.

"Whatever that glow was, it brought out the mushy side in me," Jennifer admitted softly. "May I be the first to greet you back." Jennifer smiled at the thought, and headed out the door for she had other patients to tend to that night.

After she left, the glow briefly returned, but its source was no clearer to her than before, for she was now too preoccupied to notice it.

CHAPTER 8

A Good Cup of Tea

Lilly Austin was awakened by the sun shining into her stately bedroom. She reached over to find her lover, and instead found an empty bed with a scribbled note. The sight of both made her angry. She felt cheated and used. She exhaled audibly and slipped out of bed. "Nothing a good cup of tea and a dram can't cure," her father used to say. He relied on the dram, and she relied on the tea.

Reluctantly, she accepted her fate and cursed her weakness the night before. She gave him everything, sparing nothing of herself, of her generous skills and luxurious frills. She gave all and got little in return. The arrangement was starting to wear thin. Maybe it was time for a change. He had once again fallen short. No man could seem to replace the gap left by her passing father, and the candidates of late were sorrier than ever. Her father was a gentleman and would never use a lady, never. "Nothing a good cup of tea and a dram can't cure," she repeated to herself, deciding to exclude the dram.

For company within her palatial home she had her two domestics. One was the maid who doubled as her cook, and the other was the butler who doubled as her chauffeur. Presently, he was the butler. "Andrew, I would like a nice cup of Earl Grey," she paged, "and some of those lovely blueberry scones that Martha makes. Thank you, Andrew."

Andrew and Martha were a middle-aged couple who had served Lilly's father when he was alive. When Lilly inherited her father's fortune, which included this spacious estate in western Pennsylvania, she offered to keep them on per her father's wishes. Her father, a native of western Ireland, had been a history professor at McLaren towards the end of his career. Despite relocating his household to Pennsylvania, he never sold his small castle in Ireland, for it was too closely associated with his late wife, Camille, Lilly's mother, who had died when Lilly was still a child. Although it had been over seven years since the relocation, she, Andrew and Martha felt grossly out of place here and missed their Irish manor. Little kept her here now, except for a mistake. But that too would soon be resolved, and Lilly was certain that by the end of the summer, they would return to Ireland. In fact, she was so certain that she had decided to place her Pennsylvania estate on the market by the end of the week.

In this determined mindset, she dismissed her dissatisfaction with her lover from the night before and enjoyed her tea and scones. "Andrew, when is Phillip expected to arrive? Was it 2 or 3 this afternoon?"

"At 2 pm, Miss," replied Andrew as he refilled her tea cup. He was careful not to say "Madam" for he knew that she was sensitive to that word. "Will you join me in picking him up at the airport, Miss Austin?"

Lilly sighed. She did not wish to go to the airport to pick up her elderly husband, who served simply as a tool for assuring her luxury on two continents. He was the mistake that she had made ten months ago, when she finally agreed to marry him. She considered him a fool of the worst kind, a fool who thought he was loved when he was disdained. "Why are men such a bother, and yet such a seeming necessity?" she pondered silently over her cup of tea. Her lover had stamina, vigor and lust, but he was a fool, like her husband, Phillip. To her they were all fools, except her dear departed father, of course.

A woman of her youth and passion craved to be satisfied. The young fool who had shared her bed last night was simply a fulfillment. Her husband had none of the traits of a lover and "could not satisfy a drunken barmaid" as she had recently explained to an old girlfriend in Ireland, yet he had money, fame and clout. After all, he was Phillip Austin, the famous American writer and playwright. But the thought of having sex with him tonight, which he would certainly demand upon his arrival, was enough to make her regurgitate her scone, clotted cream and all. "Why must life be so complicated? Why cannot one man have it all? So frustrating," she mumbled.

"What is frustrating, Miss?" Andrew replied.

"You men are frustrating."

"Yes, Miss. My wife says the same, but if I may be so bold, you ladies are not easy either," Andrew added with a smile.

"Spare me your wisdoms, Andrew. More tea please, my dear. You're an exception and Martha is a lucky lady."

"You are most kind, Miss. Will you be accompanying me to the airport to meet Dr. Austin?"

Lilly hesitated. She knew that she should, but what did she care about this man that she called her "husband".

"Yes, of course. When do we leave?" she finally surrendered.

"By one o'clock, Miss. I will bring the car around, as usual."

"By the way Andrew, regarding my visitor last night, neither you nor Martha are to say anything. Do you understand?"

"I do not know what you are talking about, Miss," the wise butler lied.

"Oh, stop. I may be young, but I wasn't born yesterday. Just remember who pays your keep!"

"Yes, Miss, as you wish."

"Also, if you do happen to see that 'visitor' again, throw him out. Do you understand? I'm done with him."

"Yes, Miss."

"I don't need him. He's not worth the bother. In a few months, God willing, we'll be back in Ireland and all this will matter little."

"I'll throw him out with pleasure, Miss," Andrew replied and sincerely meant it. He and Martha did not care for Lilly's latest lover in the least. He was the worst of the bunch, having no respect or manners. "Is our return certain, Miss? Martha will be most pleased. Has Dr. Austin approved of the move?" Andrew asked.

"He has no choice if he wants to be with me, and that desire, I assure you, remains unchanged."

"Yes, Miss."

"Thank you for the fine cup of tea, and please thank Martha for the excellent scones."

"My pleasure, Miss."

"Yes, pleasure is a fine thing," she replied as she rose from the table, "but until we return to Ireland, I may have to take care of that myself." She did not care that Andrew overheard her as she headed for her bedroom.

"Odd one that," Andrew reflected to himself. "Old Professor Collins treated her like a princess, and now we have little choice but to deal with it. I miss Mary. She's the opposite. Too bad she broke all ties soon after the old man died. All ties except the one with me, that is. That reminds me, I have not paid her a visit in nearly three weeks. I better look her up tomorrow. I promised her father that I'd look after her. Jealousy can turn love into hate like little else. Miss Lilly can never forgive Mary that their father loved her more, or so she thinks. Mary's everything that Lilly's not. God bless our Mary."

Anger filled Andrew's heart as he remembered the horrible falling out between the two sisters that occurred after their father died. Mary simply wanted peace, but Lilly wanted it all, even all the memories of her father's love. She completely disowned Mary. But that was not enough. She tried to steal all that she could by hiring a jackal of a lawyer, another of her numerous lovers. With his help, she used discrepancies in the will to rob Mary of a sizable portion of the family estate. Mary stood little chance against her sister's cunning. Although Mary tried to make peace, Lilly would not have it.

Andrew warned Mary every chance he had of her sister's treachery, but to little avail. Mary seemed disinterested in the feud and its material implications. She did not want to talk about it and felt somehow responsible. It was a point of great unresolved pain for the younger sister, and a point of unfulfilled greed for the older, for a large part of the fortune still belonged to Mary, despite the legal battles.

"Well, I promised the old man that I would look after them both regardless of what would come, so I better call on Mary tomorrow when Miss Lilly's occupied," Andrew concluded and headed upstairs to share the good news with his wife that soon they would return to the Emerald Island.

CHAPTER 9

Mr. Chesterfield

The house on Ryan Ridge Road was small and poorly insulated. The wind could enter at will and it often did so uninvited. There were countless cats perched on countless collectables, and the yard resembled a testimonial of man's temporal supremacy over nature. The weeds were showing little power over the heaps of rusting relics of mechanical advancement. The 1943 sedan, whose wheels were nothing more than cornflowers, shared space with an equally rusty washer and dryer, each with its assortments of native shrubbery. An ironing board, turned into a trellis for vines of poison ivy, was edged out by a cadre of abandoned pressure cylinders, whose content was long forgotten. These waited, armed like torpedoes, for the war between man and nature to start anew. Little was added in recent years for there was not much room for improvement. The exception was a rusty old school bus whose bare axles rested on four pairs of cinderblocks. It was added three years ago to extend the run-down shack, and to provide a new living room with no shortage of seating.

To say that old Mr. Chesterfield was a collector was to underestimate his talent and his long roots on the east side of town. He was a descendent of three generations of collectors whose hard labor now rusted all around him on the two acres that were the last remnant of a once mighty estate. But besides collectables and cats, Mr. Chesterfield had one other endearing quality: he was a natural on the saxophone. That talent went mostly unnoticed by all except one and she alone often braved the hazards of the the surroundings. The old school bus driver was also a dormitory security guard, her security guard, for she lived in that very dorm. That one kind and appreciative soul now lay comatose in room 328 in the trauma ward of the nearby hospital.

Old Mr. Chesterfield never forgot Mary's kindness, and as soon as he could excuse himself from his two jobs, he went to visit her. It was nearly 7 pm on Tuesday, and as luck would have it Jennifer was tending to her favorite patient when the scruffy old man entered the room. He nearly scared her out of her uniform, which was not an easy feat given that Jennifer had much more control over her fears than most.

"My apologies, Miss, but I'm a friend of Mary's. I would have come sooner, but this is the soonest I could come," he explained in a very logical way.

"You scared me to death. I thought you were a ghost or something. In this room you never know what comes a calling," Jennifer replied mysteriously.

The reply was much too complex for old Mr. Chesterfield, who was a simple man except for his two acres of possessions. "My apologies, Miss, for the fright and all."

As he saw Mary, he broke into tears. They wormed their way through his furrowed skin and fell silently onto the floor. "My God! She looks so peaceful and beautiful, like an angel. Who would harm an angel, I ask you?" He slowly neared the chair beside the bed as Jennifer finished checking Mary's vital signs.

Jennifer was about to leave the room, but his words stopped her. Here was the first person who seemed to have an idea as to what actually happened to this poor unfortunate girl. Jennifer's curiosity could not be restrained. "Did you say that someone did this to her?"

"Yes, but I don't know exactly who. I suspect it was that young professor-type or that arrogant boy or his girlfriend, but I don't know for sure. They're all very self-centered, you know. You can tell that pretty quickly about people, the way they look at you when you're not one of them." He shared his logic and insights with the patient nurse.

"As I told that short inspector with the mustache, I know that Mary was pushed because I know my Mary, and she'd never take her own life. You see, Miss, one in love with life can't take a life, not even their own. It's like laughter souring joy, or a rainbow ruining the rain. It's impossible for they are the beauty within that very thing," he continued logically, and rather profoundly for an old bus driver and security guard.

"I'm not sure what you mean, Sir." Jennifer was drawn to this odd stranger for he somehow held a clue to how this girl, the subject of her newfound sisterhood, ended up motionless on her ward.

"It's simple. You see, I know Mary very well. She loves my music and comes to see me twice a week, Tuesdays and Fridays. I play for her. I play better than ever 'cause of her, 'cause she cares. I'm happy 'cause of her. She's happiness, and she brings happiness. So, you see, happiness can't destroy itself. Mary can't and didn't do this to herself as that inspector tried to imply. Nor did she slip. She's no klutz, she's a climber. Few know this, but she's an avid climber. She showed me the pictures from her climbs. She says that on a mountain top she can really feel God. A person like that does not end up this way unless someone else caused it," he concluded. "And someone else caused it," he repeated as if to assure Jennifer.

"You're sure? That would be attempted murder." Jennifer starred at him in disbelief.

"Oh, I'm sure, and that murderer is still out there."

"Hopefully she will make it, and it won't be a murder," Jennifer consoled them both.

"It's murder regardless 'cause it was intended as such," Mr. Chesterfield added his simple logic. "That murderer's still out there, and I told that nosy inspector that it's one of four 'cause I saw those four disappear behind that bluff just before that horrible scream. I ran out of my bus, but I was too late. There she lay at the base of the cliff, my dear Mary. I don't know what I'll do without her. So, if you don't mind, I'll sit here awhile and pray for her, even though it has been over twenty years since I prayed. But, I'll pray as hard as I can. But, if I ever find out who did this, and I'll find out, why I'll…. Well, I better not, is all I can say," the old man got emotional again. He reached for a small flask in his pocket for courage, but then decided that this was a sacred place, with Mary there and all, so that he had better wait.

"I have prayed for her every day since she got here," Jennifer replied, still standing over Mary's bed while facing the seated old man. "She'll get better." Jennifer was trying to convince herself of the possibility of a miraculous recovery, although her professional training told her that the longer the coma, the worse the chances. "Are you sure someone pushed her?" she asked still bewildered by the revelation.

"Yes, I know someone did, and I know it was one of those five. Maybe it was a conspiracy, although I can't imagine why someone would hurt a person like Mary." He moved the chair up against the bed and looked at the eternal smile on Mary's face. It somehow made him feel lighter and younger.

Jennifer decided to leave them alone and continued on her rounds.

"I missed you coming round this week, Mary. I wrote you a new song. It's called 'Mary' since it's about you, and all." He reached out his quivering old hand and gently placed it over Mary's. There he held it as if he were holding on to life itself. She had brought life back to him and now he was determined to repay the favor.

"I'll play for you and it'll make you feel better," he concluded and pulled an old saxophone out of the case he had brought into the room. In no time, the ward was treated to one of the most beautiful and soulful saxophone solos ever delivered. The old man was a musical genius, and only Mary had appreciated it.

Unfortunately, the trauma ward is not the ideal setting for even the most inspiring of saxophone solos. Old Mr. Chesterfield did not get much past the first stanza when he was interrupted by a rather anxious Jennifer. "I'm sorry, Sir, but I'll have to ask you not to play your saxophone. It's beautiful, but it's arousing all of the patients from their sleep," she explained.

Mr. Chesterfield had forgotten about the other patients, and even about the trauma ward. He had simply wanted to share his latest creation with his muse that had inspired it. With an expression of confusion and sadness, he ceased his musical tribute and simply repeated. "Sorry! Sorry, Miss! Sorry! Sorry, Miss! Sorry..."

"It's quite all right. It was beautiful, and I can see why Mary enjoyed listening to you play. You're a very talented musician," Jennifer replied, seeing his genuine concern.

Mr Chesterfield was embarrassed. As his face reddened, he simply replied, "Thank you, Miss. Thank you very much, Miss. Sorry about the noise, Miss."

"It was hardly noise, but simply not the right place and time. But, I'm sure Mary enjoyed it."

"Thank you, Miss."

"Well, I'll leave you two alone", Jennifer replied, and once more slipped out of the dimly lit room.

Mr. Chesterfield was a child at heart and his mind seemed to follow. He simply sat by Mary's side and stared at her in anticipation that his short but sincere musical tribute would awaken her at any moment. There he sat and every few minutes he would say, "You're my angel, Mary, and I know you'll be all right soon. I know it, but when I find out who did this to you, I'll, well I just might, I might." Then he looked at her some more, never letting go of her precious hand. There Jennifer found him 40 minutes later, sound asleep. When he awoke, he was confused and soon hurried off, for he had a school bus to drive at 5:30 am the next morning.

"Odd old man, but he sure loves her and can play one hell of a saxophone," Jennifer thought. "You've got some unusual visitors, Mary," Jennifer concluded aloud.

If Mary could answer, she would have replied along these lines, "Jen, brace yourself, for this is just the beginning."

CHAPTER 10

Randy and Suzy

Randell Twiner and Suzy Kurtz had always dated, or so it seemed to all of their friends and relatives. Thus, it came as a shock to everyone when Randell decided to pursue other venues. Having both grown up in Brennantown, the home of McLaren University, they were the local king and queen of the present McLaren junior class, just as they had been in high school. Randell was the football star and Suzy headed up the cheerleading squad, same as high school. It was just as it had always been in their lives. Nothing had changed and everyone liked it that way. The American dream had its mascots and they were Randy and Suzy.

The news of their breakup had spread like wildfire a few days before the Mary tragedy, in the midst of which they now found themselves as persons of interest with the police. It all started soon after their recent, much-publicized engagement.

Suzy had officially dated Randy for five years. Although she initially wanted to leave Brennantown, she decided to attend

McLaren in the hope of fulfilling her dream of marrying the hometown football legend, Randy. Everyone agreed that it was a good idea, and that the pair was perfectly matched. A union between the Twiner and Kurtz families, two of the wealthiest families in town, had been anticipated for several generations, and now it was to becoming a reality. Money attracts money and power likes to consolidate. This union had both. The parents were ecstatic about the anticipated marriage. In short, all was going swimmingly until Mary Collins entered the picture.

Mary had an unusual effect on the arrogant and self-centered Randell. She drew him out of his comfort zone and into hers by simply being. Her interest in the boy, who was a year younger and a decade less mature, was minimal. In fact, it was worse. He was the very type that she never could understand. As a result, she ignored him, or, at best, was politely detached to his unquestionable desires.

Randell, a child of no want and a man of much need, was completely unaccustomed to such a reaction. He had never encountered such benevolent ignorance from the opposite sex, having been at the top of every hometown girl's wish list since he could remember. Mary's disinterest in him spurred his ego further and stoked his curiosity. Suddenly, Suzy Kurtz, the perky prom queen, could not satisfy. She was too needy, too interested, and too easy to conquer. Why climb a hill when an unconquered mountain looms in clear view? Mary was that mountain and in his mind Randell had already staked his claim to her conquest despite his recent engagement.

Suzy sensed Randell's interests in Mary possibly sooner than Randell himself. It was not hard to do. Her initial disbelief turned to anger, but she willed herself not to betray her emotions. She instinctively knew that that would undermine her chances with the man she desired. Instead, she decided to pay Mary a visit.

Mary was struggling with her math homework when Suzy knocked on her dorm room door three days before the geology field trip.

"Come in, the door's open!" Mary yelled over her shoulder.

Suzy stormed into the room and was instantly taken back by the decor. The walls of the dorm room were covered with pictures of people, normal, ordinary people from various parts of the world, and nature, normal, ordinary places in nature. A big string of hearts ran across the top of the double window, and flowers and candles were visible everywhere. "Weird girl," Suzy concluded. "What can he see in such a nerdy weirdo?" She did not have time to answer her own thoughts, for Mary turned around to face her while still seated at her desk. The desk was covered with books that seemed to flow out of the large bookshelf beyond.

"Hey, Suzy," Mary greeted her cheerfully. "This is a surprise. How're you, and what can I do for you?" Mary asked in a friendly but slightly detached manner. She was puzzled. She knew Suzy disliked her. It was common knowledge, but she refused to dislike her back. "Have a seat! You don't mind sitting on the bed, do you?"

Suzy did not answer, but simply fell on the bed with purposeful drama, accented by a hateful exhale. Suzy was angry, while Mary remained detached. Such drama had no power over her. She had grown up with worse, having endured a far more accomplished drama queen, her older sister Lilly.

Finally, Suzy spoke, after a long pause created to enhance the effect of her preplanned and well-rehearsed speech, which she now delivered in a sour monologue. Mary listened quietly and intently until silence once more separated the two women.

"Well, what do you have to say for yourself, stealing my fiancée and all? Why I should scratch your eyes out!" Suzy added emotionally.

Mary sat silently, genuinely confused.

"Well, is it true? Are you messing around with my Randy?" Suzy forced the subject.

"Frankly, Suzy, I'm shocked," Mary replied. "Don't take this wrong, but I have, had and will forever have zero interest in Randell. There's nothing that I find attractive about him."

Suzy was not expecting this response. At first, she did not know whether to be happy with the news or be deeply offended. Since happiness was not the theme of the day, she chose the latter. "How dare you insult Randy when we all know you're flirting with him?" Suzy needed to reassure herself that the prize, Randell, was worth the cat fight. He had to be inflated. Otherwise, the entire dispute would be petty. "We all know that Randy's a great catch, or you and all the rest of the damn sluts on this campus wouldn't be eyeing him up and trying to steal him from me. Deny it if you wish, but I'm onto you, you pathetic freak!" Suzy stomped her feet in unison on the wooden floor as she rose in a sudden dramatic effort to frighten Mary. The latter, of course, was unmoved by the primitive territorial display.

"Whatever, Suzy! But do me a favor, and next time you and Randell get in one of these insecurity-fueled bouts, don't come looking to me for blame. You two belong together. That part's very clear. Now, if you don't mind, I need to return to this math problem, which is far more stimulating than your dramatic display."

"Bitch, I'll get you for this!" Suzy turned on her heels and marched out the room. Unfortunately for Suzy, the entire episode was witnessed by Mary's shy and mild-mannered neighbor, Milly Chang, who after Mary's mysterious fall relayed the story to Inspector Cabot, making Suzy a key person of interest in the case. The fact that Suzy was apparently the first to spot the fallen victim only made matters worse.

Randell was no less suspicious in the case for he clearly had a clash with Mary just before her fall. The exchange on the bus had been witnessed by several classmates on that fateful day. The witness accounts agreed that he had been clearly rejected by Mary, and that his anger towards her was visible and audible.

Now Randy and Suzy had to join forces once more to survive the bad publicity from the Mary tragedy. Under the strict direction of their parents, three days after Mary's fall, they announced that they were engaged once more and any previous rumors of a breakup were quickly squelched. Both parties were supposedly happy, especially Suzy, who actually looked the part, unlike Randy, who fell far short of the mark, despite repeated maternal coaching.

CHAPTER II

Daphne

*M*ary's hospital room was quiet, except for the sound of the medical monitors and life support equipment. Five nights had passed since Mary's fall. She remained in a coma, but that tranquil smile continued to adorn her face. It was around 9:30 pm. Jennifer was working another double shift despite her previous promises to herself. She was nearly through her first shift. The ward was fairly empty and she found herself for the first time that week with little to do. It looked like it was going to be a quiet night and she was looking forward to it.

As she settled into her chair at the nurses' station, she once more scanned the ward. There is often a restlessness among the patients when night sets in, but on this evening all was quiet, too quiet. As she turned her head toward the computer screen, something caught the corner of her eye. Looking up to refocus, she was startled to see a young woman standing nearly in front of her, as if she had materialized out of nowhere. Surprised, Jennifer looked straight at the intruder unable to hide her reaction.

The silent visitor was in her early 20s and wore a look of deep sadness. She ignored Jennifer's visible shock and remained unmoved, like a detached phantom.

"May I help you?" Jennifer asked.

There was a slight hesitation before the young woman answered in a voice that did not fit her somber appearance, for it was an octave higher than Jennifer had expected. It sounded like the voice of a little girl.

"Yes, I'm looking for Mary Collins."

"Are you family?"

"No, a classmate." There was another slight hesitation. "I'm a close friend."

"I see. Well, as you may know, she's asleep."

"Yes. Has she awakened at all?"

"No. I'm afraid not."

"May I see her?"

"Sure. She's in room 328."

"Thank you," the odd girl responded and headed toward Mary's room.

"Odd thing," Jennifer concluded. Since she was not busy and since she was becoming extremely protective of Mary, she decided to follow the youth at a distance. The girl entered the room and disappeared behind the slightly drawn bed curtain. Jennifer felt odd to be intruding and was about to turn around when something drew her back. She decided to enter quietly on the pretense that she was checking Mary's vital signs. As she entered, she was surprised by what she witnessed.

The odd girl was bent over Mary and in the act of kissing her on the lips. Jennifer stood still for a second, feeling like she was intruding on a lovers' moment. The kiss was tender, and not at all like that of a mere friend. Jennifer decided to retreat and leave the two alone. "Mary has the oddest visitors," Jennifer concluded once more and found herself uncomfortably perched outside the door. Finally, she decided to enter with a mission regardless of what she may witness. Yet, despite her resolve, she pulled back once more. What she glimpsed now dismayed her further.

The odd girl was in bed with Mary, resting herself on her left elbow while caressing Mary's dark hair with her right hand and showering her with passionate kisses. At first, Jennifer stood silently startled. The odd girl had her back to her and had not noticed her. She realized that she indeed was interrupting a private moment, but it was not acceptable for this stranger to be in bed with a patient, especially given the plethora of vital tubes and life support equipment. Jennifer cleared her throat.

To her surprise, there was no response. The odd visitor continued showering affection on Mary without being conscious of Jennifer in the least. Jennifer once more cleared her throat, but louder this time. In fact, she nearly coughed out a lung. Finally, the girl turned and quickly slipped off the bed. She was red faced and visibly embarrassed.

"Oh, I'm sorry. I'll be going now," she stuttered.

"Who are you?" Jennifer asked, no longer concerned with formalities.

"I'm Mary's friend."

"Yes, but what's your name, Mary's friend?"

"Oh, I'm Daphne," the girl was meek in her behavior and response. She looked nervously at the door, but Jennifer stood between her and the escape route.

"Daphne, you and Mary seem very close." Jennifer was curious.

"Yes! No!" Daphne exclaimed and looked down once more hiding her face with her disheveled hair. Finally, she looked up and Jennifer was struck by her strikingly green eyes, which were alluring even to her, who had never felt that kind of attraction to the same sex. She quickly dismissed it, but her subconscious reaction to Daphne startled her enough that she lost her train of thought. Daphne used the pause to excuse herself and made a beeline toward the door.

"Wait!" Jennifer heard herself object. She was curious and although she realized that she was entering a dangerous area of patient privacy, she was too curious to stop. She needed to know. "I thought that Mary had a boyfriend", she said before she could stop herself.

Daphne stopped and turned within reach of the doorway. There was an uncomfortable silence, and then she burst out emotionally in an angered voice. "It was a mistake, but I found out about it. He's not a boyfriend, but a cowardly womanizer. It was a mistake. Mary belongs to me!" Daphne exclaimed and stormed out the door.

Jennifer followed her out of the room, only to see her quickly disappear through the double doors of the ward. She shook her head and returned back to Mary's room, where she adjusted Mary's blankets and checked her vital signs. As she fixed her covers, she noticed a small, stuffed teddybear holding a heart with "Love Always" stitched across it.

"Now that's a turn I did not expect," Jennifer muttered to herself. "You're a real mystery, Mary Collins. Who would have guessed?" She smiled and checked to make sure that Mary's vital signs had not changed. She decided to leave the teddy bear where it lay, tucked next to Mary. It made her look like a little girl, peacefully asleep with her favorite toy. "Who are you really, Mary?" Jennifer asked aloud. A paging voice echoed over the room monitor, as if to answer her question.

"Angel, Angel!"

Jennifer recognized the voice of her fellow night nurse paging her. She turned and headed out of the room.

CHAPTER 12

The Hunch

Inspector Cabot was working late that night. It was already past 11 pm, and he was no closer to convincing his boss of his suspicions that the Mary Collins case was an attempted homicide. The evidence did not support an accident or a suicide, but it did not rule them out either. There was something about this seemingly innocent girl that brought out the paternal instincts in this father of three.

He and his team had checked the crime scene and had carefully reviewed all of the witness testimonies. They had interviewed countless individuals associated with that doomed field trip, and others that were simply acquainted with Mary. They had discovered that the girl's father had died two years earlier in this very town, and that her mother died in Ireland sixteen years prior. Further probing revealed that she had a surviving older sister who lived in the area, and they planned to interview her. The Inspector was convinced that Mary was pushed, but by whom? For a seemingly innocent youth, she was surrounded by mystery and intrigue. The plot thickened as did his cold cup of instant coffee.

He was tired and began a monologue with the walls of his shabby office which stood in judgement of his logic. "She was pushed. That's clear. The quarry was muddy that day, and yet there were no slip marks at the fall location. Nor were her shoes soiled with mud as one would expect in a slip. Her clothes were equally unsoiled, except by the impact. It was not slippage but a trajectory. Her clothes didn't contain any evidence of sliding such as streaks of mud or vegetation. Most important of all, her hands were not soiled by mud, nor was there any dirt under her fingernails. This girl was not struggling to keep from falling or sliding because she was pushed. She was propelled off that cliff and made contact with the muddy ground only upon impact at the bottom of the quarry. She was clearly pushed. The evidence confirms it," he concluded aloud.

The monologue continued. "Next, there's the position of the body and the nature of the injuries. The body was lying much too far from the foot of the quarry wall, which at that location was nearly vertical. If Mary had slipped, she would have landed at the very foot of the quarry wall. But she was nearly six feet away from it with no slip marks anywhere. She was not only pushed, but pushed with significant force. She appeared to have landed on her posterior, subsequently hitting the back of her head. Her lacerations were all associated with the impact, and the impact alone. Based on the position of her body and the injuries sustained, the force had projected her legs outward. Most probably, she was pushed on the lower part of the body. Her body was oriented such that her feet were furthest from the cliff face and her head closest to it. Thus, she must have been facing toward the quarry. Even if she did awaken from her coma, she would probably have no idea who pushed her, for most likely she never saw her attacker," he muttered.

The Inspector was frustrated. He had painstakingly recon-structed the case based on the physical evidence alone, not fully trusting the witnesses, for many of the key ones were primary suspects. In his mind, he was certain that this was an attempted homicide that by all indications could soon become a murder. Yet, his boss was cautious. He reminded Inspector Cabot of his past hunches, some of which were far from accurate, and he still saw all the evidence for a criminal case as circumstantial. There was too much discrepancy among the witnesses. An accident seemed to him to be the most likely scenario and politically the safest.

"Bring me a clear motive and a solid witness record, and maybe you'll have something. Right now, Jim, you've got nothing but a hunch. You know where a hunch gets you in a courtroom, especially in a murder trial?" the Inspector's boss proclaimed. "The last thing I need is to be in the doghouse with the Attorney General breathing down my neck. You got nothing, Jim! Good day."

The Inspector felt that he had a lot more than "nothing". It was after 11:30 pm when he refilled his cup with rot-gut coffee for the sixth time that night. He worked best at night when the office was empty, and he could afford to do so for he was no longer married. He had given up that love for one that was closer to his heart, his job, and he did not regret it. "Okay, back to the witness testimony," he mumbled as he looked up at the old cork board hanging in his office on which he had dozens of pictures of the crime scene and of Mary's body. "I promise I'll find who did this to you," he whispered as he looked at Mary's ashen face staring at him from the photographs. He pulled a handful of pictures from the board, and sipping his black coffee, he examined them closely, looking for something he may have missed. Putting down his coffee cup, he reached for the large magnifying glass lying on his desk. He was of the old school; while others kept all the evidence on their computer or "smart" device, the Inspector still used an old camera, paper photos and a magnifying glass.

"What's this?" he muttered as he closely examined one of the photographs. "Could I have missed something?"

He hunched under the bright light on his desk, still examining the printed photo. "Is that a small mark on her neck or is that dirt?" He was talking to himself, which was not a good sign, but he did not care. "One of you clowns pushed her and I'm going to find out which one," he proclaimed aloud, and looked up at a smaller cork board on the adjacent wall, which contained six pictures, the photographs of his primary suspects. There was the field trip leader, graduate student Jack Fulton, and Mary's spiteful rich sister, Lilly Austin. Then there was the privileged pair, Randell Twiner and Suzy Kurtz. And finally that odd shy girl, Daphne Marconi, and the self-centered jock, Tony Bond.

"Damn it! I may have missed something. I wonder if it's still there. I'll have to pay Miss Mary a visit." He looked at his watch. It read 11:43 pm. "I should be there in less than 15 minutes," he concluded and headed out the door.

When he arrived at the trauma unit, all was quiet.

"Miss, where can I find Mary Collins?" Inspector Cabot asked Jennifer.

"Right over there, Sir. Are you family?"

"No," the Inspector chuckled and pulled out his badge.

"Oh, I see. Well, she's in room 328, Inspector. It's right around the corner."

"Thank you," he replied and disappeared.

Jennifer was curious. The presence of the police seemed to confirm the story of the peculiar old man who came to visit Mary the night before. She struggled to remember his name. "Oh, yes, Mr. Chesterfield," she recalled.

Her curiosity got the better of her, and she decided to follow the Inspector into room 328. As she entered, she got another shock. Stopping just past the doorway, she saw the Inspector bent over Mary as if he were trying to kiss her.

"What's going on here?" she nearly said out load.

He seemed to be fondling her neck as if he were going to try again. As he bent over Mary, his face seemed too close to her while his right hand moved her head and appeared to caress her neck, pulling the hair back to expose it. He seemed like a Dracula ready to strike. She could not tell for sure, but it looked exactly like what she had witnessed with Daphne.

Jennifer audibly cleared her throat to announce her presence. "What a disgusting man!" she concluded to herself. The sound made the Inspector spring away from Mary and focus directly on Jennifer.

"It's not as it seems. My apologies," he muttered rather embarrassed.

"Oh, it seems pretty clear. How dare you try to grope her like that?" Jennifer was furious. "Why, I'm calling security! How do I know you're a police inspector? You appear to be some kind of a pervert!"

"My apologies, Miss. It must appear awkward, but I was simply trying to get a look at the back left side of her neck."

"How's that any better? What kind of a weirdo are you? I'm calling security!" Jennifer ran out to the nearest phone.

"Miss, please let me explain!" The Inspector followed, but it was too late. Security were on their way.

"Don't you try anything! I know karate," Jennifer lied. "You're probably the one that did this to her."

"No, I'm the one trying to find out who did this to her," the Inspector insisted.

"There they are," Jennifer said as two large men in uniform hurry into the ward. "That's the guy! I caught him trying to grope one of the young female coma patients!"

"It's an honest mistake. I was simply trying to see if there was a marking on the subject's neck as evident in this photo." The Inspector held up the photo.

"Look, buddy, you're coming with us!" the larger of the burley men replied.

"But, I'm an inspector with the State Police."

"Sure and I'm Tinker Bell," said the burly security officer, with the large snake tattoo, as he grabbed the Inspector.

"Wait, let me get my badge!" the Inspector insisted and fumbled for his badge. Finally, he retrieved it and shoved it in front of the two burly security guards, who were ready to drag him away. "Look!" he exclaimed, flashing his badge.

The two guards stopped and released him, while the larger of the two inspected the badge. "Okay. What gives? What's going on here?" the big man asked.

"As I was saying," the Inspector began, "I'm investigating the case of Mary Collins in room 328. I came here to verify that this marking was on the victim and to get a better look at it." He handed the big man the slightly crumbled photograph which showed Mary's broken body immediately after her fall.

"What marking? I don't see anything," objected the large security guard.

"It's small, but I verified that she has a marking. It appears to be a small tattoo near the back of her neck on the left side beneath her hair. If you don't believe me, you can see for yourself," the Inspector offered.

"Okay," replied the large man.

What followed was both humorous and pathetic. The three men, accompanied by Jennifer, entered Mary's room. Jennifer positioned Mary gently to expose the marking. All three men examined it with curiosity.

"Okay. I see it. Well, at least she seems content," concluded the large security guard.

That thought had not occurred to the Inspector. He glanced once more at Mary's face and saw the Mona Lisa smile. "Why was she smiling?" he thought.

"Okay. You seem legitimate. I think we're done here," the big man proclaimed.

"Good night, Jen!" the two security guards said in unison and quickly departed.

"Sorry about that, but you looked pretty suspicious and guilty from where I was standing," Jennifer said by way of apology.

"It's fine, Miss. May I take a picture of the marking?"

"Sure," Jennifer replied, but remained in the room with the peculiar inspector, just in case she had not been wrong.

"Thank you," he replied and took a few photos with his camera.

"It looks like a small tattoo, no?" Jennifer said, as her curiosity returned.

"It is. I'm not sure it will be of much help but it's worth noting. Thanks again and apologies for the misunderstanding. I really am trying to find out what happened to this girl," the Inspector said sincerely.

"I'm the one who owes you an apology, but my job is to protect her."

"Too bad you weren't there to protect her last week," the Inspector sighed.

"I didn't know her then. But if I had, I would have," Jennifer replied.

"Me too. Me too," echoed the Inspector.

They parted and Jennifer returned to her rounds. It was exactly 3:30 am when the next visitor arrived.

CHAPTER 13

Purple Haze

Jennifer was tired. She was well into her second consecutive shift and had pumped enough coffee into her system to awaken the dead, yet still she felt sleepy. It was so quiet. Mary was one of only three patients in the unit that night, and all were silent. In the dim light and silence, Jennifer felt her head fall onto the desk of the nurses' station. She knew she was not allowed. She could get fired for sleeping on the job. Yet, her body resisted her logic and prepared for sleep. She was fighting a losing battle until all was lost. Jennifer was fast asleep by 3:18 am.

Twelve minutes later she was awakened by the sensation not unlike a gentle touch on her left shoulder. Still extremely groggy, she brushed it off and in a dreamy state replied, "Leave me alone, Mary. No more visitors tonight."

She was asleep once more, but only for a few seconds, for the sensation of the touch returned. This time she awakened with a start, only to find that she was completely alone. "What the hell was that?" she muttered. The touch had felt so real that she was shocked NOT to see anyone. "I'm working too hard. Too many doubles," she muttered to herself in the silence. As she regained her full acumen, she became aware of purple haze emanating from room 328.

"It's back! That mysterious glow is back." Her excitement mixed with fear before curiosity took over. Quickly but silently, she made her way to Mary's room. As she approached, the glow grew in intensity; it was clearly not a mirage or a figment of her imagination. She stopped at the door and listened. All was silent, except for the sounds of the life support systems and monitors.

"Okay, here goes. If it's some kind of a ghost I'm gonna scream!" She allowed herself that option. Without further hesitation, she entered the room and nearly fell back, surprised.

CHAPTER 14

Tony

Meanwhile that night, Tony Bond had been drinking with his friends at a campus bar. Although he was only a junior, he was 23 years of age, having extended his McLaren University experience as a result of poor grades, an excessive lifestyle and the encouragement of his football coach. Tony Bond was becoming a football legend at McLaren, and competed only with Randell Twiner for that legacy. The two were rivals on and off the field. Randell was the rich kid quarterback with the glamorous car and cheerleader girlfriend. Tony was the opposite. He too was a hometown boy, but one who had grown up on the other side of the tracks. His father was an alcoholic who beat him regularly until Tony grew large enough to land his old man in the hospital as payback. His mother was a shadow that barely existed. Tony had it tough, but now he felt like the king of the world, at least his world.

"Damn that bitch! She had it coming. All stuck up with that Irish accent. I roughed her up a bit," Tony paused to suck on his beer, while his adoring fans, three young men of a similar age group, chuckled like hyenas. "As I said, I tried scaring her a bit. You know what I mean? Took a grab or two, but she was feisty. Damn near took my nuts out. Well that pissed me off! No snooty bitch kicks me in the nuts and gets away with it. Well, like I said, she got what was coming to her. I hate bitches like her that just think they're so f—in' great! You know what I mean?" He slugged down another beer, feeding his drunken anger, as the hyenas nervously laughed anew.

"So what did you do, Tony?" asked one.

"What would you do if some bitch kicked you in the nuts? Why I roughed her up good after that. Would you believe that that bitch tried to fink me out? She ran over to that professor friend of hers, but he was too scared to do anything about it. I frightened them both, and they both shut up. F--k, Johnny, I think you're pissing into your f—in' pants, man." Tony pointed at one of his friends, who in fact was so absorbed in the fine company and cheap alcohol that he forgot about the basics.

"Shit, man!" is all his buddy could muster as he ran off in search of the men's room.

"What a loser! You guys are all losers. Just like Mary Collins and that Professor Martin. Shit, she ran to old Martin. Can you believe it? Well I roughed him up a bit too, and then gave her a little to remember me by, and all was good. All is taken care of boys. She deserved it. I need to go, you losers!" Tony staggered out of the bar well past closing time. It was 2:20 am.

He headed to a place across town. He knew the way by heart these days. But tonight was different. He was completely drunk. On his way, he fell against trash cans, telephone poles, shrubs and fences. Finally, the momentum ceased and he settled against a large plastic cow that adorned the front of a local steak house. "Bitch! She deserved that!" He echoed to himself. "Stupid professor! Ha, ha, ha...(snore) (SNORE)." Tony fell asleep.

Tony Bond, the great running back at McLaren University, awoke in confusion. It was still dark. His face was plastered against the udders of the large plastic cow. One had imprinted itself on his cheek, leaving a red mark that resembled the hand symbol for his favorite "F" word. It was nearly 5 am when Tony resumed his drunken trek across town. Soon he arrived at his destination, a glorious mansion that looked like a transposed southern plantation complete with a circular drive.

He staggered up to the front door and rang the doorbell. No one answered. He rang again. Nothing. Rang. Nothing. Then he started banging.

Finally, one of the large double doors opened slightly, and an elderly gentleman peered out into the cold misty morning. As soon as he saw Tony, he slammed the door shut.

"Damn you, bastard!" Tony exclaimed. "Let me in, you old bastard!" he yelled. He was about to ring the doorbell again, when he heard the dogs. "Shit! He sent the dogs on me." Tony sobered quickly at the sound of the vicious dogs and disappeared into what little was left of the night.

By the time he arrived at home, there was a very tired police inspector parked in his driveway. Seeing Tony Bond staggering up the small drive, he stepped out of his car. It was nearly 6 am.

"There you are. I've been waiting for you." Inspector Cabot proclaimed with a smile.

"Go away, pig. Leave me alone!"

"I'm afraid that's not possible, Mr. Bond."

"What the f--k are you talking about, you damn cop?"

"You're coming with me for questioning."

"Like hell I am, old man!"

Suddenly, a second unmarked police car pulled into the drive, as if on cue. Two very large officers stepped out nearly in unison. "Take him in guys, but let's see if we can sober him up a bit," Inspector Cabot ordered.

"I have rights!" Bond yelled.

"Yes, you do, and these fine officers are about to remind you of those rights," the Inspector added as the two officers helped Tony into the unmarked car while reading him his rights.

"What the hell are you arresting me for, you pig?" Bond yelled at the Inspector.

"For disturbing the peace! Book him!" the Inspector answered and walked away.

CHAPTER 15

The Awakening

Jennifer Angel felt someone shaking her, but it felt so far away. "Go away," she muttered.

"Wake up, Jen! You could get fired for this."

These words immediately brought Jennifer back into consciousness. "What happened? What am I doing here?" She quickly rose. She had fallen asleep kneeled next to Mary's bed with her head on the foot of it.

"Jen, this isn't like you. What happened?" asked her fellow night shift nurse who had been covering the surgical ward since the trauma unit had been quiet.

"I can't remember. I have no idea how I got here. I had completed the rounds, which didn't take long, and then finished the paperwork. I was at the nurses' station. Oh, this I do remember. It'll sound strange, but I thought that I saw a purplish glow coming out of this room."

"You're working too hard, Jen. Two doubles and five singles in one week is enough to make anyone hallucinate. You really need to take a day off," her fellow nurse insisted.

"Rhonda, I swear that I saw that same glow in here two nights ago and then again tonight. Well I remember going to check it out, but I don't remember anything after that. It's as if all went blank until you awakened me. Is anything different in the room?"

The two nurses checked Mary's room for any changes. They checked the bathroom, the closet and even under the hospital bed, but found nothing out of the ordinary. "I swear that I saw a glow, Rhonda. It was just like two nights ago, and both times, it occurred around 3:30 am. Yes, both were around 3:30!"

"Yeah, and both times you pulled a double. Jen, you're exhausted. Look at you. You fell asleep on a patient's bed, for God's sake! The brain can do funny things when it's tired. Now that your shift's almost over, go to bed. I can finish the paperwork and the transition to day shift. I'll tell them that you weren't feeling well. How is Mr. Alberts doing in room 317? Anything I need to report on him? Did you check his meds?"

"No, yes, I mean I think he's fine, and I did check his meds earlier. He needs his morning meds. Better check on Ms. Johnson in 323, as well. She's recovering nicely but also needs her morning meds. No change here by the looks of it, and the rest of the beds are vacant." Jennifer was back in nurse mode, and it gave her a certain sense of stability, even though she had somehow lost nearly two hours of her memory while at work.

"Okay. I can handle it. Go home."

"Thanks, Rhonda. I think, I will."

Upon arriving home, Jennifer decided to relax on her couch but soon fell asleep. By the time she awoke, it was late afternoon. Realizing that she had not changed out of her nurse clothes, she undressed and took a long, hot shower. Starved, she heated a frozen pizza, which she nearly consumed in one sitting. As she relaxed with a cup of coffee, she recalled a fragment of the night before. It was a small fragment, but most definitely a fragment of reality. "There was a beautiful, peaceful woman in the room," she said aloud. "I remember now. There was a woman in the room, and she was doing something odd to Mary's head, as if she were trying to heal her. The glow was coming from her. Oh my God, Rhonda's right. I'm losing it!"

She decided to lie down on her couch again. The vague recollections seemed to be just that, vague. She could not remember anything else, or how she ended up kneeling in front of Mary's bed. But as she lay on the bed, she remembered something altogether different. She remembered the first night after Mary arrived. She remembered Jack. She remembered his story about the mysterious woman. If it was the same woman, maybe she wasn't losing her mind. But if she wasn't, who was the woman and what was she doing? Her head was spinning again. She looked at her clock. It was nearly 7 pm.

"I need to find him," she concluded. "But I don't know his last name, except that he's her boyfriend. Some boyfriend, he never showed up again."

Then, she remembered that Rhonda had just come off a day shift rotation. She decided to call her. "Hello, Rhonda, Jen here. Yes, I feel a lot better. Thanks again for covering for me this morning. Hey, has Mary in 328 had any visitors during the day, while you were on day shift this week? She has? Who? Every day. Both every day, but at different times? Do you know their names? Let me write them down. Oh, it's just that I was curious about something. No, I'm not getting too into this Mary case. I promise. No. Okay. Who are they? Both are grad students at McLaren, huh? Carl Rupert. Okay. Is the other one a Jack? Yes, Jack Fulton. Both geoscience grads. Got it. Thanks. Oh, how did you find out all this? Of course you asked. Funny, Rhonda. Funny. Both cute, huh. You're always looking for that perfect guy. I better go. Sure. Aha. You can have him. Thanks again, Rhonda."

"Tomorrow, after my night shift, you're getting a surprise visit, Mr. Jack Fulton," Jennifer vowed before getting ready for bed.

CHAPTER 16

The Interrogation

Inspector Cabot was an expert when it came to interrogations. Yet, he rarely began an interrogation himself. He would use one of his three officers to start each one. At times it was Molly. She had a strong, sultry style. Sometimes it was Chen. He had a logical approach that tired out the suspect with repeated questioning from all angles and perspectives. Finally, there was Bob. Bob was big and intimidating. He was like a gorilla with a badge. For this particular case, the Inspector quickly ruled out Chen, but was torn between starting with Molly or with Big Bob. Finally, he tossed a coin for lack of a better way to solve his dilemma. "Heads for Bob and tails for Molly." The coin spun in the air and once the Inspector caught it, he flipped it onto the back of his other arm. "Tails. Molly goes first. Good. That's a good start." He was happy with his coin toss. It was a brilliant way to decide. For had it come up heads, he would have gone for best of three. That was a sure way of knowing his preferred choice. "And no

matter who tells you what, deep down one choice is always preferred," he thought. "Molly's a good choice. She'll get to him,"
he concluded and went to find Molly.

Molly was a young officer, only two years out of the academy,
with extensive training in interrogations and a fast growing portfolio of experience and success. Her youth and "girl next door"
good looks, mixed with a raspy seductress voice, made her the top
interrogator that the Inspector had in his arsenal. He prepped Molly
and then let her into the Fish Tank. The interrogation room was
dubbed affectionately "The Fish Tank" for one of its long walls
consisted of a one-way mirror, so that the entire interrogation could
be observed by the Inspector and others from an adjacent room.

"Go get him, Molly, and remember that he's one of my prime
suspects. We've got a lot on him already, but I want to get a
confession," the Inspector ordered. "Make him uncomfortable
with the facts, but remember that he has to confess on his own.
Careful not to do too much coaching. We don't want some hot-shot
lawyer saying that we tricked the dim-wit or led him on. And let
me tell you, with this guy that may be easy to do since his IQ is
the same as his shoe size. You got all the facts, right? If not, I'll
sit here and coach you through the ear buds."

"Come on, Jim. This isn't my first time. Why are you so nervous about this?" Molly objected.

"Because I have a hunch and little else, and I need as much proof
as I can get. Calvin's not going to let me hold him if we don't get
something out of him that can really stick." Calvin was Inspector
Cabot's boss, who remained convinced that any investigation of
the Mary Collins case was a waste of time and resources because
the girl obviously fell of her own accord.

"Relax. I got it. Enjoy the show!" Molly replied as she took one
more look at Tony Bond through the observation mirror before
entering the Fish Tank to confront him.

"Good luck, Molly, and thanks," the Inspector replied.

"A pleasure," she answered with a smile, and before Inspector
Cabot had a chance to say anything else, he saw her enter the

interrogation room with elegant ease. The official questioning of suspect Tony Bond regarding the case of Mary Collins had begun.

"Hello, Mr. Bond." Molly gave a radiant smile that would melt even the most reserved of men.

"Tony will do just fine, baby. Baby, you're a hot cop!"

Molly ignored the all too common topic. "So, tell me Mr. Bond…"

"I said, call me Tony, baby. I think I have seen you before at the Skeller. You single?"

Molly ignored him once more. "Tell me, Mr. Bond, how do you know Mary Collins?"

"Hell, we're in the same class. It's that rocks for jocks class at McLaren. I haven't banged her or anything, if that's what you're after. She's not my type, but you on the other hand…"

"I'll get right to it. We have several witnesses that say that you were next to Miss Collins when she fell into the quarry. Did you push her?" Molly wasted no time.

"Hell no! Is that what all this is about? I did not f—in' touch that bitch! I don't even talk to that bitch. I was nowhere near her. I told that old cop the same thing when he questioned me at the site that day. That bitch probably fell over her fancy shoelaces. Don't talk to me about her. Why toy with the little sister, when you got yourself the princess? Come on! Makes no sense!"

"So you don't like Mary, I take it?"

"I never said that. I just don't care about her. That's all. She's not worth my care, if you know what I mean, darling?"

"Mr. Bond, we know that you do care about Miss Collins, and, in fact, we know that you harassed and threatened her, physically and verbally abused her, and molested her." Molly switched to a sharper tone.

"I didn't bang that dumb bitch. I told you that. Sure, I grabbed her and roughed her up a little. I had to do it to show her what she was missing and all. She loved it rough. Let me tell you that much. She was coming on to me. It's that football star magnetism. You know. You feel it, right? I bet you like it rough too."

"Mr. Bond, we have concrete evidence that you harassed and molested Miss Collins on at least two occasions in the past several months. In one case, she sustained bruises and when she was about to go to the authorities, you threatened her with more harm. It sounds like you just admitted to that. Is that correct?" Molly was pushing him hard to see if he would lose it and betray himself before he asked for a lawyer.

"Where you getting this crap, bitch? You're no longer my type! I said that I roughed her up a little and that's all. She deserved it and so did that old Professor Martin. They're too scared to say anything. You got nothing on me. This interview's over, and you didn't impress The Bond." Tony Bond stood up and as he did so, Molly gently asked him to sit down.

"This little chat is done, pretty thing. I'll see you in the bars, and you tell that old cop to lay off or I'll get his ass." Tony Bond made for the door just as Big Bob opened it and completely blocked his exit. This startled Tony, and he turned back to Molly. "Get this ape out of my way!" he shouted.

"Sit down, Mr. Bond!"

Tony turned and looked at Bob then at Molly and sat down again, stretching out his legs and puffing up his chest. "I know I have rights, and this is against my rights. I want a lawyer, and I'm not saying anything else to you, bitch." He crossed his arms and stared at Molly in defiance.

"No need. We're done. Please cuff him, Bob," Molly smiled at Big Bob. She received her orders from the Inspector over the ear buds.

"What the hell!" Tony got all energized. "You can't cuff me! I want a lawyer! What did I do?" he screamed.

"You have the right to remain silent..." Bob began with the official arrest.

"I know that crap. I watch TV! But what did I do?"

"You threatened an officer. You admitted to physically harming and molesting Mary Collins." Molly began listing the charges.

"Get away from me, you ape man!" Tony interrupted and started to punch Bob, who simply grabbed him and pinned him against the wall. Tony was large, but Big Bob was larger and used to this drill. Tony was in cuffs before he knew what had happened.

"You resisted arrest, assaulted an officer. Need I go on?" Molly smiled. "Take him away, please, Bob."

"You're the worst kind of bitch and you're an apeman, if I ever saw one!" Tony wailed, still half drunk, as Bob led him out the door.

Tony's anger was in full control of his every thought, word and action. It blinded him and he raged all the way to the holding cell, showering Bob with every profanity in his extensive repertoire. Meanwhile, Inspector Cabot joined Molly in the Fish Tank.

"Sorry, Boss. He went ballistic early. I couldn't get more out of him. Not one of my better sessions, I'm afraid. He actually got to me with all that. They usually don't, but this one got to me a little. He's one selfish and aggressive bastard. He could have easily done it," Molly concluded.

"Except that he probably didn't," the Inspector concluded. "But we have enough on him to make him spend quite a while in jail. You did well. You got a physical harassment confession out of him and several misdemeanors. Is Professor Martin still willing to testify to the abuse and molestation that Mary Collins suffered at the hands of this predator?"

"Yes, we already have his official statement, and he said he's ready to take the stand when he heard what happened to her," Molly replied.

"Good. Are those friends of Mr. Bond willing to testify regarding last night's bar confessions?"

"Yes, there's little bravery and honor among that lot. One look at Big Bob, and they all gave us official statements."

"Very good. At least we got one predator off the street for a while, Molly. Good job," the Inspector replied.

"It was nothing," she replied sincerely. "By the way, Sir, how do you know that he's probably innocent of pushing Mary Collins?" Molly asked.

"Because he had a bigger prize."

"Bigger prize?"

"Yes, as I suspected, he was with her sister, Lilly. As he put it, 'Why toy with the little sister, when you got yourself the princess?'"

CHAPTER 17

An Awkward Visit

It was nearly 8:30 pm when Jennifer rang the doorbell at Jack Futon's small campus apartment on Kira Lane. She had walked up to the door three times before she got the courage to ring it. The doorbell rang and there was a long pause. "Maybe he's not home," she thought to herself. She rang once more. Still nothing happened. She was about to leave when the door opened.

"Wow, what a surprise! Jen, is it? I haven't seen you since the night at the hospital last week. Is everything all right?" Jack seemed shocked and confused.

"I feel really odd disturbing you like this, but I need to ask you something, Mr. Fulton."

"It's Jack. Come on in, Jen. Please excuse the mess. I wasn't expecting visitors."

"No worries. It looks fine."

"Come, sit down. Can I get you anything?"

"No thanks. I won't be long." Jennifer was still very uncomfortable with the visit.

"No rush. So, what's on your mind?" Jack was becoming intrigued by his surprise guest.

Jennifer sat down in one of the old leather chairs that made up the living room in the small apartment. Cautiously, she confided in him her concerns about the mysterious occurrences in Mary's room. He watched her in silence. But the silence made her feel insecure and she began to listen to herself as she spoke. "This does sound like I'm losing my mind," she silently concluded, whereupon she stopped and scanned Jack's motionless face for a response. An awkward silence filled the room. She was at his mercy now.

"Are you sure you don't want anything? I have a nice bottle of Pinot Noir," he offered with a smile.

"Sure, okay, but what do you think of all this?" she insisted nervously. The attraction was returning, and she felt more awkward than ever. "What am I doing here with poor Mary's boyfriend?" she thought to herself and audibly exhaled.

"I think that you're very brave to share this with me, and I appreciate it. Not sure that I believe it, but I do appreciate it." He focused on the wine and glasses.

"Great comment. Talk about a slap in the face," she thought.

"Let's have some cheese and crackers, as well. Please don't think me rude but I'm starving. I haven't had dinner yet. Anyway, Jen, thanks for coming," he replied and looked at her longer than was appropriate as he filled the wine glasses.

"Sure, but do you think that I'm losing my mind?" Jennifer had a more pressing concern than wine and cheese, and all this flirty chit chat made her more uncomfortable than before.

"No, not at all. But if you happen to be, then that would mean that we're both losing our minds," he chuckled as he handed her the glass of wine. "I told you the night I met you about that mysterious woman, and at the time you didn't believe me. I don't blame you. It was rather odd. But I doubt that there was anything to it. I later dismissed it as some mysterious relative." He sat down and offered a toast to friendship, which only increased Jennifer's discomfort.

"How do you like the wine? It's from New Zealand. Ever been there?" He continued with a smile, innocently brushing past Jennifer's concerns. He seemed too focused on her as an attractive woman, and appeared rather dismissive of her as a vulnerable person in need of support. She was starting to second-guess the wisdom of coming to see him. It was clear to her that his real interest did not lie with her mental wellbeing. It was as if he were toying with her in order to enjoy her later, like a well-fed cat playing with a mouse. She had come to him with the hope that he would sincerely accept and encourage her, maybe even comfort her concerns and doubts, for she was out on a ledge and needed rescue. No such comfort materialized. He seemed self-absorbed and suddenly much less attractive.

He picked up on her vibe and quickly corrected himself. "Never mind New Zealand. Back to your concerns. I don't know what we saw, Jen. The mind is a complex thing as you know, being a medical professional. We know so little about how it works and how it perceives. We know even less about consciousness." Jack was trying his best to logically explain her issue with the genuine purpose of helping her get to the truth, which he concluded was that they had both seen one of Mary's lost relatives. He was trying to set her straight in an attempt to fix the problem. Using this approach, he sincerely thought that he was helping. Instead, he was pushing her away.

"Look, I know that the brain is a black box," Jennifer replied getting annoyed at being dismissed as a lunatic. "Believe me, I know more than you think." She began to get defensive. "I appreciate the wine and the conversation, but I had better get going." She began to stand up for she felt uncomfortable sharing all this and needed some air. The entire exchange had missed the mark. Feeling exposed, she had needed more empathy, and less hospitality and instruction.

"No, please don't rush off!" Jack was reluctant to let her leave. He yearned for some company and she was like a gift, a lovely surprise gift. He did not want to give her back so soon. Yet, little did he realize his thoughts classified her into a possession, ensuring all his words and actions followed suit. Within those thoughts, she was just another quest, another trophy and another conquest. Despite the fact that he was trying to correct himself, this self-centered thinking oozed out of him and Jennifer, being sensitive to it, was shutting down.

"I've got to go! I'm on night shift again tonight. Thanks for the wine and thanks for listening." She was on her feet.

"But I didn't really do much listening," Jack objected, rising to his feet as well.

She turned toward him and looked him straight in the eyes. "You know that was the first thing you said tonight that made any sense."

Jack was stunned. He had no idea how he had so quickly alienated this young woman. The remark did not resonate. It hurt. It hurt his ego.

"I don't understand. What do you mean?" he objected as he followed Jennifer toward the door.

"I know, because you think you have all the answers and you're focused elsewhere." She glanced down at her chest for she had caught his gaze there on more than one instance. "Mary was never really your girlfriend, was she?" Jennifer asked while facing him again.

He lowered his head, breaking eye contact. The truth hurt. "No, she wasn't," he admitted.

"I thought so. Mary'd see right through you, just like I can. Whatever you're playing at, I suggest that you start by looking in the mirror and understanding who you are and how your coveting desires affect others. Maybe it wasn't in your text books, but I assure you, it's a worthwhile pursuit." With those parting words, Jennifer Angel left, feeling hurt, disappointed and, most of all, alone.

"Strange girl," Jack concluded as he closed the door. "Pretty but strange." Yet, for a second he saw the reflection that she had seen, but it scared him back to self-denial.

CHAPTER 18

Molly

Molly Dvorak was not your typical cop. She had never imagined that she would end up as one. Even now she often wondered about her career selection, viewing it more as one step in a much longer journey that led well beyond this profession. She was well-educated with a degree in criminal psychology and a minor in political science from the University of Pennsylvania. Molly was sharp. She had initially wished to become a criminal lawyer, but somewhere along the way she lost the taste for that occupation. Thus, for now, she was a cop and a darn good one.

Inspector Cabot considered her the star of the young class that had joined the department over the past several years. He never showed any favoritism, for that was not his style; however, he did allow his reports plenty of opportunity for growth, and Molly took full advantage. He was proud of her. Therefore, when she questioned him, he never took offense, but used it as an opportunity for mutual growth, stressing the lessons and freely admitting his own shortfalls or mistakes. Molly loved working for the Inspector. He was a great mentor and the sole reason why she was reluctant to change her career anytime soon.

So, when she knocked on his office door, he welcomed her with his usual stern, but internally joyful, "Yes, Officer Dvorak. What can I do for you?"

"Sorry to intrude, Sir, but regarding that tattoo on Mary Collins, I have an update that you may find interesting." She offered with pride while still standing in the doorway.

"Come right in Molly. Have a seat. I just need to finish this e-mail and then you'll have my complete attention."

Molly sat in one of the two worn, sunken leather chairs that were positioned in front of the Inspector's equally worn, large oak desk. The moment took longer than expected for he was of a generation that pecked at the keyboard. This made Molly smile. She loved the old man. Finally, he was finished and looked up at her past his reading glasses.

"So, what have you got for me, Molly? I'm all ears," and he was. He was extremely adept at listening, giving anyone who addressed him his complete attention, including full eye contact. It made him not only more trustworthy and approachable, but also a much more effective investigator.

"Well, Sir, I searched and searched the web, our files, and even the local libraries for the meaning of that tattoo symbol with little luck. Then this morning, I finally found something, but you'd never guess where?" Molly liked to draw her listeners into a story, and most of all she liked to draw the Inspector into one. He enjoyed it as much as she did, if not more.

"Please, do tell. Was it the ladies room?" he chuckled.

"No, what kind of guess is that?"

"An off the wall one," he laughed.

"Darn, how did you do that?"

"Do what?" asked the Inspector in genuine confusion.

"How'd you guess?"

"Guess what, Molly? I simple threw out the first thing that came into my head. I'm afraid that you lost me. Did you discover your information in the ladies room?"

"No!" Molly laughed in a most addictive way, which started the old inspector laughing as well. Soon, the administrative assistants seated outside the Inspector's small office wondered what was happening behind those closed doors.

"No, Jim," Molly cut out the formalities. "The clue came 'off the wall.' That was the insight."

"Right. I outdo myself at times," he laughed again for a second round. He was a charming cross between Columbo, Albert Einstein and Winnie the Pooh, if one could imagine such a cross. His hair was dark black and always disheveled as was his large bushy mustache, but his mind was never so. He appeared to be almost naively lost, yet he always found his way through reason, and when that failed, by simply letting go in a Pooh sort of way. He was an investigator, a scientist and a natural Taoist, all in one, and little did he realize it.

"What wall, Molly? On what wall did you find this piece of wisdom?" he chucked again. He was having much too good of a time. A person who truly enjoys life and completely projects this fact can be most endearing. The Inspector was such a man, and Molly was always drawn to this trait for they both were made from the same mold. Although a generation apart and of opposite genders, they were nearly identical at the core.

"Stop it! Let me finish," she objected.

"Of course, I'm on pins and needles," he chuckled. "Was that comment insightful as well?"

"Okay, enough!" She mildly scolded him.

"Fine. Go on. I won't interrupt," he replied, playing the mischievous school boy.

"As I was saying, I think that I got an important insight into the tattoo that you discovered on Mary Collins. After much futile searching, I was walking by the McLaren Student Union this morning, when posted on the information wall was a note about a room for rent. You see, I happen to be looking for a new place to live since my lease is up next week. Anyway, as I read the description, I noticed, to my shock, that in the lower corner of the note was an exact replica of Mary's tattoo. You know, the small Chinese symbol, which actually means nothing in modern Chinese. I looked it up earlier."

The inspector was quiet while intently focused on Molly and her story. She felt like he was almost too focused, but in a genuinely curious way. He had a bottomless amount of curiosity. "Go on. Did you find the place?" he added to spur her on.

"Yes. I went there immediately, and it turned out to be a large boarding house near fraternity row. I knocked and a young woman answered. She appeared to be a student. I pretended to be a student and asked about the apartment for lease. After a tour of the place, I asked to see the shared space, which was most of the ground floor of the house. The young woman was very inquisitive and reluctant to show me several of the rooms. I asked to use the facilities just as she went to the front desk to pick up a phone call. This gave me a chance to be alone. I snuck back, and quickly but carefully opened the large mahogany door of a meeting room that I wasn't previously allowed to see. I had only a few seconds to peer into the large room, but it was enough," she paused a while for effect.

"Enough for what? You have me strung out here. What did you see?" he was like a little boy, which was his true nature.

It was her turn to chuckle at him. She loved to get the old man to this point of uncontrolled curiosity. "Well, let me tell you, but I need a cup of coffee first. Do you mind?"

"Yes, I mind! Get your damn coffee later! I'm too busy to wait. What happened?"

"My, you're eager, sailor," she laughed and suddenly wondered if she had overstepped her bounds. She did not want to be disrespectful or to lead him on in any way. Theirs was not that kind of a relationship. Fortunately, he felt the same way and let the comment pass.

She picked up the rest of the story where she had left off. "Well, I had only a few seconds, as I mentioned, but I saw a large room with what looked like some kind of a central platform surrounded by a circle of pillows and mats. At the far end of the room were some symbols, but the most prevalent of them was the same one as the tattoo. I had to close the door quickly and return to my host. I was just in time, too. She had finished her call and was coming to look for me. She acted very defensively when she found me down the hall near the mysterious meeting room. One would say that she acted very suspiciously. Then, she checked to see if the meeting room door was locked. Finding it unlocked, she peered inside to assure that all was well and then proceeded to lock it. Her manner became more terse and she quickly dismissed me, assuring me that someone would call me for an interview, which they did. It's set to take place tomorrow at 9 am at the same house."

"Damn good work, Molly. May I assume that you'll be going to that interview tomorrow?"

"Yes, of course."

"So, innocent little Mary was a member of some odd cult. That's truly a surprise. Good work."

"Wait! That's not all," Molly cautioned.

"It's not? What else is there?"

"Well, I also saw what looked like an Eastern religious artifact in that mysterious room."

"Oh, a religious cult! Even better! I haven't worked with one of those since the late 80s. That was quite a case. A farmer from Arkansas believed that he saw aliens in his cornfield. He got some stone tablet and started a cult, which quickly went bad. It was the oddest case I ever had. Led to a kidnapping up here, which is how I got involved. I was a young man back then. But back to this case. So, we have ourselves a religious cult. Hmmm....." he pondered. "This case is getting good."

"There's more."

"More! By God, girl, did you solve the case? You're going to put me out of a job."

"No, not that good. You still have a job. But I did discover that the symbol, although not in modern Chinese, is an ancient Taoist symbol for what they call Wu Wei."

"Woo who?"

"No, Wu Wei!"

"What way?"

"It's a belief at the core of Taoism. It just means going with the flow. It's the mindset of letting a greater power move you without your resistance."

"Oh, so it's as I always say, 'Screw it! Let's just see what comes of it.' "

"Not sure that the Taoists would favor your definition, but it's along those lines."

"I like it. I may get myself a tattoo like that," he joked. "I must admit the secret to my success as a detective is this very Wok Way that you mentioned. I guess I'm a Taoist and never knew it. So, it means Who Way, huh?"

"Wu Wei, Sir.

"Right, Whoa Way. That's what I said. Good work, Molly. Keep at it, and get into that cult."

"I plan to, Sir."

"Good, now I need to run. I have an appointment with Jack Fulton."

"One of our prime suspects."

"Yes, the very one, the elusive and mysterious Jack Fulton."

CHAPTER 19

Trouble in Paradise

Suzy Kurtz was in an uncontrollable state. She had reached a perpetual oscillation between crying and screaming. The subject of her wrath and despair was none other than Randell Twiner. "Screw you, Randy! I hate you!" she burst out and returned to profuse weeping.

"Suzy, it's not that I don't love you, I just can't get married. This engagement just isn't me. Everyone wants it but me. It's not me! I'm not a marrying kinda guy," Randell defended himself.

"You're a selfish SOB who thinks with his dick! I can't believe you! I hate everything about you!" The crying resumed.

"Ugh, you drive me nuts, I swear!" he replied.

"Is your obsession with Mary Collins over now? Or, are you over at the hospital proclaiming your love to her while sneaking around with Stacy Reed? You lousy pig!" There was more crying.

"That was uncalled for!" Randell was beginning to anger.

"Was it? I wouldn't put it past you. I saw you chatting 'em both up during that field trip. I'm going to call the cops and tell 'em that bit of news. They already think you pushed her and that'll seal the deal," she threatened.

"Like hell you'll call!" He was angry now and shoved her against the wall. "You keep your mouth shut, or I'll shut it for you! You hear?"

"Oh, there goes that famous temper. What're you gonna do? Push me off a cliff, too?"

"Shut your hole! We're through! You know I never pushed her!"

"Like hell you didn't! There were at least a half a dozen people who told me about that little conversation that the two of you had before this all happened. And then, I see you two walking together. Next thing I know she's down at the bottom of the quarry, and you are desperately climbing down to tamper with the evidence. Right? What happened to Stacy? Was she your bimbo accomplice? I saw you with her!"

"Shut up or I'll…"

"You'll what, Randy? What'll you do? Hit me again!"

Randy suddenly exploded in uncontrolled rage and began to strike Suzy. "You bitch! You'll do no such thing! What gives you the right?" he yelled, and struck her forcefully across the face making her lips and nose bleed.

Suzy screamed at the top of her lungs, in a shrill that could awaken the dead, as blood streamed out of her nose. It was the same scream she had made the day she found Mary at the bottom of the cliff.

"Damn you, Suzy! Look what you've done!" Randal looked at his bloodied shirt as Suzy crumbled into a screaming heap, bleeding from her lips and nose.

Randell was scared. He didn't know what to do. "Shut your hole, Suzy, or I'll hit you again. Shut up!" he yelled at the top of his lungs, and his anger returned when she did not obey. He ignored a loud banging on the door, and in his rage turned once more toward the crying heap on the floor. She had stopped screaming, but sobbed uncontrollably while holding her hands up to brace herself for another attack. "You're a merciless bastard," she muttered between sobs while the blood streamed down her face.

"I hate you, Suzy!" he raged, and was about to kick her when he felt a strong arm grab him and shove him forcefully against a wall. Shocked, he turned to see the large mysterious man who lived down the hall of the apartment building.

"One more move and I'll break your arm," the wall of a man growled at him with a piercing stare that could stop a charging bull. He then turned to Suzy and comforted her in a gentle voice uncharacteristic of his brawn. "Are you okay? Lay your head back," he instructed and handed her a tissue.

Scared, Randell dashed out of the apartment, while the big man checked Suzy's wounds. He did not bother to follow Randell. His priority was the girl. "You'll need some ice on that. I called 911. An ambulance will be here any minute. I assume that you'll want to press charges?"

"No! No, I don't," Suzy replied instantly. "I can't! I love him. It's okay. He just got angry. He didn't mean it. I made him angry," she reasoned between sobs.

"Look, Miss, not that it's any of my business, but you didn't make him do this to you. He needs help or he'll do it again, and next time I may not be here to save you. He could've killed you," the big man counseled.

"No, he wouldn't kill me. He just lost his temper," Suzy explained while wiping the blood off her lip. Her nose had stopped bleeding, but her face was swelling up.

"Miss, people who do things like this need help and need to be stopped. If you don't press charges, he'll do it again. Believe me. He will."

"No, he wouldn't hurt me."

"He already has. And, I bet it wasn't the first time, right?"

There was an awkward silence as Suzy looked down at the floor, avoiding eye contact with her neighbor.

"Can I get you some ice?"

"No," she sobbed.

"Here come the paramedics. Sorry about the broken door locks. I'll replace them," he smiled at her.

The paramedics streamed in and quickly took over. "Officer Braxton, what happened here? Bob, are you working on your days off now?" The lead paramedic joked with the big man.

"Shit, I hate to see this. Her boyfriend was beating her to a pulp and probably would have killed her if I hadn't stopped him, and she won't press charges. This domestic violence stuff is so frustrating!" Officer Bob Braxton replied.

"Where's the cowardly bastard?" ask the lead paramedic.

"Ran off, but I'm going to bring him in anyway, since I witnessed it," Bob confessed.

"Good for you!" the lead parametric replied. Then, he turned toward Suzy who was already being attended to by his partner. "Looks like you were pretty lucky, but for a while you're going to be pretty bruised up," he explained to his patient.

"She'll probably find a clever way to explain it to friends and family. Damn this!" Officer Braxton thought while he called dispatch to place a police alert for Randell Twiner.

CHAPTER 20

Doctor's Orders

*I*nspector Cabot stopped at the entrance to Jack Fulton's apartment building. He was reviewing his notes before entering when he was disturbed from his thought.

"Inspector, what brings you here?"

The Inspector turned only to discover the smiling face of the trauma-ward night nurse. He was confused and looked the part.

"You seem lost, Inspector. Sorry about the way I treated you at the hospital the other night, but I have to protect my patients. Anyway, I'm sorry," she continued with a smile.

"Oh, quite all right, Miss…" he scrambled through his notes.

"Miss Angel, but you can call me Jen."

"Yes, of course, Jen."

There was an uncomfortable silence as both parties looked at each other and did not know what else to say.

"Well, have a nice afternoon," Jennifer finally offered as she turned toward Jack's apartment.

"You live here?" the Inspector asked, surprised.

"No. I owe someone an apology, and I'm going to set things straight," she replied. "Well, good day." She disappeared through the front door.

"Odd coincidence," the Inspector thought and followed her in.

As he neared Jack's apartment, the awkward situation returned. Jennifer was in front of the door ringing the bell.

"Seems like we're both here to see Mr. Fulton," the Inspector looked straight at Jennifer.

"You too? Why're you here to see him?"

"I'm not at liberty to discuss. Police business," the Inspector replied. He withheld that Jack was a key suspect.

"Oh, well, he doesn't seem to be at home."

"I guess I'll have to come back later. By the way, how is Ms. Collins doing?" the Inspector asked.

"About the same, I'm afraid. No improvement but not worse either," Jennifer replied.

She rang the doorbell once more, but to no avail. "I guess my apology will have to wait."

The Inspector's curiosity needed fulfillment. "I hate to pry, but how do you know Mr. Fulton? Are you one of his students?"

"Oh, no!" Jennifer laughed. "I know him from the hospital. He was there the first night to see Mary Collins. In fact, he was the only one to show up right after she came to us. He told me that he was her boyfriend. Turns out he lied."

"Really?" The Inspector smelled a sudden windfall, and reached for his pad and pencil. Then he stopped himself. He would have to try and remember the facts. He didn't want to scare her off. "Jen, can I buy you a cup of coffee? Maybe you can tell me more about Mary's hospital visitors. It may help me with this case."

Jen looked at her watch, then back at Jack's door, and finally at the Inspector. "I guess, but I only have about 40 minutes."

"Oh, that'll be plenty of time." The Inspector allowed her to pass as they headed out of the apartment building. They found a small coffee shop around the corner, and the Inspector treated the young nurse to a cappuccino. As they sat down, he pulled out his notepad.

"Thank you for the coffee," she replied.

He could tell she was an honest soul. He felt there was little doubt that she would tell him the truth. "Can I ask you a few questions, starting with Jack Fulton and the first night that you met him?" he asked politely.

"Sure." She sipped her extremely hot drink.

"Was there anything odd about Mr. Fulton when he first arrived to see Mary?"

"Well, I guess. He was odd in that he seemed very nervous and upset, as if he were..."

"Hiding something?" the Inspector realized that he should not have completed her sentence and caught himself. He was completely focused on her, and she could feel that intense energy. She was a little afraid that what she might say may get Jack in trouble. She did not wish Jack any harm, but she was not good at lying.

"Well, kind of. He seemed uncomfortable, yet sincerely concerned. I figured out that he was Mary's boyfriend as soon as I laid eyes on him. He had that lover look, you know?" She suddenly realized that maybe she had said too much since the Inspector was taking copious notes.

"I mean that he was concerned in a good way, like someone that loves her. But maybe he's just good at acting that way. I don't know."

"Why would you say that?" the Inspector was all ears. He had completely forgotten about his cup of tea, which was still sitting where he first placed it.

"Because he's not her boyfriend at all. I don't know who he is, but he is so," she paused.

"So what, Ms. Angel?

"So damn cute."

It was out. "Oh my God, what have I said?" raced through her mind with lightening speed. "And to the police, no less!"

The Inspector chuckled to himself. "So that's the connection," he thought. "That guy's a playboy, just as I suspected," he concluded to himself and decided to tread gently. At first, he ignored the comment and switched subjects asking about the other visitors to Mary's room. He spent the most time on Daphne. She was a new person of interest. Only in recent witness interviews did it surface that this seemingly odd girl had originally sat next to Mary on the bus on that fateful day. Mr. Chesterfield didn't have her on his list of potential suspects. Until recently, it was unclear that she had been in Mary's proximity at the time of the fall.

Satisfied with the increased information that he had obtained, he returned to the subject of Jack Fulton. He realized he had less than ten minutes with Jennifer to explore the subject further. He decided to go right to the heart of the matter. "What's your present relationship with Mr. Fulton?"

"Relationship? I have no relationship with him," Jennifer blushed, but could not keep eye contact.

"I see," the Inspector replied and made a quick note. "Not yet, anyway," he thought to himself. "Does Mr. Fulton know you were coming to see him?"

"No. Why?"

"No reason. This apology, what's it for?"

Jennifer was getting a little uncomfortable with the line of questioning, and he could sense it from her body language. He knew that he had to proceed gently again. The question simply hung there. The one piece of information that Jennifer held back from the Inspector was the mysterious woman and the magenta haze. She was not prepared to share that openly for fear of being labeled as insane. She weighed her response carefully. He sensed her caution and wondered about its origins.

"Well, I had been to see him earlier," she began and paused. She was an awful liar and was starting to get herself wrapped up in fear of betraying her secret.

"Why did you go see him earlier, Miss Angel?

There was the dreaded question. She would have to confess the real reason and seem insane, or lie and risk being suspected by this curious Inspector. "He asked me to come," she decided to lie.

"Why?"

"I guess he was interested in me," she paused. "This isn't going well," she thought and nervously fidgeted in her seat.

The Inspector was reading all the signs and suspected that she was lying.

She decided to run through her lie as if it were a bed of hot coals. "I had come to see him earlier because there was a mutual interest. Since he was not Mary's boyfriend, I saw no harm in it. Well, we got into a little bit of a fight because I was feeling like he was pushing too hard. You know what I mean?" She tossed her wavy hair in a flirtatious manner. "I'm not that kind of a girl. But I was too harsh on him. He was really being a gentleman."

"I see." The Inspector was now the one feeling uncomfortable.

"I need to go. Thanks for the coffee, and if I see Jack, I'll tell him that you were looking for him." She quickly picked up her belongings and began to leave.

He realized that he had scared her away. But he needed to know one more thing. "Did Jack Fulton ask you to hide whatever it is that you're hiding from me? What is it that you're hiding, Jen?"

"Nothing! Good bye, Inspector!"

She was gone.

"That guy has her completely under his control. I suspect that whatever he asks, she'll do. I wonder what he asked Mary to do before he pushed her?" the Inspector pondered, until he finally spilled his tea.

CHAPTER 21

Big Bob

When the Inspector returned to the office, he was covered with tea stains and seeped in confusion. Once there, he encountered his other protégé, Big Bob Braxton.

"Boss, I had a coincidental break in the Mary Collins case," Bob announced.

"Really! Please tell! Come into my office, Bob."

"What happened to your shirt?"

"Nothing. I was attacked by a tea cup." The Inspector brushed off the question.

"Huh?"

Bob did not get the joke. Following his boss into the office, he sat in one of the two worn leather chairs in front of the desk and quickly shared the events of his encounter with Randell and Suzy. The Inspector had his pad out once more and was diligently scribbling in it. "That's terrible. What possesses people to do that? How is she?" the Inspector inquired as he took voluminous notes.

"She'll be okay, but I'd hate to see what would've happened had I not broken down the door. He was about to start kicking her in the face!" Bob proclaimed still taken back by the morning's events. "What's wrong with our society these days?"

"I suspect that such evil is as old as our primordial ancestors, but that doesn't make in any more acceptable. She's pressing charges, I assume," the Inspector replied.

"No. That's part of the problem. She won't press charges. But I witnessed it, so that must count for something."

"Unfortunately, given our judicial process, it doesn't count for much," the Inspector replied. "Maybe we can get her to change her mind. I'll get Molly to talk to her and maybe that'll help."

"I hope so, but I brought that punk, Randell, in here anyway. We found him hiding like a rat beneath the bleachers of the football stadium. Some football hero! Man, I wish I was still a defensive lineman and encountered that pretty-boy quarterback on the opposing team. Then, justice would've been served out legally in front of the entire community," Big Bob added.

"Yes, I'm sure, but unfortunately that's not the case here, Bob. Where is he, and how are you holding him here if she's not pressing charges?" the Inspector asked for he was concerned with a potential legal embarrassment.

"As a person of interest in the case of Suzy Kurtz's beating," Bob replied.

"Let me ask you this, Bob. Did you actually see him hit her?"

"No, but it was obvious that he had, and he was about to do so again," Bob insisted.

"Yes, but what if Suzy claims that she fell and he was helping her up?"

"But that's a lie, Boss. He was swinging his leg back to give her another kick when I stopped him," Bob defended.

"I'm just telling you how it'll go down in a courtroom. I have been through this before, Bob. But you did the right thing bringing him in because at least we can question him, if he doesn't lawyer up first. Where is he?"

"In the Fish Tank!"

"Okay. Let me have a go at him," the Inspector volunteered.

Officer Bob Braxton was an imposing man in size and strength. Yet, his personality couldn't be more opposed from his appearance. He was a gentle soul with a heart as big as his biceps. He felt anger toward Randell, for although he himself was far from a ladies' man, he had a strong protective streak toward women. As a young man, he had been raised by his maternal grandmother since his mother was always working to support the family after his father's death. He related well to the hardships and social challenges of women in society and in the family. Big Bob was a huge teddy bear, who longed to find a woman that he could love and protect.

Bob decided to watch the questioning of Randell Twiner through the one-way mirror outside the Fish Tank. Usually, he was the one in the Tank while his boss, the Inspector, watched and coached from behind the glass, but today the roles were reversed. The Inspector knew his young protégés well, and he knew that Bob might lash out at Randell after what he had witnessed. He knew that he had to conduct this interview. Besides, it was going to he a sensitive one, since Randell was well-connected, having a father who was a local, high-powered attorney. All had to be done by the books for this could easily turn against the department and against Bob, in particular. The hero would become the next victim, this time of a flawed legal system.

"Mr. Twiner! We meet again." The Inspector sat down opposite the young man who remained silent. "It appears that you and Ms. Kurtz had a little squabble this morning. Care to tell me about it?"

"Look, I answered all your petty questions about the Mary case last week. I have nothing further to say," Randell replied looking into the Inspector's eyes.

"I understand, Randell, and I did appreciate your cooperation last week, but today I'm interested in your conflict with Ms. Kurtz."

"There's no conflict. You can ask her and she'll tell you the same. She slipped and fell hard on the kitchen floor. I was trying to help her up when one of your guys threw me against the wall, threatened me and nearly broke my arm. My father is planning on suing your department and that gorilla that works here. I've got nothing to say without my lawyer. I know my rights, and I'm done answering your questions," Randell smirked. He had obviously managed to get some quick coaching from his father.

"I understand, but tell me how Ms. Kurtz fell?"

"I've got nothing to say. I want my lawyer."

"She slipped on what?"

"I want my lawyer. I know my rights."

"Okay, fine."

"I want out of here right now. Are you charging me with anything?"

There was a long pause. The Inspector knew that unless Suzy Kurtz made an official charge, this was simply Bob's word against the word of this rich kid with a powerful daddy. In fact, Suzy could even turn the tables and accuse Bob. It was a no win situation unless she stepped forward with the truth.

"No. You're free to go, but I'm watching you, Randell. I promise you that, and if you make any mistakes, I'll be there," the Inspector said calmly.

"Are you threatening me?"

"No, of course not. Let's be clear that I'm not threatening you. I'm simply making you a promise."

"F--k you, cop! You know that you've got nothing on me. I'm invincible. Now let me out of here before my dad brings in an army of lawyers to pick through your trash. That's my promise!" Randell bragged and stood up.

"Bob, please escort this young man out of the building," the Inspector said aloud and started to get up as well.

Big Bob walked into the Fish Tank as requested. At the sight of him, Randell stiffened up with a tinge of concern. "Not you again! Don't you have anybody else to escort me out?" Randall turned to the Inspector.

The Inspector ignored Randell. Walking up to Bob, he whispered, "Get him out of here, and don't do anything stupid."

"Okay, Boss."

The Inspector left without a word, leaving the two adversaries in the room alone.

Randell was feeling truly invincible, despite Bob's size, and he could not resist a few jabs. "You know I'll sue you for harassment. Wait 'til I get Suzy to squawk."

"I don't get it?" Bob played dumb in the hopes that Randell would betray himself while the recorders were still running.

"We both know what went down, big man, but you'll never get me. I'm invincible. Got it? Bulletproof." Randell laughed and made a step toward the door. "So, let's go! What're you waiting for? I got places to be."

Bob reluctantly escorted Randell out of the building. He had to keep himself in check for he hated this young man.

"Bye, bye Bob!" Randell called back as he got into the chauffeured limousine waiting for him. "I'll tell Suzy that you send your love!" he yelled at Bob.

Randell knew that the real interrogation was awaiting him when he got home to his parents' house. He dreaded that, but, for now, he was on top of the world and extremely proud of himself.

"Jerk!" Bob said under his breath. "I'll get your sorry ass someday."

He walked back into the station where he ran into the Inspector. "I hate that guy," he confessed.

"I know, but try not to make this personal or it'll eat at you. He'll get his in time."

"Come hear the tape from the Fish Tank, Boss," Bob added excitedly. "After you left, I think I may've gotten him to confess to beating Suzy Kurtz."

"Really? Let's hear it," the Inspector replied.

The two men returned to the operations room, affectionately called the Mirror Room, for it was adjacent to the Fish Tank and separated by a large one-way mirror. They played back the last part of the Randell recording.

They heard the arrogant youth over the audio, "You know I'll sue you for harassment. Wait 'til I get Suzy to squawk."

"Unfortunately, that's nothing, Bob," the Inspector commented.

"But it shows that he's controlling what she says," Bob protested.

"No, that will not stick, plus it's out of context to the case."

"Well listen to the next part," Bob insisted.

They played the rest of the tape, and heard Randell once more over the audio. "We both know what went down, big man, but you'll never get me. I'm invincible. Got it? Bulletproof."

"I got him there, Boss!" Bob exclaimed in excitement.

"It's better but not enough. He didn't admit to anything. You can tell this kid is the son of an defense attorney," the Inspector chuckled, but Bob did not appreciate the humor.

CHAPTER 22

Molly in Wonderland

Molly was early for her 9 am apartment interview. "What a concept! We now have interviews for everything, even an apartment," she huffed silently as she waited outside the spacious old villa that was shoe-horned among the many fraternities on the edge of McLaren campus. She looked at her watch. It read 9 am sharp. "Well?" she sputtered impatiently. She was rather nervous about this interview but had no idea why. The massive front door caught her attention. It was made of carved wood and in the center of it was a large oval frosted window that resembled a looking glass. "Odd place this," Molly concluded.

She waited until 9:10 and then decided to leave. As she turned and descended the worn limestone steps, she heard the door creak open. There stood the young woman that she had met yesterday. The girl had a face that never smiled, and today was no different. "Come in," is all that she said, as she ushered Molly into the great hall. "Terry will be right with you?" she added in a terse tone.

"Who's Terry?" Molly asked.

"She's the owner of the house."

"Oh, I see," Molly replied as she sat down on a small bench upholstered with a Victorian flower motif. The room seemed like something out of a historical documentary. She had not noticed all the detail the day before. In its day, it must have been luxurious, but now it was simply old.

"You must be Molly. I'm so pleased to meet you!"

The stodgy hall was suddenly filled with a bright energy as if someone had opened all the windows on a sunny breezy day. Molly was completely taken aback. The woman who approached her had an internal youth that could not be quantified and a joy that seemed limitless. It was almost too much for an average person to bear.

"Glad to meet you as well, Miss…"

"Miss Nightingale."

"Yes, of course, Miss Nightingale," Molly heard herself respond.

"I know. I'm named after a bird, but at least it's one that can sing. Right, Trudy?" She turned to the quiet, somber girl. "Trudy has been with us for three years now."

Trudy looked sternly at Molly. "I guess that's the best thing you can say about Trudy," Molly thought. She nearly laughed at the thought, but caught Trudy's critical glare. "Bit of a bulldog that Trudy," Molly said to herself.

"So, I hear that you're interested in the available apartment," Miss Nightingale continued.

"Yes, may I see it?"

"Of course, I didn't realize that you hadn't. Come, come, come!" She floated up the wide marble staircase that dominated the equally large and opulent entrance hall.

Molly followed at three paces while Trudy kept a close distance behind her. "You can check in anytime you like, but you can never leave." Molly hummed the Eagle's lyrics to herself as they reached the third floor.

"Here we are! You'll love it. Love it. Love it. It has a great view of the rose garden." Miss Nightingale opened the door to a spacious room which was decorated in old Victorian grandeur, complete with gold curtains and an old soft leather couch. Adjacent to the living room was a large bedroom accented by an enormous four-post bed. Completing the apartment was a small kitchenette and an even smaller bathroom. "It needs a little airing out, I'm afraid. It has been vacant for weeks. The former tenant paid the month's rent, but then decided not to return. What do you think?" Miss Nightingale beamed.

Molly was impressed, but felt as if she had passed through a time warp into an old English boarding school, complete with a proper and cheery headmistress. The place was nice, but not her style in the least. Yet, she knew that for the sake of the case, she had to accept the offer and appear convincingly excited by the prospect of living here. "I love it!" she exclaimed rather over the top, catching Trudy by surprise and causing her to jump back two paces while releasing a short squeal.

"Great! What excitement! I love it!" Miss Nightingale did not think Molly's reaction was out of place in the least. She herself seemed to float about on an emotional high that countered Trudy's natural low. They made the oddest pair.

"Great! Great! Great!" Miss Nightingale cheered, as if her football team had just won the championship.

"Does this mean that it's mine?" Molly asked, still expecting the promised apartment interview.

"Of course, my dear. I have a knack for reading people, and you and this room are a perfect match. Perfect! Perfect! Perfect!"

Molly realized a trend here. Miss Nightingale seemed to like to repeat herself in threes. Molly was tempted to respond, "Awesome! Awesome! Awesome!" but decided against it for now.

"What about the interview?" morose Trudy muttered.

"No need! No need! No need!" replied Miss Nightingale as she fluttered back into the hall.

"Truly a bizarre place. It's like entering through the Looking Glass into Wonderland. Where's the White Rabbit? Maybe that's Trudy," Molly concluded.

"Well, when do you plan on moving in, my dear?" Miss Nightingale inquired, singing her words.

"Is tomorrow, okay?" Molly replied despite herself.

"Great! Great! Great! Trudy can give you the keys and explain the rules and all that boring stuff. Well, welcome, welcome, welcome! I must run. Much to do! Much to do! Much to do!"

"Correction," Molly thought as she said her goodbyes to the joyful woman. "She's the White Rabbit, so Trudy must be the......Caterpillar?" Molly chuckled to herself, proud of her analogies.

In the next moment, she nearly burst out laughing as Trudy asked, "Who are you?" in complete puzzlement. "Who are you?" she repeated still stunned by what had transpired without the usual interview.

"What?" asked Molly, for at this point she was neither sure of what was real and what was her illusion, nor if the two were one and the same.

"Who -- are -- you?" Trudy slowly repeated. "Who are you to get her to act like that? She never lets anyone in without an interview. I had two interviews," Trudy huffed. "Well, come on, and I'll get you the keys and a lease to sign."

They descended the large circular staircase, except this time Trudy had the lead. Upon reaching the ground floor, they wound through what seemed like an endless maze of narrow halls lined with endless large portraits of people long departed. Finally, they entered a small room, not much larger than a king-size bed. It had a strong odor, like that of stale smoke. "Trudy must be a closet smoker," Molly concluded. "Wonder where she hides her hookah?" Molly silently chuckled.

The room had a wooden desk that was barely visible under the overflowing piles of papers and books that gave it the appearance of a large mushroom. "Never mind the mess. I do everything for her around here. She'd be lost without me."

Trudy reassured herself of her own importance. "Here're the keys, and let me find a copy of the lease. It has been a while since someone left here."

The last comment made Molly a little unsettled. "Why?"

"Why what?"

"Why has it been so long?"

"Why has what been so long?"

Again, Molly was starting to feel like she was in a storybook. She had a sudden urge to flee, but had no idea how to navigate the countless passages that they had traveled to get to this small fortress of a room. "Never mind," she sighed.

Trudy gave her a questioning glare. Molly could tell that she didn't like her. As Trudy looked for the lease, Molly noticed the numerous books stuffed into a large old wooden bookshelf that took up two walls of the window-less room. There were volumes on physics, metaphysics, psychology, neurology, anatomy, religion, mythicism and astrology. It was an odd compilation straight out of the Renaissance, except in modern publication. "Obviously, she's no dummy," Molly concluded silently. "But what an odd collection of books. No wonder she's so serious. There's not a light novel among them."

"Here's the lease and here are the rules. This key opens the front door and this one is for your room. There are rooms in the house that are restricted, so please respect that." Trudy looked at Molly suspiciously. She had not wanted this girl in the house from the minute she met her. She suspected that she would be trouble. But, Miss Nightingale had seen Molly come in the day before when Trudy provided the first tour, and instantly took a liking to her. This further infuriated Trudy. The entire sequence of events was not computing within Trudy's logical mind.

"Why are they restricted?"

"Why is what restricted?"

"What's with this girl? Is she smart or stupid? Maybe it's the content of her hidden hookah pipe that's the root cause of her odd behavior," Molly thought and nearly laughed aloud.

"Why are some of the rooms restricted?" she asked, regaining her inner composure.

"Because it's Miss Nightingale's wish, and she owns the house."

Molly knew she was not going to get any further information from Trudy, so she stopped trying and simply accepted the drab answer. Upon suffering detailed explanations of triviality, Molly followed her hostess back out of the maze and into the front hall. Along the way, they ran into a short young man with a scruffy mustache, purplish hair and a beaming smile. "There's another weird one," Molly thought.

"Welcome!" He smiled ear to ear. "Charmed!" he added in a slight British accent.

"Hello," Molly replied nervously. She could sense his physical attraction to her and it was unnerving.

"My name is Chester and yours?" He seemed to completely ignore Trudy as if she did not exist.

"My name is Molly."

"You must be the new girl we heard about."

"Word travels quickly," Molly heard herself reply.

"Time's relative. Isn't it, Molly? You're here and you're gone, like that," he proclaimed with his enormous smile. Molly turn to Trudy to see if she was still waiting at the other end of the hall. She was. By the time Molly turned back, Chester was gone.

"Who was that?" she asked Trudy as she caught up to her.

"Something the cat drug in last year," Trudy huffed.

"The Cheshire Cat, of course," she thought. "I'm going insane. This place is insane." Molly's head was spinning.

"Well, that's it," Trudy proclaimed, eager to dismiss her unwanted new housemate once they reached the hall.

"Okay. Thanks. I'll move in tomorrow. I don't have much," Molly confessed.

She was about to open the door, when it opened by itself. The suddenness of the act surprised both women. A young man entered wearing a black derby. Molly took a deep breath for she recognized him.

"Trudy, what do you think of the hat? Chester gave it to me."

He did not wait for a response for he suddenly noticed Molly. "Trudy, who do we have here?" he asked with a playful interest while looking earnestly at all of Molly at once. She felt as if she had been instantly x-rayed. Based on his smile, he seemed pleased with the results.

"This is our new tenant, Molly," Trudy replied unenthused by the handsome man's reaction to the woman she already loathed. The man's sudden interest in Molly stirred jealousy, which alienated her further.

"Well, welcome, Miss Molly," he smiled an endearing smile that even the undercover policewoman could not resist.

"Thank you, but I must run," Molly proclaimed, not waiting to be introduced.

Her sudden exit took the man by surprise for he was about to introduce himself and fell short of his goal.

"The story is complete," Molly concluded to herself as she hurried away from the house. "The Mad Hatter, himself — Jack Fulton!"

CHAPTER 23

Mrs. Allen

The Inspector was on a mission. He was determined to discover who had pushed Mary Collins. He returned to the strongest and most trustworthy testimony that he had, that of Mr. Chesterfield, the bus driver on that fateful field trip.

Mr. Chesterfield swore that, although he could not directly see the location of the incident from the front seat of his parked bus, he had kept close track of who had entered the area from which Mary had fallen. He identified the following as being in the proximity right before Mary's fall: Suzy Kurtz, Randell Twiner, Jack Fulton and Tony Bond. They remained the primary suspects, and Mr. Chesterfield's list continued to hold under increasing scrutiny.

However, some discrepancies were beginning to mount, forcing the Inspector to create a matrix of all those who participated in the field trip. On that matrix, he began to mark who was in whose company according to which testimony. There were some gaps, but Mr. Chesterfield's list remained unchanged.

One of the three main gaps on the Inspector's matrix was Miss Kelly Allen, a student attending the field trip, who appeared to have gone on vacation immediately after the incident. Several witnesses claimed that Kelly had been in the company of another girl in or near the area of Mary's fall. The inspector suspected that the other girl was either Daphne Marconi or Stacy Reed. These two young ladies comprised the other two key gaps on the Inspector's matrix. All three were persons of interest.

Based on the information that the Inspector obtained from Jennifer Angel, Daphne was suspicious, but Mr. Chesterfield had not identified her in the crime scene area, and the Inspector had nothing concrete that contradicted his key witness. Stacy was also not on Mr. Chesterfield's list, but at least one other witness, Daphne, placed her near Mary shortly before the incident. Furthermore, Stacy was suspiciously missing since Mary's fall. Despite this odd coincidence, the Inspector dismissed Daphne Marconi's claim that Stacy was also in the area of the incident, falling back on Chesterfield's testimony, which was verified by two other witnesses. He had dismissed it because only Daphne listed her in the area. Furthermore, Daphne, in her account, claimed that she herself was not in the area of the fall. Despite these minor contradictions, the Inspector remained convinced of one thing, the validity of Chesterfield's testimony. Thus, four prime suspects remained: Suzy, Randell, Jack and Tony.

The Inspector's clarity was about to get murky, for that morning Miss Kelly Allen surfaced and appeared in his office with her mother.

"May I help you?" asked the Inspector when the two women entered his office.

"Inspector James Cabot?" asked the older woman.

"Yes, and you are?" the Inspector stood up and walked around his large desk.

"Emily Allen, and this is my daughter Kelly. We're so sorry to hear about Mary Collins and her condition. We received your message asking Kelly to come in for an interview. So, here we are. As you may know, I picked up Kelly from the quarry for we were leaving on vacation that afternoon. We just returned last night and that's when I received your message. How can we help?"

Mrs. Allen seemed extremely sincere and genuine. This registered with the Inspector. But it was the young girl that was of interest in this case, and she remained suspiciously quiet.

Before the Inspector had a chance to reply, Mrs. Allen quickly filled the silence. "I'm sorry that we could not be reached. You see, we took a family trip to Africa. It was a safari. Amazing it was!" It was clear that, unlike her daughter, Mrs. Allen was not shy with words. She continued about the safari, getting into such details as the size of the elephants and the peculiar behavior of baboons, until the Inspector finally managed to stop her. "Right. Here I am carrying on and it's Kelly you want to interview. I'd like to be present, if that's okay?"

"Of course, Mrs. Allen," the Inspector replied.

"Please call me Emily, Inspector. I feel like I've known you for years."

"Right. Well, if you don't mind, I'd like us to move into the conference room." The Inspector guided the two women into the Fish Tank. He ran to one of the members of his team, Chen Lee, and asked him to step into the Mirror Room to start the recorders.

He purposely left the two women alone in the Fish Tank to see if Kelly would share any insights into the case with her mother. Nothing of interest surfaced. In fact, nothing surfaced. Therefore, he returned to the ladies fifteen minutes later, fabricating a story to explain his delay.

"Sorry, I had an urgent call. Can I get you anything?" he asked.

There was a general shaking of heads on the part of the women.

"No. Okay, then, let's get started," he began. "Let me tell you that this is an official interview, and that our discussion will be recorded as potential legal testimony. Is that okay?"

Both women nodded in agreement. He informed them of a few more items and rights, and then he began. "Kelly, what can you tell me about the geology field trip that you attended on March 22nd of this year?"

"As I told you, Inspector, we were going away that day," Mrs. Allen began.

"I'm sorry to interrupt you, Mrs. Allen, but I need to hear your daughter's testimony," the Inspector interjected.

"Please call me Emily, James."

The use of his first name startled the Inspector, who was rarely taken aback in an interview. He let it pass despite its forward nature.

"Yes, Emily. May I ask you to remain silent? I really need to hear the testimony from your daughter. Much obliged, ma'am." His southern drawl surfaced as he got tense.

Mrs. Allen found the accent delightful. "I hadn't guessed that you were a southern gentleman, James. I should've known. Why, I'm an Alabama girl. Where're ya all from? You shouldn't hide that delightful accent. Georgia, is it?"

"Yes, but…"

"I knew it. I can tell an accent, especially that lovely Georgia twang. I don't hide my accent although it's gotten contaminated by all that western Pennsylvania drawl. Be proud of that accent, James!" Mrs. Allen coached the Inspector.

At this point young Chen Lee, who was witnessing the interview in the Mirror Room, was on the ground in hysterical laughter. Now, Big Bob had joined him in the Mirror Room, and the two were rolling about laughing. Molly soon arrived and could not believe her eyes. "What're you two doing?" she asked in a bewildered tone.

Bob answered since Chen was unable to speak during his laughing fit. "That lady in there is totally man-handling our boss." He pointed at the glass wall that appeared as a mirror in the interrogation room. "I've never seen anything like it. It's hilarious. She has even got his Georgia accent going." Bob laughed some more.

"No! He never switches to that unless he's flustered or really upset," Molly confirmed.

"Yeah, well he's flustered, all right. Check it out!" Bob replied, as Chen fell over a chair in another bout of laughter.

"As I was saying, Emily." The Inspector tried to refocus the discussion.

"What's with the 'Emily'?" Molly asked, isolated from the Fish Tank by the mirror wall.

"She insists on it. She definitely has the hots for our boss. I didn't think that was possible!" Chen burst out.

Molly stayed silent.

"I understand, James. Mum's the word," Mrs. Allen replied showering him with pheromones.

"What's with the James? I can see why he's flustered. You can smell the lust from here. That woman's in heat!" Molly concluded, being well acquainted with that condition, although mostly as a recipient.

"Well, Kelly, what can you tell me about that field trip?" the Inspector asked once more of Mrs. Allen's daughter.

There was an uncomfortable silence. Since Mrs. Allen and silence were sworn enemies, she could not hold back any longer. "She's shy, James, but let me tell you what she told me. She was with her girlfriend and..."

"Mrs Allen, please! I need to hear this from your daughter." The Inspector's Georgia accent was as thick as molasses on a cold winter morning.

"Oh, now he's pissed. Maybe I better go save him," Molly suggested.

"Are you kidding? You'll mess it all up. No way!" Chen insisted.

"Of course, James. I'm so sorry, I just can't stand silence," Mrs. Allen admitted, accentuating her Alabama accent to match the Inspector's growing Georgia tone.

"Yes, I can tell," he replied dryly. "Okay, Kelly, what happened that day? Who was the girl that you were with?" The Inspector tried again.

More silence followed. Mrs. Allen looked like her cheeks were about to explode. She seemed physically pained and was painful to watch.

"I need to save him, or he'll explode." Molly correctly assessed the urgency of the situation. "If she opens her mouth, which she's about to do, he may verbally crush her."

"Come on, Molly. Don't ruin it!" Chen pleaded. It was too late. Molly was on the move.

It would take a detailed audio analysis to establish the actual sequence of the following events which were separated by microseconds while enveloped in Kelly's continued silence.

Mrs. Allen could not restrain herself any further. As Molly had predicted, she blurred out the first syllable of a word. In the same instant, the Inspector jumped to his feet while letting out the first letter of a four letter expletive, just as Molly burst into the room to everyone's surprise and exclaimed at the top of her lungs, "How's it going, Boss!" Fortunately, Molly's sudden outburst drowned the rest of the Inspector's expletive, which regressed harmlessly into audio tape history, escaping the ears of its intended recipient, the former southern debutant.

Without letting the Inspector answer, Molly took charge of the interview. "I've got it from here. You have an urgent call on Line 2." Line 2 was their code for "Get out for you're about to ruin the interview." It had never been used on the Inspector before, but he heeded the warning and stepped out of the Fish Tank without an apology.

"I'm Molly. I'll be conducting the rest of the interview with your daughter. Is that all right?"

"Sure," replied Mrs. Allen, who was confused by the sudden sequence of events.

"Can I ask you to sit outside? You can sit in the observation room. Let me show you." Molly escorted Mrs. Allen out of the Fish Tank before she had a chance to object.

"She's bringing her here! She ruined everything!" Chen exclaimed and quickly sat down at the table in the Mirror Room. Realizing that the party was over, Big Bob disappeared.

"Mrs. Allen, this is Officer Chen," Molly introduced her colleague.

"All is on auto, Molly. Nice to meet you, Mrs. Allen," Chen replied and quickly ran out of the room. After witnessing his boss's fate, he did not want to be trapped in the same room with Emily Allen.

"From here, you'll be able to see and hear everything," Molly guided.

"Wow! I never thought that these secrete observation rooms existed, except on TV!" Mrs. Allen was nearly speechless.

"Yes, amazing, isn't it?" Molly replied as she guided Mrs. Allen to a chair. "Please, have a seat right here, and you can rejoin Kelly when we're done."

"Sure. Thank you."

"You're most, welcome," Molly replied and departed.

Molly succeeded in winning Kelly's trust rather quickly, and the interview proceeded without a hitch. Afterwards, Mrs. Allen insisted on seeing the Inspector once more. She walked into his room, leaving Molly and Kelly in the hall. He was not too pleased to see her, but did not let it show.

"I wanted to tell you how much I'm sorry about my interjections. It's just that Kelly is so shy," Mrs. Allen began.

"No worries at all, Mrs. Allen. I totally understand. It's stressful." The Inspector rose from his chair and came around the desk to meet her.

"Also, I… well… I don't know how to say this. I'm getting a divorce. The family safari trip was with Kelly and my parents. I mean … I don't know how to say this, being a proper southern woman and all, but I noticed you didn't have a ring."

"I'm truly sorry to hear about your divorce, Mrs. Allen," he replied ignoring the "ring" comment. "I completely understand. I'm divorced, as well." As soon as he uttered the words, he regretted sharing them.

"Well, if that's the case maybe we ….."

"I'm afraid that work is much too busy, and …."

"Oh, my, I'm so embarrassed. Of course, I understand. I didn't really mean that…"

"No need to be embarrassed, Mrs. Allen. I'm very flattered. It's clear that you are a wonderful mother and a woman with good taste," he chuckled. This made her laugh as well, greatly easing the situation.

"Now, I must get back to my work." He bid her farewell, but could see Molly chuckling outside his office. As Mrs. Allen turned her back to him, he made a smirk at Molly and silently uttered "thank you" for her to lip read. Molly simply smiled at him before escorting mother and daughter out of the station.

CHAPTER 24

The Analysis

"Well, what did you find out?" the Inspector asked when Molly returned.

"That your hunches and theories need some reworking," she replied dryly.

"In what way?"

She looked at her watch. "It's past noon and I'm starving. I suggest a team huddle after lunch."

"Good idea. I'll set it up. Can I join you for lunch?"

"Normally, I would be delighted, but I need to run around the corner to my apartment and start my packing. I'm supposed to move to my new place tomorrow," she explained.

"Maybe next time," he replied. "What's the latest on that cult? Is it a cult?"

"I'll fill you in at the team meeting. I suggest that we carve out two hours. By the way, here's the rent estimate for the new place.

I assume the department is still picking it up since I'm making this move on police business?" She placed a paper in his hand.

"Wow! What is this place, the Ritz?"

"If you don't want me to move there, that's fine with me," she replied. "It's a weird place to say the least."

"No! Move! I just need to warn my boss before the expenses hit. Okay, I'll see you at the meeting."

"Good, thanks," she replied and left his office.

"Who's the boss here anyway?" he chuckled to himself.

After lunch, the Inspector's small case team assembled in his spacious office. There was Molly, Big Bob, and Chen Lee, who had a hard time keeping a straight face when he first beheld the Inspector.

"The reason I called this meeting is that we've had quite a few developments in the Mary Collins case since Monday and I want all of us on the same page. Also, I want to spend some time conducting another analysis of our suspects." The Inspector glanced at a cork board that had photos of several of his suspects. The board was covered with a white drape cloth to assure confidentially in case he had surprise visitors, like Mrs. Allen. He pulled back the white sheet revealing the pictures of Suzy Kurtz, Randell Twiner, Jack Fulton, Tony Bond and Daphne Marconi. He added Daphne based on his previous discussion with Jennifer Angel.

"Who's the new girl on the board?" Chen asked.

"We'll get to that," the Inspector replied. "Bob, why don't you start with your summary of the Randell incident, and then Molly can fill us in on the Kelly Allen interview and the Nightingale Manor. After that, Chen, I would like an update from you regarding the search for Stacy Reed and your review of Tony Bond's computer, which we seized when we arrested him on harassment charges related to Mary Collins. Okay, let's get started." The Inspector looked to Bob, who began to review the Suzy and Randell conflict to the astonishment of Molly and Chen.

Then, it was Molly's turn. She gave the team a summary of her odd experience in Ms. Nightingale's manor, highlighting the tie to Mary's tattoo but sparing them her metaphors with the various Alice in Wonderland characters. She surprised everyone, including the Inspector, when she revealed her unexpected encounter with Jack Fulton.

"That guy's everywhere!" the Inspector blurted out as he heard the news.

All agreed that Molly's new residence was extremely odd, while Chen concluded that it would be a perfect fit for her. Unamused by him, she now began the summary of the recent Kelly Allen interview.

"Well, Boss, first of all, thanks for warming things up for me." She smiled at the Inspector. Chen and Bob snickered, but they did not dare tease their boss on this sensitive topic.

"Go on, go on!" the Inspector replied, unamused.

"When I finally managed to get Kelly talking, she differed little from her mother in that, once going, she was hard to stop." Molly glanced once more at the Inspector. She was enjoying the teasing. He simply waved his hand at her to the sound of more snickering from Chen and Bob.

"Go on, Molly! Get to the point!" the Inspector insisted.

"Well, it appears that we may want to reconsider our suspect list. Kelly assured me that she was with Suzy Kurtz prior to Mary's fall, and that she and Suzy were together when they saw Mary's body at the base of the quarry wall. She said that when they entered the area, she saw Daphne and Tony at the far wall of the quarry on the same level as Mary. But they were not together. Initially, Randell was not in sight, nor was Jack Fulton, who appeared seemingly out of nowhere soon after Suzy screamed. She said that Suzy screamed not just at the sight of the body, but also at the sight of Randell embracing Stacy Reed, both of whom were on the wide rock ledge below the the site of Mary's fall and to the left of it. Stacy ran as they came into view, and Randell headed down to the quarry floor toward Mary's fallen body. As you know, the presence of Stacy near the scene is something that neither Mr. Chesterfield, Suzy nor Randell had included in their accounts, and only Daphne listed her in the area. Thus, Kelly's account differs in several ways from those of our previous key witnesses," she paused for discussion.

"Hmmm... it's time to plot out all of this in time and space, and to revisit the crime scene. We may need to reconnect with some of the witnesses and suspects," the Inspector concluded.

"Kelly was willing to take a lie detector test. She swears that Suzy is innocent," Molly added.

"Okay. Let's run that test on her. If Kelly's right then it looks like Suzy comes off the prime suspect list, but we leave Daphne and add Stacy. That would leave us with Stacy, Randell, Jack and Daphne, since I think that Tony's out too," the Inspector concluded.

"Don't be so sure, Boss," Chen suddenly piped up. "Just before this meeting, I discovered some interesting information on Tony's hard drive as I collected data for the harassment and molestation charges."

"Yes, Chen?" The Inspector looked straight at him.

Chen, who was the newest and youngest member of the team, was a former FBI data analyst, who transferred into the area to be with his fiancé while she attended McLaren University. He was a rebel at heart and a poor fit with his previous employer. However, he seemed to fit well with Inspector Cabot's often unorthodox style. What experience he lacked in police fieldwork, he made up for in his uncanny computer skills and sharp deductive mind. He was a key complement of the Inspector's core team.

"I finally cracked the last of the passwords on Tony's hard drive and got this little gem." Chen was never without his electronic tablet. He now passed it over to the Inspector, who read the e-mail series quickly. "These had been deleted, but I managed to retrieve them," Chen added, pleased with himself.

"Interesting! It appears that I was too hasty in dismissing Mr. Bond as a primary suspect." The Inspector corrected his previous deduction. "What Chen found," he passed the tablet over to Molly who sat nearest him, "confirms that Miss Lilly Austin, whom we now know is Mary's older sister, has our friend Tony as a lover. It appears that her attraction for Tony may have had a sinister purpose, to physically harm Mary and get her to renounce her claim to their father's remaining inheritance. The chain of e-mails suggests that she encouraged Tony to harm her sister and possibly 'do away with' her. Hmmm... so, we add Tony back to the list of key suspects," the Inspector concluded and paused.

"We can also charge Lilly in conspiracy to commit a crime and conspiracy to a homicide," Big Bob blared out.

The Inspector realized that he would have to send Bob to a few legal refresher classes. "Not so fast, Bob! First of all, God willing, there won't be a homicide and Mary will recover. Furthermore, the note isn't specific enough to qualify for a criminal conspiracy charge under court scrutiny. But, it does raise a possible new scenario for what happened to Mary Collins. Assuming that Kelly's correct, and we've no reason to doubt her at this time, then Suzy is out and Tony is very much back in. We need to interview Daphne Marconi again. She's Tony's alibi per his testimony, but not per hers and now Kelly's." The Inspector was thinking aloud. "Good work, Chen. Continue to comb Tony's hard drive. Anything on Stacy? Have we located her yet?" the Inspector added.

"No, not yet, Boss. She seems to have vanished without a trace."

"Does her family know anything?"

"No luck. She appears to have only one living relative, her father. He happens to be Professor Arthur Reed, a renown entomologist at McLaren's Biology Department. He's reported by his peers and students to be extremely eccentric and recluse. Presently, he's unreachable, doing field work in a remote region of the Amazonian jungle. It appears that he likes it that way, disappearing that is," Chen concluded.

"Seems to run in the family," Molly replied.

"Yes, indeed. However, per our request, the Biology Department left a message for him regarding the disappearance of his daughter. He's expected to check in on Sunday. Until then, he's a dead end," Chen replied. "It appears that the last person to see Stacy after she apparently parted with Randell was Rachel Parker, another student attending the field trip. I tracked Rachel down this morning, and she told me that she ran into Stacy right after Mary's fall. But, oddly, Stacy was in a great rush heading away from the scene, as if she were guilty. She's willing to testify to that encounter. Supposedly, she didn't mention it initially, when we interviewed the entire field trip class, because she assumed Mary's falls was an accident." Chen finished his report.

"Okay, we need to talk to Randell again since he appeared to be the last one with Stacy at the crime scene," the Inspector concluded. "What am I saying? We won't get anything out of Randell without a legal battle. Chen, we need to find Stacy. Pronto! Do you have a list of her friends?"

"There are only a few and I interviewed all of them, either in person or by phone. Unless someone's lying, none of them know her whereabouts," Chen replied.

"Did you check phone records, credit card transactions and a cell phone location?" the Inspector grilled Chen.

"Not yet, Sir. Will do!"

"I suspect that she either did it, or saw something and is running in fear," the Inspector concluded.

"Or, she's dead," Big Bob added.

"Doubtful. All the other key suspects are accounted for and there's no homicide, as yet," Molly countered.

"It could be a precautionary murder," Bob countered.

"What's a 'precautionary murder,' Bob?" Molly asked while knitting her eyebrows.

"Enough! We need to find her." The Inspector cut them off, as a father dismissing two feuding children.

"Yes, but if we believe Kelly, and, as you said, right now we have no reason not to believe her, then Randell and Stacy were not in the right place to push Mary," Molly piped up.

"True, but we don't know exactly how long it took between the time of the fall and the time that Kelly and Suzy arrived at the scene. There could have been plenty of time for Randell and Stacy to try to escape down toward the quarry," Chen added. "Besides, maybe Stacy and Randell were not embracing at all. Maybe Stacy was trying to stop Randell, or he grabbed her because she was a witness," Chen speculated.

"Doubtful. Why run down into an enclosed quarry, and not up or out as she did later? Also, why would Randell head down instead of out?" Molly reasoned. "Unless, she did see him from below and he ran down to silence her."

"Or, they were simply embracing," Bob chimed into the conversation.

"Okay enough! Stacy is a potential suspect and a key person of interest." The inspector broke up the discussion once more, for although the questions were relevant, it was clearly headed into more speculation. "Let's compile the facts. We still have over an hour left here." He wiped down his white board. "Let's start with Mary. What facts do we have to date?" he asked his team.

"She was a senior at McLaren," Bob spoke up.

"Yes," the Inspector replied, but did not jot down the observation. "Let's list the facts that are critical to the case."

"Okay. She has a sister as her only relative, and that sister is out to harm or possibly kill her," Bob tried again.

"Okay, good! You raise a good point, Bob. We need to map out the relationships while we do this. If Mary is here," the Inspector wrote "Mary" in red at the center of the large white board. Then, he wrote "Lilly" to the right, and connected the two with a red line. "The red lines will designate a hostile relationship. Green will represent a supportive one, and yellow will stand for a neutral relationship as it related to the case. I will use the blue line to designate links that need more information. He continued the process.

At the end of the two hour meeting, his white board looked like an airline flight chart with Mary's name in the center, as the main hub, and the suspects as individual peripheral hubs. The connections were depicted in a rainbow of colors, and under each name was an abbreviated list of facts.

"What a mess!" Chen concluded. "Let me convert that into a relationship matrix with drop-down windows for the traits. That way we can read it again," he took a picture of the messy white board with his tablet.

"Okay, Mister IT, you do that, but what this tells me is that Jack Fulton does not seem to have a strong motive, although he's extremely suspicious, and that Suzy is innocent. Daphne and Stacy are still big question marks. We need to interview Daphne again," the Inspector concluded once more.

"Chen, keep chasing down Stacy and begin to treat this as a missing person case. If her father doesn't know her whereabouts, we will turn it into an official one," he ordered. "Bob, see if you can console your neighbor Suzy. See if you can get her to press charges against Randell, and confide to you what she saw the day Mary fell. Let's see if it's supported by Kelly's statement. I need you to become her best friend. Molly, why don't you take another go at Jack Fulton. See if you can run into him again in your new digs, and also try and catch up with Daphne. Finally, see what you can find out about that religious cult now that you're practically a member of it. I'll update my boss, and take on Boris and Natasha." The Inspector set the assignments.

"Who're Boris and Natasha?" Bob asked.

"Never mind. It was an after-school cartoon that us old folks watched when we were kids," the Inspector replied.

"You were a kid?" Chen asked.

"Very funny, Chen. You're lucky that you have your IT skill. That's all I'll say," the Inspector replied.

"Seriously, who are Boris and Natasha? They sound Russian," Bob persisted. He was the most naive one of the team.

"Seriously, Bob? It was a bad joke that is thirty years too late for this crowd."

"We weren't around thirty years ago, Boss," Bob observed.

"That's the point, Bob. It was a silly reference to Lilly and Tony." The Inspector sighed while explaining himself. Suddenly, he felt very old.

"Oh, right. Ha, ha, funny!" Bob tried to pretend to be amused.

"Give it up, Bob!" the Inspector replied before continuing his instructions to his team. "Okay, since we've got a lot going on, we'll have an hour meeting on this case every morning at 8 am sharp, right here in my office. Don't be late! You know who I'm talking about, Molly."

Everyone agreed and dispersed with their marching orders.

The Inspector pulled out a few more mug shots and pinned them on the suspect board. "So, Suzy and Kelly appear innocent, but we've got Stacy, Lilly, Tony, Randell, Daphne, and Jack Fulton, who has little motive, except that he obviously slept with Mary, which could be motive enough. Regardless, he's acting very suspiciously and seems to be at all the wrong places." He exhaled audibly. "One good thing," he thought, "Miss Lilly's e-mails strengthen my case that Mary's fall was no accident."

 CHAPTER 25

Natasha

The Inspector wasted little time. He decided to visit Lilly Austin first since he already had Tony Bond in the police holding cell. No one had paid Tony's bail, so the Inspector assumed that his rich princess, Lilly, was no longer interested in her former lover. "Good. This may be the very opportunity to make these two turn on each other and confess," the Inspector concluded as he headed out the door to Lilly's palatial estate on the west end of town.

It was a beautiful spring day, and the entire Austin estate was in bloom, covered with color and fragrance. It appeared like a palace from a fairy tale.

The Inspector drove his old 1968 Jaguar XJ6 sedan around the estate's driveway, which formed a large loop in front of the white stone manor. As he pulled up to the front door, he was greeted by an elderly man with a thick Irish accent. It was Andrew, Lilly's faithful Irish butler and chauffeur.

"May I help you, Sir? My, she's a beauty! They don't make such beauty anymore. 1968, no?" Andrew asked with a thick brogue.

"You must be an automobile connoisseur?" the Inspector replied.

"Hardly, but I do know a little about automobiles, especially British ones. Unfortunately, Ireland's attempts in that market were rather short lived," Andrew replied.

"Do you mean the DeLorean? That was made in Northern Ireland," the Inspector replied.

"There's but one Ireland in the hearts of the Irish," Andrew replied as he held open the Inspector's door

"Spoken like a true Irishman. The name's James Cabot," the Inspector introduced himself.

"Andrew O'Malley. What can I do for you, Mr. Cabot?"

"I'm here to speak with Miss Austin. Is she in? I'm an inspector with the State Police." The Inspector showed his badge.

"Oh, my! Is she in some kind of trouble?"

"I hope not, but I do have a few questions for her regarding a private matter."

"I see," Andrew replied without further inquiry. "Please come in and have a seat, Inspector. I'll try and catch her before her afternoon nap. Her 'beauty rest' as she calls it. You can leave the car right where it is, unless you want to give me the keys, so that I can take it for a test drive," Andrew replied with a chuckle.

The Inspector liked Andrew. He could tell that this was an honest man. "Wonder what he knows and wonder if he'd tell?" the Inspector thought.

"Come into our humble hall," Andrew chuckled again.

The hall was the largest and most ornate hall that the Inspector had ever seen in these parts, and he had visited most local places over the years. "I had no idea that this estate was so large and remarkable," is all that he could muster, as he looked about the vaulted three-story room.

"It's grand - too grand, if you ask me. But I'm a simple Irishman. Have a seat, and I'll go find Miss Austin. Would you like to see Mr. Austin, as well?"

"No, not at this time."

"That's just as well since he's not here." Andrew chuckled upon betraying his Irish humor. "I shall not be long."

The Inspector sat down into one of the red satin covered couches that looked like they came out of a room in Versailles. He did not wait more than five minutes before Andrew returned.

"She'll see you in ten minutes, Mr. Cabot. May I usher you into the sitting room?"

"Sure. Where is it?"

"Simply follow me, Sir. It's not far, I promise." Andrew opened a large door, one of two ten-foot tall mahogany double doors on the left side of the hall. "Here we are, not far at all."

"Wow, are there any small rooms in this place?"

"Yes, the one I occupy," Andrew laughed. "May I ask you to have a seat once more while you wait for the lady of the house?"

"Sure," the Inspector replied and sank into one of a dozen patent leather chairs that were positioned about the tutor-style room. The room had a very masculine feel, as emphasized by its mahogany trim and enormous, field-stone fireplace. It looked like an old English gentlemen's smoking room, complete with dark, floor-length, satin curtains. All it was missing were the likes of Sherlock Holmes and Doc Watson, and the stuffed trophy head of some poor unfortunate rhinoceros or water buffalo.

He liked this room and decided to inspect the various portraits, old prints and plethora of oriental vases that decorated the walls and furnishings. While in the process of analyzing what looked like a large print of the Old Course at St. Andrews, he was interrupted by a young woman's greeting. He turned around to find Miss Lilly Austin standing in the open doorway in her full regalia and radiance. Instantly he could tell the resemblance between her and Mary Collins.

"This room is most dreadful, isn't it? I've tried three times now to redecorate it, but my husband insists on leaving it in this shabby state. He likes to entertain his visitors here. I'm surprised he still has any after torturing them with this horrid space. But men seem to like these drab greens and browns. Reminds me of a swamp," she proclaimed in a strong Irish accent.

"You must be Mrs. Austin?" the Inspector replied, walking toward her.

"That makes me sound so old, but it's true. It is I in the flesh." She made a model pose as she finished the statement.

The Inspector was unimpressed. He concluded that, even in a coma, Mary was more appealing than her beautiful but arrogant older sister.

"You must be Inspector Cabot with the State Police. What can I possibly do for you? Did my forgetful husband run a red light and neglect to pay his fine?"

"No, I'm here to ask you a few questions."

"Pray tell, what about? Surely not my unfortunate sister. I'm so upset about what happened. Have you discovered how she fell? Is that why you're here? You know I've been worried sick over this since it happened," Lilly turned on the drama.

"Sure. You don't look the part of the grieving sister," the Inspector nearly blurted out, but decided to restrain himself. "No, unfortunately, I don't know how she fell," he replied instead.

"Still no answers? What are you folks doing? I thought it was ruled an accident? Is it more? If so, why aren't you doing more, or are you simply waiting for her to pass?" she asked with an odd wishful look.

"I assure you, Miss Austin, that we're doing everything in our power to solve this."

"I'm not impressed, Inspector. So, please tell me to what do I owe this surprise visit?" She stressed the word "surprise".

"Well, it's a part of our investigation, ma'am," the Inspector began.

Being referred to as a "ma'am" made Lilly visibly cringe. "It's a part of your investigation to interview me? I'm honored, but let's not do so in this dreadful place. Come and follow me to my parlor!" She disappeared through the large double doors into the hallway. The Inspector had to hurry to keep up. She was a nimble woman in her mid-twenties, while he carried twice her years and nearly twice her weight.

After what felt like a sprint through three additional large rooms, including one dining room with a long table set with over twenty luxurious settings, they ended their chase in a lavender room, complete with thousands of lilies depicted on everything possible.

"Much better. Here I can be myself. Please have a seat," she pointed to one of the pink love seats that was decorated with more lilies.

"I love lilies as you can tell. My father did a great job picking out my name. He was such a dear." She sighed in genuine reflection. "Well, what would you like to ask me, Inspector?"

She sat motionless opposite him, her auburn hair framing her green eyes and classic Irish features. Her native accent was distinct, but more refined than Andrew's. She was a woman in charge of her destiny, and she was well aware of her power and fortune, being the architect of both.

The Inspector was taken aback a moment by her concentrated attention. This ability appeared to be the only thing that they had in common. They were apparently both excellent and attentive listeners. He had not expected to be intimidated by a woman half his age, but somehow Miss Lilly Austin managed to do just that.

"Yes, Inspector?" she nudged him out of his thoughts.

"May I record this, Miss Austin, since this may be the only chance I have for an interview with you."

"Please, I have nothing to hide. Record away, Inspector!"

"Thank you, Mrs. Austin."

He placed the small recorder back in his pocket after activating it. He hoped that she would forget about it soon.

"As I was saying in the other room, we're still investigating your sister's fall, and in the process we've discovered a connection to you," he paused as she pierced him with her large green eyes, nearly derailing his train of thought.

"Of course there is a connection, dear Inspector, we are sisters, Mary and I," she chuckled. "Glad to see that my taxes are being well spent on this insightful investigation."

He ignored the comment and continued, "May I ask if you've been to the hospital to see your sister since she was admitted over a week ago?"

"What kind of a question is that? Of course I have! I'm there nearly every day."

"Odd. Your name was not on any of the daily visitation records," he objected.

"That's because I don't sign in, Inspector. But I'm there most mornings. I sleep very little, and that's the best time to go. It's so peaceful then, and I get to be alone with my sister as she rests in peace," she paused and smiled. "Is that what you came here to ask me, if I visit my sister in the hospital? Your thoughtfulness is most endearing," she purred.

"What a witch!" the Inspector thought, but remained unflustered.

"Would you also like to know if I cry when I see her? In case you do, the answer is 'yes.' " She smiled a sarcastic smile.

"Miss Austin, may I remind you that I'm here on official police business and that your cooperation is advised."

"Is that a threat? Are you threatening me in my own parlor?"

"No, I'm simply asking you to show some respect."

"Well, if you want respect, provide me with a reason to respect you. It's simple as that. So far I've not seen one," she snapped back.

The Inspector was doing all he could not to get angry, but despite his best efforts, his Georgia twang was beginning to emerge.

"What's with the Southern accent? Am I to be impressed?"

Inspector Cabot's accent became thicker, and he inhaled audible. "I can't let her fluster me," he repeated to himself. "That's her plan all along."

"Miss Austin, I'll get right to the point. We have Tony Bond in custody for harassment and molestation of your younger sister weeks before her mysterious fall. Were you aware that he did this?"

"Who's Tony Bond?" she asked completely deadpan.

"We have evidence that you had a relationship with him."

"What! You came here to accuse me of infidelity with some convict that I don't even know? That's harassment, Inspector! I suggest you leave immediately!"

"I suggest you let me finish, Miss Austin," the Inspector replied in a strong Georgian accent. "You see we've legally confiscated Mr. Bond's computer and on his hard drive are numerous e-mails from you. Here's a copy of one. Would you like to see it?" He pulled out a paper copy of an e-mail in which Lilly addresses Tony as her lover and flirtatiously tempts him to harm and "do away with" her sister Mary.

"I'm not interested in your drummed up lies. I've nothing further to say. Please leave my house, Inspector. If you have any further questions, you can ask my attorney. His name is Sheldon Twiner. You may have heard of him."

"Very well, Miss Austin, if that's your wish, but we have mounting evidence that you and Tony Bond plotted to harm and 'do away with' your sister Mary."

"Sure you do! Is she dead? No! Did I ever harm her in any physical way? No! Did Tony Bond harm her in any physical way? Yes! But it was weeks before any of my e-mails and weeks before her fall. He never touched her after that. He chickened out! You've got nothing, Inspector. My sister tried to steal from me what was rightfully mine. If you want any more information, please call Sheldon Twiner. I'm sure that you know how to find him. Now, please leave!"

"So, you admit that you tried to convince Tony Bond to harm or kill your sister?"

"No! You're accusing me of such nonsense! I'll admit that I vented my disappointment in my sister to Tony. That's what those e-mails were about. Are you going to arrest every person in this town that vents his anger about someone? Good day, Inspector!

I have suffered through enough of this. Please leave! I don't wish to physically force you off of my premises."

"Very well, Mrs. Austin. You just mentioned that your e-mail was sent weeks after Tony first molested Mary. How did you know when he molested her, and why didn't you go to the police when you found out about it?"

"I didn't say that, you did!"

"You did say that Mrs. Austin. You knew that Tony Bond was harassing and molesting your sister for weeks before her tragic fall. You knew it and did nothing, and later you encouraged him to do worse, to 'do away with' her, per this e-mail right here." He waved the paper copy of the infamous e-mail in front of her. "What kind of a sister are you, Mrs. Austin?"

"Am I on trial here? No! Look, that f---en bitch stole from me! She was always daddy's favorite! She deserved what she got, and I have nothing further to say. Get out! Get out right now, or I'll call the police!"

"I'm leaving Mrs. Austin. And, by the way, in case you had forgotten, I am the police!"

"Get out you f---en bastard!"

"I'm leaving Mrs. Bond, I mean Mrs. Austin. For a second there I had you and Tony Bond confused since you seem to be prone to the same language and tone."

"Out or I'll sue you! Out! Andrew!! Where are you?"

"I'm leaving, but tell me one thing, does your husband know that you were sleeping with Tony Bond?"

"Andrew! Help! Where are you?"

"I take that as a 'No'. Did Mary know?"

"That f--en bitch knew and I knew she was silently judging me. I hate her just as I hate you!"

"So you had Tony rough her up and push her into the quarry."

"That bastard roughed her up all right, but he refused to finish the job. She never squealed to you cops and I figured out why. I know that she was going to expose me to my husband. She was going to take me down and steal all this!" She wavered her arm around the room. "That bitch never said a word, but that was her way. I knew she'd do it! Now get out! Andrew! Where are you? Damn it, Andrew, get over here right now!"

"One last thing, Mrs. Austin."

"What? Get the f--k out, you bastard!"

"You're under arrest, Mrs. Austin, as an accomplice in the harassment and molestation of Mary Collins."

"You can't arrest me!"

"Yes, I can. I was hoping to get lucky tonight, so I brought along a pair of handcuffs," he laughed a hearty laugh.

"You f---en bastard! Sheldon Twiner will have you for lunch!"

"Until then, Miss Lilly Austin, you have the right to remain silent for anything you say may be held against you in a court of law. By the way, do you respect me now? Based on that look, I think not. You have the right to an attorney, if you...", he continued as he handcuffed her.

CHAPTER 26

Odd Triangle

*J*ennifer was working another double shift. It was five in the afternoon and the trauma ward was busy. She had just started another set of rounds when she noticed a tall quiet man in his late twenties walking toward her.

"May I help you?" she asked.

"No, thank you. I know the way," he replied in a distinct Australian accent.

He seemed anxious as he headed toward Mary's room. There was a reverence to his manner as he entered the room, as if he were entering a chapel. He stopped at the door, removed his baseball cap and stepped forward in anticipation.

"Who's that?" Jennifer thought to herself.

A few minutes later, as part of her rounds, she discovered the mystery man seated next to Mary's bed and holding her limp right hand. He appeared to be having a quiet one-way conversation with her. He had tears in his eyes as he whispered inaudibly.

At first, Jennifer felt odd interrupting. But, she had to check her patient's vital signs, and today there were too many patients to allow for flexibility in her schedule. She decided simply to walk in and greet the odd mournful man. "Hello!" she said cheerfully. "Sorry to interrupt, but I need to check Mary's vital signs." She pointed to the life support machines. "It looks like you're taking good care of her," she added and smiled at the stranger.

"Yes, I've come to see Mary every day, but usually it's in the morning," he replied without an introduction.

"Well, I won't be long. If you'll excuse me, I need to get past you."

"Sure. Let me get out of your way."

Jennifer liked this shy young man. He seemed genuine, unlike Jack. "Are you her brother?" she asked in her most innocent voice in hopes of starting a conversation.

"No. I'm a friend," he answered quietly.

"I see. I noticed your accent. It's Australian, right? Did you come here all the way from Australia?" She inquired as she checked her patient's vital signs.

"Yes and no," he replied softly, being a man of few words.

Jennifer was having a difficult time satisfying her inherent curiosity. She lingered over Mary to buy more time. "I don't understand?" she turned and smiled at him, flashing her brown eyes.

He liked the young nurse. There was a sincerity about her that attracted him. "Well, yes, I'm Australian, but, no, I didn't travel here from Australia to see Mary. I'm Carl. I'm a graduate student at McLaren.

"Well, I'm pleased to meet you, Carl," she replied. "So, this is the other geology graduate student that comes around during the day," she thought. "What an odd triangle these three make. Nice guy, but he needs a new wardrobe," she giggled silently.

Jennifer decided to push her luck a little further. After all, she had nothing to lose. "Do you know the other graduate student that comes around? Jack's his name."

Carl seemed to stiffen at the mention of Jack Fulton. "Yes, I do," is all he replied.

"I figured that you guys were friends," Jennifer was fishing for more information.

"Yes," he replied and broke eye contact.

"I see. I'd better not pry, but to me you both seem like nice guys and Mary's lucky to have you as friends," Jennifer replied with a smile.

He smiled back, but did not respond. An uncomfortable silence followed, which Jennifer correctly inferred as a strong hint that the conversation was over.

"Well, I'll leave you two alone," Jennifer added and was about to leave the room when she decided to take one more liberty. Turning back to Carl, she said, "It's nice to see how much you love her. I'm sure that she'll come back to you. Have faith!" She did not know what possessed her to say that, but her words had a emotional effect on Carl.

He teared up. "I hope you're right for I've lost that faith."

"I'm sorry." Jennifer suddenly wished that she had not said anything. "Here," she handed him a small box of tissues.

"Thank you. Sorry for the outburst. I just cannot believe this happened to her," he proclaimed as he regained composure.

Jennifer felt awkward for prying. Obviously, the man had strong feelings for Mary. She wanted to know more, but dared not interrupt further. Instead, she decided to quietly walk out of the room, convinced that she had stumbled upon a love triangle that explained the two doting graduate students.

"That Mary seems to have a lot of suitors," Jennifer thought and shook her head in disbelief. "Anyway, he's truly grieving, which is more than I can say for Jack Fulton," she sighed. "Why am I always attracted to the bad boys?" she wondered. "Probably for the same reason Mary was, the challenge and mystery of it. Wonder if I'll ever see Jack Fulton again?" she reflected silently in the hallway.

As she entered another patient's room, she paused again and thought, "Mary and Carl seem like a nice couple. He really cares about her. You can tell. I'm a good judge of character and that man in there is a good man, a good man with a sexy accent and an awful shirt," she laughed aloud.

Her next patient noticed and asked why she was laughing. "Because the world's a funny place," she replied whimsically.

CHAPTER 27

A Brawl

Molly had managed to fit all of her belongings into her old rusty hatchback car. There was not much to move, except for a fairly sizable collection of clothing and shoes. The former she stuffed in several suitcases, six moving boxes and an over-sized duffle bag, and the latter fit in three additional boxes. All of this, she jammed into the small car or strapped to its roof with bungee cords. The entire vehicle had the appearance of a stochastic assortment of boxes and suitcases bound into a disheveled heap on wheels. As she gazed at her creation, she began to laugh.

"God, my life's a mess! I should just drive that thing off a cliff and start again." She laughed some more.

She was about to get in the car when her cell phone rang. It was the Inspector. "Yes, Boss," she answered.

"Molly, any chance that you could come in and interrogate Lilly Austin? I booked her on a number of dubious charges and need at least one to stick. I think she'll respond to you best."

"Oh, Boss, I'm in the middle of the move. When do you need me?"

"As soon as possible," he replied.

She took another look at the heaped up mess that covered her dilapidated car. The thought of driving that mess to the station did not appeal to her. What if Chen or Bob saw her? They would never let her live it down.

"Please! I'll buy you lunch," the Inspector pleaded.

"Okay. I'll be there in fifteen minutes, but you owe me dinner."

There was a pause, for the Inspector had never thought of taking Molly to dinner. It could look bad given that he was recently divorced. Nonetheless, he agreed. "Okay, dinner."

The deal was struck and Molly headed to the station with all of her possessions.

She arrived only to pass right by Chen and Bob, who were headed out for an early lunch.

"What the...?" recoiled Chen. "It's some kind of a moving trash heap!"

"No, it's an ugly yard sale on wheels," Bob replied as he began to laugh.

"No, Bob. I got it. It's a hillbilly float complete with Miss Congeniality."

"Oh, no, Chen! It's our Molly driving a dumpster!"

Molly got out of the car and looked at her two colleagues who were in stitches. "Don't say a word," she huffed as she passed by them and headed to the Inspector's office. "It figures. I had to run right into those two clowns," she thought as she climbed the stairs.

When she got to the third floor, the Inspector eagerly greeted her. "Molly, thanks for coming in on such short notice. I really need your help. If you can get anything out of Lilly Austin before her attorney arrives, it could help our case. Here's what happened," he quickly filled Molly in on his discussion with Lilly at her estate and the charges that followed.

"Okay, so we have a pretty shaky case against her," Molly concluded.

"We still don't know for certain if Tony really pushed Mary. It appears that he may have disobeyed Lilly. I'm not sure. It's possible that she got someone else to do it. I wouldn't put it past her," the Inspector reasoned.

"Okay, I'll see what I can do," Molly replied.

"I was thinking of bringing Tony into the later part of the interview, since he's downstairs in the holding cell. We could see how they interact. Maybe that will shake something out. What do you think?" the Inspector asked.

"Heck, Boss, it's your call. Let's just get on with it. But warn me if you decide to send Tony into the room," Molly replied in a sharp tone. She was annoyed at having to interrupt her move and having to suffer humiliation at the hands of Bob and Chen.

"Okay, let's see how it goes. I have all the audio and video ready. Chen set it up before he left. I'll be in the Mirror Room," the Inspector explained and disappeared.

Molly headed into the Fish Tank where she found Lilly waiting impatiently, her claws sharpened.

"Who the hell are you, the cleaning lady?" Lilly struck instantly.

Molly ignored her and simply introduced herself.

"Great! A cop who looks like a filthy maid! I guess they don't pay you much." Lilly looked down at Molly.

Molly suddenly realized that in her rush she had forgotten to change and was still wearing her shabby moving clothes. "Oh, hell with it!" she concluded to herself.

"Mrs. Austin," Molly began, "do you know why you were arrested?"

"Yes! Because that little prick of an inspector is high on coke or something stronger! Look, Cinderella, I'm not letting this go without a fight. My attorney, Sheldon Twiner, is on his way, and he'll have your pretty disheveled head on a platter as soon as he arrives. Get it? I've got nothing else to say!" Lilly turned toward the mirrored wall and added, "Inspector, kiss my ass! That you should be so lucky to even get near it. I bet that's part of the issue. You lust for me, you little pervert!" she yelled at the mirror before getting up. To Molly's shock, Lilly turned quickly and suddenly stuck out her leotard covered posterior in the direction of the mirror and proceeded to rub it with her left hand. "Take a good look inspector and don't salivate on your one-way mirror," she laughed before sitting back down.

"Class act," Molly thought. "Why am I wasting my time here?"

"I've nothing to say, Dorothy," Lilly turned back to Molly.

"It's Molly," the latter corrected her.

"You look like Dorothy when she landed in that land full of munchkins. You know, munchkins, like that horny inspector back there!" She pointed at the mirror once more.

Just then the door opened and one of the young officers escorted Tony Bond into the room. Molly glanced over her shoulder at the mirror with an expression of "What the hell, Boss?" She was not expecting the sudden intruder, nor was Lilly. The sight of Tony made Lilly angrier, just as the Inspector had hoped.

"What the f--k is this?" Lilly burst out and rose from her chair. "What the hell's he doing here?"

Molly was equally annoyed. She had expected a pause in the interrogation before the introduction of Tony on the scene.

"Welcome Mr. Bond. Please have a seat. You too, Mrs. Austin," Molly instructed, trying not to reveal her annoyance and confusion.

The young officer helped the handcuffed Tony into a chair next to Lilly. Molly expected the young officer to stay in the room. Instead, he immediately disappeared, leaving her in the room alone with the two suspects.

Tony looked at Lilly and smiled. "Nice to see ya, princess. Did you come to visit me?"

"Oh, shut it!" Lilly responded.

"Well, here we are," Molly said, not sure where to take this.

"Look! I want my lawyer and do not wish to be in the presence of this scum," Lilly objected and pushed her chair away from Tony.

"Scum? That's a turn! A few nights ago, you were all over me like a hot dream and now I'm scum!" Tony exclaimed, staring her down.

"I don't need to listen to this!" she objected and rose from her seat once more.

"Don't leave, princess! Why, you just got here, and I'm so happy that you came to visit. Maybe we can share a room downstairs, and you can show me that little trick you did the other night with your…"

"Shut him up, please!" Lilly interrupted.

"Mr. Bond, please wait until I ask the questions," Molly made an attempt to regain control of the situation. "Mr. Bond, did you receive e-mails from Miss Lilly regarding Mary Collins? Did those e-mails contain offers of bribery if you harmed her sister and 'did away with' her, as it was termed?" Molly asked in a professional tone while silently cursing the Inspector for putting her in the Fish Tank alone with these two barracudas.

"You don't have to answer that! Sheldon Twiner will be here soon," Lilly quickly coached while returning back to her chair.

Tony turned toward her and smirked. "On the contrary, I'd love to answer that! Miss rich and proper," he pointed at Lily, "asked me on several occasions to harm her sister, Mary, and she asked not just in e-mails. She asked between orgasms, as well."

"You bastard! You lying bastard!" Lilly growled with eyes full of hate.

"Let me continue," Tony objected in a serene voice. "She not only asked me to harm her, but to kill her. Yes, to kill her own sister. What a class act!"

"You f--ken SOB! He's lying! He's the one who so proudly harassed Mary and even wanted to rape her, but I stopped him!" Lilly accused Tony and jumped up again.

"You lying bitch! You were going to pay me, but I refused to kill her! I refused to do her in, as you had begged!" Tony exclaimed.

"Why you lying bastard!" Lilly jumped on Tony and began to claw at him.

"Get her off me!" He tried to push her away, but fell to the ground in the process, his hands still handcuffed together.

She was on top of him again, clawing, punching and kicking.

"Assault! Assault!" he screamed, trying to defend himself.

Molly was out of her chair and calling for help. Soon, the young officer outside the door of the interrogation room jumped into the mix, and the Inspector appeared in the doorway.

Among a shower of profanities and a scurry of police officers that rushed in to break up the brawl, Sheldon Twiner Esquire walked into the room. He took one look at the brawl on the floor and asked, "Excuse me, but where can I find Mrs. Lilly Austin?"

"You're in the right place, Doc!" Molly pointed at the brawl on the floor and left the room in disgust.

CHAPTER 28

The Queen of Hearts

Molly debriefed with the Inspector and excused herself. She got into her overstuffed heap of an automobile and drove out of the station. Soon, she was in front of the old Nightingale Mansion near McLaren University. All was quiet there since most of the students were still in class.

Parking her car in the small parking lot behind the four-story house, she finally relaxed. "What a day! What a day!" she repeated and exhaled.

Fortunately, her key unlocked the rear door of the building. Propping the door open, she began the slow process of unloading her belongings and moving them to the second floor using a rickety old elevator. On her third trip back to her car, she ran into the Cheshire Cat. As expected, he appeared out of nowhere.

"Welcome, Miss Molly?" he said smiling ear to ear.

"Hello, Cheshire..." she stopped herself just in time.

"It's Chester," he corrected her while wrapping up his purple and white scarf closer to his neck. "Winter just won't let up, and it's nearly April." He stretched and shuddered.

"This place is bizarre. The Inspector really owes me," Molly thought to herself.

"You need any help with these?" Chester pointed at the clothes piled on the hood of Molly's car.

"Sure, I'm in room…"

"I know where you are. Right next to Helga. Lucky you," he replied mysteriously.

"Who's Helga?" Molly asked.

"Oh, you'll meet her soon enough. Here, I can take these," he grabbed a stack of dresses.

"Are you sure you don't want the shoe boxes?" Molly objected, as the strange little man held an armful of her favorite clothes, including two long negligees.

"No, this is perrrrrfect," Chester purred, as he sniffed at her clothing.

"Great! Now I'll have to wash everything," she thought. "He better not rip them."

Soon they were crowded into the tiny elevator. There was the discomfort of extreme closeness enhanced by the complete exposure of some of Molly's most personal belongings pressed between them. The sight of her nightgowns and negligee draped over Chester made her nearly gag. By contrast, Chester enjoyed losing himself in the fragrant finery.

Upon exiting the elevator, they walked down the old paneled hall passing room 12. Chester pointed at the door. "Beware of Helga!" he warned.

Molly was not amused for he was dragging her personal belongings along the dirty floor. "Chester, please pick those up!" she demanded.

Just then the door of room 12 swung open with a bang. The startled Chester dropped Molly's clothes and flung his arms in the air. Molly was equally shocked but maintained her handle on her moving boxes. Looking down at her clothing lying on the dirty hallway, she was about to chastise Chester when she realized that he had disappeared, presumably down an adjacent staircase. Looking up, she saw a large, middle-aged woman dressed in red.

"Where's that weasel?" the large woman demanded. "Did you see Chester? I thought I just heard that fur ball."

Molly stood silent.

"Cat got your tongue? My, my, what a pretty head you have, head of hair that is. You're the new girl. Welcome neighbor!" Helga held out her large paw. Molly had no choice but to shake it.

"I'm Helga. What's your name, precious?"

"I'm Molly."

"Well, it's good to meet you. Let me tell you something, sweet Molly. Don't trust Chester. He's bad news. Why, I should have his head for what he did to my Pogo," Helga lamented in a booming tenor.

Molly was still holding her moving boxes, and looking at the rest of her belongings that lay on the dirty floor. She leaned to pick them up, just as Helga did the same. They bumped heads and Molly was thrown back. The remainder of her clothes scatted out of her moving boxes and onto the floor. "My, you're a clumsy one," Helga replied unscathed by the collision. "How's that pretty head of yours?" She chuckled to herself. "You need help with this mess?"

"No, I got it. Nice meeting you, Helga," Molly replied and began pickup up all of her soiled belongings.

"Very well, but if you happen to see Trudy, tell her that I'm looking for her. I demand an explanation as to why my mattress is so lumpy. A lumpy bed is not something to be tolerated. Do you agree?" Helga replied.

"I agree," Molly looked up as she continued to pick up her clothes.

"I'm off to the garden. Have you seen it? It's behind that dreadful parking lot. It's lovely, simply lovely," Helga replied. "I planted much of it myself." She closed her door and stepped over Molly's clothes as she proceeded down the hall.

"Full of roses, I bet," Molly said aloud, not thinking that Helga would hear. She was barely visible under the stack of clothing that she held in her arms.

"Yes! How'd you know? Did you see it?" Helga asked, turning once more to face Molly.

"No. Just a wild guess."

CHAPTER 29

An Encounter

*J*ennifer was well into her second shift now. It was past 3 am and the trauma ward was quiet, providing her a chance to slow down and sit. It was a hard shift, and she was extremely tired. Her fellow night nurse had called in sick, and she was forced to cover the ward's night shift on her own. There was little keeping her from sleep, but she tried hard not to succumb. She had not been a coffee drinker until recently, but these night shifts required an ample amount of caffeine.

"Coffee. Good idea," she thought, and got up to refresh her cup. Recently, the hospital had switched to a more premium brand and installed a small brewing machine. It made all the difference, and Jennifer was becoming a coffee connoisseur. She returned to her desk. It was 3:27 on a Friday morning. Mary had now been in a coma for nearly a week and a half, and her prognosis for recovery was dropping daily.

"Well, this should keep me awake," Jennifer concluded as she sipped her coffee. "Finally, some down time." She had had a rough night. Not only was she short staffed, with a half full ward, but one of her favorite patients had died unexpectedly. He was young, only 38, and in the final stages of a cancerous brain tumor. His sudden decline was exacerbated by a recent fall landing him in the trauma ward. At that stage, there was nothing that modern medicine could do to prevent the inevitable. Jennifer felt that she and the doctors were helpless against the aggressive and merciless disease.

The thought of it all made her tear up. She reflected on the young family that gathered around the father only hours earlier. The younger two children sensed something sad was happening, but they did not fully comprehend the details, being only four and six, respectively. They were losing their father and there was nothing they could do to change that. She reflected on the two older children who did understand and the thought of it crushed them with a merciless weight. "No child should be crushed like that," she thought.

"I hate this job sometimes!" she proclaimed for no one to hear. Finally, she reflected on the young wife, who had to hold the family together while forced to accept a shattered dream. She was so in love with her husband and her children. She was so brave and strong, and yet she was so frail, so desperately frail. Jennifer saw it all. She felt it all. She suffered it all, but not like them. She was the observer of this tragedy. They were forced to live it.

"I hate this job! I hate death! I hate suffering!" she was bawling now like a child, like they were her own family. She thought of the poor dying man, who was mercifully clearly cognizant of his family in his final moments, and capable of expressing his deep love and endless devotion to them. He did just that with every word and every glance. He was noble in death and remained strong, leaving all that was precious and sacred behind him, only to face the eternal question mark. "I'll always be there for you" he consoled them, not sure if it was true. He hugged his children as if he would hug them forever and never again. Which it would be, he did not know. No one knew. The girls cried and soon the boys cried as well. The little ones did not fully understand why they cried, but they cried the hardest of all.

"Daddy, will you come home today?" the littlest of all asked the most innocent of questions. All that was needed was a simple "yes", and all would be different, all would be whole again. But that "yes" was not to be, and the brave young man took his last breath in a seemingly endless flood of tears. "He'll be home today, mommy," the littlest one answered her own question in the only voice of confidence that remained.

"I hate this! God, why do You do this? Why do people like that have to suffer, and others much less worthy go on living? Why?" she asked aloud of the silent ward.

It was 3:30 am when she received her answer.

It started with the magenta haze that flickered at times into hues of deep purple and indigo. Its source was the usual source, room 328, Mary's room. This time Jennifer was more startled than before, for this time the glow appeared so suddenly, just as she had asked her eternal question. This time it was brighter, as well, and seemed to invite her to attend.

She did not resist. She did not question it. She simply moved toward it, slowly, as if drawn by its force, drawn by some invisible and unknown gravitational field, not unlike a planet toward its sun. There was no fear, neither within it nor within her. There was no resistance. There was no struggle, neither physical nor mental. It was as it should be, a homecoming.

She walked slowly and confidently toward room 328. All was silent with no distractions, as if all was orchestrated by a higher power. She walk in confidence knowing that whatever awaited her was there to heal, to explain, to conquer all the pettiness of existence. She was at peace and walked into the light as if she too were leaving this world. Little did she realize that for a brief moment, she would do just that.

There he stood, youthful and radiant. A glow was about him. Although he seemed mortal, he clearly was not. She rubbed her eyes to assure that her vision was true. Then, she pinched her tear-soaked cheek. Both confirmed the reality of the scene.

He smiled in a way that was all knowing and peaceful to its core. Standing over Mary's limp body and looking down, he touched her left hand before effortlessly gliding toward Jennifer, as in a dream. He moved, but did not move. As he approached, it was as if he were made of dense light, dimmed so as not to blind her. Yet, his form appeared real, appeared physical, but was little more than an illusion. "Or is it real now and only an illusion in life?" The thought entered her mind; the answer did not.

She was not afraid. The energy in the room was that of complete calmness and love. She was not afraid, but she was shocked as if her senses had surrendered, having no point of reference in their extensive, biochemical memory banks that had been accumulated over countless seconds of physical existence. Yet, something somewhere inside her knew this to be normal and completely acceptable. Something somewhere in her heart understood and responded, neither in fear nor in shock, but in delight, as if an old friend had appeared unexpectedly.

She recognized him instantly. He was the young father who had died that evening. Yet, he was not dead; he was more alive than before. "How was that possible?" Her mind was like a machine frozen in the rust of logic. "He died, right?" it tried to reason in milliseconds, as the figure approached. It was as if her mind was robotically calculating meaningless equations, like the infinite precision of Pi, while her soul was accepting, was content, was rejoicing. He did not speak, yet she could hear him clearly in that very mind that was now so split. She could hear him as foreign thoughts in the still portion, the deeper portion, of that very mind. It was some sort of telepathy that seemed as odd and as natural as his presence before her.

"Thank you for taking such good care of me, Jennifer. You're truly an angel. But, please don't cry for me. I'm more alive now than I was in form. As for my wife and children, I'll always protect them for they are my kindred souls and my eternal family. We're all united with an endless love that the mind cannot comprehend, and the heart is ill equipped to explain. I ask you only that you tell my wife that I am fine. She'll be back for she forgot something. I made sure of that. Please tell her about this so that she has faith, faith that all that we perceive, all that we comprehend and reason, is but a drop in the ocean of Truth. To deny faith is to lock oneself in an ever-shrinking cell of one's own making. The world stretches far beyond ours and far beyond the universe, and yet all is so effortlessly connected when one has a chance to step outside of the house of mirrors we call our mind. Please tell her that I love her forever as I do my precious children for we are bound by the one force that is purely Divine. And to you, my dear, Jennifer, I bestow this. Hold out your hand." His words, transmitted to her as thoughts, were so calm and poetic that she stood mesmerized.

He reached out his hand, and, through some miracle of levitation not unlike our concept of holding something, he dropped a small object into her palm, careful not to touch her. The light from his hand was too blinding for Jennifer to see what the object was, but she took it in faith. As she did, he disappeared along with the magenta light that had surrounded him.

Jennifer fell back into the nearby chair. She seemed drained as if part of her own energy had somehow participated in the mysterious encounter. She felt completely drained, yet incredibly alert, like she had never felt before. It was as if her body and mind were ultra sensitive. Her mind reasoned that she had inadvertently taken a hallucinogenic of some sort. But there were none in the ward. Her mind reasoned that she was tired and imagining things, but why was she not imagining anything before and since. Her mind reasoned that it was playing tricks on her, yet it could not explain its own tricks. Her mind rested, confused. Her heart, on the other hand, seemed so full of emotion, bursting with love and joy.

It was an odd combination of sensations. It exhausted her in its polarity. She nearly fell asleep in the chair, except for one thing. Something was pressing on the insides of the closed fist of her right hand. She had forgotten all about it in her distraction and mental analysis. Yet, it was there, demanding to surface. "And to you, my dear Jennifer, I bestow this." She still heard him in her mind, as if he just resurfaced solely within it.

She slowly opened her right hand and beheld a small oval pendant with a chain. It appeared to be silver, but was probably only silver plated. She looked at it and saw a small engraved picture of a woman kneeling before an altar that had a large cross on it. It was a depiction of a saint of some sort. She turned it over and on the back it said "Pray for Us" in simple, raised letters. It appeared as if it were still glowing in her hand, as if it had taken on some of his energy. She slipped it in her pocket, her mind confused. Her logical side was working hard to convince her that she had an illusion, that all was not real. Yet, there was no explanation. She sat there for another ten minutes in Mary's room until she was awakened from her reflection by the shrilling sound of an alarm.

Damn!" she sprung into action. "Mrs. Crawford is in cardiac arrest! What a night!" She ran toward room 318 grabbing the resuscitation cart on the way. "I need to save this one," she thought. "She has that darling husband who loves her so much. She has to live for him!" Jennifer Angel was back in action, living up to her name.

CHAPTER 30

Manna from Heaven

It was Friday morning and Molly rolled into the office more than an hour late. It was not like her to be this late, but she had barely slept all night. She was exhausted.

"Momma, what happened to you? You look like you saw a ghost!" Chen greeted her as she entered the department.

"Thanks Chen. I love you, too," she replied.

"Hey, Molly, sorry I couldn't help you move yesterday, but I had a ton of work to do here. Blame our boss," Bob explained, while peeking over her cubical as she settled into her chair.

"It's okay, Bob," she replied not looking up.

"What happened to you? You look awful!" Bob exclaimed.

"Too much partying in the new digs, or did Jekyll Fulton find you? Naughty, Naughty!" Chen chimed in as he peered over his cubical, which was adjacent to Molly's.

"Man, Chen, can you just leave her alone?" Bob came to her defense. "Can't you see that she's down?"

"I'm sorry," Chen replied like a scolded school boy. "I was just teasing. Is everything okay, Molly? Sorry I didn't help with the move, but I had a hot date. Really. No kidding. With my hottie fiancee, of course," he laughed.

Molly shook her head in silence, and started up her computer. The two men decided to leave her alone. All was completely quite, except the ticking of the wall clock.

Bob soon broke the silence as he poked his head into her cubical once more. "Come on, Molly. It's time for our morning meeting regarding the Mary Collins case. You're lucky that it got pushed back to 10 am today. Chen has some news to share. I think that he's already in there, the brownnose that he is."

Molly reluctantly rose from her chair. She felt like a zombie and looked the part.

As she followed Bob into the Inspector's office, the latter inhaled audible. "What happened to you?" he asked. "You look like you saw a ghost."

Molly sat down and did not respond. All eyes were upon her. She was known for her wit. But, no comeback came.

The Inspector started the meeting. "Things are happening quickly on this case, right Chen?" He looked at the youngest member of the group.

Chen nodded in agreement as the Inspector unveiled his board of suspects. He still had the same mug shots pinned to the cork board that had been covered by a white sheet.

"Boss, you've got to get yourself a better system. That sheet looks ridiculous. It looks like you're moving or something. Oh, sorry Molly," Chen stopped, as Molly gave him an evil stare.

"No money in the budget for such frills," the Inspector replied. "Okay, what do we have? Here are the lucky suspects." He adjusted the mug shots. There were the usual pictures pinned on the board. Suzy's picture was pulled down into the lower left corner, signifying that she was no longer under serious consideration. But there were the rest of the crew: Randell, Tony, Lilly, Jack, Daphne and Stacy.

"All right, Chen. You go first. It seems that Chen had some fortuitous good fortune."

"That's redundant, Boss," Molly suddenly uttered. Even in her exhaustion, she could not tolerate someone butchering the English language. It was one of her pet peeves.

The Inspector ignored the objection and turned to Chen. "You're on, Chen. What can you tell us?"

"Okay. How did everyone sleep?" Chen asked, and Bob had to try hard not to laugh as Molly glared at them both. "No, seriously, I'll try not to put you to sleep with this report," he added. Bob was sucking air not to burst. Molly glared once more.

"Okay, as I was saying, I had quite the wake up call this morning," Chen started again, just as Bob burst into laughter.

"Boss, can you make them stop?" Molly looked toward the Inspector.

"Kids! Behave! Chen, give us your report. We don't have time to waste," the Inspector warned.

"Right, no worries! Early this morning, after I had a long, sound, restful sleep, I..."

Molly suddenly sprang up like a female panther protecting her cubs and Chen would have been flat on the floor had the Inspector not stopped her in mid leap.

"Chen, get to your report, right now! Molly, settle down! I realize you're tired, but settle down!" the Inspector interceded.

"Sorry, Boss, but he really knows how to get under my skin. He's like the little brother that I never had and never wanted to have," Molly replied growling at Chen.

He made a goofy remark and started once more, this time with minimal jabs. "Okay, as I was about to say before I got interrupted..." He made one last jab. She mouthed "f--k you" at him so that their boss did not see it.

He chuckled. He had gotten to her. Success. "I had a windfall of new information last night and early this morning," Chen added, finally taking on a professional air. "First, I discovered some additional deleted e-mails that were still on Tony Bond's hard drive. They were hard to retrieve, which is why I could not get to them earlier. One of these gems clearly states that Miss Lilly desperately tried to get Tony to 'do in' her sister, Mary, but that Tony adamantly refused. I think that he's telling the truth. Here's the e-mail." Chen projected the e-mail onto the wide screen in the Inspector's room.

"Well, that speaks better for him than for her, but he still harassed and molested the poor girl. That's also evident from the e-mail record and our witnesses, right?" the Inspector asked.

"Without a doubt, but it appears that he stopped short of Lilly's final request," Chen replied.

"What a pair!" Bob concluded aloud.

"Okay. Tony's not cleared, but he's less suspicious. What else have you retrieved in your windfall?" the Inspector asked Chen.

"I finally got to screen the last of the pictures taken by the various participants of that fateful field trip and discovered some vital clues. Look at this set of pictures." Chen projected three pictures taken in sequence from a high point above the quarry. They depicted the exact area where Mary had fallen. Chen oriented the audience. "Can you believe it? We can actually see Mary right there at the spot from which she fell." He pointed at a small figure of a young woman in a blue shirt and jeans standing in the lower left corner of the picture. Chen had included the detailed enlargement of the figure next to the original photo. It was clearly Mary. "Over here, we have Randell. I also enlarged him and got a positive match. As you can see, I attached Randell's enlargement above. He was in fact on a terrace at a lower part of the quarry prior to Mary's fall, as he had testified. Clearly, he's nowhere near Mary in this picture." Chen placed his laser pointer on the small figure of a young male standing near the center of the picture.

"Please continue, Chen," the Inspector added, listening attentively.

"Right. Now, look at this picture taken seconds after the first from the same location. We see Mary turn away from the quarry wall as if confronted by someone, but unfortunately that someone is not in the picture. We also see that Randell is distracted by something beneath the lip of the quarry wall at precisely that moment. Could that be Stacy? Unfortunately, the angle is such that we see both Randell and Mary, but not who or what made each of them turn toward the direction of the camera.

"Could it be the photographer that distracted them?" Molly asked.

"Unlikely, Molly. The photographer was a classmate named Michael Johnson. I interviewed him over the phone last night after I discovered these photographs. He told me that he didn't remember the parties being there. He says that no one saw him up there because he'd have gotten in trouble with Fulton, who warned everyone not to climb the quarry walls. He swears that he was very discrete. I believe him, since neither Mary nor Randell are looking up toward him, but are looking at eye level," Chen replied.

"This is great, please continue Chen," the Inspector encouraged.

"Now take a look at this third picture taken seconds after the second one. Here we see Mary turned back to face the quarry. But here is the clincher. Right here, just at the lower edge of the photo, we see a mysterious set of arms pushing her forward, making contact with her buttocks. She was pushed!" Chen paused as the rest of the team stared at the photo. "Here is that portion of the photo expanded. Luckily Johnson's camera had great resolution. You can clearly see that Mary Collins was pushed," Chen repeated his conclusion for added emphasis.

"Wow, your hunch was right, Boss!" Molly let out.

"Of course," the Inspector added in self-confidence.

"Also, notice in this photo that Randell is still standing on the lower ledge. We see that he's now looking away from Mary, and is facing a figure who we can't make out. I enhanced that section and it appears the figure is a partial of someone with blonde hair. The rest is blocked by the edge of the quarry wall due to the angle of the photo," Chen concluded and paused.

"Is there a subsequent picture?" Molly asked.

"No. Michael Johnson said that he heard a scream at that point and looked down only to see no one on the ledge immediately below him. The timing of these pictures fits the timing of Mary's fall based on other evidence." Chen looked over to Inspector Cabot to get an agreement in the form of a nod.

"Michael said that right after the scream, he rushed down off his perch," Chen continued his report. "As he was descending, he heard a second sustained and piercing scream, which appears to have been Suzy's when she and Kelly discovered Mary's body about a minute after the fall. It all fits. As you can see in this last photo," Chen once more projected the enlargement of Mary and the mysterious arms, "Mary appears to have been pushed with quite a force, as we had suspected. It's impossible at this resolution to identify the perpetrator. Nor can we determine his or her gender since we can only see the hands and white shirt sleeves. But, you can see right here that Mary's body is already on a projectile path off of the cliff. Her feet are off the ground. This photo actually captured the act itself," Chen concluded in an excited voice while looking at the Inspector.

"I have notified my boss. This is now an official criminal case, an attempted homicide. By the way, it appears that as much as Randell is a violent coward, he didn't do it," the Inspector concluded, as he pulled Randell's picture from the center of his cork board and pinned it along side of Suzy's in the innocent bucket. That leaves us with Jack, Tony, Lilly, Daphne and Stacy. In addition, it turns out that Lilly has a solid alibi and was definitely not at the scene. Thus, at most, she's an accomplice and solicited the act, assuming that Tony changed his mind and pushed Mary," the Inspector concluded.

"Boss, since I spoke with you this morning, I magnified the Randell portion of this last photo to see if I could identify who was the blonde-haired person near him," Chen added. "It appears to be a woman, probably Stacy, since there's a partial view of a blue hair ribbon positioned near the top of her hair, as evident right here." Chen used his laser pointer to identify a tiny corner portion of a faint blue ribbon in the enlarged photograph. "Stacy's position on the lower ledge with Randell is supported by Kelly Allen's testimony. If you recall, Kelly claimed that Randell was on the lower edge embracing Stacy when she and Suzy arrived at the edge of the quarry, after being drawn toward the scene by Mary's initial scream," Chen reasoned.

"Agreed. Stacy's probably also innocent of this, but we still need to locate her. It could be that she had a clear view of the perpetrator based on her position in this photo, assuming that it's her in the photo. That could be why she disappeared. But where is she? Any updates on that, Chen?" the Inspector asked.

"Not yet! Still looking into it. I got distracted by these photos," Chen explained.

"This photo evidence is key. Great work, Chen. This leaves us with three key suspects," the Inspector positioned the pictures of Jack, Daphne and Tony at the top of his suspect board. "Right now we have Tony in custody on harassment and molestation charges. However, Jack Fulton and Daphne Marconi are very much at large. Anyone else have anything new?" the Inspector asked the rest of the team.

"I have a question for Chen," Molly spoke up.

"Sure, what is it, Molly?" Chen replied. He had stopped the teasing and was professional once more.

"In the photo database that we now have, do you have another picture of Stacy to confirm that she wore a blue hair ribbon? Also, can you identify which of our suspects wore a white shirt?" Molly asked.

"Great questions, Molly," Chen replied. "I was about to scan the database for those two pieces of information, as well as attempt to photographically establish the positions of Jack, Stacy, Daphne and Tony Bond around the time of the incident. Although I suspect that the latter task will come up short and at best provide only circumstantial evidence."

"Boss, I'm making some headway with Suzy," Bob began after Molly and Chen concluded their discussion. "I got to talk to her yesterday. She's starting to confide in me, but, at present, she's too scared to press charges against Randell. Not much new there," Bob summarized.

"Don't waste your time with her any further, Bob. Why don't you and Chen take copies of these pictures and revisit the crime scene to see if we missed anything. I want to verify where Mr. Johnson stood when he took these photos, as well as where the perpetrator was standing relative to Mary's position. Also, we know that both Daphne and Tony were close to Mary just before the fall. Is it possible that there's a link there, and that they were both involved? Start checking into that scenario, Bob. Also, get more background information on all three key suspects and their relationship with Mary. We need to flush out clear motives for Jack and Daphne. Also, please help Chen locate Stacy." The Inspector was formulating a plan.

"Boss, I don't mind getting more information out of Suzy," Bob objected.

Chen and Molly looked at each other with raised eye brows.

The Inspector ignored the request and moved on to Molly. "Molly, anything new on your end? How was the move and your first night in the new apartment?"

"The House of Horrors, you mean," she replied. "The move was bad, but nothing compared to last night. My room is next to the room of a very odd woman, named Helga, and she kept me up all night."

Molly had everyone's attention now. "What happened?" Bob inquired on behalf of all.

"There was this odd noise coming from her room in the middle of the night. It sounded like a war, complete with sirens and fighter planes. I was going to knock on her door, but didn't want to start on the wrong foot with her. I figured that I would bear it for one night, but if it continues tonight I'm definitely finding out what she's up to," Molly replied and shook her head.

"Heil Helga!" Chen smirked.

Molly ignored him. "Otherwise, I've got little to report. I want to head back there and see if I can snoop around this afternoon.

The place seems quiet in the afternoon, except for Trudy, the ever-suspicious guardian of the house. I hope you appreciate what I'm putting up with, Boss."

"We do, Molly. Thanks. In fact, if you want to go back right after this meeting, go ahead. We need to find out more about this mysterious religious cult and about Fulton, who seems to be associated with it. As I mentioned before, Molly, I need you to get close to Fulton. Given his reputed eye for the ladies that shouldn't be too difficult, but be careful. He's still my main suspect. There's something shady about that guy. I don't like him," the Inspector confessed.

"Great! I get all the winners!" Molly sighed audibly.

"Your reward lies in heaven, Molly," Chen chimed in.

"Shut up, Chen!" she replied and glared at him.

"Okay, enough! End of meeting. Same place tomorrow but back to 8 am, Molly." The Inspector dismissed his team. After they left, he settled into his chair and opened the top left draw of his desk. From it, he pulled out a worn photograph. It was a picture of a pretty young girl in the arms of a handsome young man. They seemed extremely happy. But the Inspector frowned at the sight of the boy in photo, who was none other than Jack Fulton in his late teens. "We meet again, Fulton," the Inspector muttered. "This time I'll get you as promised." He put the picture back and looked at a large portrait photo sitting on his desk. It was a professional photograph of the same young woman. "I'll get him for you, Angie, if it's the last thing I do," the Inspector swore into his tea cup.

CHAPTER 31

A Bouquet of Flowers

Molly was exhausted and not up for the company of her police team. She gladly accepted the Inspector's offer to head back to her new apartment. It was 11:20 am when she arrived at the house that she now called home. The thought of this as her home sent shivers down her spine as she ascended the back stairs.

Suddenly, there he was as if he appeared out of thin air. "Chester, you scared me! How do you suddenly appear like that?"

"Like what, Molly?"

"Like you appear out of nowhere!"

Chester smiled a wide smile showing his perfect teeth. "It's a gift. Speaking of gifts, someone left you a dozen red roses at the front desk. Trudy's jealous. She's been sniffing them all morning. Maybe it was your boyfriend," Chester added with a wink.

"I have no idea who'd do that. I don't have a boyfriend."

"You want one? I know someone looking for a girl like you." He smiled his wide smile once more.

"No thanks, Chester, but I appreciate the offer. By the way, who is Pogo? Helga declared that she still resents you for what you did to Pogo."

"Pogo? Oh, he was Helga's little annoying mutt. You mean who was Pogo?" Chester smiled once more, and then laughed a dastardly laugh.

"What'd you do to him?" Molly asked.

"Nothing! He was too dumb for me to bother with him. I hate dogs and he hated me, so the feeling was mutual. Last Sunday, he ran off and chased me into the rose garden. Well, it was an accident, but he ended up fertilizing Helga's roses. Come to think of it, I wonder if those are from Helga? She likes you, you know," he chuckled.

"That guy is definitely creepy," Molly concluded to herself and diverted her path from her room to the front desk. Chester followed her at four paces like a curious pet. She ignored him.

As she entered the great hall, she saw the vase full of roses on the front desk. Trudy was sniffing them as Chester had described. As soon as she saw Molly, she backed away from the bouquet and her face took on a sour smirk.

"They're for you. I didn't look at the note, but it must be a boyfriend," she said without a greeting.

"I don't have a boyfriend," Molly objected once more.

"Well, who're they from?" Trudy asked as Chester caught up to Molly. "Not you too! Don't you have any classes to attend, Chester?"

Chester looked up at Trudy, who was a full head taller than him and hissed, "Buzz off!" The two clearly disliked each other.

"Well, who're they from?" Trudy was so eager that she looked as if she would grab the sealed card out of Molly's hands before the latter could opened it. "I think I know." Trudy's face became solemn.

Molly looked at the card and was visibly surprised by the note. Her brows knitted up as she silently read it.

"Come on! Who're they from?" Trudy insisted.

Molly did not answer the question, but simply pushed the vase of roses toward Trudy. "They're for you."

"For me? No way! They were delivered for you. I was here when the florist arrived. He asked for you," Trudy objected.

"Well, I'm giving them to you, card and all. Enjoy!" Molly replied. Turning suddenly, she collided with Chester, who had been standing right behind her trying to get a glimpse at the card. In the collision, she nearly propelled him across the floor. Without turning back or acknowledging him, she marched out of the room, leaving the flowers and the opened card in front of Trudy.

"Who're they from?" Chester asked as Trudy grabbed the card and read it to herself.

"I can't believe it! That bitch is going to be a problem!" Trudy huffed, seizing the flowers and leaving the card as she stormed away.

Chester was left alone in the great hall holding the mysterious card. He read it and his face exploded into the widest, toothiest smile possible just before he vanished.

CHAPTER 32

Welcome to the Jungle

Stacy was the apple of Professor Arthur Reed's eye. She bore a strong resemblance to his late wife, who had tragically died during child birth. His only child also had her mother's sharp wit and gentle demeanor. From him, she inherited her insatiable curiosity. Stacy loved adventure and feared death, just like her father. They were together whenever possible, for she was his little girl and he was her great protector.

When Professor Reed received the message informing him that Stacy was missing, he was standing in a large tent in the heart of the Amazonian jungle. This was his favorite place, and the love he had for the Amazon Basin was second only to the love he had for his daughter. The news shocked him, sending his head spinning. "Stacy's a responsible girl. She would never disappear like that, never!" The thoughts raced through his mind. He felt weak in the knees and had to sit down to keep from falling.

"What's the matter, Professor?" asked his graduate student, Janet Lee. This was her second year in "the Jungle", as the professor called it. But this year, they were alone except for the locals. She put her slender arms around his neck and looked over his shoulder at the note.

"Janet, Stacy's missing!" he exclaimed.

"What?!" Janet sprang back and took the professor's smart phone to read the e-mail herself. Here, at base camp, they had reception. In the dense jungle, where they had spent most of their time, they were cut off from the outside world, just the way they liked it.

Their relationship was a surprise to both Janet and the professor. It started innocently enough the year before, here in this very location. At the time, she dismissed the professor's attentiveness as nothing more than his usual gentlemanly demeanor. After all, he was over 20 years her senior and a highly respected member of the university faculty. As last summer's expedition drew to a close, it was obvious that the kind professor was interested in more than explaining the local butterflies to his favorite graduate student. The relationship developed slowly, primarily because Janet felt uncomfortable with it. Then, this past spring, while alone together in the lab one night, the suppressed desires exploded between them into passion, the kind of passion that left clothes strewn over the lab floor, broke countless beakers and exposed Janet's supple curves beyond the confines of her lab coat. Before either party had a chance to reflect on the long-term consequences of their action, the action was over, and the two lay gasping for air on the cold hard surface of a slate lab bench.

That was four months ago, but the passion had not stopped. Not even here in the jungle. In fact, it intensified here, becoming primal in a way that made them both feel invincible and eternal. Nonetheless, they kept it a secret from everyone, even Stacy, who was a mere three years younger than Janet. In fact, the two young women had been undergraduates together at McLaren University; Stacy was a freshman when Janet was a senior. They knew each other, but they were never close. The professor rightfully guessed that such news would be devastating to his daughter and Janet agreed. Thus, for now, they were forced to keep the relationship shrouded in tight secrecy. This made it more exciting and more passionate. They were like two young lovers sneaking about doing anything and everything to keep the truth from the parents, in this case, the world.

"Oh my God, Artie! This is horrible! What're we going to do?" Janet asked as she sat next to her lover, and placed her left arm around his neck for support. He did not respond to her affection, but simply stood up in an attempt to run away from reality. It was as if his world had collided with an alien object of unfathomable proportions. He was being pulverized from the inside out by the massive collision.

Janet could sense it. Two people, emotionally entwined, can sense as one, age differences or not, and she knew that this news could destroy him. She had to stop it. She had to stop the internal destruction before it was too late, but how?

"Come here, give me a hug," she offered as she rose to meet him. Embracing him with all her might, she tried to press herself into him, hoping to stop the invisible, internal devastation. She tried so hard. She tried even to project her energy into him. It was not an act of logic, but simply one of love. She loved him despite what the world would do or say. She loved him here and now, and that was all that mattered to her.

Her quick selfless act seemed to work. He began to respond. He began to feebly hug her back. She was winning. She was fighting for his sanity, and she was winning. He was clearly in shock and she held on tight, taking on his full weight as they now stood embraced. He let her take the weight. Subconsciously, he let her take the weight. She welcomed it and slowly lowered him back into the chair, letting go only when he touched the seat.

"She'll be all right. You know how resourceful Stacy can be. Come on, she's fine. I bet that by now they've found her and that she's fine. Let's call the department. Okay? You want me to call?" Janet asked in genuine heartfelt support.

All that he could do was nod his head to the affirmative. She took his cell phone and dialed the McLaren University Biology Department. They would still be there. It was only one in the afternoon in Pennsylvania.

"Hello. This is Janet Lee. I'm calling on behalf of Professor Reed. We just received the message regarding his daughter, Stacy. Do you know if she has been located?" Janet asked while the professor seemed paralyzed next to her.

"I see. Okay. Can we talk to the detective? Let me take down that name and number." Janet grabbed a piece of paper and a pen off of a nearby desk. "Inspector James Cabot. Got it. Please call us at this number when you hear anything. Thank you." She hung up.

Turning to the professor, she added, "The department doesn't have any other information, but I got the number for the police. I'll call right now."

The professor was still in his trance, leaning against Janet, who was now seated next to him. She knew that if she would move, he would simply fall off the wooden chair and probably roll like a dead tree onto the trodden earth below. "Damn this!" she thought to herself, but bravely plunged onward. "May I speak to Inspector James Cabot, please?" she inquired over the phone. "This is Janet Lee. I'm calling in regards to Stacy Reed. I've got her father right here next to me. Yes. Thank you."

She turned to the professor. "They're putting me through to Inspector Cabot. I'm sure he'll know something." Unfortunately, she was wrong. The conversation revealed only more questions on both sides of the line. She hung up the phone and held the professor closer. She could feel his heart beat, but he had sunken once more into what appeared to be early stages of shock. Quickly, she used her first aid skills and proceeded to revive him. Successful, she helped him to his bed in the adjacent tent where she joined him, lying next to him in silent support.

CHAPTER 33

The Pendant

*S*even hours earlier, Jennifer Angel was finishing her night shift. She had the roughest night of her career and wanted it to end. In order to complete her paperwork, she had had to dismiss the bizarre happenings from her mind. She did not include them in her report, being sure that if she had, she would probably be placed under psychiatric care.

As she finished her paperwork, she was startled to see the young widow of the man, the ghost, the spirit or whatever he was, that had given her the pendant. As he had predicted, the young widow had returned. "I guess when you're a ghost, you can predict these things," Jennifer concluded.

"Excuse me, Miss! Sorry to bother you, but it appears that I left something in my husband's room. May I get it?" the woman asked Jennifer.

"Sure," Jennifer replied. The orderlies had taken the body away, but the room had not yet been cleaned. "Can I help you look?"

"No. I know where I left my reading glasses. I can't believe that I need reading glasses," the woman reflected. "Old age setting in early," she added, making light of her situation.

As she retrieved her glasses, she took one long look at the now empty bed, briefly paralyzed by intense sorrow. Recovering quickly, she valiantly stepped out of the room. As she met Jennifer in the hallway, there was a prolonged silence as if something had to be said but no one had the courage to do so. It was then that Jennifer, finding her voice, decided to mention the pendant. It would be awkward but she had to do it. She had to return it.

"Mrs. King, this is going to seem odd, but I have your husband's pendant. Here you are," Jennifer produced the silver pendant and handed it to Mrs. King.

"Oh, thank you. John never took that off. I totally forgot about it. It's a pendant of Mary Magdalene. It's probably only worth a few dollars, but I suppose it's a keepsake. To be honest, I don't know if I really want it. You see, he trusted in her, in Mary Magdalene, that is. He believed that she was his guardian angel. Odd, I know, but you had to know him to appreciate it. I guess I was desperate. For a while, I believed that she or God would create a miracle and cure that damn cancer," she sighed.

"I'm sorry about your loss."

"I guess miracles don't happen except in the old bible tales. You can have that thing. I don't want it. It would only remind me of broken hopes and promises. Instead, I really need to go on and be strong for the children. Here, take it or throw it away for all I care." Mrs. King was wiping her tears as she returned the pendant to Jennifer. "It's yours now. May it serve you better than it served him."

Jennifer felt awful. She realized that she had to tell this grieving woman about the encounter with her husband's spirit. She had promised it to him. Yet, it felt too odd. What if she had imagined it?

Jennifer inhaled and began to relay the night's events. She did not get very far before Mrs. King looked at her as if she, Jennifer Angel, was insane or was herself a ghost.

"What did you say?" Mrs. King interrupted. In the process, she knitted her brows and stared into Jennifer's eyes, holding them locked and bound with her intense attention.

"Your husband gave this pendant to me. I mean, he was, as I said, here in spirit. I don't know how else to say it," Jennifer stammered.

"Do you mean that he gave you that pendant before he died? Did you have an affair with him, as well? Oh, my God!" Mrs. King replied covering her mouth as if she were about to throw up. "How could you? When?"

"No, no, no! Nothing of the sort! I never met your husband until he arrived here."

"Oh, so he gave it to you before he died while here in the hospital? That's odd." Mrs. King was visibly confused and partially relieved, all in one emotion. "See, I told you that it was intended for you," she sighed deeply. "You keep it, if he wanted you to have it. I'm sorry about my reaction. He and I had some trouble in our relationship a while back just before his illness. I can't believe I said that to you. I'm losing my mind. I'm so sorry. You keep it, Miss…"

"Angel, Jennifer Angel."

"Yes. Miss Angel. That's a perfect name for your profession. Well, thank you and good bye, Miss Angel. My mother's in the car with all the kids, so I must get going. Thank you."

"Mrs. King, I'm the one who's sorry. I know what I said sounded extremely strange, but I need to emphasize that your husband gave that pendant to me AFTER he died."

"What? What kind of a warped humor do you possess, Miss Angel?" The poor woman had no room to process the information.

"Mrs. King, I know that it sounds bizarre and it is, but, for whatever reason, your husband's spirit was here after you left, and I was in the room when he appeared, and he gave me this, and he told me to tell you that…" Jennifer was determined to let it all out in one breath and fulfill her promise.

"Stop! I heard enough!" Mrs. King interrupted in an angry tone. "I've been through enough! I don't believe in such crap! Maybe he believed in that crap, but I had to be the strong one, the one grounded in reality, and not some illusion of his own making. How did he put you up to this? How could you? I've a mind to report you for this. How could you?"

"Mrs. King, I know it sounds strange but it happened."

"It happened in your head, Miss Angel. I get it. You see a lot of death around here, so that's how you cope. I suggest, my dear…" Mrs. King changed her tone as it became obvious that the young nurse was not joking. She appeared to sincerely believe what she claimed to have witnessed. "I suggest, my dear, that you get some professional help. I'm sure that for a young person all this death and tragedy is hard to bear. I understand. My husband walked around here last night handing out meaningless trinkets of powerless saints. I get it. Thank you for telling me. Wonderful news, Miss Angel. Really good news. Good bye, and it's clear that you and that pendant belong together."

Mrs. King did not wait for a response. The poor suffering woman had been through enough. Her own sanity was now hanging by a thread, the thread of her logical mind which she, an engineer, prided herself at possessing and mastering. She could take no more and simply stormed out of the ward shaking her head.

"Well, I tried," Jennifer whispered as she looked down at the pendant of Mary Magdalene. "You're not a powerless saint. I know that much. I guess this pendant is meant for me. After all, you are my favorite saint," she thought as she placed the pendant around her neck.

At first, it felt awkward wearing a dead man's pendant around her neck, but soon she dismissed it as a fitting odd ending to a very odd night.

CHAPTER 34

Wonders Never Cease

Molly was unpacking when she heard the knock on the door. The knock was soft at first but became louder when ignored.

"Damn, now what freak is coming to visit?" Molly muttered as she approached the door to open it.

There, standing before her, was Teresa Nightingale, the owner of the house. She was wearing a very revealing top and tight pants. "Luckily, she can pull it off," Molly thought as she laid eyes on the woman, who was in her late forties, but did not look the part. She was radiant as always, and her very presence transformed Molly's negativity into a warm welcome.

"Come in, Terry. Please come in. Sorry about the mess. Please sit here. I'll move my stuff." Molly moved a few boxes, and the two women sat down facing each other.

"Did you like the flowers?" Terry asked. "I don't see them." She looked around the room before refocusing on Molly. "I guess red's not your favorite. It was just a guess. You seem like a red roses type."

"Terry, I was most flattered and surprised. I had no idea. It was a lovely gesture," Molly lied. "I mean.."

"Did I overdo it? Was it too much?"

"Too much for what, Terry?"

"Oh, so it wasn't too much. I'm so glad. Ever since I laid eyes on you the first day, I felt it. You know the feeling. It's that butterfly feeling." Terry was bubbling in excitement.

"That feeling, Terry, is NOT the feeling I had with the flowers."

"I overdid it. I knew it, but I also know that there's an attraction. I felt it too. Oh, my, is it warm in here or is it me?" Terry was waving her hands about her face as if to cool herself. "I hope that this isn't too much," she looked down at her outfit. "Wroomm, roommm, roomm. Hot, hot ,hot!! Oh, my God," she fanned herself again. "What we could do is heavenly, Molly."

"Terry, what are you saying?" Molly stood up in protest.

"I'm saying that I can't wait until we get through this courtship stage. You know, Trudy and I have had troubles for a while. She's a sweet girl and I do love her, but she pulls me down. Beside, she's too young. I just don't feel it the way I do for you, you, YOU!"

"Have you been drinking, Terry?"

"Oh, a wee bit for courage."

"Terry, you're drunk. Drunk and totally confused. I'm not that kind of girl."

"What kind are you, then? Oh, you like a slow courtship. Of course. I get it. I like that too. Yes, I do. Slow and gentle. Yes, Yes, YES!"

"Terry, you're completely drunk."

"I am and I am, so here I am. Take me! No, I must resist… or insist. Which is it?"

"Terry, you need to leave and go to bed."

"Bed! Now you're talking, you little monkey!" Terry sprang up and began to chase Molly about the room.

"Terry, you sound like a drunken sailor. Look, I'm not a lesbian! Ok! Stop! I could hurt you, but I don't want to," Molly objected while trying to escape her drunk pursuer.

"Hurt me! Hurt me! PLEASE, hurt me, sweet Molly!" Terry huffed, starting to run out of steam.

"I'm not gay, Terry! I like guys!" Molly yelled and stood her ground.

Terry stopped and nearly fell over as she felt extremely dizzy. "What! Yes, you are!" she objected.

"No, I'm not! I should know, shouldn't I?"

"You're confused or playing hard to get. Either way, it's mean, mean, MEAN!" Terry exclaimed and fell on the couch in exhaustion.

"Terry, you really need to leave," Molly asked gently.

"No. I'm staying because you're lying. I knew you were into me the minute our eyes met. You have that look and that vibe. You know, The VIBE!"

"What vibe?'

"That lesbian vibe, of course. Anyone can pick up on it. Yours is so strong that I bet even most men pick up on it."

Molly was taken back by this comment. She had never heard of such a thing. Could that explain the lack of boyfriends these past two years? "Terry, I don't get it."

"Oh, I do. I get it. You're not out of the closet. Oh, my, this is the best! A virgin, no less. I'll help you come out. I promise."

"I don't need help, but you apparently do!"

"Oh, denial! How cute! How sexy!"

"Terry, please leave! You're making me very uncomfortable. Please stop!"

"Okay, I'll stop. But, I still think that you are gay and in denial."

"I am not! Not that there's anything wrong with it, of course. But I like men, okay?"

"Yeah, sure. Okay. But I better get going, I'm late," Ms. Nightingale replied.

"Late for what?"

"For the gathering tonight in the great hall, you silly. I need to start getting it ready. Are you coming?"

"Sure, when is it?" Molly realized that this was a chance to explore this strange cult, and although she had little desire to accompany Terry anywhere, she had to go for the sake of the mission.

"It's after dinner at seven in the great hall. You're in denial, Princess. How sweet! Well, I can wait. In the meantime, don't tell any of this to Trudy. I had the flowers delivered so it looked like they were from the outside. You know what I mean?" Terry tripped over a moving box as she headed for the door, but managed to catch herself.

"Too late. She knows!"

"No!" Terry turned to face Molly. "How?"

"She was there when I opened your card. She'd been hovering over those flowers all morning."

"Oh, my! That's bad. I better go see her," Terry confessed and left without saying goodbye.

Molly closed the door as soon as she could and locked it, just in case. "As soon as this case is solved, I'm moving out of this looney bin. I give off the vibe? That's ridiculous! I give off no such thing! It's not like I couldn't have a boyfriend. I just don't want one right now. Ridiculous, drunk woman!" she muttered as she unpacked.

CHAPTER 35

Harry's Vision

"Boss, we found something. Bob and I were searching Stacy Reed's credit card charges, and you were right. She's on the run and in Iowa, of all places."

"Iowa!" The Inspector looked up from his desk. "Good. Do you know where in Iowa?"

"Well, as of last night, she was in Cedar Rapids at some local motel named Harry's Vision. Damn odd name for a motel," Chen muttered. "It sounds more like an optometrist's office."

"Did you contact the local police?" the Inspector asked, giving the two men his complete attention.

"Yes. Bob did and they called back a few minutes ago, but could not locate her. But, Harry's Vision confirmed that Stacy was there, and that she was not alone," Chen added.

"Kidnapping?"

"Hard to say, Boss. According to Harry, whose initial vision was Harry's Vision," Chen was enjoying the word game. "According to Harry Vision, the owner of Harry's Vision," he began again.

"Okay. I get it. Spit it out before I turn sixty," the Inspector interrupted.

"Well, it doesn't seem like Stacy is with a kidnapper. If she is, then they're getting on smashingly." Chen raised an eyebrow and smirked at Big Bob, who was standing next to him.

"What do you mean?" the Inspector asked, still confused. "Chen can be so frustrating," he thought.

"Harry told the police that he had a complaint from an occupant, in the room adjacent to Stacy's, about the amorous sounds echoing through the walls. It appears that Harry's Vision has thin walls, and that Stacy's very happy with her kidnapping," Chen replied as Bob burst into laughter.

"Okay, can you get a trace on her cell phone?"

"No can do! She didn't take her cell phone with her on this journey of self-discovery and self-fulfillment," Chen replied.

"What are you talking about, Chen? Self-discovery and self-fulfillment?"

"Well, Harry told the police that when they checked into the motel, he overheard the young couple discussing their journey out West, and that they sounded like 'two excited youths out to discover the world,' to quote Harry of Harry's Vision," Chen explained, while trying to keep a straight face. "At least that was Harry's vision of what transpired. I mean, Harry's version of what transpired," Chen corrected and stopped.

Bob burst out again in an explosion of laughter. He contained himself as soon as he saw the Inspector's stern face. "Sorry, Boss. It's not funny. I know." Bob looked down at his size 14 shoes.

"Do we have anything on this guy she's with?"

"Harry's providing his vision of the guy to the sketch artist in Iowa as we speak, Boss," Chen added in a deadpan manner.

Bob ran out of the office and exploded once more in a spray of laughter in the hall. He returned with his eyes downcast, avoiding eye contact with the Inspector. The latter ignored the childish behavior. He liked his team, and hated to admit that the youthful bantering and goofy humor had gelled them into a strong working unit. Therefore, he wisely let it go, despite the fact that all of his peers would consider such behavior as unprofessional and insubordinate. "It's fine to a point, as long as it's only within the team and behind closed doors," he had insisted in the past.

"Once we get the sketch, we'll run some profiles and see if anyone around here knows him. Chances are that he's her boyfriend, which means that he's probably local. We're also looking into Stacy's past relations to see if there's a connection. Boss, when we do find her, what do you expect to do? She's old enough to go on her own wherever she wants?" Chen asked, genuinely confused by the plan.

"Of course she is, but we need to ask her what she saw when Mary fell. I don't care if she decided to go on an adventure of self-discovery, as you put it, but I need to interview her," the Inspector replied.

"The 'self-discovery' was simply a quote from Harry, of Harry's Vision," Chen clarified.

The Inspector exhaled audibly. "The issue with Chen is that he never knows when to quit," the Inspector thought but let the comment pass. Even Bob had become sick of the running gag.

"As I was about to say, right now Stacy Reed is not only a suspect in the Mary Collins attempted homicide case, but also an official missing person. At her father's request, we placed her on the FBI missing person's list this morning. Does that answer your question, Chen?"

"Well... no, sir."

One of the things that the Inspector did appreciate about young Chen was his blunt honesty. "Okay, what part is missing?"

"Sir, in all due respect..."

"Chen, no need to be cautious. That's not like you. What's bugging you?" the Inspector asked in a patient fatherly tone, disarming his young pupil's reservations.

"Well, honestly Sir, I don't think Stacy did it. I'm analyzing that photo down to the pixels and I believe that she's the blonde hugging Randell, as Kelly Allen testified. So, to try and catch up to her seems like a waste of time," Chen replied.

"Your logic is sound, Chen, and I admire your forwardness." The Inspector glanced at Bob, who was often too shy to speak up, despite his enormous size and strength. These two were the best of friends and the epitome of opposites. The Inspector knew his team well. "Chen, some day when you have a daughter, like I do and like Professor Reed does, you will understand that true police work isn't always about catching the criminal. Sometimes, it's about reuniting a loving father with his runaway daughter. Is that a waste of time?"

Chen shook his head in agreement but made no reply, while Bob had the perfect answer, or nearly so, given its origin. "Man, Boss, you're such a great dad! I wish you were my dad!" he blurted out.

"I am!" answered the Inspector.

"Huh?" Bob was confused.

"Never mind all that. Did Harry, of Harry's Vision," the Inspector decided to join them in the running joke, "get a make on the car that Stacy was driving?"

"Yes, Sir."

"What was it?"

"An old Eagle Vision, Sir," Chen replied and Bob burst into laughter once more, while the Inspector smiled, rolled his eyes and walked away.

CHAPTER 36

A Surprise Visitor

It was nearly 7 pm when Molly entered the great hall in the "House of Horrors" as she called her new residence. What awaited her took her breath away. The large room with the two story ceiling was a marvel in itself. Decorated in traditional colonial style and hung with murals that depicted scenes from nature, it was an odd blend of old and crunchy. She had glanced at the room before, but was so focused on the three long banners at the far end of it and on the circle of lush pillows in its center that she never registered the rest. Now she could, and it was different. That was the only descriptor that came to mind, "different." Different not in a bad way, simply an odd eclectic way. A collision of Northern California with Colonial Williamsburg, it felt awkward, just as she did as she looked for a place to sit.

"Molly, come sit with me!" she heard the familiar voice shout out. It was Terry. Molly looked about to see if Trudy was there. She was, but she sat on the other side of the circle of pillows from

Terry. Molly hesitated. She wanted neither to be in the middle of the two women's love quarrel, nor to encourage Terry's illusions. Yet, she did not want to offend the owner of the house. She needed to remain in her good graces while the Mary Collins case was active. It was her job. To alienate Terry was to risk getting alienated in the house. In the end, she chose the mission and approached Terry. As she did, she felt Trudy's hateful stare from across the room.

"Come, sit next to me, my dear!" Terry exclaimed and winked her right eye. She was not quite sober yet, but getting closer. "I'll help you understand the rituals. There are a few that are hard to understand. Do you have any questions so far, my love?'

Molly ignored the much too affectionate comment and answered truthfully. "What's this about?"

Terry began to laugh. "Oh my, you're a virgin in so many ways. How totally exciting! But I don't want to make you uncomfortable. I know that this will help you find your true self, your true suppressed self," Terry replied with a knowing smile.

"Sure, but what's this about?" Molly repeated. She decided to play the naive student, and use Terry's obsession with her to get information about this odd religious sect and its connection to Mary Collins.

"Well, my dearest, this isn't all that exciting, I must admit. But don't tell anyone I said so, since three years ago this was my idea." She broke out laughing and then stopped when her eyes met Trudy's angry stare.

"This is nothing more than a call to meditation. I have been inspired by Eastern religions since I, well, since I... (sigh)... since my dear old friend Colleen Burke turned me on to this, and more as well," she added raising her eyebrows a half inch and her voice an octave. "Fond old memories," she reflected. "This is not a cult or anything like that, Molly. You can let that conservative guard down, my dear. That's the root cause of your denial and hostility. No?"

"What a weirdo!" Molly thought. "What's that symbol over there?" Molly changed the topic, pointing at the symbol depicted on the central banner, the same symbol that Mary had tattooed in miniature on the back of her neck.

"That's something that Trudy dug up in some ancient Taoist text. She and I started this. She's the expert on all this stuff, but it hasn't lightened her load one bit, if you know what I mean," Terry glanced at Trudy, who was still glaring maliciously at Molly. "At any rate, it's a symbol for the Taoist concept of Wu Wei. This entire session, as you'll find out, is really a harmless meditation session. It's a way of letting go and being at peace, which is the essence of Wu Wei."

"Like Trudy over there?" Molly could not resist the jab.

"Poor Trudy! She studies all this stuff and yet is totally clueless about how to implement it. Look at her! She was so mad about the roses that she threw a vase at me. Good thing it was only a cheap imitation of a Ming Dynasty collectable. What a shame that we had to come to an end. I suspect that she'll be moving out before the week is out. Would you like her job?" Terry offered.

"No, thanks. Not in the least. No offense."

"No offense taken. It's a grunt job worthy of a meticulous remorseful soul, like Trudy. I'm glad that we're done. It's so refreshing, as are you, my love." Terry placed her left hand over Molly's right hand and left it there.

Trudy noticed and was ready to peel Molly's eye's out from twenty paces. Molly quickly retracted her hand. "I'm a patient woman, and you're worth the wait, my dear. Aha, here's the master of our ceremonies. I swear that if I were young and straight, I would have the hots for that man. Look at him! He's a doll, and smart too!" Terry inhaled audibly at the sight of Jack Fulton's entrance.

Jack walked into the room and greeted everyone as if they were old friends. He walked up to Terry, who was clearly the queen of this ball, and kissed her hand in old fashion chivalry. "Oh God, please!" Molly thought, but simply smiled.

"Molly, is it?" Jack asked her and looked into her eyes. "How lovely to see you. We were never properly introduced," he observed with a winning smile.

"Oh, I didn't realize," Terry replied rather flustered. "Jack Fulton meet Molly Dvorak. Did I say your name correctly? Is that a Russian name?"

"No. It's Czech. Right, Molly?" Jack replied before she could. "It's an honor, Molly," he added.

Molly retracted her hand for fear that he would slobber on it. "Nice to meet you, Jack," she replied visibly disinterested. "The name is Czech. My father is a Czech immigrant."

"Then we have something in common to talk about," Jack added flirtatiously.

"My father?"

"No. Well, if you wish," Jack chuckled. "I meant to say that my mother is of Czech heritage on her grandfather's side."

"I see. You're right. We're nearly cousins," Molly flashed her wit. She had daily practice with Chen and Bob.

"Very funny. I love a sharp wit," Jack replied.

"I love an honest man," Molly answered.

Jack had no idea how to take that comment, but he did not need to reply for Terry did it for him. "Don't waste your time, Jack. She isn't interested. You're not her type, if you get my drift?"

"Really! I would've never guessed," Jack replied.

"Where's that vibe now, Terry?" Molly thought. "Obviously, I don't have one," she concluded to herself while missing an opportunity to clarify.

"Indeed! You're full of surprises, Miss Molly. But, let me warn you to stay away from Terry. She may be alluring in many ways, but she's trouble." Jack smiled at the two women.

"Oh, you are a charmer, Jack!" Terry flirted for she enjoyed it.

"Where's Trudy?" Jack looked about and then spotted the pouting angry face. "Oh, I see there's trouble in paradise. Well, good seeing you ladies, but we must get started." He smiled and walked toward the front of the large hall to a seat at the head of the great circle.

Before Molly had a chance to ask any more questions, the lights dimmed and the soft sounds of nature filled the room along with the smell of incense. All fell silent, as Jack began to lead the attendees in a session of deep meditation, repeating the sacred Hindu word "Om". Molly had mixed emotions. A part of her was happy to know that there was no evidence of a religious cult near McLaren's campus, but a part of her was disappointed, hoping for something more spectacular than a meditation class. She felt like she was taking a class at the local YMCA, rather than participating in an undercover assignment to spy on a suspicious cult. She was about to toss in the towel when a young woman slipped into the empty seat to her left.

As Molly turned to greet her, she was struck by the odd coincidence. There, sitting next to her, was Daphne Marconi. "Wait till Cabot gets a hold of this," Molly thought.

"Hello," Daphne smiled shyly and quickly joined in the meditation.

Five minutes into the session, Molly's legs were starting to hurt. She could not reach a state of peace in a cross-legged posture. Instead, she was itchy and cramping up all over. "Damn this position! How can anyone meditate when they're tied up like a giant pretzel?" she thought. "The boss owes me one for this, but I need to stay and talk to Daphne."

Jack was in some sort of a trance. He had stopped repeating the mantra and simply sat completely motionless, seemingly lost in a world beyond Molly's reach. Terry also appeared to be deep in meditation, as was Daphne and most of the rest of the room. Only Molly and Trudy were unfazed. Molly could not stop her mind from racing and thinking about her cramped body, and Trudy could not stop staring at Molly. "How much longer!" Molly wanted to scream. She could no longer tolerate the painful knot in her right leg, which had begun to throb. At the risk of offending, she rose to her feet and tried to shake out the cramps. Luckily, no one seemed to notice, except for Trudy, who was smiling for the first time that night.

Settling back, Molly decided to simply sit there with her eyes closed and her arms holding over her knees. She sat as if she were sitting in a small tub. She felt cold as if the temperature in the room had decreased. "Odd place this, but seemingly harmless. It appears that Mary was into Eastern spirituality and meditation, end of story," she thought. "But why the tattoo?" She looked up at Jack and for the first time noticed an identical tattoo on his right forearm.

"Coincidence? Are they all tattooed?" She looked about the room at the silent figures who appeared to be sleeping, while seated in a locus position. She noticed that many had the same tattoo. "There must be some kind of an initiation in this place. Maybe that's where it gets interesting. I'll have to ask about that," she thought to herself.

Finally, the meditation seemed to be drawing to a close. "Thank God," she thought. She was ready to get up and scream in gratitude.

The various members began to awaken and greet each other. "Everyone seems so peaceful, like they had returned from a spa or something," Molly silently observed. "What happened? The only person I can relate to in here is Trudy. Now there's a sad conclusion."

"Isn't he wonderful?" Terry sighed. "He can lead a session like no one else. Wow!"

"Yes, wonderful," Molly replied.

"You didn't reach nirvana or anywhere close, did you child?" Terry asked in a motherly tone.

"No, but I have a couple of their albums."

"Funny, very funny. Oh, here comes Jack. I think he really means to impress you, but we know better, right?" Terry winked at her.

Before Molly could reply, Jack was seated next to her. Suddenly, Molly realized that Daphne had disappeared. "Damn! I didn't get a chance to talk to her," she thought. "But, here's suspect number two, so all is not wasted," she concluded to herself.

"Molly, what did you think? Terry, how was it?" he asked in a mild-mannered fashion.

"Great, as always, Captain Jack!" Terry smiled. "Went as high as ever tonight. I felt so free this time. Great stuff! Well, I had better run. I'm late!" Terry prepared to rush off. The White Rabbit was back in action. "I'm telling you, Jack, that you're wasting your time with her. She's not that type," Terry winked at Molly and departed.

Meanwhile, Molly had the Mad Hatter planted firmly next to her with little intention of leaving. "So, did you enjoy it? Was this your first time?" he bombarded her with questions. She was struck by his boyish sincerity. Yet, there was something behind that facade. She could feel it now at close quarters.

"Yes, first time. Not sure I got much out of it, though," she replied honestly.

"No one ever does at first, Molly. It takes training, like anything. It's not easy to quiet an active mind like yours," he smiled knowingly. "If you want, I'll work with you, and that's not a come on."

"Sure!" Molly responded. "Sure it's not a come on," she thought, "but I can handle myself."

"Great! When do you want to start?"

"Whenever?" she replied.

"How about tomorrow night? I'll pick you up here and we can go for dinner."

"Not a come on, huh?" Molly thought. "Sure, how about seven?" she replied.

"Great! See you tomorrow at seven."

"Okay," she replied while thinking that the Inspector really owed her one after this. "At any rate, no vibe," she concluded happily. "Not that that would be a bad thing. Actually, it would be a bad thing to have the wrong vibe. Maybe I do have a vibe. No, no vibe! " she concluded to herself. "But I do wish that I'd gotten to talk to Daphne. Now there I felt a vibe. Maybe not. Crap! Terry's messing with me even at a distance," she sighed and headed out of the room.

Terry watched her leave and returned to Jack. "You're playing with fire," she warned.

"Not sure. But, I'll test that theory further," he replied. "Were you seriously hitting on her?"

"Jealous are we? I suggest that you stick with what you got, or is there something else I should know?" As she finished her question, Jack leaned toward her and whispered in her ear.

CHAPTER 37

The Old Quarry

Bob and Chen pulled up to the old abandoned quarry near Kamerynville that had been the site of the Mary Collins crime. It was drizzling and the clay-rich mud stuck to their shoes.

"I told you we should have brought some boots!" Chen let out as he sank into the mud.

They had parked the car just off the road where Mr. Chesterfield had parked the bus on that fateful day two weeks earlier. Bob sat in the car as Chen reluctantly slugged his way to the upper terrace entrance, the area where Mary had fallen.

"Stop!" shouted Bob from the car.

Chen obeyed and stood still.

"Okay, right there's where I can still see you before you disappear behind the rocks," Bob announced.

"No kidding, genius! Once I step over there I can't see you either. What are you trying to establish with this?" Chen yelled back.

"Simply that Chesterfield had a pretty good view of the landscape up to that point. Can you mark that point with a flag?"

"Sure. Now get your butt out here! This was suppose to be your task!" Chen yelled at Bob.

Bob lumbered toward him. "So how did Chesterfield not see Kelly Allen and yet see Suzy Kurtz, when the two were together? That's one piece of this that's been bugging me. We're putting more and more emphasis on Kelly's testimony, yet it conflicts with Chesterfield's." Bob scratched his head.

"Maybe Chesterfield simply missed it," Chen relied.

"Or maybe he's protecting Kelly. He also missed Daphne. That's another discrepancy between our two key witnesses. The other possibility is that there's a second way into this seeming dead end that we missed the first time around," Bob speculated.

"Well, let's take a look," Chen replied as they entered the upper terrace. "Take plenty of pictures. Damn! We should've picked a better day for this."

The two men entered the portion of the upper quarry where Mary had been standing before her fall. As they looked around, they confirmed that, except for a path down into the lower levels of the quarry at the far end of the terrace, there was no other access. It was a dead end. The walls were too steep for anyone to climb or descend. In fact, they were sheer. The quarry terrace was surrounded by sheer cliffs on three sides and the fourth side had a sheer drop onto the quarry floor. It was off this drop that Mary had fallen. Their entrance onto the fateful terrace was limited, partially blocked by fallen rocks. Therefore, once a person scrambled around these fallen rocks, he or she was out of site of the road and quarry entrance, and out of sight of the bus driver, Mr. Chesterfield. At the far end of this terrace was a scramble down to a lower ledge, which was small and acted as a sort of step toward the main floor of the quarry. This lower ledge did not extend the full length of the upper terrace, but simply acted as a rugged descent near the terrace's far end.

The two men stepped up to where Mary had stood before she fell. They both hesitated as they looked down. "Quite a drop! I'm amazed that she's not dead," Chen whispered.

"Yeah!" Bob inhaled audibly. "Look up there! That must be where Johnson's pictures were taken. We'll need to check that out. It's clearly accessible from the back side but not this side. Right there is the scree that Fulton said he descended to get to Mary after she fell. Man, seems like a lot of risk to take if you're the one who pushed her. You could get killed going down that!"

"Yeah, unless you really wanted to cover your tracks. I wouldn't put it past that guy." Chen looked down the scree that was to the right of them as they faced into the main portion of the quarry. The lower ledge and the descending path toward it was to their left.

"Did you notice that the boss has it out for Fulton?" Bob asked Chen.

"No. Not really."

"Well, it seems to me that he does. It's as if they had a past. I was there when he interviewed him, and they acted like they knew each other. There was a lot of tension," Bob observed.

"Well, not sure what that has to do with this place. Look over there! There's the small ledge were Randell was supposedly hugging Stacy. You get quite a view of it from here. I think Kelly's right. Suzy screamed because of that," Chen chuckled. "She had a front row view of Randell's infidelity."

"So, this is where the perpetrator stood. With all these large rocks strewn around here, he or she was well hidden right up to the point that he or she pushed her. Look, Chen, I could sneak right up to you and no one would see me, if I were careful. We've got to get this fallen boulder layout on a map. Let's take some GPS readings. We should've done this earlier," Bob confessed.

He was correct. There was almost an unbroken passage of fallen rocks from the back wall of the terrace up to where Mary had stood when pushed. There were some breaks in between, but it offered a nearly continuous screen from both sides of view. Bob followed this protected passage all the way to the back wall of the terrace. "Look, Chen!" he yelled back at his partner. "I found something that we missed!"

"What?" Chen came running.

"Look right here!" Bob pointed at the ground. "This rock was recently moved. It used to be right there, and then was moved to provide a nearly perfect hiding place." Bob took pictures of the rocks.

"You're dreaming, Bob. What are you working on, some kind of a conspiracy theory? Are you implying that someone was hiding here? Did it occur to you that he or she would never know if Mary would show up here and stand right where she did. It's too random. You've been watching too many cop shows. You really need a girlfriend, Bob," Chen rebuked.

"It's obvious that this was an opportunistic crime," Chen continued. "That's totally obvious. The girl was standing there and one of the suspects used the opportunity to push her. That's why I think we really need to look at motive. Right now the only one with a strong motive that remains on the prime suspect list is Tony. Lilly's smart enough to play up the drama to keep herself out of jail. Except for the e-mails that they thought they destroyed, Lilly has a tight story."

"Agreed, but we need to go back to the time sequence to validate the positions of all the suspects at the time of the crime," Bob argued. "That's why I think it's a problem that Chesterfield's and Kelly Allen's testimonies don't match. Right now the only hard evidence that we have are the Johnson pictures, which clearly rule out only one person on the suspect list, Randell, and possibly a second, Stacy," Bob reasoned. "Molly needs to crack Fulton and that Daphne girl. Right now they have little motive, but they seem to have been in the closest proximity to the victim before she fell. Wait, did you check who wore what that day?" Bob asked Chen.

"Yes, I did. The perpetrator wore white in the damning photo. As luck would have it, all three remaining suspects wore white or off-white. Also, I'm pretty sure that Stacy was the one with Randell in the Johnson pictures because I found a group photo of her from that trip in which she appears wearing a blue ribbon and a blue dress."

"She's innocent," Bob concluded. "At best, she may be a witness for some additional evidence. Who else on the original suspect list wore white?"

"Kelly Allen was the only other one."

"What if Kelly did it and lied about the rest? That would explain why her testimony does not jive with Chesterfield's and why she disappeared right after the incident." Bob speculated while taking numerous photographs of the crime site.

"But, your little Suzy is her alibi," Chen chuckled.

"What'd you mean by that remark?"

"It's obvious that you're into Suzy Kurtz. But, be careful. Mixing business with pleasure is always dangerous," Chen warned.

"I'm not mixing anything, and I'm not into her," Bob snapped.

"Well, if Kelly did it then Suzy must be her accomplice. Right?"

"I doubt Kelly did it. She doesn't have a motive and she passed the lie detector test." Bob retracted his latest theory. "Besides, this is all speculation and I'm getting wet. Let's look at that lower ledge and determine the view Randell and Stacy had of the crime scene."

They scrambled to the lower ledge. "Wow, from here they had a great view of Mary's fall! Wonder if Randell is holding something back?" Bob questioned.

"Probably, and it'll be next to impossible to get it out of him," Chen concluded as he took more pictures and GPS measurements.

"You know, there's one witness that might have seen the entire thing," Bob proclaimed, looking up at the crime scene.

"Yeah, Stacy! Maybe that's why she disappeared."

"Maybe. There're too many unknowns. That's why I think the boss is rushing things," Bob concluded.

The two men climbed the back side of the quarry to the look-out point from which Michael Johnson took the pictures that were the backbone of their criminal case. They stood there and looked at what he must have seen. Soon the drizzle turned into a downpour. "From here, he couldn't see the perpetrator unless he was right there at the drop off," Bob pointed to the edge of the cliff.

"Man, I'm getting soaked! Let's take a few quick pictures and GPS coordinates up here and head back." Chen began to take the measurements as Bob snapped more photographs, trying to replicate Michael Johnson's perspective.

"I'm going to push back on the boss, since I think that he's running ahead of his headlights," Bob stressed, while rushing back to the car.

As they descended the back side of the quarry, Bob noticed a set of nearly washed out tracks headed away from the crime scene toward a small parking area removed from the main quarry site. "This is the first hard rain we've had since the incident, right?" he asked Chen.

"Yes. Why?"

"Let's go down there and see what we can see in that nearly hidden parking spot. Look at this set of tracks that leads right to it," Bob observed.

"Bob, I'm not sure what's going through that head of yours, but these tracks don't mean anything, since anyone could've been here since the incident," Chen objected.

"True, but let's take a quick look anyway." Bob headed down to the base of the hill to a small dirt road on the back side of the quarry. Chen reluctantly followed as the rain soaked him to the skin.

When they reached the area, Bob looked around like a bloodhound on a promising scent. Of the Inspector's team, Bob was the best when it came to crime scene investigation. In fact, Bob was thinking of joining the CSI group as his next assignment. He loved this type of work.

"Bob, this is a waste of time. I'm soaking wet and cold. I'm headed back to the car." Chen turned to go.

"Please, just take a few GPS coordinates, so we can add this to the map. I'll snap a few pictures, okay? Come on, Chen, old buddy!"

Okay, Okay. But, let's not waste more time here," Chen objected, but took the GPS coordinates at Bob's request.

They were about to leave, when Bob discovered a muddy, blue hair ribbon laying near the hidden parking area. "Look at this!" he picked it up with his latex gloves and placed it in a sample bag. "What does that look like?" he asked Chen.

"That's Stacy's blue hair ribbon. But, how'd it get back here?" Chen looked at Bob with a puzzled stare.

CHAPTER 38

A Bizarre Night

Molly was worn out by the day's drama between Terry, Trudy, Jack and the odd crew that occupied her "House of Horrors." It was nearly 8 pm and she had just finished her unpacking. Tired, she was about to take a well deserved rest when she heard a knock on her door.

"Now what? More storybook characters? Maybe it's Tweedle Dee or Tweedle Dum," she huffed as she opened the door.

Standing before her was her neighbor, Helga. "Sorry to bother you, Molly, but I need a favor. I seemed to have locked myself out of my room and need to climb in through the window. Do you mind?" she asked as if she were requesting to borrow a cup of sugar.

"Helga, how do you propose to do that? We're on the third floor!" Molly observed in complete confusion.

"Ah, no worries. Thanks." Helga stomped to Molly's window and opened it like a professional thief. She slipped out of it with surprising agility and disappeared into the darkness.

Alarmed, Molly ran to the open window and peered out into the rainy gloom. As she looked across the narrow stone ledge that connected her window to Helga's, she caught the last sight of her neighbor entering her apartment window. Before she could process all that had transpired, Helga was once again standing in Molly's doorway.

"Thanks, Doll. All set. Hey, I'm sorry if I had the TV on too loud last night. I'm not used to having a neighbor. I forgot about you," Helga chuckled. "I had a few friends over to watch old World War II clips. Well, we're having another session tonight, but a quieter one," the big woman laughed. "You're welcome to join us. We'll start at nine. My favorite cable station has World War II week until Sunday. Awesome, I tell you. Come over. Oh, by the way, I love what you did with this shabby place." Helga smiled, awaiting a reply.

"Thanks for inviting me, Helga, but I'm going to pass tonight."

"I understand," Helga replied, visibly disappointed. "Okay, we'll keep it down."

"Thanks. By the way, where'd you learn to do what you just did?"

"What was that?"

"Climb ledges and all," Molly replied.

"Well, I grew up with five brothers in Germany, Alabama, South Korea and the Philippines. My only doll was an old GI Joe that wore combat boots," Helga laughed a hearty laugh. "I'm the ultimate army brat. I served in the army for a few years, and then came here on a ROTC scholarship. Climbing ledges comes natural to me, like putting on lip stick must be for you." She chuckled some more. "I'll let you rest," she added and left.

"Odd like the rest of them, but seemingly nice," Molly concluded. "Not sure what Chester has against her." She proceeded to settle onto her couch when her cell phone rang. She looked down at the screen. It was the Inspector. "Agh! This job never ends!"

"Yes, Boss," she answered the phone.

"Sorry to bother you, Molly. But, we have a situation and I need you to get down here, immediately."

"Down where, and what situation?" Molly objected.

"Station. Your friend, Daphne, got picked up soliciting an undercover officer outside the Sweet Dreams motel on the east side of town. She asked for you when they brought her in. How'd she know that you were a cop?" the Inspector asked.

"I don't know. I had no idea that my cover was blown." Molly was shocked.

"Well, can you come down and help out?"

"Sure. I'll be there in 20 minutes."

"Thanks."

Upon hanging up, Molly rushed to change while her mind raced. She had never exchanged anything more than a "hello" with Daphne. Although they sat next to each other at the meditation session at the house, they never spoke beyond the initial greeting.

She rushed to her car and was about to climb in when she froze. "We sat next to each other," she said out load. She looked into her purse and discovered that her wallet was missing. "I bet I know how my cover got blown," Molly concluded and jumped into her car.

When she arrived at the station, she was greeted by the Inspector.

"Don't you ever go home to sleep?" she asked him.

"Sleep is overrated. I raised three kids and I got used to no sleep. It comes in handy now," he replied dryly as he ushered her into the Mirror Room. "There she is in all her frills." He pointed at Daphne, who was seated in the Fish Tank on the other side of the one-way mirror. Daphne sat there nervously fiddling with her many bracelets.

"Looks pretty risqué, all right," Molly replied. "I think I know how she blew my cover. When I attended that cult meeting earlier today, she sat next to me. She never said a word the entire time and disappeared before I had a chance to talk to her. I suspect that she has my missing wallet," Molly confessed.

"By the looks of it, she's a young lady with many talents outside of the classroom," the Inspector replied. "Can you interview her? Then, I want to know about your cult session."

"I'll interview her. As far as the cult session, it was a regular meditation session led by your favorite person," Molly replied.

"Fulton?"

"The one and the same. He too appears to have many talents outside of the classroom."

"Yeah. I can vouch for that."

"What does that mean? How well do you know him?" Molly picked up the scent.

"I don't know him well," the Inspector replied, realizing that he had shared too much. "Get in there before she decides to lawyer up!"

Molly quietly entered the room and greeted Daphne as if they were old friends. "I hear that you asked for me, any reason?" she asked as she sat down.

"Here! This belongs to you," Daphne answered softly as she slid the missing wallet across the table towards its rightful owner. "If you want to charge me with theft as well, go for it. Your money's all there."

"Daphne, what's going on? You're getting yourself into a lot of trouble and, quite frankly, you don't fit the part." Molly looked at Daphne's risqué outfit.

Daphne suddenly broke down in tears that would not stop flowing even after filling a formidable stack of tissues. After five minutes, she began to speak between sobs. "I don't care anymore! I've lost everything in a matter of weeks. I don't care what happens to me. I'm completely broke, and I've got no place to turn," she sobbed some more.

"What do you mean? You live at Ms. Nightingale's house, don't you? I don't even know," Molly admitted.

"I used to, but I can't afford the rent anymore."

"It's pretty steep. I agree." Molly smiled, but Daphne did not pick up on it. She was busy crying.

"My mother died a month ago," she sobbed some more.

"I'm so sorry, Daphne," Molly replied with genuine empathy.

"Then, Mary fell and ended up in a coma. She's my best friend. I love her." She sobbed some more. "And if all that wasn't enough, I found out that my mother was borrowing money to keep me in school. She died and left me penniless with a big debt." She sobbed some more.

"What about your dad?"

"He disappeared when I was only a few months old. For all I know, he's dead too." She continued her sobbing.

"That's a lot at once. I'm so sorry, Daphne." Molly was genuinely supportive.

"Well, I have to feed myself and try to pay my rent. So, I left Ms. Nightingale's house and live in a hole on the east side. One of my new roommates fixed me up with this job. She lent me some of her clothes and helped me with the makeup. I felt stupid, but I needed the money. She promised it was easy money. Just my luck! I finally get the nerve to hit on a guy and he turns out to be an undercover cop." Daphne cried some more. She was halfway through the box of tissues that Molly had handed her, and she was still going strong.

"I need to step out," Molly replied and left. She walked over to the Mirror Room. "So, what do you think, Boss? She's either an honest girl down on her luck, or one hell of a convincing actress."

"I don't know. We need to check out her story. The arresting officer didn't describe her as naive and innocent. So, if she's telling the truth, she came across as one heck of a quick study. Let's hold her, but not press official charges unless she forces us to do so or it turns out that she's lying."

"Okay. I'm heading home for some rest," Molly replied.

"What about the cult session?"

"It's a disappointment. I'll fill you in tomorrow, but it looks like a dead end." Molly returned to the Fish Tank and soon parted with weeping Daphne. The latter gave her what appeared to be a genuine hug of appreciation before being taken to one of the station's holding cells for the night. She did not resist. It was a far nicer place then her present residence on the east side of town.

Molly returned home only to hear World War II erupting next door. "Ugh! Helga, you're killing me!" she exclaimed aloud before knocking on Helga's door.

Helga opened it with a smile. "Changed your mind? Come on in," she offered.

Molly looked into the room, which was a bizarre compilation of red decor and a plethora of army paraphernalia. To Molly's surprise, there was no one else in the room.

"No thanks, Helga, but can you turn it down?"

"Sure. Sorry. Will do," she replied, nearly saluting.

"I thought it was a party?" Molly uttered in surprise.

"Yeah, but no one showed up, as usual," Helga sighed. "I guess the Battle of the Bulge has a limited following these days." She looked so defeated and deflated that Molly, with her kind heart, felt genuinely sorry for her.

"Well, if you promise to always keep it down, I'll stay for about 20 minutes."

"You will?" Helga was so excited that she nearly knocked over the TV trying to turn down the volume. At that point, she looked no more intimidating than a large sheepdog. In fact, she resembled one. "Popcorn?" she offered Molly a greasy old bowl.

"No thanks," Molly replied as she nervously sat onto the grungy couch.

"What am I doing here?" she thought, but before she could answer her own question, she drifted to sleep with the Battle of the Bulge raging in the background.

CHAPTER 39

Mother

It was another long night at the trauma ward. Jennifer Angel felt exhausted from her latest double shift. She knew that she was pushing herself beyond what was healthy, but she needed the money in order to continue her plans to become a doctor. When possible, she studied anatomy and biochemistry at the nurses' station. She was determined to make it on her own.

The ward was finally quiet, and although her eyelids were heavy, she cracked open the biochemistry text book. She was in the process of memorizing the Krebs Cycle when she noticed a magenta haze emanating from room 328, Mary's room. She looked at her watch and noticed that it was just past 3:30 am, the "witching half-hour" as Jennifer now called it. Quickly but quietly, she walked toward Mary's room waiting to see what was in store tonight. Mary's mysterious visitors were becoming a norm.

After her recent encounter with Mrs. King, the grieving young widow, she decided to keep these events to herself. No one would believe her anyway, and she only risked her position, which was something that she could not afford to do. She simply joined the growing numbers of people that have had such odd encounters and have decided to keep them a secret. In Jennifer's case, it was a rather big secret that seemed to keep getting bigger.

She was simply going along with it now, since to question it was to slip into a dangerous place of self-doubt, where these odd experiences, which clashed with her cultural reality, risked pulling her apart beyond recovery. It was easier to simply drift with it and begin to accept it unconditionally, as if it were normal. "Besides," Jennifer reasoned, "we know so little about consciousness, the soul and even life itself. One man's miracle is another man's morning routine. How's this any different?" With this wisely-chosen, open-minded acceptance, she once again entered the place of miracles, Mary's room.

But, tonight was different.

Neither a deceased patient nor a silent guardian awaited her. Tonight, it was a child that sat on Mary's bed and smiled at Jennifer as she entered. She was a girl, who appeared to be no more than four years of age had she been alive and in form, yet once again she appeared beyond either. However, there was something different about this vision than those of the past. She had met the other spirits, and they were spirit-like. Although she was hardly an expert on the subject, she was getting plenty of practical training.

This one seemed more real and more familiar, as if truly a child, yet not one at all. The sensation was more alarming than the previous encounters, and despite the child's jovial expression, Jennifer retreated a few steps toward the door. An awkward silence followed, during which the child and Jennifer stared at each other, neither willing to gaze away. As they stared, Jennifer became aware of a feeling not unlike the timeless fascination of childhood, when each moment lasts an adult's day and each day an adult's week. She began to lose track of time, making room for the joy of existence in the here and now. She was acutely aware of everything, even the buttons on her shirt. It was there all at once, timelessly still.

The child smiled and slipped closer to Mary. She kissed the sleeping beauty on the cheek, and then hugged her in the completely-absorbed, eternal embrace of a child. It was the most amazing embrace imaginable, not unlike what Jennifer would wish of her own child, had she had one.

A sudden shudder filled her and Jennifer began to cry. Unable to bear it any longer, she was about to leave the room, when her thoughts turned to words that were clearly not of her creation. The child communicated like the spirit of the departed young father. She communicated directly through Jennifer's mind. Frozen in fear, Jennifer slowly turned toward the child, truly afraid of this apparition.

"Mother," is all that echoed through her mind. The one word that most defined her true nature was the one she feared most from this child. "Mother, all is well," the message continued in her head as the child looked at her. Jennifer was terrified.

"There's nothing to forgive. Release me, please, as I release you," the child continued. "For although we're all connected, we're not prisoners of our past decisions." The child sat next to Mary, staring at Jennifer.

"I'm going mad!" Jennifer whispered to herself as she turned slowly away from the apparition that so haunted her. Until now, all the visitations had been external to her. She had been an observer at first, and then simply a messenger. This was different. This was about her and about… She struggled not to faint. She struggled to leave, but the child in her head, in her thoughts, forbade it.

"Come!" It spoke in her mind. "Come and look at her. She's like you. She's full of promise, full of love, and full of all that is good in mankind. Yet, she too misses the mark at times. She too falters at times, making mistakes. But a mistake is relative, except in the extremes. A mistake is just another opportunity to learn, to love more unconditionally, to forgive more sincerely, and to embrace more whole-heartedly. So, embrace me, Jennifer, for I am your child. The one that you had no choice but to surrender." The child approached her now.

Jennifer froze, unable to comprehend. Then, in what felt like the faintest brush of a feather, the child kissed her hand just before Jennifer fainted, dropping to the floor.

Moments later, Jennifer awoke only to realize that the purple magenta haze still surrounded her. She had a feeling like she was in a dream, like she was asleep, yet she was completely alert. She felt a pulling sensation across her entire body. Her body was resisting the force pulling upon it. She felt a stretching, like that of an expanding rubber band, and then her body released her with the sensation of a snapping retraction, before she was freed of form. The sensation scared her as she saw her own body laying motionless on the floor behind her. Black, shadowy, shapeshifting orbs, like rapidly moving creatures, scurried about her. The child's voice was still there. It directed her not to fear, for these shadows were solely the dark energy of her fears. She obeyed, and in the process all of the shadowy orbs instantly dispersed, as if her own free will dictated their existence and their demise.

In this dream state, she retained the vision of the child sitting and smiling on the bed above her. "I know that you fought to keep me, but necessity prevented it. Jennifer, if you had not released me, you would have died. You were too young and ill to carry a baby to full term. Please understand." The child spoke lovingly in her mind and in her heart. "In gratitude that you were willing to die for me, I have something to reveal to you."

The entire conversation was as if in a deep dream, surely she was dreaming. Yet, this dream was different. It was so real. It felt more real than physical existence itself.

"Look," the child instructed and pointed toward the door.

The hospital room was the same. Mary was still there, but she too was awake. "She is awake!" Jennifer nearly screamed. The shadowy forms returned.

"Stop your fear!" the child instructed. "Look, look to the door!"

The semi-closed door of the hospital room was aglow in bright yellow and gold. A figure stood like a silhouette behind it. It was the figure of another child. Then, a second silhouette appeared, that of a large, less-defined figure positioned further back behind the transparent bright door. The latter was pampering the figure of the child, as if getting it prepared for an unveiling.

Suddenly, the door, the glowing golden door, began to dissolve and this other child, whose silhouette was behind it, entered the room through a flood of white, blinding light. This child was surrounded by a golden aura. It was a girl with long, wavy, golden hair wearing an angelic white gown. She entered the room, not by walking, but by effortlessly floating into it. The dark silhouette, that had been behind her, had fallen away and disappeared. The new child's face was that of the dream's narrator, the initial child-like apparition.

Jennifer was not allowed to witness more, for suddenly she felt the odd sensation of being sucked back into her physical body that was still lying motionless on the floor behind her. The dream was over, and she awoke on the cold floor of Mary's room in the previously still form that was Jennifer Angel. She awoke while still wrestling with one of the fallen sheets from Mary's bed. The purple haze had faded, but in her mind echoed the words of the child-like apparition. "I will return to you in the next child and that child shall survive. As foretold, it is I." The thought drifted away and Jennifer fell back onto the hard floor, numbed by the vivid revelation.

Completely drained and confused, she felt that this time she was truly losing her mind. A sorrow fell upon her as she returned to her job, checking Mary's vital signs. All was the same. Mary was still in a coma, and Jennifer was once again questioning her mental stability, while reminded of the unborn child that she had lost in an aborted pregnancy, so long ago.

CHAPTER 40

A Grudge

It was another 8 am meeting in the Inspector's office. All were present as he unveiled his sheet-covered cork board. The process had a ceremonial quality as the days passed. On the board were the usual cast of characters in the Mary Collins case. Three main suspects remained, Jack Fulton, Daphne Marconi and Tony Bond. The Inspector called on Molly for an update. She related her experiences at the meditation meeting and stressed the uneventful nature of the session. Then, the Inspector asked her to summarize her interview with Daphne Marconi, and asked Chen to conduct a thorough database search on the suspect. Finally, the Inspector called on Chen to provide an update on the Stacy Reed missing-person search.

"Sure, Boss," Chen replied. "I'm happy to announce that as of 5:45 this morning Stacy Reed and her boyfriend have been located in the outskirts of Cody, Wyoming. She's presently in local police custody. We have notified her father, and she is expected to return here by the end of the week."

"Great news, Chen. Good work!" the Inspector exclaimed. Chen was adding up the brownie points. "Can we get an interview with her before then?" the Inspector added.

"I'll try."

"When exactly is she expected here?" the Inspector pushed Chen.

"On Thursday night. We have first dibs on her, so we should be able to interview her by Friday morning, assuming she'll cooperate," Chen replied.

"Good. We need her testimony. I've got a second interview set up with Fulton. He's coming in this afternoon. That should be interesting since he's still my top suspect," the Inspector pronounced. "Bob, I saw your report on the crime scene. Good job, guys. Anything you wish to highlight?"

Bob had been holding back until his turn was called. Now that he had the floor, he took full advantage. "Yes, there were a couple of items of interest, Boss," Bob began in a confident tone that surprised everyone. He went on to describe the particular layout of the quarry, using a newly digitized map compiled from the recently collected GPS data. Stressing the isolation of the terrace that was the crime scene, he used the three-dimensional graphics to highlight the "screened passage", as he called it, provided by the fallen boulders. He pointed out to the Inspector that this passage ran from the back wall of the terrace to the place where Mary was standing before her fall. He concluded his discussion with the discovery of Stacy's blue hair ribbon and its location on the back access road.

"By the way, Stacy was definitely the one embracing Randell on the lower ledge at the time of Mary's fall. Chen found additional photo evidence that she was the one wearing the ribbon that day," Bob concluded and looked at Chen. The latter appreciated the credit.

"This is all very fascinating, but what does it tell us, Bob?" the Inspector asked.

"Well, Boss, it tells us that there are presently more questions than answers. There's also a possibility that Stacy knows more than we suspected. Furthermore, the screened passage provides a perfect hiding place, opening up the possibility of a planned crime rather than an opportunistic one. In addition, there are issues outside of those associated with the site. Specifically, we haven't resolved the discrepancies between the Chesterfield testimony and the Kelly Allen testimony. We've taken Ms. Allen's word over Mr. Chesterfield's, but what if she's involved? Finally, we have not clearly mapped the time sequence of events and the positioning of the various suspects at the time of Mary's fall. Nor have we determined clear motive for each of our remaining suspects. Right now, of our three key suspect up there," Bob pointed at the old cork board with the three photos, "only one has a documented motive, and that's Tony." Bob paused as the room was surprised by his sudden take-charge attitude.

The Inspector was about to provide a rebuttal when Bob made a statement that was poorly received by all. "Finally, Boss, it appears to me that you're rather biased against Fulton. What's with that?"

The room was suddenly silent. The silence lasted longer than anyone had expected. Bob suddenly realized that he had gone too far for the Inspector gave him a piercing stare. But it was too late. The question was already out there, demanding an answer. The Inspector composed himself and inhaled audibly.

"Shit! I'm going to be canned!" Bob silently concluded.

"Bob, I'm proud of you in your growing detective skills and deductive reasoning. You're asking the right questions, and you're correct that we still have many gaps. We still have quite a lot of old fashion detective work to complete before we can make an arrest. Sounds like you have plenty of work to do over the next couple of days," the Inspector replied. "Anything else?" he asked, daring his young pupils to repeat Bob's final question. None, not even Bob, dared to repeat it.

It had obviously struck a nerve, and by doing so, appeared to confine the topic to further secrecy.

"If nothing else, then our meeting is dismissed. Bob, I need to speak with you in private," the Inspector instructed.

"Shit, here it comes!" Bob thought. Chen had a pained expression on his face as if to say, "Why did you ask that question?" He and Molly left the room leaving the two men alone.

"Have a seat, Bob."

"Yes, Sir. I didn't mean to offend, Sir."

There was silence as Bob sat in the seat opposite the Inspector's desk. The Inspector sat behind his desk in a position of authority. He once again inhaled audibly.

"Bob."

"Yes, Sir."

"You did a nice job thinking this through, and your crime scene work is second to none."

"Thank you, Sir." Bob was sweating. "Here comes the 'but'," he thought.

"But," the Inspector paused for effect.

"Shit! There's the 'but'." Bob braced himself.

"But, you're beginning to mix facts with your opinions. Be careful of that. A good detective sticks to the facts."

"Yes, Sir," replied Bob visibly relieved. "Is that it? Is that all there is to the 'but'?" he thought.

"One other thing, Bob. You're right about Fulton. I also need to be careful. Thanks for the warning. I didn't realize I was being so transparent. I'll tell you about my history with Fulton and you can share it with the team, as I'm sure you would anyway. But, please don't share it any further because I don't want it to compromise the investigation by making me seem biased, which I assure that I'm not," the Inspector clarified.

Bob deeply admired this man. He never ceased to amaze him in his leadership qualities. Instead of chastising Bob for daring to touch upon a sensitive subject, he was thanking him for approaching it and was about to explain it.

"Sir, I'm sure that you have a good reason, knowing your character and all." Bob voiced his respect.

"Thank you for you confidence, Bob, but as you can appreciate, any grudge on my part would be wrong."

Bob simply nodded his head, relieved that he would not be fired.

"You see, Bob, many years ago my oldest daughter, Angie, met a promising young man, two years her elder. They met here at the local high school. She fell in love. She fell hard. I could tell. This young man broke her heart when he cheated on her with another, with one of her best friends. It's not an unusual story, especially at that age. But what makes it so painful and hard to forgive is that she tried to commit suicide as a result. Luckily, we saved her and she has gone on to live a happy and stable life, but not without extensive psychological support and not without a huge pain to her and to our family. She tried to poison herself," the Inspector admitted quietly. "The repercussions of it all strained my marriage beyond repair." The Inspector picked up the picture of Angie that was on his desk and looked at it lovingly. "But, she's fine now and I must release any and all grudges. Thank you, Bob, for reminding me of my responsibilities."

"What does this have to do with Jack Fulton?" Bob asked naively.

"He was the boy that broke Angie's heart."

CHAPTER 41

The Mad Hatter

*M*olly went home early. She wanted to get ready for her date with Jack Fulton. Despite all of her attempts at remaining emotionally detached from the case, she felt a deep anxiety about tonight. She could not explain it, but she had butterflies in her stomach.

As she pulled into the parking lot of Ms. Nightingale's manor, she ran into Chester. To her shock, he was rummaging through two large dumpsters located behind the building. As he saw her pull in, he disappeared into one of them.

"Chester?" she called out as she got out of the car. "Are you all right?"

"Purrrfectly fine!" Chester replied as he popped his head out of the massive green metal container.

"What are you doing in there?"

"It's a hobby. I like to recycle," he replied wearing his large ear-to-ear smile.

"Recycle? I don't get it!" Molly was genuinely confused as to why a grown man would be inside a dumpster full of trash.

Chester disappeared, only to pop out of the bin holding a worn button-down sweater. "Look at this gem! Can you believe that someone threw this out? It's nearly new, and just my size."

"It's a lady's sweater, Chester. What're you going to do with it?"

"Wear it, of course! No one will know that it's a lady's sweater." Chester proceeded to put it on while still standing next to the dumpster, and began to model it for Molly. "Looks great! Doesn't it? Feels great, too. I'm lucky to find this. It's a purrrrfect fit! I can't believe someone would throw this out. "

"It has a worn hole on the right elbow," Molly replied as she gathered her belongings out of the car. She was no longer looking at Chester for his hobby did not sit well with her.

"It does? Where?" Chester examined his new treasure. "Oh, yes, but that's nothing. I love it. It's my favorite color, purple."

"Well, enjoy it, Chester. But be careful, it runs if you wash it on hot."

"How do you know so much about my new sweater?" Chester asked, puzzled.

Molly did not look up until she was at the back door. "Because I threw it out."

"Oh!" Chester re-examined his prize in a new light, but decided to keep it regardless.

"Odd guy, but I'm starting to warm up to him, even if he's wearing my reject clothes," she chuckled and headed to her room, while Chester dove back into the dumpster, sweater and all.

As Molly neared her apartment, she heard a deep, guttural sobbing. It was coming from Helga's room. "This place is truly a nut house," Molly concluded to herself. After she placed all of her belongings in her room, she knocked on Helga's door. There was a sudden pause in the crying. All was quiet, except for a crash from the dumpsters below. Molly ran to the window at the end of the hall. Looking down she saw the tail end of Chester, who was busy digging through the second dumpster.

She opened the window and yelled down to him. "Are you all right?"

"Purrrfect!" he yelled back looking up at her. "Look at these pants!" he exclaimed in excitement at his latest find.

"Those are mine, too!" she replied.

"Really? Well, next time let me know before you throw out these gems. Actually, on second thought, just let me know after you throw them out. I enjoy the hunt." He smiled his characteristic smile and disappeared into the pile of trash.

"What a nut!" she concluded and suddenly remembered Helga. Returning back to Helga's door, she noticed that the crying had stopped. "Maybe I should just let it go," Molly reasoned to herself. Returning to her room, she received a shock. There, on her window ledge, sat Helga, looking hopeless, her feet dangling three floors above the parking lot below.

"Oh my God! She's going to jump!" Molly rushed toward her window in alarm. "Helga! Stop! It's not worth it, whatever it is! Life's a gift!" Molly screamed as she opened the window.

Helga greeted her with a smile. "Alice! What are you doing here?" she asked calmly.

"Helga, are you all right? Please come down from there," Molly pleaded nervously, taken back by the scene and the misplaced reference to Alice. "I must've imagined that she just called me that," she reasoned in her head.

"I'm doing just great. Look at that fool down there picking through the trash! Is he pathetic or what?" Helga pointed down at Chester, who was completely in his element.

"Well, he's an odd one, but seemingly harmless."

"Harmless!" Helga suddenly snapped at Molly. "He killed my Pogo, and I'll get my revenge on that little rat!" She growled as her eyes glared down at Chester. Suddenly, she switched to the sweetest tone. "Come sit out here with me. It's most exhilarating. Come." She patted the ledge next to her.

"No thanks, Helga. I don't do well with heights. Do you sit out there often?"

"Yes, I do. I can see my little kingdom from here," she pointed at the rose garden below. "Isn't it beautiful? Do you like the white roses? Maybe they should be red."

"I like the white roses, Helga. But, can you get off that ledge? You're making me nervous."

"Oh, if you insist," Helga replied and climbed into Molly's apartment through the open window. "Looks like you finished unpacking. I like it," she looked about Molly's room.

"Thanks," Molly replied, but before she could say another word, Helga was seated on her couch, completely at home. "Do you have any tea? We could have a tea party."

"Just the two of us?"

"Sure."

Molly went into her small kitchen and began to brew some tea. She looked at her watch. It was nearly six o'clock. It was then that she remembered her date with Jack Fulton. "How fitting," she thought, "all we need is for Jack, the Mad Hatter, to show up at our tea party." She chuckled at the idea.

As soon as the tea was done, the two women sat next to each other on the couch. Helga was happy to have a friend and beamed as she sipped her tea. "I'm glad that you moved next door. You're a sweet girl, Alice," Helga replied with a smile.

"Helga, I don't mean to offend, but I'm Molly, not Alice," Molly corrected her.

"Yes, of course! Did I call you Alice? My mistake. How awful! Alice is the one that lived here before you. She was a sweet girl, as well, until she got mixed up with him."

"Him? Him who? What happened?" Molly stopped sipping her tea.

"Well, he drove her mad. She was a wreck, crying all the time and imagining that she was in Wonderland of all places. Can you imagine that? A grown woman thinking she's Alice in Wonderland?" Helga shook her head and took a long loud sip of her tea. "When she first got here, she was fine; she was a lot like you, in fact. She seemed so kind and innocent. We use to sip tea right here on this very couch. Then, she fell in love with him and all went to pieces." Helga took another loud slurp.

"Who?" Molly was on the edge of the couch. She nearly fell off before Helga could reply for she was startled by a strong knock on the door.

"Were you expecting company?" Helga looked up, raising her unibrow.

Molly looked at her watch. "That can't be him. He'd be over a half hour early," she thought, and without replying to Helga, she got up and opened the door.

To her surprise, Jack was early for the date, but just in time for the tea party. Ironically, he was wearing a worn black top hat.

"Him!" Helga cried out as she stood up in surprise, spilling her tea.

It was the last thing that Molly heard before fainting into Jack's arms.

CHAPTER 42

Chesterfield Revisited

Bob could not stop thinking about the discrepancy between Kelly Allen's testimony and that of the bus driver, Mr. Chesterfield. With the Inspector's permission, he decided to visit the recluse bus driver to see if he could shed some light on the case. As he approached the small shabby shack on Ryan Ridge Road, he was struck by the plethora of junk that surrounded it on all sides, covering the front lawn and doubling as a home for countless stray cats.

"What a mess!" Bob exclaimed as he got out of his car. As he neared the dilapidated residence, he became aware of a beautiful sound that contrasted the bedlam about him. It was the sound of a saxophone. Not any old squeaky saxophone, but the most enchanting saxophone imaginable. It lamented a loss in a powerful expression of emotions, weeping over that loss in such a moving way that Bob had to stop in his tracks. "My God!" he said aloud. "That's amazing!"

Bob knew a bit about the blues and the saxophone. Although he had mastered the instrument, he preferred the trumpet, which he played most weekends in a local blues band. But this was far beyond anything that he or his fellow band members could create. This was music so powerful that it ignited the soul, revealing it in a form that left no doubt of its existence. This was a master that had excelled at his art. Bob simply stood there and enjoyed the bewildering moment. He did not want to interrupt it. Leaning against a broken washing machine in Mr. Chesterfield's front yard, he rested his own soul and listened.

He found himself slowly slumping into the grassy lawn, while still propped against the old washing machine. He was at the concert of a lifetime. Closing his eyes, he drifted with the music into a tranquil place. He reflected on the people in his life, on all that was important and then on her. She kept coming back into his mind as the saxophone played homage to love eternal, love discovered, love unfulfilled and love lost. With the pretty face of Suzy Kurtz in his mind, Bob drifted to sleep in Mr. Chesterfield's front yard, blending between the abandoned rusty washer and a worn plaster statue of Athena.

It was dark when Bob awakened. He looked at his watch and jumped up in alarm. The music had stopped and the lights were on in Mr. Chesterfield's house. Looking back at his watch, he had a dilemma. It was nearly 8 pm, rather late to bother a man at his home. Nonetheless, he decided to approach the rusty old door and knocked softly, cautiously.

He was about to change his mind and leave, when the door opened. There stood Mr. Chesterfield leaning against the door frame. He looked like he had had a little too much gin and smelled the part. "Who're you, and what do you want?" he asked in a guttural tone as six cats ran around Bob's legs and eagerly disappeared into the dark night.

"Mr. Chesterfield, Sir. My name is Bob Braxton. I'm with the State Police." Bob flashed his badge. "I was hoping that I could ask you a few questions regarding the Mary Collins case."

"Police! Am I in some kind of trouble? I swear I didn't mean to run that yellow light with the school bus the other day. I simply didn't see it. No one got hurt or anything. The intersection was empty. Oh, did you say you're here 'cause of the Mary Collins case?" The penny had finally dropped in the alcohol-infused mind of old Mr. Chesterfield.

"Yes, Sir." Bob replied. "Can I come in, Sir?"

"I guess, but the place's a mess. I was gonna clean over the weekend," Mr. Chesterfield lied. He had last cleaned the house four years ago, when his girlfriend was still alive. Since then, Mary would sometimes clean it when she visited. He missed Mary, just as he missed Agnes, the only true love that he had ever known. He and Agnes were together for 18 years, but never married. Agnes was a free spirit, a singer. She did not believe in marriage or anything that needed the approval of a government or a church. "But, boy, could she sing! And, boy, could she make love," Mr. Chesterfield reflected to himself, as he did nearly every day for the past four years. "Boy, do I miss her!" he lamented silently, as he offered the police officer a seat on his dirty, worn couch.

"Sir, I'm sorry to intrude, but I have a few questions regarding your testimony in the Mary Collins case." Bob politely repeated the purpose of his visit to the old gentleman, as the latter sat down in his favorite ragged recliner.

"Sure, but my memory isn't what it use to be, except when it comes to music. You see, I don't have to remember music. It simply passes through me from somewhere much higher, much more beautiful than this world. The music isn't mine." Mr. Chesterfield was feeling the gin and instantly diverted the conversation to his passion, music. "Of course, I play the instrument but the music isn't mine. The music comes as it wishes. It simply passes through my heart and out through the instrument, to be released, free at last." Mr. Chesterfield shared his simple creed. "Would you like a drink?" he asked.

"No, thank you," Bob replied. "Sir, your music, or rather the music that you…"

"Channel. My dear Agnes always claimed that I channeled the music. She claimed that I was simply a way for… for it to have a voice," he stuttered and paused to take another drink of cheap gin. "Are you sure that you don't want any?"

"No, thank you, Sir," Bob replied politely. He liked the odd old man.

"Where was I?" old Chesterfield asked.

"You were talking about channeling music and how it passes through you," Bob reminded him, fascinated by this foreign philosophy.

"Ah, yes, well it's simply what most folks call inspiration. Do you think that Mozart analyzed and thought about each note that he wrote as he was rapidly scribbling some of the most inspired music ever written? No! He heard it in his head because it was simply passing through him. It was playing in his head. He channeled it. The same with many great artists that simply start with a blank canvas or a block of clay, and all comes of its own accord without a plan, without a thought, without an idea of what is to come. It's that way with the great writers, the poets, the actors and the inventors. Shakespeare's plays, channeled! Einstein's relativity, channeled! Most of the great religious writings, like the 3,000 year old Hindu Bhagavad Gita, channeled!"

Mr. Chesterfield was on a roll, which had left Big Bob miles behind, still feeling like he was somewhere between a rusty washer and the enchanting goddess Athena. "A sustained inspiration is nothing more than a channel and a channel is nothing more than sustained inspiration. They're the same thing, Agnes claimed." Mr. Chesterfield seemed much too philosophical for a bus driver, and Bob was sincerely puzzled. He felt like he had entered an ethereal world of either a true genius or a delusional fool. Yet, the old man's truths seemed to resonate even in the simple, practical mind of Bob Braxton. The sermon made sense on a deeper level beyond Bob's comfort zone.

The wise old man continued his passionate lecture, which was no less absorbing than was his music, hours earlier. "All these great inspirations are simply our connection to a higher place, to a higher self, to our very eternal soul. Agnes taught me all this and she was right. She was my muse and the music followed. I miss her so much!" Mr. Chesterfield took another chug of gin. He was a humble man in possession of deep truths and a pure heart. The two were a strain on the logical, fretting mind that was necessary for daily existence. Only the music provided him an outlet for who he was deep inside, or as he put it, "for the true me, beyond this old body".

Bob, despite his imposing size and appearance, was a sensitive man, simple but sensitive. Although his mind struggled with these truths, his sensitive receptiveness related to this old man's hard-earned wisdom. "Your music is some of the most beautiful that I've ever heard, Sir. I really mean that. It's truly soulful, as you say."

"Thank you, young man. As I told you, it's not mine. I simply have the honor to play it. Now, since you won't join me in a drink, tell me again why you're here?" Mr. Chesterfield sipped his gin.

"Of course, Sir," Bob began once more. "I'm here to ask you to confirm who you saw entering the upper terrace of the old Kamerynville quarry immediately before or about the time that Mary fell from that location. In your original testimony, you claimed you saw Suzy Kurtz and that she was alone as she entered the area right before you heard her scream?" Bob had his note pad out and was back in detective mode. "May I record this part of the conversation, Mr. Chesterfield?"

"Sure. Yeah."

"Great!" Bob turned on his mini recorder, and placed it on the stained and cluttered coffee table in front of Mr. Chesterfield.

"What's your name again, young man?" Mr. Chesterfield asked as he took another drink of gin.

"Bob Braxton."

"Well, Bob, I told all that to that short inspector with the mustache. You know him?"

"Yes. I do, Sir. He's my boss."

"Well, what I told your boss is what I'll tell you. I saw Suzy Kurtz enter, and that brat Randell, as well as that self-centered instructor that lead the trip. I forgot his name," Mr. Chesterfield paused.

"What about any others? Were there others?" Bob inquired.

"Yes, that football jock. You know the one. Italian name."

"Tony. Tony Bond?" Bob assisted the old man in remembering. Then, he stopped for he realized that he should not lead the witness.

"Yes, Tony," Mr. Chesterfield confirmed.

"Anyone else?"

"Sure. There were others, but I can't remember their names. I'm simply the bus driver. I only know the kids that stand out."

"I understand. So, you're not sure who else entered the upper terrace area where the unfortunate event occurred," Bob clarified.

"No, but there were others, if I recall. There were a few more girls, but I don't know their names."

"Was Suzy Kurtz with one of those girls when she entered the area?" Bob felt that he was getting close to unraveling the discrepancy between Kelly's testimony and Mr. Chesterfield's. He could feel it coming.

"Yes, she was. She was with a tall, dark-haired, slender girl in a white shirt. I don't know her name."

"That sounds like Kelly Allen, Sir."

"If you say so."

"Anything else that you recall? Can you describe any of the other girls?" Bob asked.

"Well, that Randell fellow was with a little blonde that was rather unforgettable. She seemed overdressed for a geology field trip. Pretty girl. If I were a young man, I'd have gone after that one," Mr. Chesterfield laughed. "But, she sure was oddly dressed for a field trip."

"What do you mean?" Bob asked.

"She had on a fancy blue dress with a big blue ribbon in her hair. She looked like a southern belle out of an old movie. It sure was a strange outfit for a field trip. That Randell was all over her like a big bear on honey, and honey she was, mind you. Even an old man could tell that. Like I said, if only I were thirty years younger." Mr. Chesterfield laughed a hearty, good-natured laugh.

"That was Stacy Reed."

"Well hallelujah, Miss Stacy!" Mr. Chesterfield laughed again. He was feeling the drink now.

"Can you describe anyone else that entered there?"

"Yes, there was the girl that sat right next to Mary on the ride out. She was acting odd. She kept doting on Mary. If you ask me, she was a little too smitten with Mary. But, when that Randell fellow was bothering Mary on the bus, this girl stood up for her, right after he got off the bus. I though she was gonna get in a fight with him. She was very protective and dressed down, a tomboy type. I don't know her name, but she was keen on Mary." Mr. Chesterfield replied before taking another drink.

"Was she rather tall, long legged, jet black hair?"

"Yeah, that was her. Sort of quiet and mousy until she got all riled up by that Randell bastard."

"That sounds like Daphne Marconi," Bob confirmed, not able to help himself.

"If you say so. I like that girl. Lot of spunk! But I tell you, I wouldn't want to get on the wrong side of her, if you know what I mean?" Mr. Chesterfield smiled and took another drink of gin.

"Can you elaborate, Sir?" Bob asked.

"Well, like I said, I thought that your Daphne was going to punch out that Randell bastard after he said something else to Mary. It was after they all got off the bus, so, I couldn't hear the conversation. But, your girl was pretty upset even though Mary stayed very calm," Mr. Chesterfield explained. "Kids! Youth is totally wasted on the young!" He took another drink to emphasize his point.

"Then, what happened?" Bob was curious.

"Well, Mary and this Daphne went off their own way, and Randell huddled with his two friends, the two boys that sat with him at the back of the bus. But as soon as he spotted that southern blonde, he was off to woo her. Nothing but hormones, that one."

"Did you hear Mary's scream?"

"No, but I heard the piercing one that got everyone excited."

"That was Suzy Kurtz."

"If you say so."

"Okay. This helps a lot. Do you mind telling me about your relationship with Mary?"

"There's nothing to tell," Mr. Chesterfield replied sharply.

"I see, but I recall from your interview with Cabot that you and Mary are very close," Bob inquired.

"Who's Cabot?" Mr. Chesterfield suddenly seemed defensive.

"My boss, the inspector that interviewed you the first time."

"The short guy with the mustache?"

"Yeah, that's the one." Bob had to chuckle to himself. His boss was universally described as the "short guy with the mustache".

"I never said anything of the sort."

"Maybe I'm mistaken. Sorry about that. Anyway, thank you for your time and for the concert."

"When did you hear me play?"

"Before I showed up."

"How long were you out there? I stopped playing hours ago?"

Bob felt embarrassed and his face flushed. He had betrayed himself and did not know how to respond. "I was here earlier, but didn't want to disturb you while you were playing. Then, I got called away on some business. But, I got to listen long enough to appreciate it." Bob weaseled his way out of the questioning. "I play the blues, as well, mostly trumpet. Have you ever heard of a local band, the Bama Blues?" Bob asked.

"No. It's a blues band, huh?" Mr. Chesterfield perked up.

"Yes, Sir."

"Good, but you're lying!"

"No! I'm not. I really do play in the Bama Blues," Bob objected.

"Not that, about being called away for other business."

"Well…"

"Look, I can tell that you're lying. I too lied to you about not knowing Mary very well. She and I are close friends. She's like a daughter to me that I never had and always prayed for." Mr. Chesterfield was tearing up while poured himself another glass of gin.

"Sir?"

"Yeah. Life sucks at times. I seem to always lose the most beautiful and precious women in my life, and I can tell you that Agnes and Mary were the best of the best." He tried hard not to cry into his drink.

"Sorry, Sir, I had no idea that you were that close," Bob felt embarrassed. He did not know what to do, seeing the old man tearing up. Luckily, before he could look for a non-existent box of tissues, Mr. Chesterfield composed himself.

"Sorry about that outburst. Being a musician, I get a little emotional. Comes with the territory," Mr. Chesterfield explained.

"No worries! I completely understand." Bob reflected at the times he cried alone for hours after his mother died. He inhaled audibly at that recollection. "No problem, Sir. I completely understand," he repeated in a sincere tone.

"I know you do. You've cried a few times too, right son? Otherwise, you couldn't play the blues." Mr. Chesterfield wisely proclaimed.

"Yes, Sir. Very true, Sir."

"Well, Mary and I met a few years ago when I was a security guard at her dorm. She was always so friendly and unassuming. She was the kind of person that noticed all the 'little' people and treated them as 'big' people." He chuckled to himself. "She laughed at all my jokes and reminded me of my dear Agnes. Maybe that's why I took to her so quickly. Yes, she reminded me of Agnes and still does," he reflected and sighed.

"Anyway, where was I? Oh, yes, there isn't much to share with you and your recorder," he glanced at the coffee table. "We became friends. Eventually, I told her that I played the saxophone. Once she found out, she wanted to hear me play. That was just like Mary," he paused and smiled at the thought of her. "After she heard me play," he sighed as he continued to reflect on those precious times, "she started coming here twice a week to keep me company and to listen to me play. She used to say that it was like listening to the angels sing." He began to choke up again and paused to take a deep breath. "I can't believe that someone would harm such a wonderful, innocent girl. It makes me so angry. She's all that's good about this world and look what comes of it." He fell silent and took a long, hard drink.

"I can only imagine your pain, Sir. Everyone we talk to describes her the same way. She has had quite a positive impact on many people. I'm sorry. I truly am. God willing, she'll recover soon." Bob too knew loss and could genuinely relate. But, in Mary's case, there was still hope, and he wanted to stress that to the old man.

"Yes, God willing!" Mr. Chesterfield echoed, accenting his reply with another sip of gin. "Anyway, on a lighter subject, you can't fool an old fool, my boy. When I went out to check my mailbox this evening, I saw you sleeping there in my front yard among my old toys." Mr. Chesterfield had a knowing grin, and his wrinkled face lit up with mischievous youth.

"You did, huh?" Bob smiled back, no longer embarrassed. Somehow in sharing their personal grief and their love of music, the two men were becoming friends.

"I figured you needed the sleep, and if you had come to see me, why you'd eventually reach the door." The old man laughed a most hardy and contagious laugh. It was clear to Bob now why a young orphaned girl like Mary would choose this kind-hearted, jovial man as her surrogate father. One could not help but like the man, especially once he laughed.

The two laughed some more in genuine harmony, as Bob shut off the tape recorder and put it in his pocket. "Do you mind if we use this as testimony?" he asked, referring to the taped conversation.

"No. Go right ahead, if it helps capture and convict the bastard that did this to my Mary."

"Oops, I forgot to record that permission," Bob observed and turned on the recorder once more.

"Mr. Chesterfield, can we use this conversation as testimony in the Mary Collins case?" Bob asked formally into the recorder.

"Yes, you may," Mr. Chesterfield replied formally.

"Great!" Bob added and turned off the recorder. "Okay, I'm done with work for tonight."

"Good, then let me pour you a generous drink," Mr. Chesterfield replied with a smile. "Gin or scotch?"

"Scotch!" Bob replied and after that the conversation was all about music and philosophy, with a touch of spirituality added by Mr. Chesterfield at appropriate opportunities.

It was nearly midnight when the new-found friends parted. "So, you promise to come to my band practice, right? We have one tomorrow night at my friend Jessie's place. Here's the address." Bob handed Mr. Chesterfield a piece of paper.

"I don't perform in public," Mr. Chesterfield objected.

"It's just practice. One step at a time. What would Mary say, if she were here?"

Mr. Chesterfield smiled at the thought of Mary. "She would be pushing me out the door. She would say, 'Pops, you must do it, and I'll go with you!' That's what she'd say. She use to call me 'Pops' of late." Mr. Chesterfield was tearing up again.

"Well, Pops Chesterfield, listen to your muse and come play with us tomorrow night," Bob replied and shook Mr. Chesterfield's hand. "You know, Pops Chesterfield is a great stage name," he added with a chuckle.

"Maybe!" Mr. Chesterfield replied. "Are you planning on sleeping next to that washer again?" he added.

"Not tonight! Once a week's enough."

The two parted joyfully. As Mr. Chesterfield closed the door, he smiled at the thought of Big Bob. "Nice lad… Good heart… I guess when the good Lord closes a door, he opens a window," he whispered to himself as he headed to bed.

The Unthinkable

As she opened her eyes, Molly saw a handsome man leaning over her while holding an ice pack to her head. He was close enough that she could reach up and kiss him. At the sight of him, she wanted to do just that in her dazed state, until she became fully aware of his identity. With that realization, she pulled back in a shudder.

"Are you okay? Is the ice too cold? You gave me a fright when you fainted," he confessed.

"What happened?" Molly asked, genuinely confused.

"You fainted when you saw me in this silly old top hat that Chester gave me as I was heading up here. I'm so sorry to scare you like that," Jack Fulton replied in an apologetic tone. "I thought it would make you laugh, not faint. Had I known that you were so sensitive to top hats, I wouldn't have worn it. Are you feeling any better? Helga left 'cause she had a class on military strategy. She's an odd one, that Helga." He smiled and removed the ice pack.

"It's not Helga that I'm worried about," Molly thought, further alarmed at being in her own room with this strange man, who was a key suspect in an attempted homicide, or worse, attempted murder. "How long had she been alone with him? What had he done to her in the meantime?" she thought as she looked to see if her clothes were in order. They were. "I'm getting paranoid," she concluded silently.

"I'm glad that you're awake. I was getting ready to call 911," Jack added, smiling at her.

"How long was I out?" she asked, still disoriented.

"About ten minutes. Do you want some water?" he asked gallantly.

"No, thanks, or maybe, yes. Water's good," Molly muttered as she sat up on the couch. "Why did you come so early? I thought you were coming at seven?" Molly was starting to remember now.

"Oh, darn it! I had entered six in my calendar. I thought that I was running late. My bad. You want me to come back later?" he asked sincerely.

"He's so damn cute," Molly thought. She now realized why she had had the butterflies in her stomach about seeing him. She was genuinely attracted to the young graduate student. "Yes, well, no, but I need to get ready. Where are we going?" she sounded confused again.

"Nowhere until you feel better. Maybe we should order out. I know a great Japanese take out."

"Okay, but I must look like a mess," she heard herself say. "Why did I just say that? I sound like I'm into him," she thought. "Damn, I am into him! Who wouldn't be? Look at him!" she concluded to herself.

"You look great. I promise. Beautiful, in fact." He smiled and lightened the room.

She felt herself blush. "Damn it! Now, I'm blushing like a school girl. I can never control that damn blushing. How do some people control that?" her mind was racing through endless fields of doubt and insecurity.

He noticed the blush and was flattered. He too was extremely attracted to this lovely newcomer at the house. She seemed to have it all. Brains, looks, confidence and even mystery. It was a hard combination to resist.

"Thanks," was all that she could muster. "Oh my God, now I'm tongue tied," she thought. "Damn this assignment! I'm attracted to a potential villain. That's my problem. I'm always attracted to the bad boys," she continued her silent, self-indulgent critique.

"So, are you okay with sushi?" he asked as he returned with a glass of water, before sitting next to her on the couch.

"A little too close," she thought. "He's a forward one. Lots of practice, I'm sure. What a casanova! And I, what a fool! I fainted into his arms for goodness sakes. How pathetic." Her self-doubt continued to haunt her distraught mind. "I love sushi," she heard herself say. "I hate sushi," she thought.

"Great! So do I. Do you like rolls, or just plain sushi?"

"Oh, for goodness sake, why's this so complicated?" she thought. "Rolls," she heard herself say.

"Me too," he beamed, as if she had just agreed to marry him. "Rainbow sound good?"

"Yeah, great! You order it. It's all good," she heard herself say. "Rainbow what? This is hopeless," she thought.

"I know, you're still shaken by all that happened. Are you sure that you'll be all right eating sushi?"

"Sure," she heard herself say. "Damn, that was may chance to get out of this and I blew it," she thought. "What's wrong with me? I'm acting like a starry-eyed girl."

"Actually, how about a cheeseburger instead?" she finally admitted aloud.

"Okay, that's a switch. Sure. We can order a cheeseburger. But where? I must admit that I'm vegetarian," he replied with a smile.

"Oh, this is getting more and more awkward," she concluded to herself. "I like vegetables. A salad would be fine." She replied staring into his eyes just a little too long. "Damn it! He knows. I just gave it away. Rule number one: 'You never let them know

233

how much you like them until they tell you first.' I just broke rule number one," she silently chastised herself.

"Yeah, salad is good. I have another idea. There's a great Mediterranean take out up the street. Do you like Mediterranean food?" he asked.

"Love it! I get it all the time. Let's do that." She was relieved to be free of sushi.

"Great! What do you like?"

"Anything. Hummus and pitas, you name it. You can pick. I like it all," she replied. " 'I like it all?' What am I saying? I sound like a desperate call girl," she chastised herself once more in her fretting mind.

"Okay, anything else?"

"You can surprise me since you seem to be talented at that," she replied.

"Yes," he chuckled. "Yes, that hat." He looked toward the door at the top hat that lay on the floor, where it had fallen when Molly fainted. "I'm throwing it out. No more hat."

"Oh, it's not the hat. The hat's really cute," she replied. " 'The hat's really cute?' What am I saying? I sound like a sixteen year old," she thought.

"Here, you wear it!" Before she could object, he playfully placed the top hat on her head. "Wow! You look pretty hot in that," he added.

She blushed again. "My boss is going to kill me if I fall for his key suspect," is all she could think about while she struck a seductive pose for Jack.

He smiled back. A pheromone-induced flirtation frenzy was firing between them before the take out arrived. Then came the wine. By the time the clock struck midnight, Molly had committed the unthinkable. She was in bed with Jack Fulton, and she was wearing nothing but a top hat.

CHAPTER 44

A Brief Debrief

When Molly awoke, she found herself alone. All that remained of the night was an old top hat and an all-encompassing satisfaction that she had not felt for much too long. Unfortunately, this state of bliss was quickly extinguished by the shrill of her cell phone. Still drowsy, she picked up the phone.

"Where are you? You missed the meeting this morning? Did you get to interview Fulton?" the Inspector asked. He was obviously concerned and irritated all in one.

Molly was taken back as she looked at the alarm clock near her bed. "Shit!" she exclaimed over the phone. "I mean, sorry, I overslept."

"Well, get in here! Did you get to talk to Fulton?" he insisted.

"Yeaaahhh," she replied slowly. "I did."

"What did you find out?" he asked.

"Oh, baby, what did I find out!" she thought. "I found out that I want to major in geology," she replied cryptically.

"What?!"

"Nothing. I mean that we talked a lot about geology. But I'll fill you in when I get there."

"Okay, hurry! Bob did some fine investigating last night and the case is getting tighter. You know that guy's really coming along," the Inspector admitted. "He really seems to be throwing all of himself into this case. You know what I mean?"

"Yes, I sure do, Boss!"

"Are you okay? You sound different," he observed.

"I'm great. Fantastic even! "

"Okay, see you soon." He hung up the phone and reflected, "If I didn't know better, it would appear that our uptight Molly got herself... no, that's impossible!" He dismissed the obvious.

Molly took her time getting to work. She was still in a state of euphoria from the night before and did not want to lose that feeling. She knew that as soon as she got to work, it would be gone. "Sleeping with the enemy. Nothing like it," she chuckled. "I guess that makes me a bad girl." She chuckled some more as she got dressed. "Me, a bad girl! Funny!" She posed in the full length mirror in nothing but her birthday suit and the top hat. "I do make a pretty good, bad girl." She giggled as she admired her reflection. She felt like a new person. How could that be? She felt wanted and cherished, which felt amazing. "It's so wrong, yet so right. Wow!" She smiled as she got dressed.

As she drove to the office, reality began to press into her mind. "I'm such a fool! He's probably the one that pushed that poor girl over a cliff after she slept with him, and here I am falling into his trap just like she must have, and just like Alice. Oh, God, I'm Alice!" She suddenly panicked and nearly hit the curb.

By the time she arrived at the office, the euphoria was replaced by self-loathing and embarrassment. "How could I be such a fool? This had better not get out. That guy's a predator. He preys on woman like some kind of a charming vampire. I let him prey on me. I slept with a key suspect in a potential homicide. If this gets out, I'm fired and publicly embarrassed to boot." She was a nervous wreck as she reached police headquarters. "Compose yourself," she instructed her racing mind.

After pulling into the parking lot at police headquarters, she rubbed her hands across her neck as if to check for vampire bites. "I'm probably just another conquest, another piece of meat. I'm a fool. What am I going to tell my boss? He must suspect. He's bound to grill me since he seems to hate this guy. I don't blame him. I hate this guy!" She concluded, having traveled a complete 180 degree mental journey since leaving the house. She walked into the office with resolve and a newfound disdain for Jack Fulton, except for the part in her that still really liked him.

The Inspector was eagerly awaiting her in his office. "There you are. What took you so long? Did you get lost?"

"Very funny, Boss. I got here as quickly and safely as I could. There was an accident on the highway, and it had everything backed up," she lied.

"Oh, okay. Well, tell me what happened with Fulton. I want to know every detail of what you found out about Fulton and his ties to Mary," he demanded, propped on the edge of his seat.

"Everything?" she thought and nearly laughed before quickly composing herself. "There's not much to tell, Boss. I hate to disappoint. He seems like a nice guy, charming for sure, but suspicious as you observed," Molly replied nervously.

"Skip the generalities, Molly. The facts, what are the facts? What was his real relationship with Mary? We know that he slept with her at least once, that predator!"

There, again, was that word associated with Jack Fulton. Molly shuddered at the thought that she was Jack Fulton's latest prey. If her boss ever found out, her career would be over. She shuddered again.

"Are you cold? You're shivering?"

"Am I? I'm not feeling well. I woke up with a headache and a sore," she paused and almost laughed at what had entered her mind at the end of that sentence.

"A sore throat?" he finished her sentence, but looked at her in puzzlement.

"Yes, a sore throat," she replied with a stern expression.

"Yes, of course. So, did you get anything else out of him?" The Inspector was frustrated by Molly's seeming lack of information.

"Nothing that words could properly describe. I mean nothing in words that would be relevant to the case," she corrected her slip. "Focus, Molly! You almost blew it!" She silently chastised herself.

"What does that mean, 'nothing in words'? What were you two doing? Playing charades?" He was getting annoyed.

"No, we weren't playing charades, Boss. What I mean is that he seemed suspicious in his body movements." She was sweating. "What am I saying? Focus, Molly!" she thought trying to regain her composure during the awkward exchange.

"Body movements? What are you talking about? You're not making any sense today."

"I didn't mean body movements. I meant body language. He seemed suspicious in his body language, and I agree that he's a predator," she clarified.

"That he is! I'll vouch for that!"

"Me too!" she added, and quickly left the room leaving her boss scratching his head.

CHAPTER 45

The Second Canary

After leaving her boss, Molly headed back to her cubical, relieved to have survived the interrogation. Once there, she was greeted by a cheery Chen, who was conspicuously staring at his watch. "Nice of you to come in before noon, Molly. You just made it."

"Shut up, Chen!" Molly dismissed him and sat down in her cubical.

"Nice to see you, too," he replied. "Ah, and there's Big Bob!" Chen said as Bob walked into the room. "What's with that grin, Bob? You look like a cat that just swallowed a canary."

"Buzz off, Chen!" Bob dismissed him.

"Everyone's so cheery, today. Even the boss expressed anger at this morning's meeting. Maybe it was because I was the only one at his morning meeting," Chen added.

"Molly, you were late as well?" Bob poked his head into Molly's cubical.

"Yeah, you too, huh?" she replied. They both ignored Chen.

"Yeah," Bob replied. "What was your excuse?" he added.

She smiled. Chen noticed the smile and added. "Another cat that swallowed a canary. What's going on here?"

"Shut up, Chen!" Molly and Bob replied in unison. That started everyone laughing and quickly broke the tension.

"So, why were you late, Bob?" Chen insisted.

Bob repeated the same smile.

"Who's the canary, Bob?" Chen added.

"I can't tell you, but I think I'm in love," Big Bob chuckled. "Oh, hell, I can't keep a secret." He now had everyone's full attention.

"Well, early this morning I got up and there was a text on my cell phone. It was from Suzy Kurtz. She accepted my invitation to go to band practice tonight. She wanted to see me play in the band. Is that cool or what?"

"So, why were you late? Did you go out and celebrate?" Chen teased.

"No!" Bob replied in an irritated tone. "Since she lives just down the hall, I went to see her."

"Yeah, and...?" Chen asked eagerly.

"Well, one thing led to another, and well.... Whew, baby! She's a hottie!" Bob was on cloud nine.

"Well, that explains one canary. Lucky for you, Bob, that she's officially cleared as a suspect in the Collins case. Otherwise, you'd have a problem. Who's your canary, Molly?" Chen asked, and all eyes were on her.

"What canary, Chen?" Molly replied in her best irritated voice. She turned to Bob and added, "I'm so happy for you, Bob, but I suggest that you keep this little bit of news a secret until this case blows over. We all know that Suzy is innocent, but it still doesn't look good if you're messing around with one of the original suspects and a present witness." As soon as she proclaimed this wise advise, she got a knot in her stomach. She realized that what she had done was far worse. At least Suzy was no longer a suspect, and obviously what transpired between her and Bob was mutually genuine, even if it was inappropriate given the circumstances. Bob did not sleep with a key potential homicide suspect. She realized what a risk she had created for herself and the department, and quickly fell silent.

"I hear you, Molly. That's good advice. So the two of you can't say a thing to anyone, especially not our boss," Bob pleaded.

"Mum's the word, Bob," Chen replied sincerely. Then, he turned to Molly. "So, who's the second canary?" he smiled.

"No canary, Chen. I hate canaries," she relied with a frown.

"Are you gay? You have that vibe," Chen added.

"Shut up, Chen!" Molly and Bob replied in unison.

CHAPTER 46

Band Practice

That evening, Big Bob headed to his friend Jessie's house to partake in his favorite pastime, playing jazz and blues. It was practice night. He had his trumpet under his arm as he entered Jessie's spacious garage. The garage had been meticulously transformed into a music studio, complete with a small stage, elaborate electronics and even a basic lighting system. Several fold-out chairs were strewn nearest the garage doors in anticipation of an audience that rarely materialized.

"Bob! There you are! We were about to give you a call. Johnny couldn't show up tonight, so we'll have to skip the sax solos." Jessie greeted Big Bob with a brotherly pat on the back. "Kenny added a fantastic drum solo at the end of the Havana Grove tune. It really rocks! Too bad Johnny's out and we won't hear it with the sax. I'm telling you, this may be the one. This may be the big hit. It's got a jazzy rock sound with a powerful blues blend, all in one!" Jessie was excited.

Kenny smiled at Bob and greeted him with a simple "Hey Man!" as he tuned his drums.

"Is Katie coming?" Bob asked in regards to their bass player.

"She should be here any minute," Jessie replied. He was clearly the leader of the band.

As soon as Katie arrived, the Bama Blues Band began their practice. They had been together as a band for over two years, although the core of the group, Jessie, Katie and Kenny, had been playing together two years longer. The Bama Blues were just starting to make a name for themselves in their hometown and had begun to have a small following on the internet. Things were looking up, except that they lacked a decent saxophone player. Johnny was undependable and often missed practices. Jessie wanted to replace him, but did not have an alternative.

Bob wanted to tell Jessie about Mr. Chesterfield, but decided not to complicate the situation, since it was unlikely that the recluse old man would be interested in the position and the commitment it required. "Last thing we need is a another sax player who never shows up," Big Bob had concluded.

The band was thirty minutes into practice, when the side door of the garage opened slowly. No one noticed as a pretty young blonde quietly walked into the room. Silently, she slumped into the nearest fold-out chair. Her energy was unavoidable and before she could settle into her seat, all of the male members of the band had their eyes transfixed on her. There was no doubt that she was beautiful. Yet, there was a inner joy about her that seemed new and made her almost sparkle. She was extremely happy. But, who was she and why was she here?

The band's energy rose with the new energy in the room, transforming an ordinary jazzy number into something much more. Once they finished, Jessie spoke on behalf of the band. "Welcome!" he said with a smile. "I'm Jessie. What brings you here?"

She smiled and was about to answer, when Big Bob leapt off the small stage to embrace her. They embraced like new lovers, uninhibited by a curious audience.

"This is Suzy. She's my neighbor." Bob introduced the young woman to the band.

"A neighbor. Is that all?" Suzy whispered to Bob.

Big Bob blushed and did not reply. Soon the entire band came forward to great their surprise guest.

"Please, don't let me interrupt your practice. I just want to sit and listen, if that's okay?" she asked in a melodic voice.

"You lucky dog!" Jessie enviously whispered to Bob as they resumed their places on stage.

Bob smiled. He was in love and that was all that mattered.

Suzy listened with a fixed smile of admiration on her face. She was genuinely happy. Her long, abusive relationship with Randell was over and a great weight had been lifted. Bob was everything that Randell was not and more. Ever since the day he saved her from Randell's rage, he was her hero, and she could not look at him in any other way.

Katie struggled with the vocals on the new, raspy blues tune that she and Jessie penned the week before. She was a talented bass player and an exceptional song writer, but lacked the vocal depth and power to propel the otherwise moving tune into passionate excellence. Jessie knew this, for he had a fine ear, but he did not dare to criticize his long-time girlfriend. It was Katie who suddenly stopped singing and admitted her frustration. "Damn, I hate that tune! I can't hit those last notes and get the gripping raspiness that's needed. Damn it!"

"It's fine," Jessie lied.

"Like hell it is!" Katie objected, for she knew better. She had written the song and knew what it needed. Then, she looked at Suzy as if she remembered her at last. "Now I know you, you go to McLaren!" she proclaimed, as she finally recognized her. "You're friends with my sister, Joanne."

"Joanne Stanley?"

"Yes, I'm Katie Stanley. She's my kid sister."

"Yeah, I know her," Suzy replied.

"Wait a minute, you sing. I've heard you sing. You played Juliette in that play last year."

Suzy smiled, "I'm not sure that I can sing, but I did play Juliette."

"She's modest. She can hit this note. I've heard her sing and she's good. Come on, Suzy. Try it! Try this number. I would gladly unload this song," Katie added and laughed.

After much convincing by all of the band members, and Bob in particular, Suzy reluctantly stepped up to the microphone. She looked at the music score and shook her head. "I'm not sure I can hit that."

"Come on! Try it! Let's take it from the top gang. Just do your best, Suzy!" Katie urged as Big Bob echoed his support.

What happened next would go down in band history, along with the rest of that magical night. Suzy not only hit the high note with ease, but she was a natural, transforming the promising melody into a haunting blues number that tugged at one's soul. Her raspy voice and her passionate delivery, energized the band to new levels.

"Wow!" Jessie spoke for the rest of the band once more. "That was amazing! You want to join the band?"

"But, I don't play anything," Suzy objected.

"No need! You just need to sing!" Jessie smiled. "That was soulful. Who would have guessed that you had that in you."

Suzy sighed, for despite her rich-girl exterior, she was a person who had suffered silently for years. All of that surfaced with the music, creating a mystifying vocal presence beyond anyone's expectations, even her own.

As the band celebrated their new found talent, they had not notice that a second surprise visitor had entered the room. Unlike Suzy, he was easily missed. Jessie was shocked at the sight of an old man sitting near the side door of the garage in one of the fold-out chairs.

"Mr. Chesterfield!" Big Bob exclaimed before Jessie had a chance to address the stranger.

Mr. Chesterfield rose and greeted the band.

"What a night for visitors!" Jessie spoke for the group.

"Mr. Chesterfield's a fantastic sax player," Bob bragged about his new friend. "I've never heard anyone better. Not even among the pros!" Bob exalted.

"Fantastic! Would you like to join us on stage? We just happen to be short a sax player tonight," Jessie urged the old man.

"I don't know. You're all young kids and I could be your grand-father." Mr. Chesterfield felt suddenly out of place. Suzy Kurtz was giving him an odd look, wondering why an old bus driver was being asked to join the band when only minutes earlier she was flattered by the same offer.

"Come on, Mr. Chesterfield! Play with us!" Big Bob urged. "Did you bring your sax?"

The old man reached to the floor for the saxophone case. Soon he produced a fine, but well-worn instrument.

"Wow! That's a classic!" Katie observed, for she had a strong interest in antique instruments. "They don't make them like that any more, with the old mechanism. Those are hard to play, but boy do they sound great if you know how," she added.

It took more coaxing on the part of the entire band to get Mr. Chesterfield to agree to play. Once on stage, Bob slipped him the sheet music for the same number that Suzy had so masterfully sang. The old man took a quick look at the music and set the pages aside. "Got it!" he added by way of explanation. "Can I improvise a bit?"

"Sure," Jessie replied looking around at the rest of the band members. They all simply shrugged their shoulders. Without further discussion, Kenny set the slow back beat and the newly transformed band performed its first number together.

This is what the local music reviewer wrote in the newspaper the following week after their weekend debut. "Wow! You have to hear these guys! Our own home-grown Bama Blues Band has reinvented themselves by the addition of Suzy Kurtz's soulful vocals and the masterful playing of Pops Chesterfield on sax.

Where did they get that guy, anyway? What a jazz and blues band! Their new tune, Havana Grove, is fantastic! You have to go hear the new Bama Blues Band. Don't miss them! They are playing next week at the Rusty Nail."

As so often happens when we let destiny do her bidding, this small garage band from a little town in western Pennsylvania went on to make a lasting impact on the world stage of blues and jazz.

CHAPTER 47

A Confession

Molly returned home that night feeling confused and violated. Despite her regrets of having surrendered to Jack Fulton, she felt a growing attraction toward him. The entire affair was making her head and heart spin in opposing directions. Thus destabilized at the core, she sought safety on her soft couch with a cup of hot chocolate. Hot chocolate was her refuge, ever since she had left her parents' home, so many years ago.

Curled up under her favorite blanket, she wanted nothing more to do with this world, at least not for tonight. "Damn me for being so weak!" she muttered as she sipped her hot cocoa.

It was then that she heard the knock on the door. "Now who could that be?" she thought as she glanced at her watch. It was nearly 9 pm.

Slowly and reluctantly, she approach the door and opened it. The sight took her breath away. Standing there was Jack himself. He looked dapper and his smile was too much for her to resist. She wanted to kiss him, but knew that it was wrong. Holding back, she put on her sternest expression and addressed him before he had a chance to say a word.

"What do you want?" she asked firmly.

"Sorry to disturb you. May I come in? It'll only be a moment. I wanted to clarify something." He had such begging eyes that she let him enter.

"Okay. But, I was about to go to bed, so make it quick!" she heard herself say in an angered tone.

He slipped by her and sat in a sofa chair facing the couch. Quickly, she closed the door. She did not want anyone seeing Jack in her room for fear of raising further suspicions. He noticed her reservation and fear, but did not comment.

"Why're you here?" she asked as she fell back into her safe couch haven and resumed sipping her hot chocolate. She made no efforts to be hospitable. She was angry at him and at herself for succumbing so easily to his masterful ways.

"I came to apologize."

"Apologize?" she thought. "Was it that bad that it needed an apology?" This thought unnerved her more than any other. She had not thought of that. She remained silent awaiting his next word.

"I came to apologize for coming on so strong last night. You're the kind of woman that I'm attracted to, and the wine must have gotten the better of me. I mean that I enjoyed it and all, but it wasn't right," he paused.

"At least he enjoyed it," she thought. "That's a relief." She reflected but remained silent, unsure of where he was going with his apology.

He wished that she would speak, for it was hard to guess what she was thinking. Her body language gave mixed signals; both attraction and rejection. He decided to break the awkward silence once more.

"I meant to say that I enjoyed it very much, but that I, well, I…" he paused again. He had to rethink this. He did not want to say something that he would regret. To release her was stupid, yet to draw her closer was selfish and felt wrong. His heart and loins were aligned against his conscience. A tug of war presently ensued within him as he gazed into those beautiful green eyes, and could not help but recall the glorious curves that even now made themselves evident through her sheer robe.

"Why are you apologizing, Jack? I'm not about to repeat my mistake, if that's what you're after," she stated boldly, as if reading the lust racing through his mind. "What happened between us was a mistake," she emphasized her point. A part of her cringed at the sound of those words. She was releasing him, although she was so incredibly attracted to him. She knew that he would struggle to do the same, and suspected by way of his introduction that this struggle had brought him back to her door.

A part of him was relieved, yet another equally deep-seated part was panicked. He was losing her. The attraction between them was so evident that it took all of their individual resolve to oppose it. "I agree. It was a mistake," he heard himself say while a part of him screamed at the foolish reply.

"Agreed!" She smiled while she felt sick in her stomach. She did not want to release him, but it was wrong and there was no way of making it right.

"Good, well that's that." He stood up and she did the same.

As they approached the door, he unintentionally brushed up against her breast, feeling nothing but the sheer robe between him and the eternal memory of her. He stopped to look into her eyes, and she did the same, excited by the contact. They seemed to communicate without words. Instinctively, she looked up at him and he kissed her passionately once more. She did not resist. She could not resist.

Then, it happened in the form of another knock on the door. This time a firm knock, demanding an answer.

"Who's that?" he said in a panicked whisper.

"I don't know. I wasn't expecting anyone," she replied. The mood was broken and guilt poured into the void. "I can't afford to be seen alone with you," she burst out.

"Are you married?" he asked in complete confusion.

"No, but this isn't right!" she replied.

"I know! That's what I came to tell you. This isn't right."

The knocking continued, unanswered.

"Why's this not right?" she asked him transfixed on his eyes.

"Because… because I have feelings for another!" He let is out. It was out and all had instantly changed between them.

"I see, well good! Good!" she reluctantly echoed. Her stomach was churning again and the knocking, that damn knocking, persisted like an alarm.

"You need to hide in my bedroom until you can sneak out of here," she instructed, making little sense.

"Okay," he complied and ran into the bedroom.

Finally, she answered the door. It was the Queen of Hearts, Helga herself, holding a bouquet of fresh-cut, white roses.

"I figured that you were home. I saw the light. I just picked these for you." She handed Molly the bouquet of roses. "Thanks for being such a good friend. I forgot what it was like to have a good friend." Helga added before entering the room uninvited. "Did I wake you?" she added seeing that Molly was in her robe.

"No, but I was getting ready for bed." Molly hoped that Helga would take the hint and leave. No such fortune occurred. Helga was on a mission. Having rediscovered true friendship, she was determined to proclaim its importance to the world or at least to her new friend. Without any further hesitation, she marched into Molly's small living room and fell into the sofa chair, the very chair that Jack had vacated moments earlier.

"Also, as your friend, I came to warn you about Jack Fulton," Helga whispered as if she sensed his presence.

"Warn me! Why?" Molly was intrigued and resumed her seat on the couch. She too was whispering for she knew of Jack's presence.

"Well, don't fall for his charms for he's a predator," Helga whispered.

There was that word again associated with Jack Fulton.

"What do you mean, predator?" Molly asked, still whispering.

Helga looked around as if to see if Jack was listening. It struck Molly as odd that Helga was acting as if she were somehow aware of Jack's proximity.

Helga said even softer now, "He preys on pretty young things like you. Oh, he leaves me alone, I assure you of that. He thinks I'm ugly. But you, well, you're irresistible prey to him, just like Alice," she paused for effect.

"Alice? What happened?" Molly was intrigued.

"As you know, Alice used to live here. He courted her before you arrived. It took no time at all before she slept with him, and then he had her. The games drove her insane. He'd play with her like a cat with a mouse. He'd push her away only to reel her in again, and then excited her to the point that she felt sure that she was in love. That's when he would drop her, squeezing her heart and slamming it on the cold ground. It was cruel to watch. He drove a wedge between us. Alice and I were friends, just like we are, and he destroyed that. He destroyed everything! Stay away from him. He's evil!" Helga looked earnestly into Molly's eyes. "Now that we're friends, I had to warn you. You don't want to end up like Alice." Helga paused and looked about once more before suddenly changing the subject. "I need to get some sleep. I have an 8 o'clock class."

"Okay." Molly felt exposed and angry. She felt for Alice. She felt like Alice. "The Mad Hatter is truly mad!" she thought. No, she knew it without thinking.

As soon as Helga departed, Molly closed the door and headed to the bedroom to confront Jack. She found him lying on her bed.

"Please get off my bed!" she insisted, looking straight at him.

"Sorry, but I couldn't help but reminisce," he flirted.

"I want you out of here, and don't come back!" she ordered.

He was shocked and rose to his feet. She was nearly pushing him toward the door. Her demeanor had changed. The spark of attraction had been replaced by hot ambers of anger.

"I want you out of here! It was a mistake and we're through. Understand?" She was certain now. There was no longer any room for hope. At the door, she did not hear another word but simply closed him out of her room and her heart.

CHAPTER 48

No Wonder It's Wonderland

The next morning, Molly awoke with a feeling of dread. Her bold decision of the previous night had haunted her dreams. The sleeplessness wore on her physically and mentally. Her head ached, yet her heart ached more.

Molly never called into work claiming to be ill, but on this day that is exactly what she decided to do. She desperately needed a break. Seeking refuge on the couch with yet another cup of hot chocolate, she decided to ponder her next steps. The pondering lead to doubting, which spurred loathing and finally triggered curiosity. What if Helga had been wrong? After all, what had Jack done other than shown her affection? Besides, he had come to tell her something, apparently to break up the relationship, not to control her. He was attracted to another. Who? Something was not right, and she needed answers. After another cup of cocoa, she decided to do what she did best, investigate.

While getting changed, she formulated a plan. Her headache had mysteriously disappeared and her heartache had been replaced by a new light of hope. Or was it simply denial? She was not sure for that was part of her investigation. The answers to her growing number of questions lay not just without, but within her as well.

"I need to find Chester," she concluded. "That oddball knows more than he lets on."

Without further delay, she crept out of her room, so as not to alert Helga. She wanted to verify Helga's account of Jack and Alice, for that was one of the keys to the mystery. "What really happened to Alice?" she thought.

The house was quiet. It was nearly 11 am and most of the odd occupants had dispersed in pursuit of their daily rituals and scheduled classes. Descending the back stairs, Molly had an insight that struck her like a brick of wisdom: "Most of us spend our lives unfulfilled by daily rituals, rarely embracing true joy. What a shame!" she concluded.

The idea was much too deep to ponder further, so it simply passed through her as do so many insights in each of our lives. Her quest was not to solve this eternal riddle, but to simply find Chester, and the truth behind Jack Fulton, the man that had wormed his way into her heart.

"Maybe Chester's in class," she reflected after five minutes futilely spent knocking on his door. Chester lived in the basement of the large manor. It seemed a fitting place for him for it was equally odd and mysterious. The old oak door of his quarters looked like a portal to the Victorian era. The entry down the damp stone basement stairs added to the time-warp effect, as did the plethora of spider webs and rejected pieces of antique furnishings that lined the dark passage. "This place gives me the creeps!" Molly concluded and without further ado, turned to leave. "How can he live down here?"

It was then that she heard the odd noise. It started as a gurgling of sorts, like that of a bubbling cauldron. It was faint, but distinct. No, it was close as if it were next to her. She paused to allow her senses to sharpen. Fear rose in her stomach, but she quickly quelled it with her curiosity. The noise persisted, but was joined by another, much less distinct reverberation, like that of a running engine that protested in coughs and sputters. It became clear that the noise was coming from Chester's mysterious residence.

She returned to Chester's door and, without further hesitation, used all of her force to pound on it. Her curiosity was in charge of her actions. She did not pound for long before the door gave way with a sinister creek, ready to reveal its secrets.

There, standing at three quarters of her height, was Chester himself, dressed in what looked like an old baby-blue leisure suite. He seemed out of place even in this creepy setting. "Why, hello Molly. To what do I owe the pleasure?" he greeted her with a wide, toothy smile. With the opening of the oak door, the noise had doubled and now reverberated down the dusty hallway.

"What's that noise?" she asked without further cordiality.

"Oh, that! Well come in, and I'll show you." Chester led her through the door. What awaited her was a quirky combination of a bachelor pad intertwined with a mechanical workshop and a cobweb-ridden warehouse, all packed full of the oddest items imaginable. It was like walking into the mind of the occupant. It defined him, but confused the intruder.

The noise seemed to permeate from another room closer to the west wall at the rear of the mansion. She was struck by the enormous size of Chester's quarters. He seemed to occupy an extensive portion of the basement. As he led her through yet another room filled with a hodgepodge of collectables hardly worth collecting, the noise grew louder until it completely drowned out their conversation. Finally, they reached the back end of the basement and entered a set of garages, complete with rusty dilapidated bay doors. One of the bays was open, revealing the sunny rear courtyard of the manor. Standing within this bay was a 1904 Stanley Steamer automobile that looked like a small chugging, horseless carriage.

"That's my pride and joy. I finally got her running this morning, but she's much too noisy. What do you think? To the best of my knowledge, she has got only one sister still in existence, and she's down in Virginia." He beamed with delight.

The old automobile was indeed a marvel, although apparently far from restored. The solution to the mystery relaxed Molly. She smiled, realizing that Chester, for all his oddity, was by all accounts genuine, quirky but genuine.

"She isn't ready for the road, but I hope that by this summer I can give you a ride around campus. What do you say?" he asked, smiling with pride.

"I'd love that, Chester."

"Is that why you're here, to find out about Old Betty?"

"No, I came to ask you a few questions regarding the house. Do you have some time to chat?" Molly asked sincerely.

"For you, Molly, always!" Chester beamed and his whiskery mustache gave a hopeful twitch. He seemed to purr at the thought. "Let me shut Old Betty down, so we can hear each other. She's a loud gal at present, but once I get her working right, she'll be nearly silent. Can you believe that?"

"No, I can't, but I'll trust you on that, Chester."

Chester shut down the old steam engine and offered Molly a grungy seat on a dumpster-supplied sofa in the far end of the garage bays. "Can I get you a cup of coffee or something?"

"No thanks, Chester. I don't have much time this morning, but I really wanted to speak with you."

"Sure! What about, Molly?" Chester sat down next to her, so as to be as close to her aura and form, as possible. He had always been attracted to the pretty red head that had recently arrived, and he made no attempts to hide his feelings.

She was a little uncomfortable at his proximity and the musty smell that seemed to be his trademark, but she decide that to help him trust her, she needed to sacrifice a little.

"I wanted to know about Jack Fulton and the young woman who had previously occupied my room."

"Oh, you mean Alice. Well, that's a mystery for sure. You see, Alice appears to have disappeared. No one knows exactly what happened to Alice. She was beautiful like you." He smiled his big ear-to-ear smile as Molly blushed. "And, well, Jack Fulton was certainly interested in her. Rumor had it that they were dating. I had seen them on several occasions together, and once I caught them kissing right there in the garden." He pointed his finger at the rose garden that was barely visible out of the open bay door. "It was late one night, a few weeks before she disappeared. I think she was in love with him. You can tell, you know," he added.

"So what do you think happened to her?"

He fidgeted noticeably before responding. "I can't say, but I know who might tell you?"

"Who?"

"Why Ms. Nightingale, of course. Don't let her deceive you with her quirky ways. She knows about everything that goes on around here." He paused to sip his stale coffee.

"Chester, what is going on around here?" Molly decided to go straight to the heart of the matter. "This is the oddest place I've ever experienced."

Chester let out a laugh that sounded almost like a combination of a sneer and a chuckling purr. He smiled his wide toothy smile and chuckled his odd chuckle once more. "It is indeed, Molly! It is odd, indeed, and I'm no exception. I can't tell you much more for I'm sworn to secrecy. We all are, you know." He smiled again.

"I'm not!" she objected.

"I know, and that's why I can't tell you."

"Oh, Chester, please. You're the only one that I trust. This place is like a fairy tale or something out of Wonder..." she was about to say it.

"Wonderland!" He chuckled louder and smiled wider.

"Yes! Wonderland, and where's Alice?"

Chester chuckled some more, breaking out into the oddest laugh that sounded like a severe bout of the hiccups. "Let's hope that she found her way back out of the rabbit hole," he replied.

"That isn't helping, Chester. Please tell me what's going on. I promise that I won't tell anyone, or ever reveal that you and I had this conversation," she genuinely pleaded, locking her green eyes with his.

Chester felt empathy for her, and looked about to see if anyone was near. He got up and closed the open bay door. The room suddenly fell into a shadowy, semi-darkness fitting for the secrecy that was about to unfold. He sat back next to her, closer now, almost in her lap, like the cat he so resembled.

"Okay. But, you mustn't tell anyone that we had this conversation for what I'm about to reveal is kept secret by the Society," Chester whispered into her left ear. She could feel his breath upon her cheek. She wanted to pull away in disgust and alarm, but forced herself to endure.

"Okay," she replied, glancing at him. "I won't tell a soul."

He looked about nervously before continuing to whisper in her ear. "You see, Molly, although this house is a dormitory of sorts, it's first and foremost the seat of a very secret society that dates back hundreds of years. In fact, legend has it that this society is far older, dating back to the early middle ages. It's reputed that it originated somewhere in the heart of France, or so they teach us when we go through our initiation," he paused and licked his lips, pressing them ever closer to her left ear.

She wanted to push him back, but feared that he would stop his revelation. Instead, she used the excuse of a question to reposition herself away from him. "What's the name and purpose of this society?"

"Well, I'm about to get to that," he purred and resumed his proximity. "The society is called Société de Magie Noire, and it has numerous branches around the world. The locations are known only to each Branch Master, in our case Ms. Nightingale. But it's rumored that there are at least fifty or more branches worldwide, with the highest concentration in Europe, as you might expect given the legend of its origin."

"Fascinating!" Molly was so intrigued that she ignored Chester's ever growing proximity.

"Yes, but what's more fascinating is its purpose. As the name implies, it's magic but not black magic. The 'noire' is more for dramatic effect of some form or another, although historically there appeared to be some dark elements infused among us," Chester paused and sipped his foul smelling coffee.

"Say more," she asked sincerely.

"You mustn't tell anyone that I told you this. I'd be expelled or worse."

"Or worse?" she asked looking directly at him.

"Yes, publicly exposed."

"Exposed? What do you mean?"

Chester resumed his place nearly on her lap. He loved it there and took this opportunity to fully enjoy the position. "I'll tell you, but listen to me, for this is imperative. The purpose of this secret society... you can't reveal this to anyone, promise?" he paused and looked straight at her.

"I promise," she heard herself say.

"Okay, then. I trust you. Don't let me down on this. Okay?"

"Okay."

"The purpose of this society is to network people that are psychic and ones that have the gift."

"The gift? What gift, Chester?"

"The gift of being a medium. Not that it's that odd anymore, but being in the society makes the budding talents feel safe and free to grow. Plus, we like our secrecy," he purred.

"Mediums? Are you card readers?"

"Where have you been?" he objected.

"I don't understand," she countered.

He returned to her ear and whispered some more into it. He could smell her perfume, which excited him and put him further at ease. "Mediums can connect to the other side."

"The other side of what?"

"You know, death!"

"I don't understand." Molly was completely naive to the subject, and never a believer in such supernatural rumors.

"Molly, I'm a medium! It doesn't make me any more special or a better person than you. I simply have had, since childhood, the power to communicate with Spirit. You know like the movie, Sixth Sense. I have that sixth sense!" he confessed. "When I was young it was more visual. I could see spirits at times, like my grandfather after he died. Later, as I got older, it became more like a connection through my thoughts when I decided to use it, or when Spirit decided to use it. I know it's odd, but it's true. You must believe me," he pleaded in genuine honesty.

"Okay, I believe you," she gave out a big sigh. This was stretching her logical and naturally skeptical mind. "Please go on," she asked, having decided just to ride along for now.

"As I mentioned the Société de Magie Noire probably originated in the middle ages as a safe haven for the craft, or gift, often misinterpreted as witchcraft, and for alchemy and other such forces of a darker reputation. Now, it's simply a haven for folks that are not ready or able to come out of the closet about their gift." Chester paused to get a sense of Molly's reaction and to take another sip of his stale coffee.

"So, this place is a secret haven for mediums?" she summarized.

"No."

"No? What else is it?"

"It's a safe haven for psychics, not just mediums, and it's a private dormitory, of course. You see, our society is like the numerous secret scientific societies that existed throughout Europe before the Renaissance. Science had to hide from the ever-probing eye of the Church. Well, now we feel that we need to hide from the ever-probing eye of a science-dominated society that fears anything that may erode its very foundation. It's no different than before, except that now the religion is science, and we, the psychically gifted, find ourselves the outcasts, not unlike the early scientists of the middle ages," he paused. "Luckily, no one is getting burnt at the stake these days."

He cleared his throat and continued, "Of course, just as in the infant days of science, there were many quacks and impostors, or even abusers, so it is with us and our greater company. These impostors dilute our truth and give fodder to our critics, making us ever susceptible to ridicule, and often ostracizing any that try to bridge the gap between science and spirituality. But we're after the same thing as the scientists. We're after truth and a better understanding of our world, but unlike most scientists that define this world simply as one of physical evolution and survival, we explore further, beyond the mortal walls and into the greater realm of the soul. We are often at odds with traditional religions that may be threatened by our continued probing and growing understanding of what lies beyond death. All this contributes to our need for refuge during this fragile infancy of our craft, and this secret society has evolved as one such haven." He stopped his monologue and pulled away to sip his nasty brew.

She had neither expected such a revelation nor such a philosophical synopsis from such a seemingly plain and odd man. He sat there looking at her with his Cheshire Cat smile while she paused to ponder his perspective. Sensing her need for reflection, he gave her leave to do so by rising to refill his coffee cup. There was something sad yet noble about his revelation, although she needed more time to ponder its significance or validity. Presently, she was simply investigating, like the very scientists that he had eluded to in his explanations.

"Tell me, Chester," she asked from across the room, "how did you find this place?"

"Oh, well, how does one find all great things in life?" he answers with a question. "The secret my dear is to let go and let it find you. It works for love, as well." He smiled his ear-to-ear smile as he walked back toward her. She looked at him in a totally different light. He seemed wise despite his appearance and manner. "Now, about your other question, the one regarding Jack and Alice..."

"Yes, please go on," she replied while noticing that Chester's demeanor had changed. He did not press himself upon her now, but sat opposing her in a separate chair, as if the revelation that he had confided in her freed him of his lusts and fears. It seemed to have given him a sense of confidence.

"Well, there's a rumor going around that your friend, Jack, is one such impostor infiltrating these walls. That rumor is fueled by his seeming psychic inability and his continued insistence on leading our meditation sessions, when to some of us it's quite clear that he's faking it. I believe that Alice, who had a strong gift as a budding medium, got close enough to him to reveal him for who he was, a fraud. Some of us feel that she may have paid a high price for that revelation, not unlike Mary Collins, who was the next to get close to him. Coincidence? Is it a coincidence that the two young women that belonged to our society, both attractive and romantically entangled with Jack Fulton, ended up surrounded by mystery and tragedy when they got too close to him? Some of us think not. Take that to your police inspector, Molly!" Chester smiled his ear-to-ear smile.

"What! What are you talking about?"

"I know your true identity, Molly."

"What? That's ridiculous!"

"Is it? I know that you're a cop, Molly. There, now you hold my secret and I hold yours." He once again smiled the smile of the all-knowing Cheshire Cat.

"How did you know? Was it your gift?" she asked naively.

"No. It was your trash," he laughed. "It's amazing what you discover while dumpster diving," he laughed some more and soon disappeared.

CHAPTER 49

But Where's Alice?

*M*olly was visibly shaken by her interaction with Chester. It was evident that he and all that were around her were not what they appeared to be. All about her were deceptions and dualities. She returned to her haven on her couch with yet another cup of comforting cocoa. Her world was rapidly shrinking around her leaving her with this last refuge — her couch and her cocoa.

Worlds of differing realities appeared to be silently colliding before her. Reality was no longer safely defined and compartmentalized into logical bits of memory and proof. The mystical was lurking all about, released from its confines of religious antiquity, a time when miracles were allowed to occur to ancient prophets. Surely the miracles of old were myths that we had grown to accept, believe or simply tolerate. Yet, had we not proven with science that all such mysteries were false? Had we not grown as a society around this orderly duality of historically acceptable miracles and our present reality in which such miracles could not exist? But such a socially acceptable order was no longer true if Chester's revelation foreshadowed a broader truth. Or, was it all simply an illusion? If so, which was the illusion? She was no longer sure.

She pondered the unfathomable, for such faith was not yet hers to grasp. All was fresh and this world, so alien, pressed upon her without her desire to seek it.

The mysterious case of Mary Collins was beginning to consume its primary investigator. Had she gotten too close? Had she opened a Pandora's box that she had no power to close or comprehend? Was Jack, her lover, a plausible killer? Was Chester a madman or an odd empowered prophet? Her head was spinning while her heart desired the one at the heart of this mystery, Jack Fulton. She knew she was lying to herself. She wanted him and the forbidden fruit that they had tasted together, of each other, completely fulfilled, in that one moment.

"Damn it, Jack got to me! I want him! How's that possible?" she cursed and pondered. Despite two strong warnings now, she called him, and it was he who was knocking on her door. Afraid yet hopeful, she abandoned her sole refuge and rose to answer the soft knock.

"Hello," he greeted her with a boyish smile that made him irresistible. "You really surprised me when you called. I didn't think that I would hear from you again. May I come in?"

She did not answer for her body had done so for her. She could not control that body now. He controlled it. She was his for the night, and he sensed her surrender. Like two planets caught in a gravitational tug of war that only brought them closer with every rotation, Molly and Jack were together again for another taste of that which poets enshrine in songs and timeless prose.

She did not want to engage her mind or wrestle with verbal foreplay, so she surrendered to the inevitable and simply lead him toward her bedroom. Her mind was too confused to resist him. Her heart and loins had won, yet again. He too could not resist her, and soon their opposing worlds collided in euphoria once more.

Morning came and with it another oscillation in this dance of magnetic attraction and repulsion. Molly awoke wary, before the sun, only to find her bed filled with Jack. She was taken back by her weakness the night before and regretted her decision.

"Damn it! What have I done?" she cursed as she quickly rose from her bed and headed for her couch. She did not want to be next to Jack Fulton, the suspected villain and potential killer. She barely sat on the couch when she realized that she had to shower. She had to wash all traces of him from her body. Without further thought, she did just that.

When she surfaced, there he sat, violating her sacred haven, her precious couch. "Wow, you sure are something!" he rose to embrace her as she pulled away. "What's the matter?" he questioned.

"Nothing. I need to get to work," she objected, crushing his romantic hopes.

"What do you do, anyway? I never asked you." He smiled, trying to charm.

"Oh, nothing of importance. I work in a stodgy government office," she replied and headed for her bedroom to dress. She felt very exposed with nothing but a towel between her form and Jack's roving eyes.

"What office?" he yelled after her as she disappeared behind the bedroom door.

"Agriculture!" she lied as she dressed quickly.

"Oh, a farm girl!" He chuckled, trying to bring some lightness back into the budding relationship.

"Hardly!" she replied as she appeared in the bedroom door fully dressed.

"Wow, that's the fastest that I have ever seen a woman dress," he laughed.

"You sound like you have a lot of experience with that." She took a jab at him.

"Very funny! Can you join me for a quick cup of coffee at Ricky's?" he asked hoping for more of her time.

"No, got to run. Last night was a mistake," she proclaimed, as she headed for the door. "You had better leave," she added.

"What's with you? You're so hot and cold. Look, I'm sorry that I'm attracted to you. Does that help? You have that effect on me. I can't resist you, but I think I had better." He too was pulling away now.

"What happened to Alice?" she blurted it out, no longer holding back.

"What?" She had caught him off guard. "Alice who?"

"Alice! Hell, I don't even know her last name! The one who lived here before me. The one you slept with in this very bedroom before I arrived. You seem to recall how fast every woman dressed, don't you recall anything else about them?"

"Ouch! What has gotten into you?" he objected and began to look for his coat. "You're right, I better leave."

"Oh, running off when the questions gets too close to your precious secrets!" She was angry now.

"What're you talking about? You're starting to scare me."

"I should be the one who's scared of you. But you know what? I'm not, because you're nothing but a sexual predator that feeds on innocent women. Yet, I won! I enjoyed you for my satisfaction without any further attraction," she lied.

"That would make you the sexual predator," he replied.

"Hardly! I can't imagine Jack Fulton as the victim of any woman's passion."

He fell silent for he knew that she was right. A pain appeared on his face as he reached for his coat.

"What's the matter? Does a strong woman scare you?" she pounded him some more.

"No, but a completely irrational one does!"

"What happened to Alice?" she insisted.

"I don't know," he replied and left the room.

She fell back onto the couch and started to weep. She was so confused that she had forgotten why she was crying. All the emotion surfaced, asking to be acknowledged as her own. "Damn that lying bastard! Why am I always attracted to lying bastards? Why?" She wept and wept until Ms. Nightingale appeared in her half-ajar doorway.

The sight of the landlady sobered Molly instantly. She looked at her watch. She would be late for work once more. "Damn it!" she muttered to herself, before trying to feign a smile to greet her surprise guest.

"What's the matter, child?" Ms. Nightingale rushed into the room. She seemed forever in a hurry, and this morning was no exception.

"Nothing. It's personal." Molly objected as she rose from her couch.

"Sit, sit! I heard you crying, so I rushed over here. Are you all right? You are much too young and pretty to be in such misery," Ms. Nightingale comforted her.

"What does any of that have to do with it?" Molly objected.

"It has everything to do with it. You weep for love. I can tell. I was in love once or twice myself, and wept over it more than I wish to admit." Ms. Nightingale smiled and sat next to Molly to console her.

"I can tell when two people are in love, but he's not ready. Whatever the two of you shared, I assure you was genuine, but he's not ready for another serious commitment. I thought that he was, but he's not. He's like a son to me. I know him. I raised him. He tells me everything. He's a good boy, or man now, but he runs deep," Ms. Nightingale paused. "As much as I love him like a son, I think it would only break your heart to get involved with him right now."

"What are you taking about?" Molly objected.

"Why you and Jack, of course."

"What? What has he told you?" Molly was appalled and embarrassed, all at once.

"Nothing, but a mother knows."

"You're his mother?"

"Not physically, but spiritually," Ms. Nightingale replied.

There was that word again. Molly was about to grill this woman about the secret society and all that Chester had revealed, but she caught herself. To betray Chester was to lose her credibility in the house. It could jeopardize the Mary Collins case. She had to play along. She had to be the detective.

"I see. This house seems to have a lot of spirituality," Molly began fishing to confirm Chester's statements. Ms. Nightingale noticed the sudden topic switch, but did not object.

"Yes, it does. We're a sort of spiritual enclave here as you saw in our meditation session the other day. It's all good and innocent, as is Jack's attention." Ms. Nightingale returned to the subject.

"What happened to Alice?" Molly asked bluntly.

The question somewhat startled Ms. Nightingale, but she recovered instantly. "Why do you ask?"

"Because it seems that Jack had some sort of a romantic interlude with her. What happened?"

"Well, I suppose there's no harm in you knowing since you have some of her traits. I was certain of it as soon as I laid eyes on you." Ms. Nightingale took control of the discussion once more.

"Traits? What're you talking about?" Molly objected.

"Let me back up a bit, my dear. Alice Wadsworth came here two years ago. She was strong-willed, self-assured and confused to the core. Sound familiar?" Ms. Nightingale did not wait for Molly's reply, but continued. "She was a sweet child and possessed a power of which she was little aware. But I could tell that she possessed it," she explained as she smiled at Molly. "Anyway, she stayed with us and soon opened up to her gift."

"What gift?" Molly interrupted.

"Her gift. She was a medium, but only recently aware of it. I am one, too. Unlike some people you may meet here, I'm not afraid to admit it. I help foster people with such talents, especially young people. That's my mission and I run this house as a haven for such psychically gifted youth, such as yourself," she paused and smiled once more.

"Stop right there! I'm not psychically gifted or a medium, so you got that wrong," Molly objected. She was still feeling like she had fallen into a freak show, and the White Rabbit was once again leading her down a mythical rabbit hole.

"But, you are! You simply don't realize it. All people have some form of the gift, but only a few open up to it. Many are aware of it as children, but soon forget for they are often told that it's ridiculous or only their imagination. Yet, a few retain it from those childhood years. Others rekindle it later in life, and still others have it thrust upon them, like me. But that tale is for another time. Most, however, are either in a state of denial or ignorance when it comes to their potential. You see, it's no different than creativity, intuition or inspiration," Ms. Nightingale explained with a knowing smile similar to Chester's toothy grin.

Molly could not help focusing on Ms. Nightingale's two pronounced front teeth. "She does look like the White Rabbit," Molly thought. "This place is making me crazy! I'm imagining things, and if I stay here much longer the only gift that'll befall me is that I'll become mad like the rest of them," she concluded, while staring at those two front teeth that seemed to be growing with the length of the monologue.

"All of this is a higher-self connection of your soul and its anchor in Heaven," Ms. Nightingale continued. "We're souls in form, thus avatars of sort. But, we have a connection to our source and our true home, Heaven, and so few of us realize it. In the distant past, that connection was publicly encouraged, even revered. Look at the native American culture for example and its shamans. As I said, many young are innocently aware of this natural connection, but lose it by school age, partially because of their education," she sighed, as she revealed her truths to Molly.

"Don't get me wrong," she admitted. "I'm not advocating any huge shift in our western society. Any such rapid shifts are unhealthy. I'm simply providing a haven and acting as an advocate for the spiritually gifted who are willing and ready to embrace that gift. But, I'm a firm believer that we, as souls in form, are all spiritually gifted. Many are actually on the verge of awakening to this very fact; just like you are, Molly."

Molly tried to focus on the conversation, but those teeth, those rabbit teeth, kept her from hearing anything that Ms. Nightingale shared. "I'm so rude! She probably noticed that I'm staring at her teeth," Molly thought and tried to look into Ms. Nightingale's eyes, which seemed redder than usual. "Crap! Now, it's her eyes!" Molly thought and decided to simply look away as if in deep thought.

"At any rate, regarding Alice, that lovely girl finally accepted her predisposition about a year ago. It was then that she began to work with me to open up to her higher self. The odd thing is that once she really began to excel at it, she simply walked away," Ms. Nightingale sighed. "I don't understand it. Maybe she got scared. Self doubt is a formidable monster to overcome. She moved away about a month ago, but I assure you that she's perfectly fine."

There was a pregnant pause as Ms. Nightingale awaited a response to her lengthy monologue, while Molly tried to recall its content.

"You can open up to your higher self as well, Molly, if you really want to learn," Ms. Nightingale dangled the bait.

"Really. How?" Molly took the bait but ignored the hook. The investigator's curiosity prevailed.

"I knew you'd be curious. Genuine, unbiased, open-minded curiosity is the path to a broader understanding of your true self and your full suite of God-given powers." Ms. Nightingale smiled knowingly. "It's no different than a child's innocent curiosity and acceptance when first exploring this physical world."

"Honestly, Terry, the idea of it sounds hokey to me." Molly decided to share her true feelings.

Ms. Nightingale did not seem offended in the least. "Of course it does, and I'd be surprised if it sounded like anything else, given your background and position."

"What do you know about my background and position?"

"Don't be so defensive, Molly. I know very little for you reveal little, but I know that you're a child of western culture, and thus share in our collective ignorance and disbelief in such powers. It doesn't matter. This gift mustn't be forced on anyone. Free will must always be respected, especially in such personal matters. Therefore, I'm not here to force an alternative view on you or on anyone. I'm simply sharing with you my own view since you asked, but I don't claim that it's some holy truth. It's simply a broader perspective than that of most." Ms. Nightingale paused to see if Molly was comfortable with this position.

She seemed to be. She was either accepting or tired of the topic. Regardless, Ms. Nightingale continued, "I didn't try to convert Alice, either. She came to me because she was curious. I simply pointed her to some literature and coached her when she asked for help. She willingly took it from there. By making amazing progress in a matter of months, she opened up to the gift that I had sensed within her when I first met her. And, then, it happened."

"Then, what happened?"

"She fell for Jack, of course. As you can imagine, she's not alone in this weakness." Ms. Nightingale smiled a knowing smile.

"Yes, it is a weakness, for he is truly evil!" Molly proclaimed aloud before she could stop herself.

"No! Hardly! No more evil than you or I. He's mostly confused and deeply cares for a young lady that he cannot have. I thought that he was over her, but all this has brought more pain."

"What? Who?" Molly was shocked.

"Let me finish the Alice story first for it's all linked. Alice fell in love with him. He surely contributed to this, and briefly believed that he too was in love with her. However, soon he realized that his attraction was simply passion and nothing more, for his true love was budding elsewhere. He confided this to me, but you should know," she paused and cleared her throat before continuing. "Part of the issue is that, although he is very in tune with his senses, Jack lacks the ability to connect to his higher self in a manner that Alice was able to do. He hides this inability from all in this house for fear of being perceived as inept. Odd as it sounds, the leader of our meditation sessions feels inept. If you ask me, it doesn't matter in the least, but apparently it's a threat to him," she paused and shook her head.

"So far Chester's story is validated, even Jack's inferiority complex," Molly thought.

"Regarding Alice," Ms. Nightingale continued, "Jack pushed her away once he realized that he did not love her, and soon after that she disappeared. I don't know exactly where she went, but one day, about four weeks ago, I found an envelope from her on my desk. It contained a check for the remaining month's rent, and a short note in which she thanked me and said her goodbyes. It was all very sudden with no explanation of why or where she was going. One day she was here, and the next day she was gone. But, I assure you that she left of her own free will. I suspect that she couldn't stand the fact that Jack had fallen for another."

"Another? Who?" Molly asked with an eagerness that betrayed her.

"Why poor Mary Collins, of course. They have kept it a secret since he's a graduate student, and her field instructor this semester. So, please don't say a word to him or anyone. However, I heard you crying and wanted to make sure that you were all right. You deserve the truth. Jack confided in me that he was going to tell you about Mary. I assumed that he had already done so," Ms. Nightingale smiled, but Molly sensed something odd, something untold, hidden behind that smile.

"No. He hadn't told me, nor is he acting the part."

"I'm sorry, my dear. I guess I said too much. Maybe he changed his mind given poor Mary's dire condition."

"Said too much or not enough?" Molly intentionally pushed her, as if she were conducting an interrogation.

"What do you mean, my dear?"

"Why are you telling me all this? What is your motive?" Molly asked, getting right to the point.

"My motive? I don't have a motive, my dear. I simply want you and Jack to be happy."

"Sounds more like you want me to push him away. Ms. Nightingale, I am not interested in you or Jack, and, by the way, I don't have the vibe."

"No worries, my dear. Trudy and I made up. You helped us, you know. You helped us realize what we have," Ms. Nightingale admitted with a smile.

"Glad to be of service."

"But, you most certainly have the vibe and you ought to do something about it. It sets off confusing signals," Mr. Nightingale added with a mischievous chuckle.

"I have no vibe and no psychic gift. You have me all wrong," Molly replied forcefully.

"Do I, or is it you and Jack that have it all wrong? Regardless, I have both of your best intentions at heart. At the right timing, it would work, but not now, my dear. Not now."

"Sure you have good intentions," Molly thought. "I need to get to work," she replied. "Thank you for enlightening me, Ms. Nightingale. I believe that 'enlighten' is the right spiritual term? I don't want to get your terms and vibes confused."

"Now, Molly, I meant no harm. I assure you of that."

"No harm, no foul," Molly replied tersely.

"Molly, please don't misunderstand me. I really am trying to help you. Be very careful not to misinterpret Jack's affection, as Alice had done."

"I appreciate the advice, Ms. Nightingale, but I really need to get to work."

"Okay. By the way, where do you work?"

"Didn't Jack confide that in you? I work at the Ag Department."

"Oh, no he didn't. That sounds exciting," Ms. Nightingale lied.

"Yes, very. In fact, it's so exciting that I dare not miss any more of it. Good bye, Ms. Nightingale."

"Good bye, my dear."

Ms. Nightingale departed, thinking that Molly still had the vibe, and that although she was very odd, she had some promise. Molly closed the door thinking the entire situation was very odd and devoid of any promise. Thus, the two strong-willed women agreed and dissented.

As Molly prepared to leave the building, she ran into Chester in the hallway. He pulled her aside and whispered in her ear. "I neglected to tell you something extremely important. I think I know where Alice is buried."

"What? Buried?" Molly retracted in horror.

"Look in the rose garden!" Chester smiled and vanished. The image of his smile was all that remained.

CHAPTER 50

Stacy's Secret

*M*olly entered the police barracks in a daze. She did not even respond to the usual hazing from Chen, or the usual questioning by the Inspector. She was confused and torn as to what to say to her boss regarding the happenings at the house. She knew that she had a duty to the department and to the case, a duty to share all of this information, but she also knew that the more she shared, the more certainly she would be implicated in sleeping with Jack Fulton. She could lose her job and her career, if she was not careful. Torn on all fronts and exhausted by the forces pulling her apart, she fell back to her sense of duty.

She was about to tell the Inspector of the odd happenings in the house, including the secret society and mysterious disappearance of Alice Wadsworth, when he surprised her. In doing so, he closed the door on her confession, at least for now.

"Well, Molly, glad you seem better, although you're still very pale. Maybe you had better go home once we finish this interview," he began.

"What interview?" she asked, awakened from her dilemma.

"Guess who contacted the department and is coming for a visit later this morning?"

"I have no idea."

"Who's the key person of interest that has been missing since the day Mary fell?" he insisted.

Molly was so tired and confused by what had transpired over the past 24 hours that she had completely lost track of the Mary Collins case.

"Oh, Molly! You're still not yourself. Why, Stacy Reed has surfaced and is coming here in about an hour. I'll need you to conduct the interview, a young woman to young woman sort of chat. You're the best candidate for this. Are you up to it?" the Inspector asked eagerly.

Molly did not feel up to it, but she did not want to refuse him. She knew she would have to get Chen to debrief her and help her formulate her questions. "Sure. Let me get prepared. Is there anything you want me to ask her?"

"Molly, where have you been these past few days? You know what to ask," the Inspector replied.

"Yes, of course, but is there anything that you, yourself, wish to add to the list?"

"No, but touch base with the team before you start the interview. Chen and I will be in the Mirror Room watching and recording. Stacy should be here at ten."

"Okay, Boss. I'll be ready."

"I know you will be, Molly," he replied and walked away.

Molly went to find Chen, who quickly reacquainted her with the key facts and questions regarding the case, but not without considerable teasing as to her recent whereabouts and seeming bout with amnesia.

It was just before 10 am when the Inspector buzzed her to come into his office. "Are you ready? She's in the Fish Tank waiting for you."

"Sure. Let's do this," she replied confidently. Molly had regained her footing despite a difficult few days. She decided that for now she would get through the Stacy Reed interview before relaying to the Inspector her recent findings. She would have to be careful not to implicate herself in a relationship with Jack, but she could not keep case-relevant facts to herself. That was not right.

Bravely, she walked into the Fish Tank where a petite young blonde awaited her. "Hello, Miss Reed. I'm Molly Dvorak. I'll be the one conducting the official interview regarding the Mary Collins case. Shall we begin?"

Stacy Reed nodded nervously. She seemed uncomfortable sitting in the police department interrogation room, but few were ever comfortable there. Nonetheless, she seemed more scared than most. Molly decided to attribute this to the nature of the young woman. After all, she did run from the scene and disappear for over two weeks. Molly would have to excel in this critical interview. Clearing her mind, she focused on the case and nothing more.

"Stacy, please tell me about the geology field trip that took place on March 22nd of this year. What did you see and what happened, in regards to Mary Collins?" Molly began.

The interview lasted over an hour. It was a brilliantly executed dance of questions, trust-building dialogue and even a few smiles. Molly worked Stacy, without Stacy knowing that she was being worked. She unlocked the doors of reservation and gently coaxed the secrets out of hiding. The dance was one of light empowerment and delicate trust. The Inspector was correct in picking Molly for the role. The two women fit and the results were eye-opening. By the end of the interview, Stacy was completely at ease and the Inspector was beaming with satisfaction behind the cloak of the one-way mirror.

Minutes later, Stacy Reed was escorted out of the station by Big Bob, who soon returned to share in the team debrief. He had observed most of the interview, having been summoned into the Mirror Room by Chen at the Inspector's request.

"Great job, Molly! You're a star. That interview just about seals our case," the Inspector proclaimed while still beaming.

"What she saw and testified to today jives with the other key witnesses and answers the remaining questions. It's clear that he did it. Wow, I never truly believed that she'd be the key witness to all this. This is great! I'm so pleased! Y'all did a fantastic job. Great work, team! We can arrest him, as soon as we locate him," the Inspector proclaimed in a Georgian accent, which betrayed his genuine excitement.

"Boss, I know that you're eager to close this case, but can we review the facts once more to make sure it all fits?" Bob asked, being the most conservative of the team.

"I agree," Molly supported the idea.

Not to be left out, Chen added, "Me too! Let's just run through what Stacy Reed provided and how it fits with what we have to date," he echoed.

"Of course, of course!" the Inspector exclaimed with a satisfied smile. "I was going to suggest that very thing. That's why we're here. Y'all are right. I'm simply excited to see the light at the end of the tunnel. To think that initially my boss wanted to close this out as an accident. Now, here we are about to press charges in an attempted homicide. Exciting is the world of detective work!" The Inspector beamed, being completely in his element.

Molly liked the old man, and his passion for his work made him even more endearing. But she questioned his conclusions and was horrified at the potential outcome. Where the case was headed seemed to seal her own fate, and, ironically, she appeared to be the one who had sealed it with this interview.

"Okay, let's play back the interview and we can conduct our final analysis together. Chen, can you play back the Stacy Reed interview, please?" the Inspector asked. "Be prepared to pause it, as needed. Everyone okay with that?"

They all nodded in agreement, while Molly's head was starting to spin once more. The Mirror Room began to take on a double meaning. For in it, she felt exposed in a mirror of truth, soon to be revealed.

"Okay, pause it right there, Chen. So, what did we hear?" the Inspector asked before answering his own question. "Based on this first portion, we know that Stacy ran because of two reasons. First, she was angry with her father because she recently discovered that he had an active relationship with her college friend, Janet Lee. This was the same Janet Lee who was now his graduate student. Second, she saw quite a bit of what transpired with Mary, for she had almost a perfect view from her position on the ledge below. After her embrace with Randell, which we know took place right before Mary's fall, as documented in the Michael Johnson photos, she claims to have looked up at Mary when she heard her scream. She actually witnessed her falling and had a brief glance at the person who pushed her.

Then, the group reviewed Stacy's testimony as it corroborated the Johnson photos and the testimony of the other witnesses, especially that of Kelly Allen. "It all seems to check out, Boss," Chen concluded on behalf of the team, although Molly was noticeably silent.

"Okay, let's continue! Please play the next section of the interview, Chen," the Inspector requested. They all listened for the next eight minutes, until the Inspector once again asked Chen to pause the recording. "Okay, what did we hear in this section?" This time, he decided to let his team answer the question.

"Well, Stacy seems pretty certain that both Tony and Daphne were nowhere near Mary when she fell. She places them exactly where Suzy, Kelly and Daphne Marconi had placed them," Chen observed.

"We are, therefore, left with one and only one remaining suspect. Correct?" the Inspector asked.

"But, according to his testimony, Tony placed Daphne within striking distance of Mary. Why the discrepancy?" Bob asked.

"It happens. Witnesses don't always completely agree. Besides, Tony's not a highly credible witness given his track record with Mary. We already have him in custody for harassment, as well as assault and battery against her, with ample witnesses to back up those charges. I'm not too concerned about that discrepancy, Bob," the Inspector concluded.

"Besides," the Inspector continued, "we have the photographic evidence from the Johnson files that confirms the relative positions of Randell and Stacy, which matches the testimony of the other witnesses. We also have two independent witnesses, Stacy and Kelly, that place Daphne near the far wall of the quarry ledge at the time of Mary's fall. She was simply too far from Mary to be the one that pushed her. That, and we have no clear motive for Daphne. If anything, she seemed protective of Mary and close friends with her," the Inspector clarified. "Any other questions or discrepancies on that portion of the interview?"

All were silent.

"Okay, good. Please play the next section of the interview, Chen," the Inspector asked.

Once more the team listened for what seemed like eternity to Molly. She was visibly nervous. "Cat got your tongue?" Chen leaned over and whispered to Molly.

She did not answer, but thought the comment was ironic, given that it was Chester, the Cheshire Cat in her silly analogies, whose revelations had gotten her tongue tied. It was that and her unforgivable transgressions with Jack Fulton.

"Okay, let's pause there, Chen," the Inspector instructed. "What did we learn here and how does it fit the evidence to date?" He was in instructor mode now, and his team were his students.

"We learned that Stacy was planning to leave her father in protest to his actions and to elope with her boyfriend. We also learned that her boyfriend was waiting for her on the far side of the quarry, near where we found her blue ribbon, the one she clearly wore in numerous evidence photos. Apparently, she lost it in her flight to rendezvous with her boyfriend, who did indeed whisk her away from the scene," Chen concluded.

"Correct, and she now had another motive to flee, right?" the Inspector added with a smile.

"Correct!" Bob chimed in. "It was in her horrified flight up from the lower quarry terrace, just after Mary fell, that she ran into Jack Fulton on the main terrace. While appearing extremely nervous, he forcefully demanded to know what she saw. She claimed that his behavior scared her further making her run toward her boyfriend and away from the scene. She admitted that she should have run toward Mary to see if she was all right, but that she had panicked upon witnessing the horrific act and enduring Fulton's threats."

"Right!" the Inspector affirmed Bob's summary. "Any questions? Molly, you've been silent all this time, any observations about the interview? Any issues with the sequence of events that transpired on March 22nd, according to this testimony?" The Inspector picked on Molly.

"Well, the only reservation that I would have is that Stacy was a little hesitant in revealing what she saw just as she looked up to see Mary falling over the edge of the quarry cliff." Molly grasped at the one thread of hope.

"How so?" the Inspector asked.

"She said that she saw a man in a white shirt and blue jeans, and that he had dark hair. When I pressed her to reveal who she had seen push Mary, she replied that she had seen Jack Fulton standing over the spot from which Mary had fallen. She did not see him push her. The evidence is circumstantial," Molly objected.

"No. The evidence is clear. Jack Fulton was standing at the top of the cliff just as Mary fell. This Stacy confirmed in the final portion of the interview. Let's listen!" the Inspector signaled to Chen.

After they listened to the closing portion of the interview, the Inspector resumed his argument. "Right there in the end, Stacy confirms that it was Jack," he concluded and looked up at Molly.

"In all due respect, Boss, she states that she did not see Mary being pushed, but that she did see Jack Fulton standing at the top of the cliff right after Mary fell. Then, she states that he disappeared, reappearing later when she reached the fall site. It was there that the two ran into each other. Jack was running toward the scene as she was moving away from it. He wasn't running away from it as you would expect if he were the one that pushed Mary," Molly objected.

"He was running toward it to play the part of the concerned instructor, when in fact he had been at the scene only moment earlier as the heartless villain. Why wouldn't he run down to Mary after the fall? Running away would implicate him. Besides, he already had a suspect running away and that was Stacy, the one key witness that could implicate him. He threatened her. She ran. He returned, acting innocent and playing the concerned teacher. Why would he initially turn away from the scene only to seek out the one witness to the crime, Stacy, in order to threaten her before descending the quarry to reach Mary, unless he was trying to cover his own tracks?" the Inspector argued.

"Or, he was not at the scene when Mary fell but was running toward it when he encountered Stacy, as he testified," Molly objected.

"But, he was there! Stacy just testified that he was there — white shirt and all. He lied! I suspected it and Stacy just confirmed it. Play that back, Chen!" The Inspector was getting excited. "Right there! Please pause it right there, Chen. Right there, Molly, Stacy admits that she saw Jack Fulton on top of the cliff just after Mary fell. Not only that, but we have the Johnson photos that clearly show Jack's arms pushing Mary off the cliff, as evident by the white shirt sleeves, which we all know he wore at the time of the crime. He did it, Molly! Why are you defending him?"

The last comments silenced Molly instantly. Was she trying to defend Jack, or was she trying to block the inevitable to clear her own conscience? She was no longer sure.

"Are you suggesting that we bring Fulton back in here for another interview? You want an official shot at him?" the Inspector asked Molly.

She was dumbstruck. If Jack came in for another interview and she had to interview him, what a mess that would be. He would find out that she was a cop, and he surely would turn on her and reveal that they were sleeping together. The thought sent waves of fear throughout Molly's mind and body.

"No. I guess not. I guess you have him, Boss," she reluctantly conceded.

"Damn right I do!" the Inspector proclaimed victoriously. "Damn right, I finally have him!"

CHAPTER 51

The Final Encounter

Jennifer was not eager to return to the trauma ward. She had finally taken a few nights off after the last encounter in Mary's room, which had shaken her to the core. She did not want to return, but her sense of duty prevailed. She had been questioning her own sanity, finally dismissing the argument all together in exchange for time — time to forget and simply allow her loyalty to her patients to drive her actions.

It was in this fragile but noble state of mind that she resumed her place as a night nurse on the trauma ward. It was a quiet night and she was grateful for it. Not wishing to neglect Mary's care, she nonetheless avoided her room as much as possible. The memories seemed too raw there, as was the inexplicable energy surrounding the comatose girl.

Jennifer knew that given Mary's condition, her lack of a living will and her sister Lilly's official approval to terminate the coma, that it was only hours before Mary would be taken off of life support. She knew because her boss had warned her that they expected the paperwork in the morning.

This had an unnerving effect on Jennifer. She had grown close to Mary, although the latter had never once opened her eyes or in any way reached out to her. She cried over the news that Mary's life would soon be terminated. As a medical professional, she knew that there was little that could be done, but until now there was hope. The loss of that hope was gut wrenching.

With a heavy heart, Jennifer Angel took to her nightly rounds. She had left Mary's room for last. It would be the last time that she would bath her. The hope of the miracle would soon die, and something in Jennifer would die with it. She knew this. Subconsciously, she knew. She had prayed for a miracle ever since Mary arrived, and with all the odd happenings, she was starting to believe in its eventual fulfillment.

Taken back by tears again, she bowed her head to her folded arms as she rested on her desk. She had to find the strength to enter Mary's room. In this position of complete surrender, she prayed with all her heart one last time. "A miracle is needed, and miracles do happen. You can make miracles happen! Please, Lord, grant Mary a miracle!" Jennifer prayed with unconditional love and a pure heart. All of the recent events had strengthened her faith, despite shaking her sense of reality.

"Please, God! Please let our dear Mary awaken tonight for she has so much to live for," Jennifer cried as she prayed. Completely consumed by her prayer, she was not aware of the invisible, swirling energy around her. Nor was she aware of the time. Not until the clock in the hall announced the magical half hour. "It's 3:30, maybe hope is not dead," Jennifer sighed.

Coming out of her emotional trance, she recognized the light. It had a purple, magenta aura, and its source was none other than Mary's room. She sprung to her feet with a lightened heart and hurried toward the light, which symbolized her hope.

As she entered Mary's room, she was struck by the power and clarity of the light on this night. At the core of the light, at the source of its aura, was a figure. She was surrounded by a pure bright white glow that oscillated into hues of deep purple and sharp magenta. In the intense brightness, she appeared translucent as if part of the light itself.

Hope gave Jennifer a confidence that until now had escaped her. In prior encounters, she was a daunted observer or a surprised recipient, but now she was a willing participant. Eagerly, she stepped toward the glowing figure of the mysterious woman that she had seen before. Willingly, she pressed herself closer into the light, closer to Mary.

With a welcoming smile, the mysterious woman invited her forward. Beautiful and radiant, she had all the making of the angels described in ancient literature and depicted by the old masters. What appeared like two bright wings on either side of her was the intense white glow that emanated from her very being. There she stood, as if in form, yet only a shadow of it. Her true essence was far more powerful and far more vibrant. Her true essence was the very light that emanated from her, that was her.

Now Jennifer dared not to enter any closer. Already, her entire form was consumed by the powerful aura of this energy being. She felt her within; she felt her without. She was one with her. How was that possible? Her mind raced and in doing so she began to separate from the light, as if her very doubts extinguished it.

Then, it happened.

The mysterious woman spoke, but not in audible sounds, rather in thoughts that were clearly not Jennifer's thoughts. She seemed to be inside Jennifer's head, as if tapping into her mind in some inexplicable way. With this telepathy, she made herself completely clear and her voice was bright, feminine and distinct. Jennifer did not resist. She could not have resisted, had she wished to do so. She was simply passive now, awaiting what would come, knowing it was to be.

"My dear Jennifer, blessed are thou among your fellow brothers and sisters. You have a pure heart and a gentle soul, and we have come to answer your selfless prayers. For you are the guardian of your sister's soul that lies before us. You are her sister soul and her guardian angel in this life, not I. I am her guide in Heaven, but you are her guardian in form. You see, we are all guardians of those around us if we forget ourselves and embrace this most sacred of roles and most blessed of opportunities," the Spirit paused. Jennifer felt the loving energy, intense and electrifying. It surged through her unresisted.

"Dear Jennifer," the Spirit continued, clearly audible in Jennifer's mind, the alert mind that she had willingly surrendered for this purpose. "Thank you for all that you have achieved. Thank you for embodying love unconditional to all that you touch every day, especially this young woman, who in form is a stranger to you, but beyond form is far more. We are pleased that at last you are united with Mary, your soul sister. It is as was planned before you both entered this life, and is manifested through your unconditional love and faith. Trust in that very fact, my dear. Do not try to understand with your limited mind, simply accept that which your soul already knows to be true." The mysterious angel grew in size and energy, enveloping both Mary and Jennifer in a bright white aura that was so intense that Jennifer could no longer keep her eyes open. Closing them, she fell on the floor to her knees.

The healing light made Jennifer feel completely free of her body and gave her a lightness that defied gravity and all points of reference. It was so odd, yet so familiar. She was floating in the light, her body lost and eagerly relinquished. A joy and peace permeated her mind. No, it was not the mind that was affected. It was something far more personal. It was her true nature, her soul. Her soul in that moment was completely free and one with the light. In its freedom, it embraced the soul of another freed of form. Thus entangled, the two souls recognized themselves as extensions of one another and of the light. There were no differences here. There were no judgments, no conclusions, no deductions or questions. All was known. All was congealed into formless perfection. All was eternally at peace, a humbling harmonious peace.

Jennifer did not want to leave this euphoric state. She wanted to stay. She wanted to remain part of the light, part of this mysterious angel, part of her sister soul, whom she now recognized. This was Heaven. Surely, she was in Heaven. Surely, she was home. She remembered it all for just a timeless moment before being sucked back into form, as if by some merciless drain that emptied her vessel of all this tranquility and pleasure. She was falling back now, separated from this eternal joy, only to cry out in vain for mercy, mercy to remain formless and free.

As if all was part of a deep dream, Jennifer saw the mysterious woman kiss Mary's form on her closed eyes, transferring what looked like part of her light into Mary's body. With that mysterious kiss, Jennifer knew that Mary's soul passed back into her form. She saw all, while in a state of physical awareness in the deepest sleep. In that recognition, she knew that the soul so closely entangled with hers only moments earlier was that of Mary Collins.

Jennifer awakened on the floor at the foot of Mary's bed in the very spot where she had fallen to her knees. The light had faded. The mysterious woman was gone, and Mary still lay in a coma before her.

"I guess that I was just dreaming," Jennifer concluded. Reality had extinguished the spark of hope and sadness filled the void.

CHAPTER 52

The Rose Garden

*E*arlier that evening, Molly made her way up to her room. Her mind was still racing in fear of what was, could be, and had been. She was drained of all energy by the rushing, swirling fears that completely overwhelmed her mind.

"I have slept with a killer," she confessed and felt violated. With no place to turn, she dove for the sanctuary of her couch. She was too tired to make her hot chocolate. Reaching for the blanket, she fell fast asleep. Her bed had been soiled by that evil man. She would sleep on the couch.

It was 3:30 am when she awoke. Just as Jennifer awakened to the purple light in Mary's room, Molly awakened to the faint sound of digging beneath her window. Still drowsy, she wisely decided not to turn on the light, but simply crept to the window that overlooked the back of the mansion that she now called home.

There, hidden by the moonless night and the scraggly branches of a large oak, was a large dark form digging in the rose garden.

An extensive pile of excavated soil was visible beyond the periphery of the tree branches, but the form remained hidden. Molly had a sinking feel in her stomach as she recalled Chester's final revelation. "Was Alice really buried in the rose garden?" Molly reflected. Until now, she dismissed Chester's final revelation as a prank. After all, he was an odd prankster.

With every muffled sound of the shovel, her fears were coming to life. Looking again, she witnessed this mysterious dark form get down on its knees as if to pray. But rather than pray, it reached into the ominous abyss and extracted a stiff bundle that had all the dimensions of a corpse.

Molly drew in an audible gasp and held her breath as her shock settled into her consciousness. "Oh, my God! It's a body! Chester was right!" she thought. Then, it struck her like a brick. "The killer is there in the garden below her! Is it really Jack Fulton?" The figure had the stature of a large male, that part was clear, but his face remained obscured. He had his back to her, and the dark night and ample tree cover provided Molly little chance of recognizing him from the safety of her room. She had to get closer and risk detection. She had to dissolve her fears for she was a police officer sworn to her duty.

Quickly, she dressed and silently she snuck out of the room. Creeping past Helga's room, she noticed that the lights were out but another late night war movie was audible in the hallway. "At least she plays them softer now," Molly thought.

Once on the stairs, she crept slower for fear that at any moment she could run into the killer returning from the garden. "Damn it! My gun's not loaded!" She suddenly realized that she had forgotten the bullets. "Oh, well, I'll have to bluff it. He won't know that it's not loaded. Only I know," she consoled herself.

She was down the stairs and at the back door. Cautiously, she opened it, but to her horror the door let out a loud squeal that seemed to holler a warning to the dark form in the garden. "Damn this door! I never noticed that it squeaked like that!" she cursed under her breath as she slipped through the partially opening.

Coming around the back of the house and into view of the garden, she saw only the shadow of the hole at its far end. A crescent moon peeked from behind the clouds to solemnly greet her and to be her torch. With its white light, she saw an empty grave and nothing more. The killer and his quarry had mysteriously disappeared.

She walked up to the dark hole and found it completely empty. The pile of dirt and the fallen shovel were all that remained of the perpetrator and his quest. Bravely, she looked about the garden, but found no evidence of the villain or the body. The garden was walled on all sides except the one facing the manor. The only egress was through the gate to the back parking area, the very path that she had just traversed. "Surely, the killer could not have taken the body over the five foot wall, or could he?" she wondered.

She decided to investigate this option. Leaving the garden, she crept around the thicket covered wall. As she suspected, the killer had to flee with his evidence through the front gate, for nothing of interest presented itself along the periphery of the garden's outer walls. He would have had to head toward her as she approached from the stairwell. "How could she have missed him?" she wondered.

She checked around the house itself, but did not find any evidence of the killer or the body. Exhausted and frustrated, she returned to her room. All was silent, except for the raging battle footage in Helga's room.

Molly settled back on her couch. It was nearly 4 am. "Should I awaken my boss?" she wondered. Turning on her lights, she made a cup of hot chocolate. She needed to rest her nerves and to make a decision.

Turning off the lights again, she settled back on her couch with her hot cocoa, safe once more. It was nearly 4:30 am when she became aware of more shoveling. Creeping to her window while keeping her room dark, she again saw the dark figure in the rose garden. To her horror, the hole was filled and the figure, shovel in hand, walked out of the garden toward the house. He was most certainly a man, but she could not recognize him for the moon had gone and the dense trees obscured her view. She decided to head back out into the hall. The battle was still raging on Helga's television set, but all else was quiet. Molly had her loaded gun now as she once again approached the stairwell. She peered down the stairs, but heard and saw no one. The killer had vanished.

With the loaded gun, she made her way down the stairs and out the back door returning to the rose garden. The moon greeted her again, but all was silent. All was still. No one was there and the hole was gone, and in its place she beheld three white rose bushes that appeared ominously grey in the resurrected moonlight.

CHAPTER 53

Once Upon a Miracle

Meanwhile, back at the hospital, Jennifer had shaken off the odd encounter, not certain if it was just more of her vivid imagination. She began to take Mary's vital signs. The doctors had decided to stop all medications since the patient was now beyond all statistically valid chances of recovery. The finality of Mary's situation sank deeper into Jennifer's reality.

Mary's heart rate was normal. Her blood pressure was normal. Neurological activity was normal. Jennifer checked all of the vital signs. "Neurological activity normal?" She paused as the relevance of her last observation sank into her logical mind. She double checked the monitor. As she did so, she heard a voice, one that she had never heard before.

"What time is it?" the voice demanded. It was the voice of a young woman. Startled, Jennifer looked back toward the window where the mysterious woman had appeared earlier that night. No one was there!

"Where am I?" the voice inquired in a light melodic tone.

It was then that Jennifer Angel realized that the statistically impossible had occurred. Mary was sitting up on her bed, asking her questions.

"Mary! Oh, my God! Mary! You're alive and awake!" Jennifer was more shocked at this sight than all of the previous visitations combined. Her medical background had not prepared her for such a miracle.

"Yes, and you must be my guardian angel, Jennifer," Mary smiled at the shocked nurse.

"How do you know my name? I assure you that your guardian angel is far more powerful!" Jennifer was screaming in excitement.

"I know your name because of your name tag," Mary replied with her charismatic smile. "And, since I assume that you took good care of me, you must be my guardian angel. No?" Mary giggled. Joy seemed to emanate from her.

"Can you get me a piece of paper and a pen before you summon the doctors? Please! I need to write down all that happened to me while I still remember it. Please?" Mary pleaded.

"Sure!" Jennifer replied and quickly returned with a clean pad of paper and a pen. "Here you are."

"Give me a few moments, please. I just need to try and remember. It was most fascinating," Mary replied as she began scribbling onto the note pad. She was so light and joyful, so peaceful yet energized. It took about twenty minutes before Mary paged Jennifer. The latter had respected her request and had not informed anyone, although she was getting nervous as her duty was to inform a doctor, immediately.

"Thank you. That's better. I know I'd forget the details if I didn't write them down. May I have a glass of water, if that's all right?" Mary seemed cheery and completely normal.

"Yes, certainly, but I can't give you much," Jennifer replied, while excitement filled her thoughts. "Mary isn't going to die! Mary is very much alive! Thank you, Lord!" Jennifer whispered quietly as she fetched the water. "Miracles can happen! Thank you! Prayers are heard! Thank you!" She was nearly crying with joy.

Returning quickly with a glass of water, she sat at Mary's bedside. "Jen, first I need to thank you for taking such great care of me. Thank you!" Mary looked into Jennifer's eyes and smiled. Her blue eyes sparkled. Jennifer realized for the first time how strikingly blue they were when filled with life. They had such power and depth. When in the coma, they were extinguished, hidden from view by endless sleep. Now, they were vibrant, powerful and free.

"Second, I wish to tell you that all that you experienced was as real as us sitting here. You were meant to experience it. That was their gift to you. I know that it was a lot to take in, but trust me that it was real. Okay?" Mary smiled and locked eyes with Jennifer.

"I'm glad you're awake, Mary. I just don't know about the rest." Jennifer looked up at her. "How'd you know about that? You were in a coma!

"Precisely, why!" Mary replied with a smile. "But, it was all real, Jen. I assure you of that!" Mary proclaimed in complete confidence.

"Okay, but it's a lot to accept. I'm just glad you're all right. I need to let the doctor-on-call know that you're awake, or I'll get in trouble," Jennifer replied.

"I understand, but can you do me one more favor and get a hold of Jack Fulton? Please tell him that I've awakened, and ask him to come at once," Mary requested. "Do you know who he is? I'm not sure that I can recall his number just yet," she added.

"I know who he is," Jennifer replied and her expression changed. "Why do you want to see him?"

"I need to forgive him for something, and I want to make sure that he's all right," Mary added, detecting Jennifer's change in demeanor, but not reacting to it. "Can you ask him to come here as soon as possible?"

"Okay, if you wish, but I really have to call the doctor now," Jennifer insisted.

"I understand. Thank you for everything, Jen," Mary smiled. She knew what would follow: the doctor's questions, the tests and the police investigation. She had somehow witnessed the near future. Calmly, she readied herself for the public reaction.

"Okay, I'll call the doctor and then I'll call Jack," Jennifer replied.

"If you don't mind, can you call Jack first?" Mary asked.

"Okay, but then I need to get the doctor in here," Jennifer warned.

"That's fine. Thank you, Jen. You're a dear. Can I step into the rest room?" Mary asked.

"That will have to wait." Jennifer used her authority. "We have you hooked up, so you can go in the bag. Okay?"

"Forgot about the bag," Mary laughed. "I'll hold it," she replied with a chuckle, completely alert and seemingly completely healed. "I understand, Jen. You need to tell the doctor, first. But, please don't forget about Jack."

"I'll call him right now and then the doctor. Once the doctor says that it's fine to disconnect you, you can use the bathroom," Jennifer explained.

"Deal!" Mary replied and laid back against her pillow, still reflecting on her experience.

Jennifer did as promised. She called Jack at home after looking up his number. To her surprise, he sounded very awake, despite the early hour. His reaction was one of disbelief and it took her a while to convince him, but soon he was on his way.

Next, she contacted the doctor-on-call. He was completely shocked and asked her to repeat her statement. "I'll be right there!" he exclaimed and hung up.

Soon the doctor arrived and the official investigation into the miraculous recovery of Mary Collins had begun.

CHAPTER 54

A Remarkable Journey

As soon as the doctor had conducted his first round of evaluations, Jack Fulton was allowed into the room at Mary's request. Mary's doctor was in contact with the police and knew about the ongoing criminal investigation. Recently, he had been informed by the Inspector that Jack Fulton was a person of interest in the case. Therefore, he was reluctant to allow Jack a private sitting with Mary and insisted that Jennifer remain in the room. He himself departed to call the Inspector and tell him the news. He reached the Inspector's answering service, but was sure that the Inspector would soon return his call, despite the early hour.

Jack was excited to see Mary. "Thank God you're back! You had me so worried," he confessed. He looked at Jennifer inquisitively for he was uncomfortable with her in the room. "Can we have some privacy, please?" he asked her.

"I'm sorry, Mr. Fulton, but it's the doctor's strict orders that I remain here while you're in the room," Jennifer replied.

"Why?" Jack asked for he was visibly annoyed.

"Because that is his request, and I must follow the doctor's orders," Jennifer said frankly.

"That's absurd!" Jack objected.

"Maybe, but I have my orders to protect the patient," Jennifer replied.

"Protect her? From me? That's ridiculous! I take personal offense to that statement!" Jack was getting angry.

"Calm down, Jack," Mary instructed in a tranquil voice. "She's just doing her job. Besides, she's the one who cared for me all these weeks. I want her to stay. Regardless of the doctor's orders, I want her here," Mary replied and smiled reassuringly at Jennifer. "Jen and I have no secrets. Right, Jen?"

Jennifer felt awkward. Her sole response was a smile.

"Mary, I'm glad you're back, but that statement made no sense," Jack replied in a caring tone. "You don't even know this girl. You met her only an hour ago," Jack objected. "She's here to spy on us, so that the cops can continue to harass me." Jack glared at Jennifer. The latter retracted in her seat, more uncomfortable than before.

"Jack, I know more than you suspect. At least Jen has been faithful to me." She smiled once more at Jennifer.

"What's that suppose to mean?" Jack objected, while he tried to understand how Mary could know about his infidelity with Molly. "Did Jennifer spy on me and tell her? Did the cops know and tell Jennifer, who ratted to Mary? That would be too weird!" he thought.

"You know very well what it means," Mary replied calmly. "I know that your weakness got the better of you. She's charming and has a good heart, but you must make a choice, Jack. To love someone above your own self is the only meaningful love. To romantically love two people at once is sincere confusion at best. That in itself may not be wrong, but it's wrong if you imply or proclaim sole commitment to one or the other, or both. You know of what I speak." Mary looked square into Jack's eyes.

He lowered his head, breaking her stare, and by that act, admitting his guilt. She knew all, and he was baffled as to how that was possible. His anger at Jennifer intensified until it lashed out. "How'd you know?" he turned to Jennifer. "How'd you know what I did? You're a police spy, aren't you!"

Mary answered for her. "She's exactly what she claims to be, honest and true. Take an example in that, if you wish to have me back, Jack."

The strong words sank into his mind and heart. He was torn and Mary knew it. He was genuinely attracted to two women at the same time. Yes, it was selfish. He knew it was wrong, but he simply didn't know which one to choose. He was still searching and enjoying the search. But he also knew that he had to fully commit to one or the other. He knew in his heart that to lose them both would be a grave mistake.

"Enough! You'll figure it out in good time, but don't wait too long." Mary changed the subject. "More importantly for now, I wanted to share with the two of you my journey while I was asleep."

She asked Jennifer to move closer to the bed, thus including her in the inner circle. At first, Jack objected, but apparently he had no choice in the matter.

"What journey, Mary? You were in a coma for God's sakes, not touring Europe!" Jack objected.

"There, my dear Jack, is the source of your spiritual bottleneck," Mary replied.

"What're you saying? I don't have a bottleneck!" Jack objected. "What happened to you? You sound and act different, like you're a clairvoyant prophet or something."

"No. I'm still me, only a little wiser. As for you, you talk the walk, not walk the talk," Mary replied.

"What does that mean?" Jack felt attacked once more.

"You proclaim yourself as spiritual, yet you have so little faith," Mary explained.

"What's this, beat up on Jack day?" he was getting angry again. The reunion was losing its luster.

"No. I'm simply trying to help you," Mary replied.

"Well, you're failing miserably!" Jack objected.

"My apologies, Jack. Let me start again. May I?" she asked sincerely and respectfully.

"If you promise to give me a break with the lecturing," he replied.

"I promise." She smiled and waited.

"Well, go ahead, tell us about your fantastic journey," Jack replied.

She looked at him to make sure that he was sincere and then began anew. "I was in a coma, of course, but what happened to me while in that state was truly amazing. I don't know much about near-death experiences, but I do know that although my body was functioning and my mind was not, I was beyond both. It's hard to explain, but I feel that the two of you would understand and should know," she paused to see if they were still willing to delve into these mysteries with her.

They seemed to be, so she continued, "The last thing that I remember was the fall itself, and then there was extreme darkness. I heard noises, like those of this world, but they were more fearful and more confused. They sounded like some kind of a mixture of memories, mine and those of others. It was a dreamlike state with the same level of seeming confusion. I was in this state for a time that I can't quantify for it may have been minutes or days. I'm not sure," she paused. It was obvious that her recollection of this first stage was not a pleasant one.

Then she smiled, staring ahead as if she were reliving the experience. "Next, I saw a light. It was like the sun shining through an endless sea of dark clouds. But it was brighter and whiter than the sun. It was very sharp and intense." Mary glanced at her notes, to make sure that she had not left anything out. Her brain was straining to fill in all of the details.

Jack was quiet now, but still brooding. Jennifer was eager, for she too had experienced many odd things in this very room, and she wanted to understand.

Mary once more glanced at her notes. "What're the notes for? Did you write while in your coma?" Jack asked irreverently, still expressing his anger at her earlier critique of him and his recent behavior.

She did not react to his anger. "No. I took these right after I awakened," she replied calmly. "I knew I would forget the details if I didn't write them down. Is that okay?" she replied and then smiled at Jennifer. There was a growing distance between her and Jack, and he continued to widen it.

"Please go on, Mary," Jennifer insisted.

"Is it okay if I go on, Jack?" Mary looked at him.

He nodded his head in approval.

Mary continued, "I, of my free will, entered that bright light. It was beckoning me, but it was somehow made clear to me that I had to chose to enter. Upon entry, the experience was unlike any other. I felt propelled through time and space, through some kind of an energy field. It was not unlike passing through a brightly-lit tunnel at tremendous speed or a long, narrow, bright spinning vortex. Soon it was over and I was greeted by the most angelic being, who introduced herself as my guide. She had a magenta glow that oscillated to a deep purple hue. I lost track of time, or more precisely, time seemed less rigid as if it had lost track of me." She chuckled and raised her eyebrows in an expression of bafflement.

"No offense, Mary, but maybe you were just dreaming?" Jack interjected.

"The medical facts do not support that conclusion. The part of her brain that creates dreams was dormant, in fact, it was completely shut down," Jennifer interjected.

Jack raised his left brow at Jennifer, in a sign of distrust, but said nothing.

"I understand how that would be your first reaction, Jack. But, it didn't feel like a dream," Mary continued. "I don't know how to explain it, but it was all so vibrant and distinct. The time sequence was linear throughout my journey, unlike the randomness of dreams, but the events seemed to speed up at times, and at other times, they appeared to be much, much slower," Mary replied, still smiling as if the recollection brought her joy.

"One thing that was very evident was the extreme positive energy, best described as compete joy — joy in the moment, like that of a small child. That joyful energy seemed to unite everything. I was content to stay, but my guide informed me that it wasn't my time, that I had to return. Oddly, I recall feeling torn about that fact. I really wanted to rest and stay, but my guide would not permit it." Mary did not need her notes any longer. It was all coming back to her now. Jennifer and Jack had her full attention and the room was completely still, except for the sounds of her quiet voice fused with the backdrop of the medical monitors.

"The oddest thing about it all was that this Heaven seemed to be extremely similar to Earth. The landscapes were there, the trees, the mountains and the streams, even the ocean. It was as if it were on our planet, on Earth, yet it was different. My guide told me that it was too complicated to explain, but that Earth and its Heaven share the same space-time field but at vastly different energy spectra. I remember that part but it still doesn't mean anything to me. Does it make sense to you, Jack?" Mary looked at the scientist.

"Not really, but there's still so little that we really understand about quantum physics and the time-space continuum," he sincerely admitted.

"Right, well, at any rate, I was taken, or more precisely, flown across and beyond these Earth-like landscapes. It was like something out of Peter Pan," she chuckled. "There was neither weight of a body nor any physical restrictions to hinder me. I simply glided with my guide like I had wings, but I didn't of course. In fact, I seemed to have lost a sense of form yet retained my own entity, which still makes no sense to me. At any event, it seemed more like being transported quickly, without any effort." She tried to explain the unexplainable.

"This last part was the oddest of all," she continued. "I was guided to appear before a group of higher souls, or so my guide revealed to me during our effortless flight. That flight ended at a place that had no resemblance to Earth. The energy was much more intense there. An omnipresent peace permeated this nondescript place. I felt incredibly light, happy and loved. My guide and I entered a room for lack of a better description, but it lacked walls. It was more like a particular location in the midst of endless space. Anyway, as I said, it was extremely odd." Mary paused and began to tear up.

Jack was going to ask Jennifer as to what kind of hallucinogenic drugs they were using on Mary, but seeing Mary's reaction, he reconsidered. Jennifer was much more receptive, having experienced her own share of unbelievable marvels of late.

Mary continued, "Then, as we waited there with my guide, seven orbs seemed to materialize out of the empty space itself. Their aura was that of royal purple, not unlike shades of my guide's aura, but more intense and vibrant. Mine seemed to be more yellow. Somehow these colored auras defined levels of a soul, but I have little recollection of such details. All that I recall is that these orbs of light were the high-level souls. I know this must sound too weird. It does even to me, as I'm relating it," she sighed, "but it was so."

She checked her notes once more before resuming her story. "These high-level souls surrounded me and my guide, forming a semi-circle of light. They almost fused into one, but I think it just appeared that way. But, I clearly remember that the soul orb positioned in the center of this semi-circle intermingled his or her energy with that of my guide. They didn't speak, but in this shared energy, the two seemed to exchange information. Since these souls were simply orbs that didn't speak, I couldn't tell if they had any kind of a gender preference as did my guide. That's why I mentioned that this lead soul was a he or a she, or maybe neither," Mary explained.

Mary stopped again and looked at Jennifer, and then at Jack. "Guys, I realize how odd this sounds as I'm retelling it. It does sound crazy, but I swear that I experienced it," she shrugged her shoulders realizing that she was stretching their ability to trust her and to comprehend.

Regardless, she continued, "At this point, my guide turned to me and summarized the information exchange between her and this one high-level soul. Using some sort of telepathy as before, she related to me that these souls confirmed that I must return to form for my time on Earth was not yet over. She stressed that I should make an effort to teach others and to heal wounds, both new and old. She clarified that most of all, I must use my remaining time in the 'Earthly School', as she called it, to learn to be more unconditional and selfless in my love, my forgiveness, and my grace to all souls, for all souls are of the one Divine and connected in that one Divine."

Mary paused again to check her notes. "She also told me that she would always guide me. Then, she explained that this group of highly enlightened souls was one of a few that presided over Earth's Heaven, adding that I was fortunate to have this time with them. Finally, she revealed that they are pleased with my progress. All this happened so quickly, as if instantly, and before I knew it, we were flying back over the familiar Earth-like land-scapes. My guide and I parted at the same place that we had met. As soon as she disappeared I was sucked into that tunnel of bright light just before I awakened here." Mary stopped to reflect, and sighed audibly. "I know it all sounds crazy, but you must believe me," she insisted.

"Sounds like one hell of a trip," Jack observed. "But, I believe you, Mary, although I can't comprehend it. It sounded like one of those tales of an alien abduction or something equally bizarre. Sorry, but I'm a scientist and this kind of stuff is hard for me to comprehend. I'm truly trying to be more open to all this, but this is still a bit too much for me," he confessed in all sincerity.

"I totally understand, Jack. It's a lot for me to accept, as well, and I experienced it," Mary confessed.

Jennifer was quiet, patiently waiting her turn to speak. Finally, all eyes were on her as she too reflected on what Mary had shared.

"Since you arrived here, Mary, I have become more interested in all this and have begun to read about near death experiences, or NDEs, like the one you described. Fortunately, there's a growing volume of data on the subject that seems to align fairly closely to what you related to us, especially to the first parts," Jennifer replied. This entire experience had increased Jennifer's interest in the subjects of neurology and neuropsychology, including the mysteries of consciousness and NDEs.

"Jennifer, I don't doubt your sincere efforts but I think that there needs to be much more solid research done on the subject of NDEs before we can scientifically accept such claims. No offense, Mary," Jack concluded.

"I agree about the need for additional research, but I hope that we always keep an open mind and not simply dismiss as lunacy the growing number of such experiences and their surprising consistency," Jennifer replied. "Many are even experienced by highly reputable scientists and medical professionals. As our medical abilities grow, and we often return patients from the clutches of death, the numbers of NDEs grow in proportion," she added.

"Thank you, both, for your support in all this. It means so much to me," Mary replied and smiled at Jennifer, before turning to Jack. "Jack, I know that this is hard for you to accept. It's a lot for me to accept, as well. I simply know that it was real, just as I know a dream is not real. I don't ask that you believe in it. I simply ask that you allow me to do so."

"Of course, Mary, you're free to believe whatever you chose to believe. But tell me this, what did your guide look like?" Jack asked.

"Most of the time, she took the form of a beautiful woman with black hair and light violet eyes, but, at times, she was a child or even old, very old, and at other times she was formless, as when we entered that meeting with the high-level souls. In fact, her form was less distinct then her aura, which was always the color of...."

"Magenta, with hues of deep purple," Jennifer completed Mary's sentence.

"Yes," Mary smiled. "You know her?"

"Yes, both Jack and I have seen her here in this room, while you lay in your coma," Jennifer replied. "Right, Jack?"

"Well, I wouldn't go that far. I admit that I did see a mysterious woman with an odd glow seated next to you, right over there, on the first night I arrived." He pointed at the empty chair near the window. However, I must also confess that I only saw her that first night, and I was not in a very sound state at that point." He admitted the sighting, which made Jennifer smile. She was not imagining it after all.

"Wow! Okay. So, you guys know her," Mary chuckled.

"Jen knows her. I know only rocks and minerals," Jack corrected.

Mary did not respond, rather she changed the subject. "One last item that I need to share and then I'm done. My guide left me with a key point, stressing that I share it often and never forget it."

"What was that? Don't do drugs!" Jack added, for he could no longer hold back his skepticism.

"Very funny, Jack. Now I know where you really stand on all this," Mary fired back.

"I sincerely want to know," Jennifer added.

"Ok, so this is for you, Jen. Just before we parted, my guide asked me to remember three words," Mary replied.

"Three words? That's it?" Jennifer asked in puzzlement. "What are they?"

"Renounce and Rejoice!"

"Why's that so important?" asked Jack. "Sounds like a fortune cookie."

Mary once again ignored Jack's skepticism and continued. "My guide explained that joy is the clearest expression of our connection to the Divine, along with unconditional love, of course. Yet, the joy of a young child that binds he or she so closely to Heaven is that which so often eludes us as we grow older and more responsible. She simply advised that we try to renounce all that is not of love or that does not increase our joy. She stressed that this doesn't mean that we will not have times when we're sad or stressed or challenged, for there too lie the lessons of this 'Earthly

School'. But, we must try and renounce all that's not of the heart, so that joy may flow through us to brighten our lives and those of all that we encounter. This joyous light will never fail us if we don't let it fade through greed, lust, fear, hate, anger and other dark forms of the 'self-centered ego', as she put it." Mary paused as she too pondered the importance of this message, confirming it once more by rereading her scribbled notes.

Upon further review of those notes, she continued. "My guide stressed that joy and unconditional love form the torch that's there to light the path to the Divine. Therefore, we must take care to keep it bright, through our thoughts, words, acts and grace, as often as we can, until we too simply become that very joy and that very unconditional love. She stressed that the most enlightened teachers in human history all mastered this inner joy and unconditional love, which kept them closely connected to the Divine."

Mary checked her notes again. "Then, my guide reminded me that,

'I of myself can do nothing for it is the Divine in me that does the work.'

She explained that this does not give me permission to expect rewards without effort, or to give up and feel powerless. On the contrary, it means that within me, in my soul, I am an extension of the Divine, and, if I allow that greater connection to work through me, miracles can and will happen. It was then that she disappeared. In her place these words echoed through my mind like a timeless tune until I awakened.

'All that matters is the love you give and the joy you share.'

I know what she meant. Love freely given of your heart and joy freely shared from your heart is all that defines you as a soul and your life's work as a soul." Mary stopped for she was in tears.

Jennifer came to her to console her, while Jack silently reflected on what he had done.

CHAPTER 55

The Arrest

Mary was getting tired. Despite her remarkable recovery, her mind and body were stressed by the recent ordeal. Jack was about to leave, when Dr. Murphy, Mary's neurologist, appeared. He cordially greeted Jennifer and Jack, and quickly turned his attention to his patient.

"My dear, you're a miracle and nothing less. I've been practicing medicine for over twenty five years and I've never experienced anything like this. Sure, I've read of such cases in medical journals, but to experience it is something all together different," he proclaimed with a smile. He was an old school doctor with a tremendous empathy for his patients.

"How was this possible?" Jack asked.

"Your guess is as good as mine, young man. You see, Mary not only had a severe head trauma, but also the part of Mary's brain that makes us human, controlling our emotions and thoughts, was completely shut down. There was no ability to think or dream, or even function beyond basic physiological activity as governed by the more primal portions of the brain. But, even those were failing, as evident by her increased dependence on life support systems. The vast magnitude of this medical miracle is indisputable," the good doctor proclaimed, smiling at Mary once more. "You're my miracle, my dear. Few doctors get to witness one of this magnitude. But, most of all, I'm so glad that you're back with us. You must rest. I must dismiss your company for you must rest." He checked her vital signs as Jack waved Mary goodbye, still pondering the impact of the doctor's words as it related to what Mary had shared.

Jack did not get far down the hall of the trauma ward. He was in deep introspection when he found himself face to face with Inspector Cabot. The latter was flanked by two uniformed police officers.

"There you are! We heard about Mary's miraculous recovery. Lucky for you, huh?" the Inspector addressed Jack. It was clear that he did not like him.

"Are you coming to see, Mary?" Jack asked, still confused. The feeling of disdain between the two men was mutual.

"Yes, for a moment. But first and foremost, I'm here to arrest you for attempted homicide!" the Inspector exclaimed with a smile. "You thought that you would escape me, Fulton. Well, I got you now. Please arrest him, officers!" the Inspector ordered.

"You can't arrest me! I didn't do anything wrong!" Jack objected.

"Sure, sure, sure. They all say that. We all know better, don't we, Fulton? It'll be my pleasure to place a social predator like you behind bars. That's what I enjoy about my line of work, to capture guys like you, and keep them off our streets and out of our lives," the Inspector proclaimed. "Book him!"

The two police officers began to read Jack his rights as they handcuffed him. At that very moment, Jennifer walked out of Mary's room. She was shocked by the sight of the arrest and ran up to the scene.

"What's going on here?" she asked.

"Miss Angel, is it?" the Inspector addressed Jennifer. "We're arresting Mr. Fulton for attempted homicide and a number of other related charges, all associated with the case of Mary Collins," the Inspector explained.

Jennifer looked at Jack, who was now in handcuffs, and then back at the Inspector. She retained a shocked expression on her face. "Jack's certainly a womanizer, but a killer? Hardly!" she said aloud, as Jack cringed at Jennifer's review of his character. "You can't arrest him!" she objected.

"We definitely can and just did, Miss," the Inspector replied, feeling fully empowered and justified.

Jennifer ran back to Mary's room and interrupted the doctor. "Mary, they arrested Jack for your fall. What should I do?" she blurted out.

"Ask the Inspector to come see me, so I may have a word with him. I assume the Inspector's making the arrest," Mary stated calmly.

"How'd you know about the Inspector?" Jennifer asked, but decided not to wait for an answer. She ran back to the Inspector, who was already on his way to see Mary, having left the two officers to dispense with Jack.

"Mary wants to see you!" Jennifer proclaimed, while still rushing down the hall.

"Good! I want to see her as well." As he entered the room, he greeted the doctor first. "Thank you for your support and your notification, Doctor."

Dr. Murphy appeared nervous and reluctant to admit his part as the Inspector's informant. He was simply following the Inspector's orders, but felt odd nonetheless. He quickly left the room, trying to stay clear of such judicial matters.

"Mary, I'm Inspector Cabot with the State Police. I handled your case. May I say that I'm so pleased to meet you and to see that you have miraculously recovered, as the good doctor informed me over the telephone." The Inspector addressed Mary in a sincere tone. He was a father of three daughters and a kindhearted man, who took pride in protecting young women, like Mary, as if they were his own flesh and blood. Thus, he persistently pursued predators like Jack Fulton. He was expecting a thank you from Mary for capturing her assailant.

"Hello, Inspector. The pleasure is mine," Mary began in a soft, confident tone. "First, I'd like to thank you for your sincere and tireless efforts to protect my rights and to do what is just. We need more men like you," she praised, sounding much wiser than her years.

The Inspector nodded his head in acceptance of her praise. This was why he had come to see Mary, to meet her and to accept her gratitude. "Glad to do so, my dear. You see, I've got daughters like you, and I wouldn't want any harm to come to them, either. We need to stick together and keep the predators off our streets," he added.

"Yes, and you and your team excel at that effort," Mary praised.

The Inspector ate it up. "Thank you, Miss. Let me share with you that we've apprehended Jack Fulton after clearly identifying him as your assailant. I hope that he was not here to harm you. I assure you that we'll keep him away from you. Where he's headed, he wont harm a fly." The Inspect chuckled for he had his man. He was proud of his success. All was as he had expected, except that which followed.

"Inspector, my sincere request is that you please set Jack Fulton free, immediately," Mary proclaimed with a smile, placing her request calmly, as if she were ordering breakfast.

"What!" the Inspector exclaimed, nearly falling backwards. "What kind of a fool is this girl?" he thought instantly.

"Yes, Inspector. You see, I asked Jack to come here this morning. He's very dear to me and I don't wish him any harm," Mary proclaimed gently and smiled once more.

"But, he tried to kill you! We have clear evidence and testimony to that effect. We know that he pushed you off that cliff. You survived only by the Grace of God," the Inspector objected.

"By that same Grace, I ask you to release him. In all due respect for your efforts and authority, Inspector, there was no ill will or harm done, and I don't wish to press any charges against Jack Fulton or any charges related to my fall. That's my wish, Sir. I don't believe that you have a case against Jack, for I'll testify that he did not push me. So, please release him, immediately," Mary requested firmly but calmly.

"Miss, you're making a grave mistake. This man's not what he pretends to be. He has you in his spell. That's how guys like that operate and how they succeed. They're the foulest form of offenders. They're the killers, the rapists, the child molesters, the manipulating wife beaters of our society. We must eradicate them at every opportunity. If you release him now, he'll not only potentially harm you in the future, but most certainly harm others. He has probably already harmed others before you. In fact, I know he has," the Inspector reflected on the case of his own dear daughter, who had her heart broken by the very same man that he now held in legitimate custody. To allow this villain a free legal escape was unthinkable.

"I wish him released. That's all. Thank you, Inspector. Once you do release him, please ask him to come see me." Mary was in charge and she knew it.

"I'll do no such thing! We have pictures of the man pushing you," the Inspector objected.

"Or trying to catch me?" Mary replied with a smile. "You're not sure, are you? You have no case, Inspector. I'm completely fine, and I do not wish to press charges since my fall was an accident!" Mary insisted.

The Inspector let out a big sigh. He realized that now it would be nearly impossible to successfully prosecute Jack Fulton. Besides, he could not afford the negative publicity with his boss or the public. However, he could not accept complete defeat. He had the facts proving that she was pushed by none other than Jack Fulton. Yet, if she insisted that her fall was an accident, and medically she was fully recovered, he had a weak case and his boss would never let him prosecute. He was trapped and she knew it.

"I'll release him, but I'll not relay your message to him. You're making a huge mistake, Miss. Good day!" the Inspector turned and left, thwarted once more.

It did not take more than a few minutes before Jack returned to Mary's room. He was visibly deflated. "Thank you," is all that he could muster.

"You're welcome, but I know all, Jack. We're not meant to be, so goodbye," she replied.

He looked up at her in disbelief. "Did she just save me only to release me out of her life?" he thought.

She could read him like a book. "You're not ready to have a relationship with me or with any other woman. Grow up, Jack, and fix all that you've done," she replied and looked away.

He left the room without another word.

CHAPTER 56

Through the Looking Glass

Although it was a perfectly sunny spring day, a violent squall was brewing in the local State Police headquarters. Inspector Cabot was furious. He had finally captured Jack Fulton and was about to reveal to the world the true nature of this social predator. It was to be a great day of victory. Instead, it brought defeat. "That stupid, stupid girl!" is all that the Inspector could manage the entire long ride from the hospital. "That stupid, stupid girl!"

Once at the station, he was forced to publicly accept his defeat and this brought more anger. That anger burst forth at the team meeting that he hurriedly assembled.

"Darn, that girl! It's this kind of stupidity and naive sense of forgiveness that allows predators, like Fulton, to continue to walk our streets and even teach our youth. This is ridiculous!" the Inspector raged. "If we were in most other parts of the world that guy would be rotting in jail. Damn this game of cat and mouse! Who would have thought that that stupid girl would wake up and not press charges? She should be kissing my feet, not blocking justice!" He stormed about the room at the marvel of his team. They let him vent without a word. They knew better than to step into his path of fury.

Finally, the good Inspector ran out of steam and collapsed into his office chair. Prior to that act, he had ripped the sheet off of his suspect board and threw the pictures of the various past suspects about the room. Poor Suzy Kurtz's picture ended up in the trash from which Big Bob gently extracted it when the Inspector was not looking. Tony Bond's picture ended up in a potted plant, and even Stacy Reed was not spared, for her picture landed in a stale, half-full cup of cold coffee. Only the picture of Jack Fulton received special attention. After the Inspector swore his vengeance on the photo, he proceeded to rip it into tiny pieces, which he scattered about the room like confetti for the cleaning staff to recover.

"Damn this case and damn the laws! But, most of all damn that Fulton and his naive girlfriend! Any woman that falls for that bastard is stupid!" the Inspector proclaimed, and suddenly sobered, after recalling that this own daughter had once fallen for the charms of the same young man.

Molly felt herself sinking into her chair at the thought of being on the list of Jack's stupid conquests. Yet, she loved the Inspector as a father and felt compassion for him. It was in this love and compassion that she finally overcame her fear of being exposed as Jack's latest romantic conquest. Jack, the predator, should serve justice. In her mind, the Inspector was right. She had to take the high road regardless of personal consequences. She could not let Jack kill again or attempt to do so.

"Sir, I think I found another lead that may help," she suddenly blurted out.

"What? What are you talking about, Molly? This case is dead! The victim is fine and will not press charges, claiming she fell accidentally. There's nothing more to do here. Fulton won!" the Inspector publicly proclaimed, while clenching his teeth.

"Not if there's a second victim, and we can prove that he did it," Molly added.

"A second victim? Who?" The Inspector stopped his ranting. She had his complete attention. "Was there hope?" he thought and began to calm down.

"You know the odd house that you had me move into?" Molly began. "Well, first of all, you were right, there's a secret society. I just found out last night." Molly did not admit that she already knew for three days. "It's some kind of a haven for mystics and psychics, nothing violent or crazy, simply odd. But, the society's not relevant to this. What is relevant is that a young woman is missing from the house, and that she may have been murdered by Jack Fulton," Molly proclaimed.

The room was completely still and all attention was on Molly. "Has she gone mad?" Chen thought in alarm.

Finally, the Inspector broke the shocked silence. "Please say more, Molly."

Molly related the story to the team. She left out any referenced to her involvement with Jack, and decided that if any such details were to surface, she would deny them or claim that she was doing everything in her power to extract pertinent information out of him. After all, she needed to win his trust. No one needed to know that she fell for the charms of a killer. Besides, she was now aligned with her boss. Jack was a predator, a liar and a two-timer, that part was clear. He had never let on to her that he was committed to Mary Collins, not even now that the girl had recovered. "What kind of scum sleeps around when his girlfriend is in a coma?" she concluded. "If he can stoop so low, then maybe murder is not out of the question," she postulated to herself. Molly was now convinced that Jack Fulton tried to kill Mary and succeeded in killing Alice.

The Inspector took rapid notes. "We must investigate that rose garden immediately, assuming that he didn't move the evidence. We may have to investigate the entire house. I'll get Judge Preachy to issue a warrant as soon as possible. Great work, Molly!

I'm always amazed at this team. What a team!" The Inspector was excited again. There was new hope. His prey would not get away after all. He would find that body if he had to turn over every brick of that house.

As the team parted with new marching orders focused on Alice Wadsworth and the Nightingale Manor, the Inspector asked Molly to remain behind in his office. "Thank you, Molly!" he exclaimed with a smiled. "This will go a long way towards your promotion," he added with a wink. "But tell me, how'd you get so close to Fulton?"

She smiled while thinking to herself, "If you only knew!"

He sensed her reservation and added, "Maybe, I don't want to know."

Molly did not answer, but simply left the room.

CHAPTER 57

White Roses

Following the Inspector's orders, Chen contacted Alice Wadsworth's parents and discovered that they were convinced that she was doing field work in a remote location as part of her anthropology studies. They had received several texts from Alice before she left and additional ones after her departure. These messages documented her trip and the on-going work in East Africa. During Chen's interview, Alice's father mentioned that he and his wife were perturbed by their inability to contact their daughter by phone. But, this too Alice had explained in her texts, blaming poor cell coverage and a busy field schedule.

Next, Chen followed up with the McLaren Department of Anthropology, which was supposedly heading up the trip. They had never heard of such a trip. They did share with Chen that they had been informed, via an e-mail from Alice, that she decided to withdraw from the program due to family matters related to her father's sudden death. Yet, Chen had spoke to Alice's father minutes prior to his call with the Anthropology Department. The roots of suspicion were growing deeper.

Unfortunately, no one had questioned Alice's whereabouts for nearly a month, until now. It appears that either Alice truly wanted to disappear, or someone was using her cell phone and computer to make her disappearance look unsuspicious to those closest to her.

When Chen dug into the cell phone records, it turned out that Alice's phone was inactive as of three days ago. The last texted message, corresponding to the field updates described by her parents, were four days ago from Brennantown, the home of McLaren University and not from East Africa. Alice Wadsworth was now an official missing person as her parents requested immediate police involvement.

The warrant to search the rose garden at the Nightingale Manor was granted, but the judge did not feel that there was sufficient evidence to warrant a search of the manor itself, which would be much more intrusive to the rights of the owner and the occupants. Nonetheless, the Inspector had his room to maneuver, and the hunt for Jack Fulton was active once more. Late that afternoon, the Inspector, along with an excavation contractor, two uniformed officers and his team, minus Molly, whose cover he wished to protect, descended upon Ms. Nightingale's manor.

When the Inspector rang the doorbell at the old residence, Ms. Nightingale answered the door. She was visibly shocked to see such a police presence. Her shock broadened when she discovered the cause. "That's crazy! You can't do this! I have rights!" she protested. "You won't find anything! Alice moved out of here nearly a month ago," she assured the Inspector. "This is a witch hunt in which we're being singled out!" she proclaimed, as the Inspector began to mobilize his team. She was angry, but presented with a warrant, she had no legal means to resist. "Just make sure that you restore that beautiful garden back to its full splendor. If any of those roses die as a result of this, I expect them to be replaced in kind."

"I assure you, ma'am, that we'll do so. Now, where's that garden?" the Inspector asked.

"In the back of the house, but you'd better not damage my property or anything on it, or I'll sue you!" Ms. Nightingale threatened. She did not like the police. They scared her.

The Inspector and his team invaded the rose garden like a swarm of hungry locusts. "Look, Inspector! Molly's right. Look at the white roses! They're freshly planted," Big Bob observed.

"That may be good or bad. If what Molly thinks she witnessed is true, then Fulton may have moved the body," the Inspector clenched his teeth.

Soon the backhoe was digging in the area of the recently planted white roses. A few minutes later, it became obvious that the area was free of any evidence of wrongdoing.

"Damn it! He moved her and planted white roses! While we have this warrant and the equipment, let's dig throughout this place, just in case," the Inspector ordered, and the excavation contractor complied. Before the hour was up, the once graceful rose garden looked like a construction site, complete with trenches and countless piles of earth.

"Nothing! Damn it, nothing! But we have you on the run, Fulton!" the Inspector proclaimed, while shaking his fist at the setting sun.

It took two days to restore the rose garden to Ms. Nightingale's satisfaction, but the police intrusion had created great anxiety within her and the entire house. Rumors were sweeping through the manor like waves of foul weather. No one was spared, and few slept soundly.

"Damn, the cops!" Ms. Nightingale confided to Trudy later that night. "They're probably using this drummed up nonsense to harass us." She was determined that all of this was a conspiracy against psychics and mediums.

The next evening, Molly returned to the manor. She intentionally kept her distance from the house for the past day and a half, so as not to risk exposing her true identity to her fellow residents during the police activity. None of the residents, except Chester, knew that she was an undercover detective. She hoped that she could trust him, for it was more imperative than ever that she maintain her cover. Her life could be at stake.

As she entered the back door of the manor, she ran into Chester at the bottom of the stairwell. The latter was smiling his characteristic ear-to-ear smile. "Boy, Molly, your boys sure made a mess of the rose garden. I bet Helga's furious," he laughed, for he disliked Helga.

"Chester, watch what you say or you'll blow my cover," Molly whispered, looking about suspiciously.

"I'll whisper, my dear. You know that you're wasting your time digging in the garden. The body's moved," he added.

"I know. I saw him move it the other night, but my boss didn't believe me," Molly admitted.

"Did you see, him? Did you see Jack moving the body?" Chester's eyes widened until they looked completely cat-like.

"I saw him, all right. But, I don't know where he moved it," Molly whispered back.

"Shame."

"Chester, is this a wild goose chase? I mean, it looked like a body, but what if it was something else?" Molly began to doubt herself. Deep down she did not want Jack Fulton to be a killer. That would mean that she slept with one, not once, but twice.

"What else could it be? Besides, despite what Ms. Nightingale told you, Alice didn't leave willingly." Chester looked about to see if they were alone.

"How do you know?"

"Because, no one throws ALL of her things out before leaving."

"What? I thought that Ms. Nightingale had a note from Alice that she was leaving?" Molly was puzzled.

"I sincerely believe that Ms. Nightingale is telling the truth, but is the note really from Alice or did someone write it to look like it was?" Chester questioned.

"You're right. That's a key piece of evidence that we didn't check," Molly admitted. "But, how do you know that Alice threw her possessions out? Does Ms. Nightingale know this?"

"I doubt that she knows anything beyond what she told your boys. I know she's odd, but she's honest to a fault." Chester was serious now. He too seemed honest, and certainly odd.

"So what happened?"

"The night Alice disappeared, I heard a lot of noise in the far part of the basement that had been divided into individual storage. I was tired and simply dismissed it. I had no reason to believe that it was in any way suspicious for Alice was very much alive that day and in no apparent danger. In fact, I had talked to her that afternoon," Chester confessed.

"What was the noise?"

"I don't know. I don't have access to that part of the basement. It's divided into separate storage facilities. But, days later, when I was doing my treasure hunting …"

"Do you mean dumpster diving?"

"To me it's treasure hunting," he corrected her. "Regardless, there, in one of the dumpsters, were many of Alice's possessions, including her photos, text books and many of her clothes. Later that night, I found Alice's gold necklace kicked under some of the old furniture that lines the basement hall leading to the storage facilities. Now, you tell me, if you're moving away, why not take those items with you? Why throw some away and throw others in the hallway in the basement. Also, how did her necklace end up down there in the basement, when Alice lived on the third floor and didn't have one of the storage areas. Why would she? She wasn't moving! She never mentioned moving, not even to me on the day she disappeared, except for that note that Ms. Nightingale received that night," Chester reasoned.

"Did you retrieve any of her things from the dumpsters?"

"No, she wasn't my size. Too petite."

"Chester, you're awful! Why didn't you go to the police?"

"At the time, I did not know she was gone. I did not find out until a week later and by then all that evidence was gone. Besides, at the time, I believed Ms. Nightingale when she said that Alice suddenly moved out. People are odd around here," Chester replied.

"That's an understatement! Who has access to the storage rooms in the basement? Who rents them?" Molly asked.

"I know that Jack rents one, as do Helga and Trudy. The last two are Ms. Nightingale's. That's as much as I know."

"Did you report the odd noise in the storage area that night?"

"No, but I continued to investigate weeks later, since something didn't feel right. That's when I discovered the freshly dug earth in the rose garden. When I approached Ms. Nightingale with the garden item, she simply replied that Jack and Helga had been planting some flowers. Helga's very fond of Jack, if you haven't noticed, and uses their mutual love of gardening as an excuse to be with him. I recalled seeing them planting white roses in the very spot that seemed so disturbed. A few days after you arrived, I did a little probing about using a long, thin iron rod and found that something was buried there. It was hard, yet soft as well," Chester inhaled audibly.

"I was going to call the cops, but since you were a cop anyway, I decided that I just needed a chance to tell you. When I tried, you and Jack were rather busy, if you know what I mean," he winked at Molly, whose heart sank. "At any rate, I did tell you. Unfortunately, your lover was on to us and moved the body." Chester gave his Cheshire Cat smile once more, but this time out of fear, more than anything else.

"I'll call my boss, Inspector Cabot, as soon as I get into my room. We need to open up those storage rooms," Molly concluded. "Thank you, Chester. You're a true pal."

"Pal? Great! I guess that's all I'll ever be. Jack gets laid and I get to be a pal," he thought.

Unbeknownst to both of them, someone had been hiding in the shadows of the upper stairwell, listening to their conversation. Undetected, the figure slipped silently up the stairs.

CHAPTER 58

Painting the Roses Red

*C*hester's new revelations had Molly's head spinning. There appeared to be a killer in the house, and, what was more, he was now standing in front of her door. She gasped and froze, as she stood at the end of the hall. The moment seemed to last a lifetime as time slowed to a near halt. She could see every muscle move in his neck as he slowly turned his head toward her. There was no room to react. Jack was already upon her.

She was about to scream when he addressed her in a soft tone. The tone made her pause and look at him anew.

"I came to explain myself. I heard everything," he said calmly as he stepped between her and the stairwell door.

"Everything?" Molly's heart nearly stopped. She instantly replayed the conversation that she had had in the stairwell with Chester moments earlier. "If he heard everything, then he'll surely kill me!" she thought. She realized that she was unarmed and very vulnerable.

"Yes, everything, and I think that it's time we stopped pretending. I know you know all that has transpired," he paused to accent his message.

Molly noticed that he was reaching into his jacket pocket for a gun. She could see his right hand grasp it. The muzzle was pointing through the fabric. "He's going to kill me right here in the hallway. He won't get away with it. He must be desperate!" she thought.

Keeping his hand in his coat pocket, he asked her if they could go into her room, which was right past Helga's door. "I got something for you, but not here in the open. There're too many ears about," he added.

She began to protest, but he insisted, maintaining his hand in his coat pocket. "Molly, I don't want to do this in the hallway."

"Hallway is fine," she heard herself reply.

"Please open the door! I insist!" He sounded urgent. "Don't force me to do this out here in the open," he warned.

She scrambled for the key in her purse and opened the door. He quickly followed her inside. "So, this is how it'll end," she thought and felt sweat running down her brow. Suddenly, something in her awakened. "Damn if I surrender to this predator without a fight!" flashed through her churning mind.

It was then that it happened. Jack Fulton closed the door and in the process instinctively looked back toward it. Molly used that moment to pounce on him like a cornered tigress. Before he knew it, he was the recipient of her years of martial arts training. With his mouth bleeding, he found himself doubled over on the floor, excruciating pain shooting up from his testicles. He could barely breath for the intense pain.

Not a shot was fired as she sat on top of him, pinning his arms behind his back. "So, you thought I'd just surrender to you. Think again, Jack! You're not playing around with naive Alice or innocent Mary. This is me that you're messing with, and I don't take crap from anyone, especially a psycho like you!" She pulled his right arm back to the point that it nearly popped out of his shoulder.

The pain was so intense that he could not answer, except for a dulled moan. As she held him down with her knees and left arm, she used her right hand to reach into his coat pocket to extract the gun. She rummaged around in the large pocket of his coat, then felt the cold metal. "So, you thought that you'd use this on me, huh?" She uttered between her teeth while giving his arm some slack, so that he could answer her.

He had finally found his voice. "Ahhh, you're killing my arm! What the hell's wrong with you? I came to invite you into the Society," he managed to blur out.

Just then, she extracted the object from his pocket. It was not a gun, but a small metal casting of the Wu Wei symbol that was so prevalent in the main meeting hall of the house. It was the symbol of the Société de Magie Noire.

"What?" she released him further. "You didn't come to kill me?"

"Kill you? Have you lost your mind? You're a scary woman! Please get off of me!" he demanded. He just wanted to run away from her.

She released him, but blocked the door. "We need to talk. What conversation did you overhear?" she asked.

"The one between you and Ms. Nightingale. I returned here to make up after our quarrel the other night because I thought I heard you crying. When I got here, I found the door partially open. You and Ms. Nightingale were in deep conversation, so I didn't want to interrupt. I know I shouldn't have listened, but I did listen. After talking with her about you, I convinced her to let you into the society. It took some convincing, but we were going to initiate you in the next meeting, if you accepted this token. But, all this was obviously a huge mistake on my part because you're not right. You're seriously disturbed! Let me out or I'll call the police," he insisted.

"Jack, I am the police," she confessed in a moment of weakness.

"What? You're truly insane! I need to get back to Mary and apologize to her. I need to get her forgiveness. Somehow, she found out about my transgressions with you," he was speaking his mind aloud in a stream of consciousness.

"What about Alice? What did you do to Alice?" Molly pressed him and would not let him leave. "I saw you dig her up in the rose garden."

"What drugs are you on? You're completely insane! Let me go!" he pleaded.

"You can leave once you tell me about Alice," she insisted.

"I told you, and so did Nightingale. Alice left on her own. I made a mistake with her, like I did with you, but that was before Mary came along. Once I met Mary, I knew I had to leave Alice. By the way, you and I are so through! Please don't bother me any further or I'll call the police. I never want to see you again. Let me go, you psycho!" He eyed the door in a desperate attempt to flee.

Molly was not sure if this was just another lie or if Jack was being truthful. He seemed sincere, but often the worst criminals excel at leading double lives, for they believe their own lies. "Damn, I shouldn't have told him that I was a cop, but he didn't believe it anyway," she thought. Her mind was racing. She decided to try and back out of this situation. "Look Jack, I'm sorry. I think that I made a big mistake," she admitted.

"Just leave me alone! You're insane! Regardless of who you think you are, you're liable for assault and battery. Let me go or I'll sue you for this!" He glared at her.

She stepped aside, and he ran out of the room, disappearing down the hallway.

"Damn, I really screwed up this time!" She shook her head, and went into her kitchen to make a cup of hot chocolate with plenty of Baileys.

Sitting on her couch, her last sanctuary, she pondered all that had just transpired. "What if he's truly innocent? But that makes no sense," she reflected. Looking down, she saw the metal casting of the Wu Wei symbol. She picked it up off the floor and placed it on her coffee table. "It's more likely that he's just a great liar or seriously delusional," she decided.

As she sat back on her couch, she heard a knock on her door. "That must be him coming back to make things right again. He's the unbalanced one," she huffed and got up to answer the door. As she opened it, she encountered Helga.

"Hello, Helga. Sorry about the noise. I guess it was my turn to be loud," Molly chuckled.

"Hello, Molly," Helga replied in a sincere voice. "I heard Jack Fulton rushing out of here. Are you all right? You really need to stay away from him. He's dangerous," she warned.

"Yes, I believe you," Molly replied.

"May I come in? I won't be long. I just wanted to warn you about something that I think I saw happen in the rose garden the other night. Did you hear a commotion out there? I was watching a late night movie and thought I heard someone digging out there, and then the other morning the police destroyed all my precious roses. It was my haven. What am I to do now? My white roses are all gone! Those cops planted red roses instead!" she seemed genuinely distraught. "My roses are red!"

"I'm sorry, Helga, but I need to get some sleep. It was a long day," Molly replied hesitant to entertain another guest.

"Molly, I would love a cup of your hot chocolate," Helga said in a sincere tone. "That would make me feel so much better. Please!"

"All right, Helga. Give me a moment," Molly retired into the kitchen. She decided to make herself a second cup, as well, but with plenty of Baileys.

"Oh, thank you, Molly, my dear friend," Helga shouted across the room and sat down in the chair opposite Molly's couch.

"There's no way that Helga is associated with Jack's crimes," Molly thought. "She's extremely odd, but harmless," she concluded to herself. "I can read people. That's why I'm a detective. Just as I know that Jack Fulton is a coward and a fraud. What the hell was all that about tonight?" She was still reflecting on her exchange with Jack as she returned to the living room with two cups of hot chocolate.

Entering the room, she saw Helga inspecting the Wu Wei statue. She was looking at it with visible envy. As soon as she saw Molly, she placed it back on the coffee table.

"Here's your hot chocolate." Molly handed Helga the cup.

"Thank you, my dear friend, Molly," Helga smiled. Molly thought that she noticed something odd in Helga's smile.

"Molly, did Jack Fulton give you this?" Helga pointed at the small Wu Wei statue.

"Yes, as a matter of fact, he did, but I'm planning on returning it," Molly replied honestly.

"I see. He did the same thing with Alice, you know. The two of you are so similar, not in appearance, but in your relationship with Jack. You see, Molly, I know that you're having sex with him. But, so did Alice. I know. I'm not as dumb as I appear!" Helga's voice turned sharper.

"I'd never for a minute think that you're dumb, Helga," Molly instinctively replied, noticing Helga's sudden mood swing while taken aback by the personal nature of the accusation.

"Do you love him?" Helga asked.

"Love who, Helga?" Molly was completely blindsided by the forwardness of the questions.

"Jack, of course! I can tell that he loves you," Helga continued, while avoiding eye contact and staring at the Wu Wei statue.

"Why are you asking these things?" Molly knitted her brows.

"Because I'm your friend, and that's what girlfriends talk about, isn't it?" Helga replied with a sweet tone once more.

"Maybe, but I don't have any close girlfriends at present," Molly replied honestly.

"How dare you?" Helga got up suddenly and sprang for the door, locking the pad lock.

"What're you doing?" Molly asked and rose in alarm.

"How dare you say I'm not your close friend? Why, we're very close, you and I. We live here, next to each other, and we have the same interests, right Molly?" Helga was acting very strangely.

"What do you mean, Helga, and why did you lock the door?" Molly was standing in front of the couch, concerned with Helga's erratic behavior.

"I locked it so that he won't return. He may kill you, like he killed Alice," Helga replied.

"Did he really kill Alice?" Molly asked, growing alarmed at the turn of the conversation toward the subject of murder.

"Of course he did! He killed her, all right, and gave her one of those just before he did so." Helga stood blocking the door while pointing at the Wu Wei statue. "That's his lure to get you into their exclusive little club, so that he can possess you. They never asked me! He never gave me one!" she huffed in growing anger.

"I see, and how do you know that Jack gave Alice a similar statue?" Molly tried to remain calm, ignoring Helga's bait regarding the secret society, yet wishing to learn more.

"I know! Just like I know that you love him. Well, I love him too! And I too want to belong! Anyone care about that?" Helga was growing very angry. "You don't care that I love him! Does he care that I love him? No! He cares about you! He's into the pretty girls, like you, Alice, and that little bitch, Mary. I wish that I had gotten to her first, before he did. He's warped, you know. But I like that!" Helga smiled, still blocking the door with her large muscular frame. "He doesn't love me because I'm too ugly and too big," she growled.

"Helga, you're scaring me. Please leave!" Molly tried to run back toward the kitchen to get to her cell phone.

"Stop right there, Alice!" Helga yelled and pointed a gun at Molly. At the sight of the gun, Molly froze.

"Helga, what're you doing? Put that away! I'm not Alice. I'm your friend, Molly!"

"Oh, Alice, my dear Alice. Now that you're back, I have to kill you again. Ms. Nightingale told me about reincarnation. I know what you're up to Alice. I just didn't expect you back so soon!" Helga approached Molly with the loaded gun.

"You made me do it the first time and I'll do it again. You see, Alice, Jack did kill you because he fell in love with you and not me." Helga's voice deepened. "He killed you with his affection that belonged to me. You stole him, and now you want to steal him again! No way, Alice. No way! You're going right back! You deserved to die, Alice. I need to kill you again since you rose from that rose garden. You painted my roses red, Alice! My white roses are gone, and they're red instead!" Helga was furious as she pointed the gun at Molly.

"Helga, please put the gun down. I'm not Alice. Jack doesn't love me and I don't love him. You're wrong!" Molly tried to stay calm and tried to slowly back away toward her bedroom door to reach her gun, which she now kept loaded.

"I killed you once and I will kill you again, Alice! I will kill you a thousand times if I have to, Alice. If you keep springing up like Ms. Nightingale said you would, I'll continue to kill you!" The anger in Helga's voice reached a crescendo. "You don't belong here. He's mine, not yours! You don't deserve him!" Helga raged and neared Molly while pointing the gun straight at her.

Molly decided to try and buy some time. "Helga, you can have him back. He told me he loves you and not me."

"You lie, Alice! You're such a liar, Alice!" Helga screamed.

Just then, there was a pounding on Molly's door. It grew louder and momentarily distracted Helga from her task. Molly decided to make a run for the bedroom. As she sprang for the bedroom door, Helga turned and fired the gun straight at her. Molly fell to the floor, feeling an excruciating, burning pain in her right thigh. As she looked down at her wound, she saw a dark red blotch appear and grow on her white, rose-patterned robe — painting the roses red.

"I'll have to kill you again, Alice. Maybe you'll stay dead this time! Don't you pull this resurrection crap again!" Helga screamed. The pounding on the door grew into a frantic screaming. Molly recognized the voice on the other side of the door as she lay on the ground in front of her bedroom door. Her right leg refused to support her. "Damn this case!" she muttered to herself. "I'm not going to die!" she roared and overcoming the most intense pain that she had ever known, she stood up to face Helga once more.

"You sure are tougher this time, Alice," Helga said quietly. "But, now I'll kill you like they do in the war movies. This time it won't be a quiet strangulation while you're asleep, as I did when I snuck through your window the last time, Alice. No, that didn't keep you away. That won't do at all. This time I'll simply shoot you, point blank!" Helga smiled and stood facing Molly. She pointed the loaded gun at Molly's head and took aim.

Just then the front door of Molly's apartment crashed open and a man leapt through it. Helga turned to face him and fired on him. He charged at her like a raging bull, ignoring the gun fire. She fired again, and this time hit him as he flew toward her. But, he had no intension of stopping despite his wound. He reached Helga before she could fire the next shot, and ran her down with the force of a runaway train.

Molly was losing consciousness. The last thing she saw was the image of a large man tackling Helga to the ground. As Helga's head hit the wooden floor with a crash, her wig parted from her bald scalp, clearly revealing the head of a man.

CHAPTER 59

A Room Full of Flowers

When Molly awakened, she found herself connected to intravenous drips and numerous monitors. She could not remember how she had gotten to the hospital. Then reality reminded her with the throbbing pain in her right leg. Without intending to do so, she triggered a room alarm, alerting her nurse.

"Ah, ya're awake!" the kindly old nurse proclaimed as she entered the room. "Please don't try to get up. Ya'll only make things worse."

The nurse introduced herself, adjusted Molly's position and checked several of the monitors. "Ya're a lucky one!" the nurse proclaimed. "Doctor told me if that bullet been a fraction of a centimeter off, it'd have cut the femoral artery and ya'd have bled to death before the EMT's got to ya." The nurse checked a few more gauges before adding, "Ya just missed ya boyfriend. He was here all day 'til 10 minutes ago. But, I'm sure that he'll be back soon enough. He's so sweet and handsome. Ya're a lucky one!" the old nurse smiled.

"Who're you talking about?" Molly responded honestly. "I don't have a boyfriend."

"Oh, I'm sorry! I forgot ya're still on strong meds. Don't ya mind me! I talk too much," the nurse confessed. "Let me check your vital signs," she insisted.

"Who comes to see me? Is it Inspector Cabot?" Molly was curious.

"Short fella with the dark mustache? He's been here, too. He and ya boyfriend don't seem to get on, do they?" the nurse observed. She was a keen observer of human nature and prided herself on that fact.

"Actually, ya had many visitors, my dear. Look at all them flowers!" The nurse pointed at the table and the large window sill. Molly had not noticed until now that her entire hospital room was filled with flowers. "A lot of people must love ya, my dear. Ya're a lucky one!" the old nurse repeated.

"I guess you're right," Molly agreed, still in shock at the sight of so many flowers.

"I've never seen this many flowers. Ya're a celebrity, ar' ya? I don't keep up with them reality shows. Ya seem like one of them reality show celebrities," the old nurse observed and looked questioningly at Molly.

"No! Hardly!" Molly replied and chuckled. The old nurse was visibly disappointed as she left the room still mumbling "Ya're a lucky one!"

Molly laid back on her pillow. Her leg was still throbbing. She remembered being shot by Helga, right after Helga admitted that she had killed Alice. It was all coming back to her now. Helga confused her with Alice and shot her. Then, she remembered Jack Fulton rushing into her room and tackling Helga. The rest was a blank.

The idea of Jack Fulton trying to save her made her smile. "I guess he saved me," she concluded. Then, she became concerned.

"What if Helga killed him while he was trying to save me? Oh, I hope not. I had him all wrong. I owe him my life! I owe him an apology!" She silently concluded just before she closed her eyes and fell asleep, confused by the pain medicine.

She was awakened by a gentle male voice. Opening her eyes, she saw Jack. "Thank God you're not dead!" she exclaimed without thinking.

He smiled his usual charming smile. "You're one odd but lucky girl, Molly Dvorak."

"What happened? I remember getting shot and that you showed up to save me. By the way, thank you. I had you all wrong," Molly confessed.

Jack audibly sighed. "No worries, Molly. I'm simply glad that you're all right," he added sincerely.

"What happened after I passed out?" Molly asked.

"Well, I managed to get shot as well," Jack smiled and showed her the bandage on his left shoulder. "It's a flesh wound, no worries." He added to console her worried expression.

"Oh, no, you have a black eye, too," Molly observed.

"Yeah, Helga, or should I say, Franz Gunt, is a proficient fighter. Turns out that she was a he, and rather mentally confused, at best. He's wanted for several suspected murders in Canada, committed nearly five years ago," Jack revealed.

"Is Alice dead?" Molly asked.

"I'm afraid so. Poor dear Alice. She was so genuinely kind-hearted. It's often true that the good die young, and it's certainly true of Alice. That bastard, Franz, murdered her. Your boss, the Inspector, discovered her body in Helga's basement storage area, after Chester tipped him off. Poor Ms. Nightingale. She's so upset about you and Alice that not even Trudy can console her. I have tried to calm her down, but it's useless. It'll take time. She feels responsible even though Franz had her fooled, notes and all. But, I feel even worse for Alice's parents. Parents shouldn't have to bury their children. That's not right," Jack concluded.

"True, so true," Molly agreed, and they fell silent reflecting on Alice and the tragedy that surrounded her.

"You know, Helga, or whatever is his name, was jealous of Alice because you fancied her," Molly shared. "She, or should I say he, loved you."

"Hard to believe, isn't it? It's all crazy! Franz was mentally extremely unstable. I can't believe that we never figured out the disguise," Jack replied.

"That explains why I was certain that I had seen a man digging in the rose garden the night that he exhumed Alice's body. I saw a man because it was a man," Molly recalled.

"Yeah, he had apparently buried poor Alice there after strangling her and writing the notes, texts and e-mails in order to make it seem like she simply left of her own free will and went on an anthropology trip or something," Jack explained.

"What happened to him? Did you kill him?" Molly asked.

"No," Jack chuckled. "I'm not a killer as your boss suspects. The entire idea is ridiculous."

"I agree," Molly replied, reflecting on how she too had suspected Jack to be a killer. In the next instant, she silently reflected on the unsolved mystery of Mary's fall. After all, Jack was the only remaining suspect. She paused and pulled away from him a little.

"Franz is in custody. Your boss is handling the case. He'll have more details. You can ask him when he comes in this afternoon. He'll be here in the afternoon. Oddly enough, he still acts weird around me. You see, Molly, I must confess that I dated his daughter in high school, and after we broke up, she tried to commit suicide. He still blames me for it, even though she and I are good friends now. I was the one that talked her out of it, but no one else knows that fact. We never talk about it. But, old Cabot blames me. I suppose that when I'm a father some day I'll feel the same if some jerk messes with my little girl. I was a jerk back then," Jack admitted.

"And not now?" Molly chuckled.

"I don't know. You tell me?" Jack replied, while shrugging his good shoulder.

"Jack, did you push Mary Collins at the quarry? I need to know," Molly blurted out. She was still under the influence of strong pain killers and her usual guard was down. She knew that she couldn't be friends with Jack if she suspected him of that hideous act.

"What! I can't believe you just asked me that! I thought of all people, you'd know better." Jack was shocked. He stood up, deeply offended. "I forgot. You're a suspicious cop, first and foremost. I confirmed that you're a cop, you know. It shocked me. I suppose all that happened between us was part of the police investigation. Thanks for reminding me."

"I didn't mean to offend you, Jack. I realize that you saved my life and I'm grateful, but all the evidence in that case pointed to you. I can't be friends with you, if you did that." The medicine was like a truth serum. She could not lie, and all her thoughts seemed to spill out of her lips unhindered and unfiltered.

"I need to go now, Molly. I can't believe what I'm hearing. You know what? The feeling's mutual. I can't be friends with someone that doesn't trust me and doesn't believe in me. I need to go see Mary. She's still in a recovery room upstairs. I just wanted to make sure that you were okay. I cared. My mistake. Have a nice life, Molly," Jack replied in a cold voice and walked out of the room. He was deeply hurt, and didn't want to be near her any longer.

"Jack, I'm sorry!" she cried out to an empty room.

"Ya're a lucky one," the nurse muttered as she entered the room in response to Molly's cry.

"Maybe I am. Yes, maybe I am," Molly reflected. "Good bye, Jack. I release you," she said in a whisper and soon fell into a peaceful sleep.

CHAPTER 60

Mary's Secret

Seven months had passed since the apprehension of Franz
Gunt. Gunt had been convicted of the Alice murder in a swift
trial, and was scheduled to stand trial in Toronto for two additional killings in Ontario, Canada, that had occurred nearly five
years earlier.

It was late autumn now and McLaren University was well
into a new school year. Jack Fulton was instructing several field
classes of eager students on another Teaching Assistant stipend.
Often he shared teaching duties with his good friend and fellow
grad student, Carl Rupert. Meanwhile, Mary Collins had completely recovered from her ordeal. Upon graduating that summer,
she accepted a position with the local school district as a 1st
grade teacher.

Jennifer Angel received early acceptance at a nearby medical
school for the following year. For now, she continues working as
a trauma nurse at the local hospital. To her deep disappointment,

her night shifts were devoid of further spiritual visitors. Molly had fully recovered from her gun shot wound and resumed her post on Inspector Cabot's team after receiving a promotion to detective. Ms. Nightingale finally forgave herself for the Alice tragedy and has recently taken on a new promising protégé, Jennifer herself. Fortunately for Ms. Nightingale's continuing relationship with Trudy, Jennifer did not have the vibe.

Big Bob Braxton quit the force and was planning to propose to Suzy Kurtz on an upcoming cruise he had booked to St. Croix. Suzy was certain to accept since she had never been so in love. Their band, the Bama Blues, recently signed a large record contract that included a national tour. By next summer, their breakout album, Suzy's Petals, would go platinum and Pops Chesterfield would adorn the cover of Rolling Stone.

Tony Bond was serving his time for his attacks on Mary Collins. Unfortunately, Lilly Austin escaped justice thanks to her rich husband, Phillip, and a small army of legal support. She and her husband had recently moved to a grand villa in Costa Rica, leaving Pennsylvania for good. Lilly's domestics, Andrew and Martha O'Malley, were content to be rid of her, and, with Mary's support and insistence, returned to Ireland. Randell Twiner escaped a jail sentence for his attack on Suzy Kurtz because she never pressed charges, but his father discovered the truth and financially disowned him. He's now flipping hamburgers at a local diner.

Upon graduating, Daphne Marconi had gotten over her girly fetish with Mary Collins and moved to New York City to study fashion design, where she recently met the love of her life, a Russian runway model named Katrianna. Kelly's mom, Mrs. Allen, who's now officially divorced, is happily dating Inspector Cabot. She's extremely happy, and he's not talking about it since he cannot get a word in edgewise.

Chen, who continues to tease his boss about his newfound romance, is still with the force. He is planning to marry his fiancé in December, being deeply committed to her and to his computer games. Meanwhile, Kelly Allen hopes that the Inspector will elope with her mother to a far away land and never return. She has expressed this as a sincere wish at several girlfriend lunches to her closest friends: Jennifer, Stacy and Mary.

While not dodging Mrs. Allen, the Inspector is chasing new predators in town, but he remains convinced that Jack Fulton pushed Mary Collins off the quarry wall in an attempt to kill her. He has gathered further evidence to support his claim, including another witness that validated Stacy Reed's testimony that Fulton stood over the edge of the cliff right after Mary's fall, only to return soon after in a failed attempt to appear to be her rescuer. He has vowed to keep his promise to get Jack, the social predator, off the streets of Brennantown.

As for Stacy Reed, she made peace with her father and his new found love, her former schoolmate, Janet Lee. On this particular fine autumn day, she was walking through McLaren campus, when she spotted the car.

"Oh, my God!" she exclaimed. "That's the car that I saw hidden behind the quarry the day Mary fell. I'm certain of it," she said aloud. Then, to her amazement, she saw him get out. "Oh my God, he did push her after all! I wasn't imagining it," she concluded in horror and ran off to find Mary Collins.

She and Mary had become close friends through Mary's ordeal. Now it was time to tell Mary all that she knew and get her advice as to what should be done next. Unable to curb her enthusiasm at solving the Mary Collins case, she rushed to Mary's apartment. Finding the door unlocked, she entered.

"Mary, where are you? I need to tell you something! It's really urgent! I know who pushed you in the quarry that day. I was right all along!" Stacy exclaimed, as Mary stepped out of her bathroom wearing nothing but a towel.

"What's with you, Stace, don't you knock? You look like you saw a ghost or something," Mary observed, and walked over to her bedroom to get dressed.

"I just saw the car that I told you about!" Stacy shouted through the half-open door of the bedroom. "It was the car that was hidden in the bushes on the far side of the quarry the day you fell. I just saw it on campus, and guess who I saw driving it?" Stacy was so excited that she was nearly hyperventilating.

"Jack Fulton," Mary replied, as she stepped out of her bedroom wearing a flowered dress.

"Right! How'd you know that?"

"Just a wild guess based on your enthusiasm," Mary replied. "Did you have breakfast, yet?" she asked, completely unfazed.

"Yes, I have," Stacy replied, while following Mary into her kitchenette. "I saw Jack step out of that same car," she continued excitedly. "I knew that he did that to you. I knew all along that it was him. Why did you forgive him? How can you still be friends with him?" Stacy was truly baffled. She was trying to protect her friend, who had become like a sister to her. Stacy, Kelly, Mary and Jennifer had become inseparable friends.

"Stace, have a seat and calm down." Mary had fixed herself some cereal and sat down at the small kitchen table. Stacy sat next to her. "I guess it's time that you knew the truth, but you can't tell anyone. Promise?" Mary looked her straight in the eyes.

"I promise, but what's this about?" Stacy objected.

"It's about my accident in the quarry last spring," Mary replied.

"Mary, why do you keep calling it your accident? I saw the police evidence when they interviewed me. You were clearly pushed by someone in a white shirt. It was there in color on an enlarged photograph. You're lucky that you didn't die. The fact that you are sitting here as if nothing happened is a miracle. For all practical purposes, you were nearly murdered by Jack Fulton." Stacy was upset and shifted to the edge of her seat. "I saw Jack standing over that same spot right after you fell. I saw him and so did Andrew Peterson, who happens to be that little police inspector's latest witness. That inspector will nail Jack. I'm sure of that. He hates him." Stacy paused and glared at Mary. "And, he should nail him for this," she added.

"Do you want some coffee, Stace?" Mary asked calmly, as she rose and poured herself a cup.

"No thanks, but let me tell you how I know this." Stacy looked extremely serious.

"Okay. How do you know this?" Mary echoed as she sat back down and continued to eat her cereal.

"I know because I know! I mean, I know that the Inspector is pressing to reopen your case and prosecute Jack because he approached me to be a witness along with Andrew Peterson!" Stacy exclaimed.

"And will you be? Are you sure you don't want some coffee? Your soon to be stepmother, Janet Lee, brought it back from Brazil," Mary giggled.

"Shut the hell up, Mary! You know how I feel about all that. I can't believe my dad has proposed to her. I mean, she's a nice girl, but she's only three years older than me, for goodness sake! Anyway, you're not listening. How can you calmly eat your breakfast when I'm trying to tell you that Jack Fulton tried to kill you?" Stacy was fit to be tied.

"I'm listening, Stace!" Mary replied and locked eyes with her to reassure her.

"Okay. Please tell me why you refuse to punish Jack and continue to have a relationship with him?" Stacy was angry at Mary. She could not understand her friend's level of forgiveness. "Maybe this will change your mind. I just saw him get out of the very car that was parked behind the quarry. He's guilty! He did it!" Stacy proclaimed.

"Why would Jack park his car in the quarry that day when we both know that he was on the bus with us leading that field trip? How would he even get the car there and get back to campus?" Mary questioned. "Why would he even need a car there?"

"How the hell should I know, but he did! Maybe he was planning to run," Stacy reasoned.

"No offense, my dear Stace, but you were the one planning to run. If he were planning to run, why did he risk his own neck to get to me as soon as possible?" Mary countered.

"Hell if I know! He wanted to seem innocent and make it look like an accident. But, remember that he stopped me right after you fell and told me that it may be in everyone's best interest, including mine, to forget what I saw. He said that because he knew that I saw him push you! Unfortunately, his threat worked because I was too scared to come forward until much later when the cops caught up to me out West. I assure you that I wouldn't run now, Mary. I would kick his sorry ass for doing that to you!" Stacy proclaimed.

Mary reached over and placed her hand over Stacy's. Stacy was starting to cry. "I simply don't understand why you're protecting him when he tried to kill you," Stacy sobbed.

"Oh, Stacy!" Mary stopped eating and moved her seat right up against Stacy's chair, placing her right arm around her friend. "It's time I share my little secret."

"What secret, Mary?" Stacy pulled back, looking up at her.

There was a prolonged silence as the two women looked at each other, as if for the first time.

"First, can you describe the car that you saw Jack driving today?" Mary asked.

"What does that matter?" Stacy refuted.

"Why, Stace, wasn't that the reason for your visit today to tell me about this car and how it confirms Jack's guilt?"

"Yes, but what are you saying? What secret, Mary? Why do you have secrets from me? Does Jen know?" Stacy asked.

"No, and she best never know. You'll see why," Mary replied.

"What's your secret? Are you and Jack engaged or something?"

"No, hardly!" Mary laughed.

"So what is it? Don't try and tell me that Jack's innocent because I saw him do it with my own eyes " Stacy held her ground.

"You saw him push me?" Mary asked calmly.

"Yes!"

"You saw him push me, Stacy?" Mary repeated the question.

"Well, no, but I saw him standing at the lip of the quarry right after you fell. God, that sound of your scream and that awful sound of you hitting that rock floor still haunt me at night. You know that?"

"It haunts me as well, at times," Mary replied and embraced her friend to whisper in her ear.

"What?" Stacy pulled back. "What did you just say?"

"You heard me," Mary replied.

"I don't believe it! So, how was it that he was..?" Stacy suddenly stopped, for Jack walked into the room.

"Hey, Mary! Hey Stace! Is this a bad time?" he asked.

"Yes!" Stacy exclaimed unhindered.

"No!" Mary countered.

Jack laughed. "You two are a pair! You can't agree on anything, and yet you're such close friends these days. It's quite baffling." He laughed again.

"Mary, I need to call Carl," he continued. "I need to find out when he needs that old car of his back. I know it's his spare, but I hate to leave it sitting out there on the main road. It's bound to get a ticket. Can I use your phone? My cell just died." Jack explained with his usual charming smile.

"Sure, Jack. Help yourself," Mary replied.

Stacy sat on the couch as if she had just seen a ghost.

"What's with you, Stace?" Jack noticed her odd behavior.

"That was Carl Rupert's car? That old gold Chevy is Carl's car?" Stacy repeated.

"Yes, but why do you care?" Jack was confused by Stacy's sudden interest in cars.

"Go call Carl, Jack! I need to tell Stacy something in private," Mary instructed.

"Okay, but are we still up for going out tonight? Should I invite Jen and Carl along? Those two lovebirds need to come up for air from their little love haven in Carl's old place. I swear the last time I walked by his place, all the windows were fogged up from all that steamy passion," Jack laughed a hardy laugh at the expense of his friend Carl.

"Sure, invite them along," Mary replied. "Are you going to bring your usual date?" she asked.

"Yes, if she's willing," Jack teased. "You gonna come? What about you, Stace?"

"Hmmm… I don't know if I want to publicly associate with you," Mary teased back. "What would your fellow grad students say, if they saw us?"

Jack rolled his eyes at Mary. "Who cares! Besides, I owe you one for setting me straight, Mary. You really are the best!" He smiled, gave her an affectional squeeze and headed toward the refrigerator.

"Yes, you do owe me one!" Mary yelled across the room. "You owe me big, Mister! You're lucky that I'm so forgiving these days," she correctly assessed.

Throughout all this, Stacy sat frozen in time and space, unable to utter another word. Jack looked at her and shook his head. "Stace, we need to find you a steady boyfriend," he chuckled, before walking out of the kitchenette toward the far end of the living room to call Carl.

"What was Carl's car doing behind the quarry that day?" Stacy asked Mary in a whisper as she finally found her voice.

"Well, I need to give you a little history lesson first," Mary began. "Before I met Jack, I had a brief and rather innocent exchange with Carl. You can't say a word to Jen, but Carl had a thing for me. It was so obvious. He wasn't like he is now. Jen has done wonders for him. He was very shy. It was cute, but I didn't feel the chemistry, plus he was a grad student and all," Mary paused.

"That didn't stop you with Jack!" Stacy countered.

"No, but with Jack it was different. Carl and I weren't a good fit. He was simply smitten and confused. I don't know. I guess I should've pushed him away more than I did, but he was so attentive and sweet. I simply decided to avoid him, which in hindsight was rather cowardly of me. Eventually, Jack and I hooked up, and Carl found out. I discovered later that unbeknownst to any of us, including Jack, Carl freaked out and took it really hard." Mary looked at Stacy.

"Where are you going with all this, Mary? How does all this make Jack innocent?" Stacy wondered.

"Well, the day of my fall, Carl surprised me at the quarry. I guess he knew about the trip from Jack and decided to wait there for me since I was avoiding him," Mary whispered.

"Carl stalked you on the field trip?" Stacy was shocked.

"I don't know if one would call it stalking, but he did surprise me. I understand now that Carl simply needed a chance to express to me his feelings, and I hadn't given him that chance. Like I said, he's different now, but, back then, I must admit that he was scaring me a bit," Mary reflected.

"No way! Carl, a stalker? Funny, easy going, Carl?" Stacy was in disbelief.

"Don't underestimate the effect of a good woman on a man," Mary laughed. "Carl's lucky to have Jen. What a sweetheart that one!"

"Based on what he told me when we all went out last week, he's smitten and values what he's got," Stacy added. "But, I still can't believe that about Carl."

"I sincerely believe that he simply got too obsessed, which stemmed from his inexperience in relationships," Mary explained as if she were a psychologist. "By the way, I'm glad to hear that Carl values Jen that much. I just hope that they never break up for I'm not sure that he'd handle it well," Mary observed.

"Okay. So, Carl was stalking you at the quarry and his car was the one that I saw parked on the other side of the hill," Stacy summarized.

"Yes, well not about the stalking, but about the car. But as I said, Carl did surprised me at the quarry that day. He was waiting there, hidden by some fallen boulders near the very spot from which I fell," Mary continued.

"Mary, he was stalking you! How creepy!" Stacy exclaimed. "I can see why you don't want to scare Jen. But shouldn't we warn her? You think that she's okay with him?" Stacy was concerned for Jennifer.

"He's fine. He had a sheltered childhood and simply didn't know how to approach a woman or deal with love. Jack and I discussed this extensively. I really believe that it was all innocent," Mary defended Carl. "He's a sweetheart to Jen. He worships the ground that she walks on, as he should by the way," Mary added.

"It's still creepy. So, what happened next?" Stacy asked.

"Well, he snuck up on me to confess his love and his broken heart, and to ask me to leave Jack. I was so shocked to see him there that I wanted to scream, but I knew that he wouldn't hurt me. He insisted that he simply wanted to warn me that Jack didn't appreciate me like he did, and that Jack was a womanizer. He was extremely sweet, but I was too freaked out by the entire encounter. I simply wanted to run away. At that point, I had no idea that he even knew about my involvement with Jack," Mary explained.

"You were playing with fire, Mary," Stacy concluded and shook her head.

"Yes, and I payed for it. But, as I was saying, he insisted that I leave Jack. I wanted to run away. But, before I did I told him that I was falling for Jack and that he needed to accept that fact. Then, I rushed off." Mary paused and took a long sip of her coffee.

"Unfortunately, I rushed toward the edge of the quarry wall. Once there, I spotted Jack, who had seen and recognized Carl, and, sensing my plight, was coming to rescue me," Mary paused again. It seemed hard for her to relive those moments.

"Are you okay, Mary? If you don't want to say more, I under-stand." Stacy sensed Mary's reservation.

"No. You should know the truth. I have never told this to anyone, but it's good therapy for me, as well." Mary inhaled audibly and continued. "Anyway, where was I? Oh, yes, Jack was running up towards me and Carl. He too was sheltered from view of the Inspector's witnesses by the numerous large quarry rocks at that location. When Carl spotted Jack, he panicked. He ran after me and tripped. I was facing him when he tripped. I had only enough time to turn to try and get out of his way as he fell, when I realized that I was standing at the edge of the quarry wall. It was then that I felt the horrific push forward as Carl fell full force against me, unintentionally shoving me over the edge." Mary paused, reliving that horrific moment. Then, she turned and looked straight into Stacy's eyes. "You see Stacy, I know that Carl tripped. I saw him trip. He didn't mean it. Jack saw him trip, as well." Mary paused once more.

"So, it was Carl that pushed you," Stacy confirmed.

"Yes, but it was an accident," Mary confessed.

"Oh my God, Mary!" Stacy threw herself at Mary and hugged her tight, as if she were trying to keep her from falling into that quarry once more.

Then, Stacy pulled away remembering what she saw. "So how did Jack end up standing there?" she asked, still baffled by what she had witnessed that day.

"Well, obviously, I didn't see that part since I was already unconscious at the base of the quarry wall," Mary replied. "But Jack told me that he tried to grab me, but to his horror, he couldn't reach me in time. He found himself standing at the point where I fell, looking down at me. His first instinct was to head down the cliff after me somehow, but there was no way to get there. Then, he remembered Carl. Carl was aghast at what happened and Jack had the presence of mind to protect his friend. He didn't want Carl to be arrested for he saw Carl trip and fall into me," Mary explained.

"Why didn't they just tell the police that it was an accident?" Stacy asked.

"They should have, you're right, but instead he thought he could hide Carl and let it appear as an accident. After all, it was an accident. But in hindsight, he underestimated that police inspector's perseverance. He instructed Carl to leave, which he managed to do unnoticed, except that you saw Carl's car before he drove away." Mary looked directly at Stacy. "I guess they underestimated you, as well."

"Jack took the rap for Carl all this time?" Stacy was amazed.

"That's Jack for you, always playing the stubborn fool!" Mary laughed and glanced past Stacy.

"So, what else happened?" Stacy was on the edge of her seat.

"Well, I heard Suzy Kurtz scream and I was in a complete panic. I rushed back toward Mary as fast as I could, but ran into you, Stacy," Jack suddenly spoke up. He had long ago finished his call with Carl, and had been quietly listening to Mary's confession from across the room.

Stacy was startled by Jack's sudden intervention in the conversation. Mary had seen him listening, so she was not surprised that he had finally joined the revelation.

"I ran as fast as I could, but I ran into you, and then I recalled that when I had first looked down on Mary's fallen body," he paused reaching out his hand and placing it on Mary's shoulder. She covered it with her hand to give him the strength to continue. She knew that this was hard for him as well, for he had never stopped loving her.

"I recalled that when I had first looked down to see Mary," he repeated, "I saw your horrified face, Stacy, looking straight at me, and so I pleaded with you not to say anything. I may have, in my excitement, come across harshly, and I apologize for that, but I was simply scared." He sighed and looked straight into Stacy's eyes.

"I did see you there, Jack, and that's why and only why I thought it was you this entire time. Knowing you better now, I've struggled to understand how you could have done such a horrible thing. Well now it makes sense." Stacy shook her head. "I'm sorry, Jack, that I suspected you."

"Oh, Stace, you simply related to what you saw. Thank God, Mary's okay. That's all that matters." He smiled at Mary

"So, Stacy, now you know our secret," Mary sighed and looked back at Jack, "for Jen's sake, it's best to keep it that way."

"Yes, for Jen's sake," Stacy replied, still bewildered.

The Afterword

The rain danced on the tin roof. He awoke as thunder echoed through the last remnant of his dream. It was nothing more than an autumn storm, yet this time there was something that touched a nerve rarely awakened. He relaxed and listened to the rain. The old tin roof was alive with the harmony of countless fleeting raindrops, each adding its note to the enchanting melody. He was engulfed in the moment, savoring each drop.

It was 3:30 in the morning when he was aroused from this tranquility by a violent flash of light, instantly echoed by the crack of sound that ended with a thundering crash. The warm body next to him made her presence known with a soft sigh as she rolled over to meet him, her arm searching for his comfort. He reached out to reassure her and without the intrusion of words, kissed her. The kiss led to another, and soon the music of the rain and the rhythm of the wind provided the tempo for their passion. Now the roll of thunder was overpowered by a more piercing, more intense confirmation of the miracle of existence. The two lovers fell back exhausted but still intertwined, inseparable as the thunder and lightning slowly drifted into the past, or simply moved on. No matter, the sacred moment was gone. As she drifted back to sleep, he listened to the rain, savoring the night as if it was his first and last.

There is something magical about complete contentment, the kind that permeates your entire body, mind and soul, and in that precious moment all is fulfilled, lacking nothing, perfectly whole. This was that rare moment, and, he was wise enough to recognize it and awake enough to savor it. Kissing his beloved Molly gently, Jack fell into a blissful sleep, completely content at last.

David Stockar is a fiction writer with an appreciation for classic literature and story telling. In his work, he explores the complexities of relationships and motivations, often taking the reader beyond the foreground of daily existence into deeper, more eternal mysteries. He enjoys multi-layered plots that juxtapose complex characters and supernatural elements. His favorite media are mystery and adventure novels. He is happily married with four children and currently lives in Pennsylvania.

CPSIA information can be obtained at www.ICGtesting.com
Printed in the USA
BVOW08s0637260315

393248BV00001B/69/P